Lavinia's War

CLAIRE GARTRELL

Dedicated to Lavinia and Dorrie, c. 1916 - 1989, the years of their friendship.

Contents

Acknowledgments

My first stop after I had read through Lavinia's archives was my alma mater, Wolfson College, University of Oxford. Whilst here in the 1980's researching for a doctoral thesis on Christian Science, I learned the basics for writing academically. Now, I used similar research methods for a novel set in colonial Malaya, about which I knew next to nothing. Treading the familiar cobbles and breathing the rarefied atmospheres of the libraries, I gradually groped my way towards a beginning for Lavinia's book. What I learned at Oxford was my only guide throughout, as I worked without the benefit of agents, publishers or writers' grants, supporting myself with either my aged pensions or my job. Thank you, Oxford, for all you have taught me.

Lavinia had few living relatives, apart from distant cousins. I was fortunate, before leaving for Australia, to meet her cousin Daphne and her son Dave Bean, who has collated much information about the Coates family and provided me with encouragement, enthusiasm and more archival material. I have been unable to contact him lately and I hope he reads this.

I would never have been able to achieve the computer formatting of the manuscript without the help of my dear friend and partner Dr Alun German, ex-Jesus and Wolfson Colleges, who also acted as primary reader and critic, never failing to give me an inkling of the quality of my scribblings in no uncertain terms. For his candour and unfailing support, I am grateful.

My landlord Richard Jackson, himself a writer, read through the whole manuscript in the final stages and offered incisive insights and encouragement.

My three dear children, Susannah, Raymond and Giles have all contributed in their different ways. Susannah and her partner Anthony Trinkwon have proofread the manuscript prior to publication, which involved many hours, days and weeks of close work. They have been generous with their suggestions and support. Raymond's author photos have given me a "face" and identity for important publicity work and Giles, also a writer and actor, has been a reader as well as giving professional judgment and opinions. To everyone, I give my heartfelt thanks and gratitude.

Finally, Peter and Caroline of Bespoke Book Covers have gone above and beyond in providing a friendly and reliable service on all kinds of topics related to publishing. As a complete novice, I would not have managed without their professional help.

Introduction

The Real Lavinia

Anyone thinking they knew about nurses were often mistaken with Lavinia, or Val to her friends. Val was an enigma. You might have thought, on first meeting her, that here stood a no-nonsense yet kindly soul, an upholder of traditional values and above all, dutiful. She liked to have fun, perhaps as an antidote to her work, but here the similarity ended. She devoted herself to her patients while on duty, yes, but only she knew that her career was her means of escape. Before the war, only those who knew her well saw the occasional gleam in her face and an expression of unmistakable longing in her eyes.

Perhaps the writing had been on the wall when Tommy died but she had not entered her profession as a result of that. At eighteen years of age, she had a handful of choices open to her - marriage, teaching, secretarial work or nursing. The year was 1926. World War 1 had wrought many changes to the position of women in society, and it was acceptable, even expected, that girls should enter the work-force – until marriage. This option, however, proved very difficult during the inter-war years as so many eligible young men had been killed on the battlefields of Passchendaele, Ypres or the Somme. She would have to travel.

Many years later, I knew her as an older Val, but if she grieved as a result of her experiences, she kept it well hidden. She had retreated once more behind her façade. She had always been known to us children as Auntie Val, a tiny, bustling, capable-looking woman with a quick walk and a cheerful smile. You never would have known that she had had any shadows or regrets in her life. She always, unlike many adults, gave us her full attention and listened to our prattle, gazing at us, or at anyone who happened to be speaking, intently. Sometimes she would break out into a squealing laugh at something you might have said.

Val was my mother's oldest friend, reaching back to their young childhood in Tonbridge, on the River Medway in Kent, during the Great War. There were always Christmas presents from the Aunties, including Val. These were modest, but welcome in the dreary days of post-World War 2 – handkerchiefs, briefs, a colouring book, wrapped up in thin Christmassy paper with a neatly written tag. It is strange how even the most ordinary, every day items took on a magical quality at Christmas when presented as gifts, and I would arrange them and rearrange them for the rest of the day and gaze at them. To me, Val was a real, although not blood-related, Auntie.

From my mother's descriptions, their childhood had seemed an idyllic age. Blissfully unaware of the world outside their sphere, they had enjoyed, as daughters of the small shopkeepers and factory owners of the town, a freedom and security which I envied in the 'fifties. Among the English middle class, families were often small, and the "County" schools, later transformed to grammar schools, offered a sound education for a modest fee. The daughters of the good citizens of Tonbridge grew up together and rode their bicycles along a largely traffic-free High Street and the leafy lanes of west Kent. All the families knew each other - their mothers took lunch or tea in the Cadena café and their fathers talked shop in their clubs.

Their paths had diverged after School Certificate – my mother's taking her to secretarial college and Lavinia's eventually into nursing. As a child, I had little idea of Val's past life after she left school. She appeared leisured and unstressed in the years after World War 2, although I now know she was employed in a multiplicity of jobs. Sometimes we visited her home in Hildenborough – a village situated just north of the town, and saw her parents. Percy Coates was a retired leather goods manufacturer and Florence always seemed to be in delicate health. It was not until I read the letters and archives that I got to know them better, and their personalities filled out a little. The Coates family lived in a detached Victorian villa on the London Road, filled with the usual hotch-potch of heirlooms and heavy furniture. The garden was a child's dream, with unexpected twists and turns among heavy foliage and large shrub-bordered, daisy-strewn lawns.

Lavinia had had a younger brother, Tommy, who had tragically died at the age of fifteen under a general anaesthetic. It left Val as their sole remaining child, a situation which would prove significant in her later life as she assumed full responsibility for the care of ageing parents. After their death, Lavinia moved to a little semi-detached house in Southborough, near Tunbridge Wells, which as a young woman sometimes invited for lunch during one of my trips home, I found rather depressing. The house was among others identical, with small rooms and a curved staircase and although in a practical sense it suited her changed circumstances, I could never resist remembering the elegant house which had been the Coates's family home. It was, however, not far from the Common, a beautiful area where they still play cricket on the green and visitors pausing on the busy road to Tunbridge Wells explore the old church and the woods beyond.

During her retirement, Lavinia involved herself with literary societies in Southborough and Tunbridge Wells, and had a circle of friends among the social and intellectual elite in this most conservative of areas. Lavinia had a lively mind and among her papers, articles have survived which deal with topics commenting on contemporary issues. Her middle-class, conservative background and her work as a health visitor with mothers and babies came through in her views on working mothers, for instance, in which motherhood was idealised and sanctified. Perhaps this reflected her often-expressed wish for children herself, which was not fulfilled.

Her diaries, letters and articles testify to her literary creativity and her observation and interpretation of the world. She left a lifetime's record of a woman of her times. The importance she attached to these papers is shown by the survival of her Malayan letters and journals in 1941-42. She bore these in her luggage, throughout her flight southwards down the Malay peninsula ahead of the Japanese invaders, carrying them to safety through her subsequent voyage through the treacherous, torpedoed waters of the South China Sea and on to Western Australia. The meticulously recorded experiences of the previous year included her impressions of the colony during the declining years of British rule. Showing physical signs of the times, they are a telling resource.

In 1989, after Val's sudden and unexpected death, the sad task fell to my mother, as a beneficiary of Val's will, of searching through her possessions with my daughter's help, to find the records. They discovered her fiancé George's letters tied firmly, as if they must never be opened – like a pharaoh's tomb. The tie was thin red ribbon. "We felt as if we were wrong to open them," my daughter said. Val, I'm sorry for the trespass.

For two years then, the papers lay in an old leather suitcase in the attic of my old home in Tonbridge with other family papers and photos until my mother's own death and the sale of the house in 1991. After this, they came into my possession and were transported with other effects in the wake of our many moves: to Oxford, then again to Kent, to cardboard boxes in a cupboard in my son's photography premises in Crowborough during our sojourn in France, and latterly to Pontypridd, South Wales. Here, they survived several years in a school trunk in the living room of my student property, after which they were rescued by my son-in-law and again brought to Tonbridge. They currently reside with me in London, but this will not be the end of their journeyings, for in a few weeks I will travel with them via Malaysia where after seventy years they will have a brief homecoming, before the onward journey once more, to Sydney, Australia.

I have now read them all, and it has taken the best part of a year to decipher, amongst them the many letters Lavinia received from home during wartime and the daily correspondence from George, almost illegible, written on the thinnest airmail notepaper and affected even more by the vibrations of his mining dredge in Taiping, or the smudging of the ink caused by the splashes of the washing of the ladder by the "coolies". A rich resource, they bring to life a vivid picture of the details of colonial life before darkness fell, in the defeat of the British regime by the invading Japanese forces and its effect on the lives of these two people. In the telling of their story, I feel a huge responsibility, but as their voices come through so clearly down the years, they have in fact facilitated my task, and this will be theirs, expressed as far as possible by their own British colonial speech and views on life. It was their world.

Claire Gartrell
Blackheath, London.
January 2014.

Chapter 1

The Beginning

I have often wondered how it would have been if the invasion had never happened, and if, as we had dreamed, I had returned to Malaya well again. Like most of the British residents at that time, our blind arrogance – and unquestioning faith in our military commanders, could not permit, or even conceive, ideas of the humiliating defeat that was the beginning of the end for us as an imperial power.

Once we were married, we had planned to spend a year together in Taiping then book a passage home, whatever happened with the European war. We would have settled with my parents in their Kentish village. In all my youthful optimism, I could never have envisaged anything obscuring our happiness. It would all go on as it had before the war - Germany would finally succumb and we would regain our place on the world stage. The idyll George and I inhabited in Malaya now seems arcadian. Of course, it could not have lasted. Looking back with the cynicism of age, I wonder now. Would we have survived a post-war world together? Perhaps not, but we never got the chance to try – to settle into ordinariness, the daily dull, happy routines that I would have welcomed.

How often we talked about our children! When we looked at the future it was always with at least the three of us. In his daily letters he buoyed our spirits during the long separations with his visions of the voyage home to England, how our names would be on the cabin door - Mr and Mrs G. Powell and Baby. How innocent and how silly it was – our lovers' talk, but the images sustained me through the long, dreary days lying sweating in the European hospital in Batu Gajah. All through the worst times I lay flat in bed, listening to the monotonous hum of the ceiling fans, willing myself back to health, while dear Dr Shelley tried all sorts of treatments on me. I wanted to bring a healthy body to marriage as I thought he deserved, not the thin, feeble frame I looked down on– its pitiful, emaciated arms protruding from the cotton nightgown. But George had been patient and kind, travelling the two hundred miles from Taiping to sit by my bed. It was a few months before I had progressed enough to be able to go with him to the flicks, to the Clubhouse or the swimming pool.

I wrote home to my mother that I was engaged to the best-looking man in Malaya. Aware of his charm and success with women, he had treated it with insouciance. In a letter to me, he had described how women had thrown themselves at him, almost if it had happened to another person – without vanity - just as a curiosity. I had not suffered jealousy because of my confidence in him. Madge had, he said, profoundly affected his view of women of a certain kind – I suppose in me he had seen her antithesis – steady, sensible yet pretty enough, from the sort of solid well-to-do family background he had always wanted. Yet he beat me in the creativity stakes. My upbringing, education and profession as a nurse had paradoxically anchored me so firmly that my aspirations in writing and intellectual pursuits eluded me. I could not relinquish my self-control and on the few occasions I had, I later regretted it. I kept that cool head, even at the height of our affair, which sometimes he mistook for frigidity, while his passion often seemed to get the better of him. It must have been true, although I wonder myself at my *sang-froid* after all these long years of loneliness. From his letters, it seems as if the thought of our togetherness consumes him, at home in the bungalow with Jock and Ian, or on the dredge, pacing out the endless nights of duty or writing those long letters on the thinnest of paper. I, on the other hand, devote only a small portion of space to George in my diaries. I follow the war news avidly, cutting out clips from the newspaper as I go. I feel like a bystander, a witness to world events from my hospital bed or in the gardens, in an outpost of empire that would become a second theatre for war. He often complained that I held back my feelings and sent him letters filled with trivia - about friends, colleagues, people we both knew, about the latest gossip rife in the colony. Perhaps I feared losing that iron control to a man I loved but could see so clearly, carefully schooled as I had been in the transience of men's passions. How could I know that I would spend a lifetime reliving every moment.

Lately, I have written articles, leading me to remember and relive the past. It seems very real to me and recent – a typical trait in the elderly, as I am only too painfully aware from past experiences - not only from the many old people I have nursed, but from my own parents. I can't help trying to imagine George as an old man with white hair – he had a beautiful head of black, wavy hair when I knew him – but I have digressed as usual. Some time ago, I wrote of the moment which determined my future career. I called this article *The Turning Point* and submitted it to the local paper. These days, my memory operates selectively and there are long stretches of nothingness, but I recall this event vividly.

I remember it happened just after the end of the Great War. It had rained heavily that day and as I walked home from school I saw, incongruous in an English puddle of rainwater, glimpses of vibrant, exotic colour. Some foreign stamps had fallen out of an envelope, showing fantastic images of mosques, palaces and tigers. They came from Malaya, and immediately fired my child's imagination and my ambition to travel. Eagerly, I showed them to my mother when I reached home. She presided over tea in the dining room, looking fresh and rested after her afternoon nap in a crisp white blouse and calf-length skirt. Little Tommy, my baby brother, nearly four years old, was being supervised at tea in the nursery by his nanny.

"Oh, there you are, Lavinia," said Florence. "I was beginning to worry. There have been so many new cases of this dreadful flu that I was sure you must have been taken ill."

Florence took the tea cosy off the pot and felt its temperature while I hurriedly took off my hat and coat. Mother was always so anxious, but perhaps she had good reason to be. At ten years old I tended to be something of a dreamer, which later turned into wilfulness as I clearly saw the obstacles which my gender put in the way of making those dreams reality. Full of eagerness to show my poor mother my fascinating find, I took the stamps over to her.

"Look, Mother! Aren't they beautiful? They were in a puddle but I can dry them. The colours aren't spoiled."

Florence frowned slightly and pushed back a long strand of fair hair which had escaped from its fastening on the top of her head. Her delicate, pale face, with its early worry lines, reluctantly showed an interest in what I proffered. The late afternoon light grew dim and she took the little package over to the window to see its contents more clearly. She carefully examined the stamps, their garish colours and fantastic depictions out of place amongst the muted tones of the "tasteful" English room. Unfortunately for me, Mother did not share my wonder or, if she did, she kept it well hidden. Like most parents of a respectable ilk, she took my moral education deeply seriously and seemed far more concerned with what presented as the morally and socially correct course of action.

"May I keep them, Mother? May I?"

Similar to many other children of my age, I had a rudimentary stamp collection but most of them were rather dull, just showing the be-whiskered head of King George V. I could see them now, in my mind's eye, having pride of place in my album and showing them off to my friends.

"Certainly not, Lavinia," answered my mother, to my acute disappointment. "Some poor child probably dropped them. Let's see now, there's a Chinese family at the top of this road – Mr and Mrs Wong. These stamps probably belong to one of their little girls. After tea we'll go straight up there to ask them." She paused and then relented a little, to my delight. "I suppose if they have no idea who they belong to and nobody claims them you may keep them – I will put them away in the meantime and you must not play with them."

A tense meal followed, as I tried to swallow my bread and butter and wash it down with warm tea. To my chagrin and acute disappointment, the Chinese family did claim the stamps and I had to relinquish my precious little package. The lady of the house, Mrs Wong, smiled at me graciously as I handed them over with all the good grace I could muster but thereafter she waved whenever I saw them out and invited me to play with her daughter.

The Wong family, to me, always had an aura of the exotic. Minting, the little girl, went to my school, and thereafter became included in my small circle of friends. I learned, in good time, how they had lived in Malaya in a place called Penang but that her father's work, for the British government, had brought the family to live in England. Minting had attended an English school in Penang and spoke the language fluently. The stories she told us about her life in Malaya, where she had left many friends, fascinated me. She described it as a place full of sunshine and colour, with peoples of many nationalities and of wondrous, sweet-smelling tropical plants, strange animals and highly coloured birds flying wild in the trees. I couldn't wait to grow up so that I could go there and see for myself. By contrast, England seemed mundane and dull in the extreme.

It seemed like only a few years later that I came to the full realisation of my likely destiny in this life. Unlike many female explorers and travellers of the nineteenth century who had hailed from the aristocracy, I had been born into a rigidly respectable family of the middle class, and knew that I would face rigorous opposition to any proposals of lone travel. However, unbeknownst to me, the First World War had been to my advantage. As the 1920's continued, I began to see possibilities in the nursing profession providing a means of escape from the inevitable fate of marriage and family. This represented a strange contradiction in my vision of the future – I knew that at some time in my life I would want these things too, but not at the expense of a life and career of my own. In a sense, the Great War had both facilitated and limited my choices. Unless I wanted to bring disgrace on my family, I would have to remain a "spinster" while I pursued my ambition. However, the slaughter of the First World War had significantly reduced the numbers of eligible young men available, which helped in its way. Although ideas of greater freedom of choice for women, brought about by their variety of war work, progressed, marriage often put an end to a woman's career.

I found the prospect of a career in nursing exciting and became more focused in my studies, filling my schoolbooks with carefully drawn botanical and biological diagrams. I loved what I imagined would be the strict discipline of the profession, the almost religious devotion to duty, the long hours and the sacrifices – for the benefit of others.

The moment I entered St Stephen's Hospital School of Nursing on the Fulham Road, I loved the atmosphere and prospective challenge of the environment. I felt nervous, in an excited sort of way, on that first day on the wards in September 1930 as I walked through a myriad of corridors and up and down the echoing stone staircases of the Victorian hospital, previously used as a workhouse. Clanging and rattling noises reverberated against the walls as oxygen cylinders and trolleys clanked along, pulled or pushed by hurrying nurses or orderlies. An all-pervading aroma of antiseptic and ether filled the air mingled with the sweet scent of flowers wafting from private rooms as I passed. All the floors seemed identical, with walls painted a glossy cream and green, the parquet floors highly polished, so that my new black lace-up nurses' shoes squeaked as I walked. I tried to straighten up and look like a competent nurse, conscious of the rustling of my starched apron and the one stripe on my cap, signifying a first-year student.

A friendly-looking hospital porter, wheeling an empty trolley, nodded as he rattled past.

"Morning, Nurse," he greeted me.

I grasped my opportunity.

"Good morning," I replied. "Could you please direct me to Men's Surgical? I seem to be rather lost."

"First day, is it?" replied the porter. "You'll be alright, Nurse. That's Sister Haynes' ward. I go there a lot myself. I'm Tom by the way." He held out a hand.

"Val," I said, pleased to see a friendly face but conscious for the first time, as I always would be during my training, of being caught loitering, talking when I should be working – even sitting down. Tom had a round smiling face over his brown work overall coat, topped with a mop of black hair falling over his eyes. I felt cheered by the encounter and went in the direction he pointed out to me. I arrived exactly two minutes late for report, at two minutes past seven.

As I entered the ward on the top floor of the building, the space opened out before my eyes. Early morning light streamed in through the large windows at the other end of the ward. Designed on the "Nightingale" plan, about ten white-counterpaned beds stood down each side of the room facing a long central table holding several large vases of flowers. Near the door where I entered were two or three private rooms and an office. At the near end of the ward stood a smaller desk around which about six or seven uniformed nurses sat writing on notepads. The night nurse sat alone on the other side of the desk holding a large sheet of paper. She looked up as I entered. She looked about forty and wore her dark brown hair pulled back severely under her cap, which showed the wide blue stripe of a staff nurse. Her eyes, red with fatigue, surveyed me through round, horn-rimmed spectacles. Despite her obvious exhaustion, she smiled kindly while I felt more pairs of eyes focused upon me than I needed at that particular moment.

"Lavinia?" said the staff nurse. "Come in, we're expecting you. I've only just started."

She indicated a spare seat at the end of the semi-circle and I sat down, taking a fountain pen from my uniform pocket. My nearest neighbour, a young blonde woman whom I had seen once or twice in the distance in the nurse's home, smiled at me before we gave our full attention to the report. The night nurse handed me a sheet of paper containing a list of patients with their diagnoses and current treatment. Next to each patient's name a space for our notes had been provided. I tried to concentrate and jot down a few words as the staff nurse went through the list but she spoke rapidly and referred to the procedures and equipment in abbreviated terms and although I had revised handover methods and the medical shorthand used, I struggled to keep up. I hoped it would become more familiar with time.

After the report had finished, everyone seemed to know what to do except me, and I stood to the side waiting for directions feeling, once more, a little lost. Sure enough, as the night nurse took her things and left the ward to her well-earned rest, the senior nurse in charge came up to me.

"Hello," she said, "I'm the junior sister here – Nurse Clarke's the name. Sister Haynes will be here about nine and I expect she would like to welcome you to the ward. For the time being, I'm putting you with a second-year nurse who will show you the ropes. I understand you're familiar with the charts?"

We had been shown samples of the observation charts for recording the blood pressure, temperature, pulses and respiration of our patients and the fluid charts, for recording their input and output, all of which had to be measured accurately for the doctors when they came round. During our first six weeks in the school, we had covered the basics of bedside nursing to equip us least partially in our first placements. Luckily, once I had settled into the routine of the ward, I picked it up quite quickly and became proactive in my observations of what needed to be done. By the time Sister Haynes arrived, puffing into the room with her stout frame squeezed into her dark-blue sister's dress and her permed grey hair escaping the elaborate frilly hat, I was happily bed-bathing a patient, surrounded by the patient's toiletries, clean linen and a large bowl of soapy water. The second-year nurse I thought rather remiss, and I felt that I would have done a better job of supervising me. I made a mental note of her omissions for when my turn came for supervision.

The curtains which I had pulled round the bed for the privacy of the elderly man occupying it, parted as I was in the process of removing his pyjama trousers and I just managed to cover him with a towel as we had been taught, when Sister Haynes' large, red, perspiring face peered through the crack.

"Good morning, Nurse Coates. When you've finished bathing this patient, could you see me in my office, please?"

I acquiesced, returned the Sister's greeting and said that I would be there as soon as I could. The elderly patient grinned.

"That was a close one, Nurse!" he chuckled. He had a twinkle in his eye and I guessed that he was not as old and infirm as I had originally thought. He beckoned me to get a little closer.

"You've got to watch that one," he said in a low voice, gesturing to where the curtains had parted. "Keep on the right side of her. She's been here since the dinosaurs and knows all the bigwigs here."

I acted innocently in response to his well-meaning hint but smiled to myself as I went back to the bowl to re-soap the flannel. I showed vestiges of the smile to the patient. He grinned back, as if we shared a secret.

"You'll be alright, Nurse," he said. I took that to be a compliment and hurried to clear up before I assisted my patient into his bedside chair.

I looked outside the curtains, rather desperately, for assistance. Everyone seemed busy, with most of the beds shrouded by curtains and I was obliged to carry out the procedure alone. As I lifted him into his chair, I felt the strain in my back and grimaced when he was not looking. This was how it would be – the exhaustion which I had heard about and which I already felt, after only a few hours on the ward, culminating in a broken body at fifty. I would have to use my wits to get off the wards and into a less physically demanding role, and the sooner the better.

Sister Haynes was writing at her desk when I approached her office. She gestured to me to sit in the chair in front of her. In a few moments she looked up, unsmiling.

"Well, Nurse Coates, welcome to my ward. I've heard some good things about you from your tutors in the school. It seems you've made a good start already this morning but don't get complacent. You've got to live up to the example of two excellent nurses who've just gone on to other wards – a tough act to follow. I was sorry to lose them."

I knew who she referred to - the pair always stuck together and constituted star material in the world of nursing. Their theory consistently showed a high standard and they collaborated only with each other, as if the other students in their group ranked beneath their attention. I felt relieved that the preceding set had the honour of their membership and not mine. I can see them now – how they looked as young women, in their crisp uniform dresses and aprons. One of them, a tall blonde with a peaches-and-cream complexion called Hazel, had married and thus earned the honourable title of "Mrs" rather than "Nurse" as a concession to her status. I wondered, and still do, how her husband coped with the demanding training she undertook. In those days, limited co-operation existed between married couples (and some stay it still does) in matters of work. I will never forget the day I saw Hazel crying with distress in the hospital carpark and calling frantically with tears in her voice after a receding car, as her husband drove off and left her standing there. She had a sensitive soul, in spite of her undoubted ability and intelligence, or more accurately, probably because of it.

I can see now that I inhabited a more fortunate position than Hazel and had no competitors for my devotion to duty. I survived Sister Haynes and many more like her, in my quest for the Holy Grail of registration. Fortunately, when I began my training I carried the advantage of youth, which played no small part in my success.

Nurses worked long, arduous hours – more so than they do now. I swallowed the rationale for this, hook, line and sinker. In a sense they tried to break our wills as our bodies were broken – a brainwashing on the same lines as an army private has to endure. By the end of a shift, pain racked the weakest parts of my body but I felt strangely euphoric. All the boxes were ticked, the charts were complete and the patients had survived under my care. I felt cleansed, almost holy, and even managed a smile to my patients as I finally left the ward, even anticipating the next day's shift with pleasure.

"See you tomorrow," I would say to them, feeling sorry that they had to stay where they were while I at least had a respite. This was the only reward. There was never any praise, only dreadful castigation (usually self-inflicted) and guilt if anything should be omitted.

It was to be nearly seventy years before nursing degrees and diplomas were awarded from universities. I did not live to see this day. There was a belief for many years that such a practical skill could not be intellectualised and research into best practice outcomes was unheard of. What made a good nurse, it was believed, was a combination of women's intuition, individual experience (the longer the better) and old wives' folklore. It was thought then that the discipline of learning menial tasks from scratch formed the basis of a good training. So, in my first year I cleaned the ward bathrooms, dusted and cooked from cooking lectures teaching us invalid cookery – from raw meat sandwiches to baked custards. The practice of cooking for patients survived for many more years, as I remember. We learned bed-making for patients having different kinds of surgery, bandaged figure-of-eight and reverse figure-of-eight on different parts of the body and prepared and administered soap-and-water or turpentine enemas using a long rubber tube and a funnel at one end.

Even though the training challenged my less-than-optimally-strong constitution (I had narrowly survived as a very delicate infant) I had a strong will and a good brain. I stuck it out, using my intelligence and not a little cunning to survive. My methods varied from "helping out" other students on the ward who fell behind in their studies – these hapless nurses willingly shouldered some of my donkey work - to becoming "Sister's pet" by being startlingly familiar with patients' treatment and diagnoses and volunteering to assist the doctors in their procedures.

Sister could often be heard calling out on the ward for my assistance.

"Nurse Coates!" was the familiar cry, echoing down the ward during a particularly busy shift, when the doctors' rounds rendered a chaotic morning even worse by consultants trailing an entourage of their own students behind them.

"Nurse Coates! Go and check that infusion. It should be nearly through by now."

I would cover the poor patient I abandoned and race to stare at the said drip, checking the rate with my fob watch and calculating when the bottle would be finished. Brand new nursing students gazed at my apparent expertise with respect and awe. I felt sorry for them, but I recognised this as a survival game and Sister's trust endorsed my actions.

Nursing then constituted a disciplined and exacting science, and the patient was a passive bystander in his own treatment. To them, the doctors appeared as gods and the nurses, as their representatives, strictly to be obeyed. We spoke of patients not as individuals but in terms of their complaint, their bed number or their treatment. It was,

"The hernia in 17."

or,

"The transfusion in the side ward."

We did not see ourselves as unkind but our rigidity, manifested in our bustling starched presences must have intimidated our patients. We meant them to be intimidated. Like schoolchildren listening obediently to their teacher from among their rows of desks, so our patients from their neat rows of beds submitted to our authority. In our turn, we submitted to the authority above us, just as the wider society was based on hierarchy and class. We lived in dread of Sister

Tutor's disapproval, and Matron was an exalted being only occasionally seen in the distance.

My comparative success within this system gave me a certain confidence and reinforced my manner in dealings with others, which became a part of my outward personality. It was a slightly patronising manner which assumed that I, the nurse, knew best but was encouraging and kind in any case, as a mother to her child.

"I think I'll take a little walk up the corridor today, Nurse," ventured one of my long-stay patients on Women's Medical, my last ward at the end of the second year. She was a timid woman, used to living under the shadow of a domineering husband, by whom she had borne five children in quick succession.

"That's right, dear," I would say. "I'll get one of the auxiliaries to look out for you."

My tone was both comforting and reassuring as I finished making her bed. Lately, I had noticed that I often used this very tone outside the hospital to my friends, especially Dorrie, my oldest and closest.

I would watch the slight, frail form of my patient, clad in its quilted housecoat as she made her slow progress towards the doors of the ward, seeing the pink fluffy slippers disappearing around the corner. I reflected in that rare, quiet moment that however hard my life was, at least I was free, independent and able to make my own decisions.

By the summer of 1933 I had progressed to lectures on *Materia medica* - on different kinds of drugs, their origins and uses, and on different kinds of operations and anaesthetics, given by one of the professors who lectured to medical students as well. I now had more responsibility on the wards, frequently left in charge at night with a night sister on call or overseeing several wards. It often occurred that after the evening rush was over, about 1:00am saw me in splendid isolation at the central table, writing letters or studying for a test or exam. Occasionally, I and the two auxiliaries were rushed off our feet, especially if we had an emergency or an admission, but I relished these quiet times.

"I am writing this in the middle of the night," I would write to my mother. *"I have two pneumonias, one mad man and about 20 others, so I am in the midst of things again."*

I loved the solitariness of night duty, the peace of the ward, the autonomy of making my own decisions and most of all, the eventual emergence into the light of early morning and a new day, back to the Home and to sleep. A dreamlike existence....

My busy life often curtailed my trips home, much to the disappointment of my mother, who loved to hear my tales of the wards and funny stories about Matron or Sister.

"I'm sorry, Mother. I'm off on Wednesday and Thursday again this week, but unfortunately, I will have to go to the Theatre on Thursday morning and I have a lecture Friday morning so I shall have to come home on Wednesday afternoon about 3 pm and return back at night with a late pass. I hope you don't mind, Mother, but I can't see anything else to do."

My four years of hard work and sacrifice paid off, when in June 1934 I attended my own graduation ceremony along with dozens of other newly qualified nurses. We occupied the first six rows of the Great Hall of the hospital, under the austere gaze of the portraits of august personages: governors of the hospital past and present, leading consultants and stern matrons. My intake of 1930 was considerably reduced to about two thirds of the original numbers, I noticed. I turned and grinned at my parents, who sat proudly among the visitors behind me, only to receive a sharp nudge from the survivor squashed next to me. The dean of the medical school, paunchy and a little crumpled in his tweed suit and monocle, stood on the podium and, after checking his pocket watch, had started speaking.

"What an attractive sight," he was saying. "I see from this stage what appears to be row upon row of our finest young women, looking as ethereal as lilies in their caps and aprons."

He turned to look at Matron, who occupied the stage along with several others, forcing a smile of gratification from her usually dourly inexpressive face. Several of the graduates round me suppressed giggles behind their hands. I heard a loud snort from someone behind me, fortunately inaudible from the stage. The dean continued.

"Yet ladies and gentlemen," he continued, "it is these delicate flowers who will smooth the brows of our sick and spare themselves nothing in being the handmaidens of the medical profession."

He went on, for what seemed like hours, in a similar vein, but I had stopped listening.

Later that afternoon, I collected my suitcase from my room and walked with my mother and father out of the gates of St Stephen's Hospital for the last time. A short holiday awaited me and a job hunt – my prized certificate was in my hand and I was ready to take on the world.

Chapter 2

Retrospect

I had dreamed of Malaya again. When I awoke, not to the steamy heat nor the droning of the ceiling fan but to the pale English sun infiltrating my bedroom, I felt disorientated and confused. In my dream, I had been young again with the optimism of youth stimulated by the novelty of my surroundings. I had woken each day fresh and eager, as to the start of a new chapter. My body had felt light, healthy, had not felt the stiffness of age. I was newly arrived and not yet drained of the vigour which I knew later when my body weakened to sickness.

Then I remembered. The year was 1989, and I would celebrate my eightieth birthday in a few days. Malaya had been nearly fifty years ago and in between, I had watched the world change, watched my mother and father grow old and pass from it and seen other people's children grow to adulthood. Sometimes, I had pondered the purpose of my existence but then realised that I did not need one, except to adhere to the principle of some grand design, and I had never been particularly religious. The natural impetus was to keep living, to keep moving, to keep the cogs of life turning and that, since Malaya, had provided my default survival mechanism.

The church clock on the green struck eight. I heard a key in the lock and a cheery voice floated up the stairs. My dream was enclosed in its own sleep cycle and I had overslept.

"'Morning, Miss Coates!"

Mrs Roberts, who for years held the position of daily help at Hildenborough, had been gone many years and Janet (it was only recently that I had come to know her surname) was her replacement after the move to Southborough. I thought I had better answer now or she would assume the worst.

"I'm just coming, dear! Give me a minute!"

Hastily, I forced my legs over the side of the bed and sat up, getting my bearings. Dressing gown and slippers on, I looked vainly for my stick. In recent years it had become my rock and support, having multiple purposes too numerous to mention. Too late. Janet, whose approach had been muffled by the thick fitted carpets, was in the bedroom.

Janet's meek, grey, unassuming persona, complete with a much-worn tweed skirt, flat brown lace-up shoes and blue nylon overall, suggested subservience, however unnecessary in the modern age. I had naturally thought of her when looking to replace my daily – she had worked for Dorrie's family and remained the soul of quiet discretion. Now she quietly and without a word, handed me my stick which had fallen behind the bedside table. Although not hired as a nurse, she helped me to make that first effort of the day, rising to my feet.

"What sort of a day is it, my dear?" I asked, trying vainly to see through the heavy net curtains. November had announced its dreary arrival and the weather had settled lately into a long stretch of cold, grey, drizzly days.

Janet attempted to be upbeat and brighter than she felt.

"It's not raining at the moment, Miss Coates," she said, assisting me to the top of the stairs. "On the forecast it said that we'd have a bit of sunshine later."

There was a large mirror attached to the wall at the top of the stairs. Goodness knows why I had put it there when I moved in. It only served to reinforce to me the cruelty which time effects on the human body. Although I usually tried to avoid my reflection, now I stopped and looked, no doubt curious to see whether by some miracle my dream had had some basis in truth and that some of it may have lingered. Alas, it served only to emphasise the comparison.

I saw a rather overweight, dumpy old woman, hunched over a stick, wispy grey hair in disarray and misshapen white legs with feet stuffed into fluffy slippers. My somewhat chubby cheeks, which a smile usually lifted, sagged from my bones, looking pallid without their usual application of rouge. I suppose, I thought, first thing in the morning fell short of the ideal time to make a self-appraisal, but this did nothing to lift my spirits.

The stairs always posed an obstacle. One of these days, I knew, I would not survive the descent without a mishap. Usually, Janet went down ahead of me, and guided me down one step at a time. I could make the descent on my own but preferred to wait for help. The ascent later in the day presented a similar risk but I managed this alone, usually a kind of mountaineering feat. The bend in the stairs halfway up would, I know, break my fall if the worst happened. I knew my days in this house rapidly approached an end but I purposely delayed the decision to enter a nursing home, preferring instead to rely on home help, which could be increased to a "care package" if needed. I knew, however, that it would only take one incident before my independence would be taken away from me. Thank heavens, though, my brain was still good.

Once ensconced at the kitchen table, waiting for Janet to put my breakfast in front of me, I put that brain to use. I looked over the garden at the back while I reflected. One of the reasons I had bought this house after Father died, it reminded me of the garden in the old Hildenborough house, although much smaller. Now, the November chill had brought nearly all the leaves from the trees. They lay on the grass, sodden and brown. The autumn mist still lingered and everything was still. My thoughts returned to Malaya involuntarily. My dream had lasted longer than I thought, and I recalled not only the events but the passion, the feelings long-forgotten, like the young woman I had been then.

Janet put down the teapot on the kitchen table and poured me a cup. I downed the refreshing brew immediately and tried to pour myself a second, before she respectfully, and with my assent, took the teapot handle and performed the task herself.

"The garden's still looking tidy, Madam," she remarked. "I remember the garden in your old house, years ago. Your father used to keep it nice. I'll have to get my Bill to come and sweep up those leaves for you."

Janet's husband acted as gardener and general handyman when the need arose, but the help's reference to Percy set off another train of musings in my mind, always, these days, tending to look backwards rather than forward. For how could one look forward at eighty? Quite apart from natural lifespan, one simply lacked the energy to think with any enthusiasm on the future. Refreshed by my tea, I felt in the mood to think about the past now.

"Janet, did I ever tell you about my first job as a qualified nurse? It was at New End Hospital, Hampstead. In those days they specialised in glands, you know. Endocrine disorders, and all that. It was cutting edge stuff back then in the 1930's and I was proud to be a part of it."

Janet, her hands now in the sink and covered with bubbles, turned dutifully to look at me.

"Really, madam?"

I felt "on a roll" as the young say nowadays – even more so with a captive listener.

"Yes, and it was there that I met Duger. She was one of my patients."

"Duger?" interposed my daily help, looking puzzled.

"Yes, dear. She was Danish. It all came from the way she signed her name you see. Illegible. It *looked* like Duger. It became a kind of nickname."

"What was her real name, then?" asked Janet, interested now.

"It doesn't matter. She was always Duger to me. Honestly, I can't really remember, anyway. I'll tell you about her one day. My goodness, she told me things that would make you blush! She was a character alright – wild! But she fascinated me. She certainly fascinated me..."

Here I tailed off, and concentrated on finishing my breakfast of bacon and eggs, which, in spite of my stubbornly large waistline, I insisted on eating. My mind, however, still remained busy with Duger. Janet, patient as ever with my ramblings, went back to her tasks and I released her to attend to a few of the essential ones, such as making my bed and preparing my meals for the rest of the day. To stretch my legs, once I had finished my breakfast, I got up out of my chair with some difficulty and, leaning heavily on my stick, passed through the small lounge to the French doors at the back of the adjoining conservatory, opening the door onto the patio. Stepping out, I heard the village church clock chime again, and counted. Nine strokes. The sounds lifted and carried on the wind, drifting away into the clear air. I looked up into the pale blue of a perfect autumn sky. How different it had all seemed then, in London. And Duger. I hadn't thought of her in years. I wondered if she were alive or dead and what had happened to her.

At first, I thought her outrageous, semi-conditioned as I had been by the militaristic training and the general ambience of dedication and duty. Desperately wearied by the work itself, acceptance was the easiest option and even held rewards of its own. Although it remained, in my case, a role, success resulted in a sense of achievement in service itself and in efficiency in performing the multifarious tasks expected. But Duger turned all this carefully developed philosophy on its head. We became friends because despite my prim exterior, she sensed a hunger in my psyche for excitement, kept rigidly under control. I hung onto her stories, both on the ward and later in her letters, recognising in her perhaps my *alter ego*. I knew that what I recognised in her existed in me too, although she in no way subscribed to the values in which I thought I believed.

I thought back to the autumn of 1934. The weather was similar to the way it is today – cold and unsettled but with sunny interludes. Duger was on holiday with relations in London from her home in Denmark, when she developed a Bartholin's cyst[1] which had become infected, possibly as a result of her carefree, if not promiscuous, life-style, which she had lived to the full in London. For nearly a week she had needed a lot of nursing care as she found walking excruciatingly painful. Duger was close to me in age, beautiful, tall and from a wealthy background. She lived with her aunt and uncle in Snekkersten, across the water from Sweden, having left her parents and younger brother for some unknown reason into which I did not pry. Her uncle was a well-known actor and she may have been a protégée of his, with her looks and personality.

Between my duties, in the quieter times of the afternoons, I would sit by her bedside, drawn into her world - a welcome escape from continual, exhausting duty. She lightened my life, and the atmosphere on the ward, which developed something of a party atmosphere. I do believe that the recovery rates improved on that ward during her stay.

"How tired all you poor nurses look!" she would say, in her charming and broken English. "Why do you work so hard?"

My feeble explanation about ethics and duty of care only served to deepen her confusion, so I would change the subject and instead ask her about her home in Denmark and her way of life there.

The notion of work ethic and sacrifice for the good of others escaped her. Her personal charisma shone so brightly that she made me question my motives. She was unashamedly hedonistic, romantic and pleasure-seeking in the extreme and, as the other patients on the ward looked on bemused, flirted outrageously with the doctors. Dr Hodgkiss, the duty doctor at the time, amused her because of his stern demeanour, which in no way decreased in his dealings with her, despite her best efforts.

"Miss Brinch, you should be taking some exercise around the ward now," Hodgkiss would say when he got to her bedside. "You will become weak if you lie in bed all day."

Duger would move aside the movie magazines which she loved and which occupied much of her time.

"Oh doctor," she would say, looking up at him coyly through her lashes. "Will you help me to walk? I think I would do it so much better if I went with you."

Dr Hodgkiss was not fooled.

"Nurse!" he called over to me. "Miss Brinch would like to take a walk now. Take her up to the end of the corridor and back, please. Twice daily walks from now on. Report to me if you have any problems."

He winked at me conspiratorially. Duger was henceforth compliant with her exercise and soon afterwards was to my regret, discharged, to travel back to Denmark. I missed her, hoping one day that I could travel across the North Sea to her home. In the meantime, she wrote regularly, lightening the effects of the tense pre-war days with accounts of her exploits. She wanted me to go and live with them in Denmark as a kind of au pair.

"We live nearly one hour from Copenhagen by the sea so we have a lovely view over to Sweden. People here in Denmark call it the Danish Riviera."

But I could not see myself just idling away the days. My upbringing, family and my training in nursing amalgamated in a moral code which did not allow the pursuit of pleasure for its own sake. But I did not rule out a visit. I wrote to Duger that I would think it over, but in reality, I had exams coming up and could not see myself throwing it all away. She was restless, in any case, in her aunt's house where the yearly apple-picking and trips with her aunt to Copenhagen to see her uncle in plays did not satisfy her wander-lust. She was longing to have a love affair. She missed her time in London where she had stayed in the Regent Palace Hotel with Margaret, a dear friend of mine, and before that Paris, with drunken parties and waking up next to people with whom she did not remember going to bed. It seemed that her moods could be strongly influenced by the condition of her love life, at that time in a sad state, with a German boyfriend planning to marry a girl in Berlin. It never seemed the right time for me to travel to Denmark. Perhaps, if truth be told, I feared to become caught up in her lifestyle. I could not free myself from a slightly disapproving stance, and, true or not, felt that I was not fundamentally influenced or changed by knowing her. I was curious and it was part of my education.

While Duger's letters provided a welcome distraction from the gloom of the 1930's, I began to forge my career in the direction of health visiting. I knew that there was much work to do but I felt confident in my ability. In the autumn of 1935, I left New End to undertake a year's nursery education course at Dr Barnardo's St Christopher's Nursery College in Tunbridge Wells, only five or six miles from home. The training, severe but well regarded, would open the way for health visiting. In the 1970's, I wrote about it for an article submitted to *Nursery World*.

"There stood two Edwardian houses in the centre of a Royal Borough (Tunbridge Wells was named "Royal Tunbridge Wells" in 1909 by Edward VII partly to commemorate his mother Queen Victoria's fondness for the town). They were double fronted and joined together on three floors by smoked-glass cover-ways and wooden floors. The basements had a direct route through the kitchen to the pram room and cloakroom. The founder/principal of the college took into her care children whose parents were engaged, either in high official positions under the Crown Agents for the colonies, the diplomatic service or professions anywhere in the world. She was the pioneer in the practice of "humanising" cow's milk, which was the addition of whey into the feed. This was at a time when babies were dying from being fed on patent foods that had come into popularity as an alternative to (and liberation from) breast milk and which in many cases had resulted in many infant mortalities. I was very nearly a victim of this practice

myself. A few of the graduates from the college had taken posts in Royal households and the stately homes of England.

"From the college, during the day could be seen a retinue of nurses pushing various types of prams up the long hill to the Common. They wore long grey coats and hats to match in winter and plain pink dresses with white collars and frilly cuffs to their short sleeves in summer. These nurses were on "Nursery Duty" and their day's work would be against the law today. It began at 6.30 am and consisted of washing piles of stained and dirty terry-towelling nappies in the cold, austere basement in winter and a clammy hot-house in summer. Four wooden tubs were used to ensure thorough washing and rinsing, wrung by hand and later hung outside on lines where sometimes in icy weather they froze on the line. There were babies from a month to children of five years old, usually about thirty of them. Those over six months had to be bathed, dressed and fed in time for the morning walk by 9 am. The younger babies were left in comparative peace, either in cots or prams out in the garden if fine or in the pram room if wet. I often had to push a large bassinet up the long hill and across a busy highway to the steeper hill on the common. Two sturdy toddlers sat in the pram and another held the handle. On strict orders we were not allowed to sit down on the wooden seats on the common or even to speak to one another.

"Those nurses who were not on pram duty were engaged either in feeding the babies, scrubbing floors, washing paintwork, kitchen duties, ironing, mending and other sundry duties. The dispenser was the most skilled of the students as she had the precarious duty of getting the correct temperature for the addition of the whey. When I was on this particular duty, I was called back on duty to remake all the foods because they had junketed from the whey. Added to the other duties was the stoking of the colossal boiler fire, which if allowed to go out involved the very hazardous job of relighting it. The last duty of the morning was the laying of tables for the pram pushers and their retinue.

"On their return, the college was in a state of pandemonium. The

necessity of urgent calls by the demands of nature resulted in hurried short cuts through the hallowed kitchen passage to the toilets. The cook's irate shouts echoed through the whole building. The worst crime of all was the use of the out of bounds staircase, which was a short cut to the dining room. The offence was met by a special punishment by matron herself – a severe admonishment on the office carpet, on the subject of erroneous short cuts.

"As a respite to this plethora of work, the off-duty consisted of a half-day a week and alternate morning and afternoon on Sunday. In the week, we were given two hours off during the day, while work churned on in the college until eight o'clock at night and sometimes with the addition of night duty, starting at 10 pm – 6.30 am.

"While St Christopher's benefited from our free labour, the reward for the year's enterprise for the cost of a hundred pound fee was the graduation ceremony. On this auspicious occasion, one was allowed to wear a white starched apron, a nurse's cap and strings tied under the chin with a bow and a stiff collar and cuffs, under which a specially made grey dress was worn. The final accolade was a certificate of merit and a silver badge embossed with the design of St Christopher. The promise of a further award for the service of one year's employment was to be a real silver button engraved with a "C". This was to be worn in the place of one of the buttons on the long grey coat and considered an emblem of much distinction!

"Paradoxically, I loved the college enough to return a few years later for a period of temporary staff duties, which was considered a very elevated position so soon after training. No doubt my willingness to return was also due to the allure of the babies whose faces still remain in my mind and quite a few are in the daily report book, which I still have in my possession today."

In the Southborough garden, a cloud had covered the sun, instantly altering the previously sunny aspect to one of dullness, devoid of colour. I had kept warm enveloped in its rays but now I pulled my dressing gown closer around me and shivered. After all, it was November. Janet appeared in the doorway with a duster in her hand. She looked at the grandfather clock in the lounge.

"Goodness me, Madam. It's coming up to ten. Let me get you washed and dressed and then I'll bring you a cup of coffee in the lounge. It's not so nice now."

Looking up at the sky, she came out onto the patio to help me over the step.

"What have you been doing out there all this time?' she asked curiously, and I thought, somewhat impertinently.

"Oh, just thinking about the past," I said. "It keeps me amused you know. It's better than television."

Once ensconced in my favourite armchair in front of that television set, I let Janet fuss around me.

"Do you want it on, Miss Coates?" she enquired.

"There's never anything on at this hour, only rubbish," I replied. "Just the newspaper will be fine. And the coffee."

It happened while I sat there, drinking my coffee and munching on my favourite bourbon biscuits. I wondered how I would occupy the remaining twelve hours or so before the church clock chimed the summons to mount the stairs again. It was then I suddenly knew that I had to write. Time pressed too heavily on me these days, and despite my advancing age, I felt convinced that I still had the ability, provided I could sit typing at the desk for hours. The last time had been nearly ten years ago, but I still had my contacts with various magazines and newspapers who had previously welcomed articles about my nursing experiences in the 1930's.

I had a tiny, decorated ceramic bell next to my chair that I now rang to summon Janet again. She rushed down the stairs, having mounted them only five minutes before, putting even herself at risk of falling – she was getting on in years too.

"It's been a long time since I heard you ring that, Madam!" she said anxiously, somewhat breathless. Her features relaxed once she had assured herself that this was no emergency.

"I'm so sorry, dear," I said. "I didn't mean to startle you but I think if I have to spend another day just sitting here, I'll go mad. You remember that suitcase with all the old letters and diaries in it? Do you know where it is?"

Janet thought hard. Her Bill had helped with the arrangement of furniture and odd items after the move from Hildenborough. Then she remembered.

"I think it's in the spare room, Madam," she said, wondering what her employer was going to ask her to do next. She thought if it involved lugging a heavy suitcase down the stairs, she would ring Bill to get him to come round and help. "It's going to be a bit heavy for me, Madam, but I'll ring for Bill to come round and bring it down for you if you like."

I nodded, and let Janet use the phone to summon her husband. Ten minutes later he appeared at the French windows. He removed his shoes carefully before entering the sitting room. Well, I thought, at least if nothing else comes of this morning, it will be a bit different. Already I felt better, and the house developed a bustle of things happening.

"'Morning Miss Coates!"

Bill was a surprisingly good-looking man, a little younger than his wife and well-preserved, with a slim yet muscular frame kept in trim by his manual work. Not for the first time, I wondered how somewhat "plain" looking women often ended up with attractive husbands, who remained faithful. Obviously, it would remain a sacred secret from which I was excluded, and part of the great mystery of marriage. In less than five minutes, Bill, with Janet directing operations, carried the suitcase, with consummate ease, down the stairs. I had risen from my chair and stood watching them from the hall, leaning on my stick.

"Where do you want it, Miss Coates?"

I thought about it.

"Better put it in the dining room for now," I concluded, as I looked into the room which bore that title.

This room rarely saw use these days as I had my meals either in the kitchen or on a tray in front of the television. Dining rooms had become obsolete, I reflected. The mahogany table and six matching chairs with their green leather seats looked too perfect, polished regularly by Janet. The room had a slight smell of dust and old-fashioned lavender polish, which I preferred over the "spray-on" variety. What plans I had had for dinner parties when I moved here! I think Dorrie and Roe had been the last to have a meal with me in this room years ago, and then the lingering smell of cooked food (fish we had had) had permeated it for days afterwards.

"On the table, please," I could stand and go through the papers at leisure, and when I got tired, I could sit down on one of the chairs and continue working that way, putting them to use. "But be careful of the surface, won't you."

Bill carefully lifted the heavy case onto the table, taking care not to scratch the pristine mahogany surface. "There you are, Miss Coates. I'll unclasp it for you, shall I?"

I nodded. I would wait until everyone had left the room to start looking through the papers, letters and documents in the case. It would not do to open it under the eyes of Mr and Mrs Andrews, honest, "salt of the earth" people as I knew them to be.

Bill did a half-bow and backed out of the room. I had some notes ready and slipped them into his hand. He gave a mock salute in thanks and turned to leave.

"Oh Bill," I said, waylaying him. "I think that apple tree at the back could do with a prune as all the leaves are off now, and when you come, can you do a general tidy up? Those leaves on the patio are getting hazardous. I nearly slipped this morning."

"I can do it now for you if you like, Ma'am," (he pronounced it "Mum") "then, when Janet has finished, I can drive her home."

I agreed, impatient to start looking at my papers. I would have to check up on him later - a nuisance, but I could see his reasoning. If only I could do things for myself, I would not have to involve people. I turned back to the suitcase. There it was, all of it. The letters, in separate folders - Duger, George, Dorrie, Margaret, and many more. Where to start? And what to write? I pulled as many folders as I could from the suitcase, stacking them on the table at the side. My little pocket diaries that I used to keep before the war came last, at the bottom, saved by my mother and father. I had not taken them with me to Malaya. I turned the pages, seeing the tiny writing of the entries, almost as tiny as I had heard the Bronte sisters had written while concocting their imaginary worlds. I opened Duger's folder and started reading a letter from November 1936. What had I been doing then? Ah yes, I had become a pupil midwife. My career was blooming, while Duger's stagnated, if she ever had one. But I lived a fuller life, vicariously, through her.

In the carpet-hushed, stultified atmosphere of the stuffy dining room, the October London of over fifty years ago became to me as vivid as if I saw it now for the first time before my eyes. My days, I remembered, overflowed with lectures and practical experience. I relished being back in London, and especially St Thomas' Hospital, after Tunbridge Wells, even though my parents were reserved on the matter, I recall. The evenings continued as busy as the days, as I met up with any friends staying in London to go on the town.

That first day, in October 1936, I recalled, seeing the diary entry, Dr Hodgkiss, the "Obs/Gynae" consultant from New End, had given a lecture on breech and vertex presentations and the next day I practised in clinic. "Just like St Stephens!" I wrote on 22nd. The following weeks, I assisted in deliveries, simple and complex, played golf, saw Charles Boyer and Katharine Hepburn in "*Heartbreak*" and met up with Dorrie and Rita, two of the Raymond girls. Dorrie had just moved into new digs and worked as a private secretary at *Good Housekeeping* magazine. I kept an eye on my smoking, and decided to note in my diary whenever I got through a packet of cigarettes. I went home every few weeks as well, much to my mother's joy. That Christmas at home I sang carols in church on Christmas Eve and received plenty of presents on Christmas Day. Parties continued until the weekend, then on Sunday 29th I delivered my thirteenth and fourteenth cases. I also got a letter from Duger. How different her Christmas seemed compared to the Christmas of 1934, as she remembered it at New End.

A deep but gentle voice startled me. Bill stood in the doorway behind me.

"All done for you, Miss Coates. Janet's finished now and we'll be on our way. She says she's left your lunch and dinner in the fridge and you can put it straight into the microwave. The table's all laid for your lunch, she says and she'll see you in the morning."

I turned to thank the thoughtful Bill, who, with Janet had raised a family of four with very little money, and gave him a smile of appreciation. I would stop for lunch now and continue with my reminiscences later.

---

1. A fluid-filled swelling (cyst) in the Bartholin's glands, located at the either side of the vaginal opening, due to infection or injury (Google, accessed 24/12/22).

Chapter 3

Influences

I woke the next morning with more purpose than I had felt for a very long time. Now that I had begun to sort through the letters, papers and diaries, I would try to make some kind of story out of it – an autobiography. That sounded very grand – usually only famous people did that, but my life had become significant in a way and I had always kept careful records. Janet looked pleased to see me busy, working my way through the suitcase, annotating and making notes on a notepad.

"Don't overtire yourself, Madam," she said to me after breakfast, as I got up from the table and set out with a determined air for the dining room. I had even washed and dressed that morning before she had arrived.

I pretended not to hear her and closed the dining room door firmly behind me. In actual fact it slammed shut, which was not my intention, but it conveyed the message that I wished not to be disturbed. I opened the door again two seconds later.

"Coffee in here at eleven, please Janet!"

I hoped I did not behave too cantankerously as it would inconvenience me if Janet left, but I remained confident that she knew me of old, and I was paying her, for heaven's sake.

"Thank you!" I added as an afterthought.

Duger's letters particularly, had rekindled the memories of the 1930's as I exercised my rusty faculties and, perhaps for the first time ever, saw a causal effect between meeting her and my journey to Malaya. She spoke to me from the pale blue pages of embossed notepaper, persuading me of existences beyond the one I knew, which beckoned enticingly like mirages.

"*I think I told you once my uncle dislikes me,*" she had written in 1936 on 23rd of November. "*He has been awful to me the whole time. Well! I have just bought a new evening dress, lovely, of dark blue silk. My aunt was unfortunately or fortunately for me ill that evening, and I went out with my uncle alone. He used to be completely passive without saying a word to me. Then that evening I thought, if he continues in that way I could not bear it, and I began to speak about everything that makes him thaw. In the party he was very nice to me, more than I could expect from him. It was a party for dinner, and dinner parties in Denmark are simply with a lot of wine, maybe for that reason he was so kind. When we went home, Oh dear!*

"*First in the taxi to the station he take around my leg so hard I couldn't say anything except: "But Carl, what are you doing?" (I never say Uncle or Aunt, only Carl and Fenja)*

"*Then he said: "Dear, you look beautiful tonight, and I have been dreaming about you the whole evening. I should like you to be mine."*

"*Then he kissed me very brutally, I never knew he could be like that, so excited after everything he has been to me. Of course, I have had a lot to drink, so I didn't mind, but kissed him again. Then in the train we were still alone and he said:*

"*I think you must hate me very much.*"

"*Oh, never, Carl, I loved you from the first day I came here.*" (*A terrible lie but in that moment useful!*)

"*Then he says:*

"*Is that so, even when I was malicious?*"

"*Yes, even so, only then I was very sad.*"

"*Yes, I understand dear, but you see there mustn't be anything else between us now, I am too old.*"

"*Then I told him just what he wanted to hear:*

"*Of course you are not too old, you will never be anything else but a big naughty boy.*"

"*I know it was a very bad trick of me to be like that, and not fair against my aunt, but I wanted to play with him only for a moment. He himself is a very big actor. He plays every evening comedy, why shouldn't I try only for once? And now he can't be malicious to me any more, I have him in the hollow of my hand. Dear! I clap myself on the shoulder intellectual for that, if I can only say it in English. Certainly I don't love him, not even like him, but I don't know how to explain it, there is something with him, he is full of charm. At the stage, people is mad after him, and when we walk at the street people say:*

"*Do you see? It was Carl Alstrup!*" [1]

Duger's letters fired my imagination. I was transported back to the frivolous world Duger inhabited and shared with me. There could not have been a greater contrast in our lives. After reading the account of the taxi, a vague memory came to my mind. I think the year was 1936. I looked at the date on Duger's letter in the January of that year which mentioned an Austrian man connected with me and tried to jog my memory a bit more. The scenes shimmered like water in my mind's eye and I concluded that I must have over-imbibed on that particular evening, for I dimly remembered going to a night club in Piccadilly with Margaret and a friend of hers, who had brought along a blind date for me – German perhaps? Surely not. No, he *was* Austrian, and I have hazy memories of a hotel room with dingy striped yellow wallpaper and a cheap, dusty chandelier above the bed. What I had done about the hospital curfew I dare not think, but I had probably scaled the wall at the back of the hospital and crept through the cellar door which was always left unlocked.

"I think it was very interesting that you wrote about the Austrian man. I know quite well how it is to be lone with a passionate man like that, but I never thought you would come in such a situation..."

Why had she thought that? I wondered, when she had written to me of escapades far beyond what I had ever contemplated. Did she think I appeared prudish perhaps?

"...About that prescription you asked for," Duger continued, *..." it is a little difficult to write, but I will try. The girl must take, that day she expect her month, a dose about five quinine tablets...at one time and a big spoonful of castor oil. After that she goes in a hot bath as hot as she can take it after that she needn't be afraid any more....since I got your letter I have searched into the dark room of my brain to remember how Caesar was born. I don't know whether I have learned it or forgotten it. I think the first. Is he not born the same way as other babies? It must have been wonderful and interesting for you to help with that.... "*

Perhaps, I thought, I had asked Duger for this "prescription" out of clinical interest? Or did I experiment, very dangerously, with the lifestyle she presented? Not for the first time, I recognised this tendency in myself to throw caution to the winds, especially under the influence of alcohol. The comparatively new freedoms women now enjoyed were heady and dangerous. We walked alone. But I managed to keep my head and miraculously, stayed out of trouble.

Now, eager and engrossed with the prospect of composition, I tried to marry up Duger's letters with my corresponding miniature diary entries.

8th March 1937. I peered short-sightedly at the tiny script, trying to decipher it. It had been written with the aid of much younger eyes. "Patient Carter, 1 am. Severe PPH (Post-Partum Haemorrhage). Called for the doctor. Fundal pressure immediately. Endeavoured to express the placenta by Credes method. Not successful. Patient passing big clots every 20 mins when fundus was pressed. Condition very poor. Waited 2 hours. Manual removal of placenta...... Hitler wishes to denounce the Versailles Treaty and the Locarno Pact. He wants to institute a new Treaty with reservations for France and Belgium......war clouds...."

Duger became ill again in the April with some more of the same trouble she had had in New End in 1934. A "boil as big as an egg" in a "very discreet place" had developed, but at least she had a good doctor, and according to her a very good looking one, with "black hair and eyes". I remember I laughed when she compared him to Hodgkiss.

"I began to cry and couldn't stop it again. It is terrible to be so weak but I can't help it. A doctor always frightens me to dead with all his knives and other instruments but I am very glad it wasn't Dr Hodgkiss who maked the operation. He would never have done it so soft and kind. This charming man didn't laugh at me, didn't tease me, didn't told me that he could cut one leg of his own son, and the boy wouldn't say a word, like Hodgkiss did to me." I could never remember Hodgkiss being so insensitive but I suppose it was true. *"Maybe it's because he hasn't any son. I simply love him, only one night with him and then die..."*

I surmised that Duger probably found more in common with her Danish doctors than she did with the English ones, whom perhaps she found more adherent to the Stoic philosophy. In January 1937, she had been in Berlin with her uncle and aunt, and stayed with her German boyfriend Karl-Heinz – I concluded that this boyfriend had decided against the marriage he had previously considered. He lived in Potsdam, near Berlin, with his parents, and it was impossible for them to be alone together. On her last day in Germany they went to some friends in Berlin who conveniently went to the cinema and left them alone at last.

Duger may not have thought comment on her impressions of Berlin at the height of the pre-war Nazi era necessary, but I felt sure that, even at that younger age I would have shown keen interest. However, I had accepted Duger for the way she was and her talent for getting into interesting and compromising situations. She literally thought of nothing but men and falling in love.

"*I was crying at the station,*" she wrote. "*I love Germany and hate Denmark.*"

In the New Year of 1937, I had begun my health visitor's course and felt myself on the home stretch, career-wise. It could not be long now before I could apply for an overseas posting and fulfil my long-held ambition to travel. In the meantime, I had to be content with Duger's accounts, which reflected an increase of activity in her life. In May, she wrote that she had a position with an English family in Casablanca and was sailing there before July.

"*My aunt doesn't like it, but I don't care,*" she wrote. "*She is going to adopt two children here, one of two months and one of two years old, so there will be a lot to do with them now. Then Karl-Heinz will come about the 8th June and we will stay here 8 days. He would that I should go with him to Rugen afterwards and stay 14 days with him there....I have been longing for that the whole time, and how my aunt will not give me permit to do it.....There will soon be a Kronborg play here in Helsingor.* (Kronborg was a castle in Helsingor immortalised in Shakespeare's play *Hamlet*) *There will be played Hamlet with English actors Laurence Olivier as Hamlet and Dorothy Dix and 18 others and dear! I am going to play also. I did get the engagement today and I am very excited. Of course it will not be as Ophelia or Gertrude, but even so I shall say a few things in English. I didn't tell it to Carl (Alstrup) yet. He will be ill if he hear that I am going to play in an English play. It's unfortunately only for 6 days. Anyway I am very glad they did take me, and I think it's very funny my beginning in that way. Ha! Maybe a theatre direction. We can see how talented I am[2]. Oh dear! Don't laugh...*"

In the close, confined atmosphere of the Southborough dining room, the light was becoming dim and I could barely see the fading script. On another unpredictable November morning, heavy cloud hid the sun and only an obscured light penetrated the front window. As I heaved myself up from the dining room chair to put on the main light switch, a clatter of cups was heard from the kitchen. I fervently hoped that Janet was taking due care with my tea service. In a moment, the knock I was expecting sounded on the hollow wooden panel.

"Miss Coates, shall I bring your coffee in there for you, or will you come out?"

"I'll come out, thank you!" I called back through the door. I did not want to risk any spillages onto the precious archives, and anyway, a break for refreshment would be welcome.

Janet poured coffee for us both and drew a chair for herself from the kitchen table. I sat silently for a few moments. I had immersed myself, as surely as if I had lived there, in the reality of a past age, more vivid now than the present.

"How are you getting on with the papers, Madam?" Janet ventured.

"Very well, dear, thank you," I returned. "I would like others to benefit from my experiences."

I had set myself a bold task but I could only try. At least I could make a start and write down as much as I remembered, then someone who came after me might take up the rest. It was all there – my life in a suitcase.

On August 3rd 1937, I started a temporary health visitor job in Shoreditch and thereafter became peripatetic, acting as Visitor in the poorest area of London. I witnessed appalling squalor and poverty but somehow remained generally unfazed, shocked as I felt at times. I dealt with it by being aware of the knowledge that I must have appeared like a visiting being from another world and possessed a protective aura – of professionalism, education and background. I felt privileged to have inside knowledge of these people in their homes and challenged myself to provide the best I could for them. In October, the Board confirmed my permanent position at Ealing Hospital as Health Visitor.

In stark contrast, Duger's life seemed frivolous in the extreme, and yet provided a welcome relief from my days in the squalid slums of 'thirties London. In August she had written to me from Casablanca, at last seeming happy. On the ship from Hamburg, countless men had run after her, including the captain and a Danish professor of music. However, she preferred Hans, the First Officer, although she strung the other two along.

"I couldn't help playing with them. I still gave both of them a tiny little hope, and every morning their faces grew longer and longer. I still played the game of love with Hans. The last evening I have been sitting in the room with Hans where the captain was running up and down so Hans went out to see what happened to him, and as soon as he saw Hans he asked him in that way,

"I used to have 12 passengers and now I can't find more than 11. Do you know where the other one is?"

"Then he called the steward: 'Go and find the twelfth passenger!'

"Hans came back and told me, and we laughed very much – he never saw the captain so silly before...."

"At ten o'clock we were in Casablanca, but we would stay in the sea until early morning. How can I explain in a letter how sad I felt. Hans was free that very evening and we saw Casablanca together only the light, it looked like a fairy town, and I tried to think, in one of all those lights will be my home for a whole year, maybe longer".

The family's name was Lennox.

"The life here is more than wonderful. Until now I haven't done anything. I can go up in the morning what time I like, and just tell the boy what time I want my breakfast. It is an Arab boy who makes the meals and then we have a Fatima and an Arab woman who does the work. The little girl is all playing by herself."

In the meantime, at the end of that October in 1937 I had gone flat hunting in Ealing, thinking at least to give myself a convenient base while I established myself at the hospital. The job had started on 1st November at Ravena Park, where I had Visited in the morning and had taken part in the afternoon clinic. I still had time for leisure and I had gone to the cinema, seeing "*Lloyds of London*" with Tyrone Power and Madeline Carroll, which I had pronounced "very good indeed. It is the story of Lloyds shipping insurance and also introduces Lord Nelson." At the end of November, the typhoid epidemic in Croydon reached its zenith and there were four cases in Kensington. Luckily, Croydon and Ealing were a considerable distance apart, but nevertheless, my mother always worried herself to distraction, despite my reassurances.

Duger's next letter in December reiterated some of the havoc she had caused among the crew on the *Oldenburg*. It all seemed unreal to me. I remembered when I had read it for the first time and compared her experiences with my own. Certainly, if I attracted attention at all, it was usually only as a nurse, for I wore uniform more often than not. I did not begrudge Duger her beauty. It rendered her attractive to both sexes, for different reasons. I had in some ways tried to emulate her when she had been in England – her clothes, some of her mannerisms and the way she did her hair.

She had seen Hans again when his ship had docked at Casablanca, but he now worked on the *Centa*. After she had left the *Oldenburg* the captain, who had resented Hans' success with her, had fired him.

"*They know all about it in Hamburg and on Centa, and the captain on Centa told him he had to stay on the boat here in Casablanca and not go into town. They speak about me as that terrible Danish girl who broke all the hearts on Oldenburg.*"

Despite the captain's orders, Hans did leave the ship in Casablanca and they drank champagne in a hotel, where Hans told her he wanted to marry her. But Duger just wanted to flirt with him and dreaded the day when she would have to break his heart.

"*I have never had so much success as here,*" she wrote. "*If I am going out alone I have a tail of men after me, am I sitting in a restaurant they are simply eating me with the eyes.*"

I leafed through the wad of stiff, slightly dirty, yellowing, blue vellum and tried to ascertain just how much material Duger had provided me with. I could not include it all in my work. How had she affected me? Looking back from such a distance I could see more clearly. Certainly, re-reading her vivid descriptions of a visit to Marrakesh near the Atlas Mountains had whetted my appetite for travel to parts of the world whose culture existed as different to my own as the landscape of the moon contrasted with the fertile valleys of Kent. An initiation into a harem for tea in that city provided a glimpse into a world unknown in the West yet familiar in the way I had heard of such things in childhood tales of the wonders of the East or the *Arabian Nights*. It fascinated yet appalled me as it must have had an even stronger effect on Duger. I read it again.

"In the afternoon," Duger had written, *"was the old Mrs Lennox invited to a harem to tea. She asked the young Mrs L to come with her but she has been so often with her and asked me to my great surprise if I want to go instead of her. I was more than willing. It is not every day we get a chance like that. It was by a rich man and it was a big wonderful house. When we came in a very big room was all the women in there. There was about 10, in all ages very old and the youngest was only a child. First did I think they were all his wifes but then Mrs L told me that only the 4 was his wifes the rest was only slaves, but still he used them as his wifes too, and had children with several of them. They were all very pleased to see us, and so terrible curious feeling on all my clothes, and one did lift my frock up to see what I had on under, just like small monkeys. They had all beautiful dresses on of thick coloured silk. Wonderful big rings and bracelets and the hair covered with a most lovely expensive silk thing with hand-made flowers. We had tea that yellow sweet Arabish tea with the big green leaves swimming in it in the glass. A lot of terrible sweet cakes all sorts. They were all so sweet talking and laughing and asking about everything outside their little world. I have learned some Arra-bish now it is necessary because our boy and Fatima don't understand a word of French what of course is the language here. But it will take me a long time before I can make a conversation of that awful difficult*

language. When we again stand in the street, and the door was locked behind us with a very big key, was it if I had been in a tale and seen something who is not true. I will never forget it, this beautifully black eyed girls so sweet and childish without sorrow. who never came out of the harem when first they are getting in living in their own little world, and don't know anything except what they hear nobody can read or write and they are never longing out, they are happy and proud to have a husband who has money enough to lock them in. How interesting it must be, they only can have their own little war sometimes, and nothing else to do as give birth to his sons, it must be sons, how can a rich man love a wife who only can give birth to girls. Some of the older ones (it means over 20) have to give place for the youngest the favourite, and wait until he wanted her..."

7th February 1938. Current events. Hitler's purge in Germany. Places himself as head of army. 1st sign of Germany weakening. Discussion on defence and possibility of war. Then on 21st – Austrian professor: Austria's value to Germany. Wood from forests + cellulose which forms explosive for bombs. Iron ore. Paper. Electric water falls. Most decisive event in European history, annexation of Austria. Very fateful to whole of Europe. Czechoslovakia next to be annexed is in a very dangerous position. Next in annexation Poland, Yugoslavia. Denmark. Roumania richest oil fields. Will probably be sold obsolete arms by Germany. Italy will be too weak to resist. Result of Germany annexing Austria. Economic life poor. Complete Nazification of police and army. Miscellaneous. Spain war. Franco will win. Balance of power policy by Sir Edward Grey.

I noticed in my next diary entry that with war clouds gathering I absorbed the beauties of the English countryside, no less. One never appreciates what one has until it becomes under threat, I thought. At that time, I kept company with another man called Bill - something of a stuffed shirt and Oxford bags - but nevertheless an amiable soul upon whom one could rely for such activities as walks. On the 6th of March, Bill and I went on a fourteen-mile hike, taking the train from Baker Street to Chorley Woods, and then hiking to Chalfont St Peters, Chalfont St Giles, Jordans Coleshill and Amersham. Nature had surpassed herself in putting on a show that day. I took a second or two to gaze out at the dismal November afternoon. Already, darkness descended, although I had hardly noticed the creeping gloom gradually encompassing the room. By contrast, that day in 1938 dawned glorious like mid-summer and the thirty-year old woman I was. With the trees still quite bare of foliage, the unnatural warmth had created an ethereal mist over the landscape. I remembered the belts of barely visible vapours that Bill and I had passed through and watching the sun setting behind the trees.

About that time, Duger made a reference to something I must have said about plans of mine to work in South Africa and I wondered now at my youthful restlessness after just having procured a worthwhile job at Ealing. I could only guess at the different course my life must have taken if my plans had come to fruition. Duger wrote from *El Minzah*, rue Charles Lebrou:

"Do you really want to go to South Africa?.... I know an English nurse here who did help with the baby...

Would I have wanted to go to Casablanca to live and work in close proximity with Duger? Perhaps a lucky escape as things turned out...

"She is living in the mountains near Marrakesh and help all the Arab there when they have their babies or other illness"....

Duger had already told me that her employer's parents, the older Lennoxes, worked as missionaries and Duger must have had an opportunity to journey into the mountains to visit them and witness their work.

"...It was terrible but interesting to hear all she..." (the nurse) *"... did see, how primitive everything is, none of the native have a bed or chairs, only a carpet and they are so dirty it is nearly impossible to work with them, but it is not the worse part of it. They have their own*

idea about everything if somebody is death they smear honey round the lips and do all kinds of awful tricks with ill people it is very difficult to let them understand not to do it....there is a terrible typhus epidemic here in Casablanca. It comes from all the Arabs, and it is not allowed to go in the native town except it is necessary. A big boat full of tourists was not allowed to go into port, because they know they still would go in there even if it is told them not to. We all have to go with a little strong-smelling stone in our pocket to keep the louses away, the most of the natives is full of louses. Thousands die from typhus now and a lot of Europeans too."

Slowly, I became aware, engrossed as I was, that the house seemed unnaturally silent. I heard the firing up of the central heating boiler in the kitchen and the faint click-clicking of the radiators, usually a pleasant sound to me as it signalled the end of my economically enforced restriction of the heating system during the day and the beginning of a period of warmth and relaxation in the house. Now, however, I felt a sense of foreboding and aloneness. I checked my watch. It was exactly five o'clock. Janet must have left at least an hour ago. Why had she not come in to tell me first, or at least shouted out?

I opened the door to the hall and was met with the same slightly hostile near-darkness in the impeccably clean and tidy house. As I reached for the hall light switch to dispel the shadows, sinister in the gloom, I mentally shook myself. How ridiculous, in my own familiar house where I had happily spent time alone for many years. I wondered at myself, and yet Janet's actions struck me as strange and unlike her. As I wheezed up to the hall phone to dial her number, it did not occur to me that the reason Janet had left without disturbing me may have been directly related to my behaviour that morning.

It was Bill who answered.

"Oh Bill," I said, trying to make my voice sound calm. "Is Janet home yet?"

"Is anything wrong, Miss Coates?" Bill sounded genuinely concerned.

"Well, she must have left very quietly, Bill. I didn't even hear the front door close!"

Bill made a concerned and surprised noise and Janet came on the line.

"Yes, Miss Coates?"

Janet sounded like her usual self, inscrutable and impeccably polite.

"Janet! I just said to Bill, you must have been very quiet leaving, I didn't even hear the front door close! Why didn't you tell me you were going?"

"Oh, I'm very sorry, Madam! I knew you were very busy with your papers and was afraid of disturbing you!"

I was so relieved that I felt myself growing irritated.

"Well, never mind this time," I said to the unfortunate daily. "In future, please at least knock quietly and put your head round the door, will you?"

"Yes, of course, Madam," said Janice, chastened.

Really, she (must have) thought, her boss was getting worse. Ringing her up like that when she'd done nothing!

Later on, unbeknown to me, although I could imagine it, the Andrews' chatted over their late-night cup of cocoa, sitting as ever in perfect harmony. The gist of their conversation centred on me and my unpredictable behaviour and whether or not I became worse with old age. Should Janet try to get another job, they wondered? Half an hour settled the issue. I had undoubtedly shown generosity and kindness in my time but being clever and very advanced in years, I not unusually had particular and peculiar ways.

Janet stayed.

------

1. Carl Alstrup was a Danish actor and film director. He appeared in 22 films between 1908 and 1942. He directed four films between 1909 and 1910. He and his wife Fenja lived at "Fenjahus", Snekkersten, where he died in 1942 (Wikipedia, accessed 24/12/22).

2. Laurence Oliver and Vivien Leigh played together in *Hamlet* at Kronborg castle at Helsingor, Denmark, in 1937. He was 30 and she was 23. At that time, they were having a love affair and both were married to other people. No evidence has been found of Duger's participation at Kronborg, which leads one to conclude that either she had a very small role or that she did not, after all, take part.

Chapter 4

World's End: A New Beginning?

Casablanca 6/5/38. "Everything seems to wrong for me this moment. I have been ill again, it was a boil in exactly the same place as usual, very uncomfortable......."

These words seemed to herald in a period of worry and foreboding, both for my Danish friend and for the world in general. In September, I had sent in my forms for South Africa with some trepidation, deciding whatever the outcome not to turn back now.

Duger had continued: *"The doctor, a nice handsome young chap, wouldn't cut it without put me to sleep. I came up in that chair there for me is awful, as the electric chair is for a murder. First they bound my legs and then my arms. I have always been afraid to chloroform or whatever they use. I am afraid when they press the mask over my face, and gave a feeling I can't get any air. And there were two big men against one and that was poor little me, bound so an Indian couldn't have done it any better..... but it is not the worse. I will have to have a operation. Something is invisible on that spot who was to be cut away, otherwise I will have the same trouble every 6 month or a year. I had it twice in Paris and twice in Snekkersten and now again. It was I will have to go to a Hospital, and it will take about a month. I am so sorry about it. It is still not the worse. Something terrible is happened to me. I am going to have a baby. It is still only 2 month, but I am nearly going mad of thinking about it. I thought it was impossible for me I have never taking care, and nor have the men. So I thought of course there was something wrong with me, and didn't dream of that it should happened to me. I have done everything, and am now going to have an operation for that, as soon as possible. Can't you imagine how I feel this moment. It is my Danish friend who is master for that..."* (she meant, of course, the father)... *"and he does not seem to be at least worried about it, so I have to keep it for myself and do what I can, but it is not funny at all. It must be done before we go to England, and if you have enough money it is not at all difficult here. They do it for 600 franc. It isn't even 3 pound, but I have only 200 francs a month so you see it is not easy at all...."*

I had conflicting feelings about Duger at that time. I cared for her but I clearly saw signs predicting an end to our continuing friendship. Perhaps my intrinsic sense of self-survival or the sobering fact of now being thirty years of age (as indeed was Duger) ensured that for the first time I felt critical of her actions. Of course, I sympathised, but failed to understand fully her professions of ignorance of male and female anatomy and physiology. She was a healthy young woman and put simply, her luck had run out. Her grief and surprise at the desertion of her Danish friend I also found hard to credit. I reflected then as I did now, that although the English education system may have produced generations of women whose behaviour amounted to prudery and caution in the days before the "sexual revolution" and "the pill", the better and brighter ones emerged equipped with enough knowledge to keep out of trouble. Whether or not they chose to adhere to it remained another matter, but in the event of misfortune, they should expect to assume responsibility for the consequences of their actions.

I wrote to Duger commiserating, genuinely anxious for her welfare and privately hoping that she would learn from her experience. My little diaries told me, in their usual stop-press style, the European news of the day.

"12th September 1938. Hitler's speech at Nuremburg: Defence of Sudeten Germans. Refuses to tolerate the condition of the Sudetens under the Czechs. He states he cannot help the attitude of the French and the English if they as a Democratic Nation wish to uphold the Czech they must do so at their own risk."

I must have heard very little from Duger for the next year until the August of 1939. Perhaps some of my reserved attitude to her later exploits had seeped through in my letters to her? At this point I was puzzled by an unexplained gap in the blue sheets about which, according to her replies, I had left unremarked upon. Here, my memory was a blank for nearly a year. I remembered that I was turned down for South Africa, but why? In all likelihood they were inundated with applications and at that stage I had not sufficient experience. I still longed for sunshine and continued with my health visitor job in Northolt, waiting for the right opportunity to make further applications. The war came ever closer.

In the August, Duger wrote:

"I understand quite well that you want to go away from England. I couldn't live there forever. I love the sun and climate here. In the meantime I have been in the hospital here 3 weeks. How different a Moroccan hospital is to an English one. It was that damned boil who came again, so I had to jump in it and get the operation.... I was in a ward with 13 other women most Spanish. The flies were awful in the daytime and the mosquitoes in the night so we had to cover us with the sheets and make a little breathhole, and it was so hot I couldn't stand it. It was awfully dirty too. The floor was only washed twice a week of an Arab who emptied the BP (bed pans) too. But the nurses were very sweet to me all of them. In the night we had only useless nuns, who preferred to give it all over in the hands of God, and thought it helped us better when they prayed over us. Perhaps! We never know. But the most of the time we had to lie alone, every 3 hours did they come through the ward, so if we needed anything we had to say it in that

time otherwise we could call and scream nobody came. The bedpans stand beside the bed and was emptied 4 times the day and two times during the night. Unfortunately my bed was besides an old lady's and she always went just after they were emptied, so I had a terrible smell beside me and it was permanent, I could get so angry with that old goat...."

Her last letters in 1939 told me about a position offered her with a millionaire "several times over" who lived in Fez in a large villa, about sixty years old. He travelled most of the time and wanted Duger to accompany him on his travels for 1000 francs a month, firstly to the American Exposition.

"...I know he like me but there is another thing I know too that I will have to make love to him, but he will be large in every way. I will be a fool if I do not take it. First of all I will see the world as never before, second it will be an easy job in every way. He showed me two lovely big silverfoxes together and told me it was for me when I have decided. I will get all these lovely frocks I have dreamed about".

By the end of March 1940, she had decided not to accept and go back to Denmark. She had not appeared to take the beginning of the war into consideration when coming to her decision, which appeared largely based on her erstwhile employer's physical characteristics and sexual inclinations. I did not blame her.

"First of all I would have to stay in Fez until July and then I would go with him in car through Spain and France to Denmark and then after to America. Well! In July I am going to Denmark anyway, and with him I wouldn't be so free. Second he is a Jew, and I don't think it is amusing to travel with a Jew in this awful time. Third, I had to sleep in the same bed as him, and if you have seen him undressed, or in his nightshirt (not pyjamas) a fat tummy and hair all over. Terrible! That's still not the worse but if I have to make love I want it natural anyway perverse people is an awful thing, and that he was. Of course I would be nicely dressed and he would give me everything I needed, but he was very careful in small things, very afraid to give a penny more out than necessary, and that I hate."

Duger and I had both had our "coming of age" of thirty years. As she said, she had had so much experience in her best years and now wanted to go home to Denmark. What would she do there? I wondered. It seemed like the end for her - that her life had flared brightly for a few short years and that now she would settle into a dull, perhaps spinsterish life in Snekkersten - but I felt I had not even begun to live. Did I judge her? For me in 1989, the Duger interlude had died a natural death and her letters had ended shortly after the outbreak of war – a natural and perhaps unavoidable conclusion. Two years later, perhaps her shadow was over me in my dealings with George and perhaps I felt a wariness through knowing her.

All my friends seemed on the move. Even Dorrie was now in Sydney having, by her own accounts, the time of her life – I and her mother, Violet Raymond, had seen her off at Southampton on the ship - all of us in our fur coats in early 1939, war clouds or not. She was in a safe place – a European war could never reach Australia, we all believed. I had seen an old black and white photograph somewhere – here. I pulled it out from among the letters. The trio – me looking as black as thunder (but perhaps I was merely sad) before that final, deep, blasting hoot from the huge bulk of the ship alongside which we stood on the wharf – the *Ormonde*. It could only be moments before Dorrie would go on board. Another photograph showed Dorrie, her handkerchief fluttering, behind the railings on deck, already diminishing in size as the *Ormonde* pulled out, finally breaking the coloured streamers binding her to the wharf and to those who stood watching. On impulse, I picked up the phone and dialled Dorrie's number. No answer. Perhaps she was at church. I had wanted to ask her for her memories and impressions of that day fifty years ago as she sailed off to a new life and left me to an uncertain future.

The war had finally broken out in September 1939, almost a relief after the years of worry, uncertainty and vainly trying to delay its advent at all costs. In the early summer of 1940, the Churchill government changed the mood of the country to one of positive patriotism which had my friends joining up – my dear friend and former flatmate Margaret in the WRENS and others in the WAAF. I applied to all three services in my capacity of nurse, only to get my application forms back vetoed by the medical officer of Ealing, with the words in bold script: "**RESERVED OCCUPATION**". There seemed no way out, but I kept on banging my head against various brick walls, hoping that someone would give me release from my apparently inescapable fate serving the housewives of Ealing. My situation was laughable if it hadn't been so tragic. My whole career had been forged with the ambition of utilising it as a means of escape, and now it was the career itself which became the reason for my bondage to duty.

Each weekend, I went home to Tonbridge and returned on Sunday night to Ealing, leaving my parents nearly worried to death for my safety as I crossed London to my digs by underground. Nowadays, I often watch archive film of people sleeping in the underground stations during that war – not intentionally, as they could never come across convincingly or impart the reality of the experience. I never had to sleep like that but I had to tread over the sleepers as I got off the trains in the weird partial gloom of Bank Station, say, where I changed for Ealing, from the darkness of the blacked-out train. One evening, as I emerged from the carriage, I was hit, almost physically, by the low murmur of chatter echoing off the shiny green and cream walls, and a stench of fear from the mass of bodies in a confined space. The clamminess of the humid environment, where once prevailed the business-like, private orderliness of the day-to-day lives of city folk struck me in a poignant way. I remembered even now that I had reflected on the changes that wartime wrought in people as I walked among their incumbent forms on the concrete platform, that it stripped innocent people of their normal human dignity, even if they were not directly involved in it.

On one particular occasion at Bank, as I made towards the green fluorescent "exit" sign to await the "all clear", there was an uncanny silence, which led me to the conclusion that this raid was a bad one. Muffled by seventy feet of rocks and earth above my head, the repeated thuds of the falling bombs penetrated, every thud sending cold fingers of fear through the bodies of London's citizens. Each wondered if their homes and lifetime possessions would have been spared when they emerged. Mothers comforted their crying children, focusing their fear into their care, while the older women looked at each other philosophically and the old men, sitting dangling their hands between their legs, wished fervently for the return of their youth. In the corner, near the exit sign, a girl of about fifteen stared in glassy-eyed panic around her, her breath coming in short, shallow pants. As I watched, seeing the first signs of hysteria, her whimpers of terror gave way to screams in response to a series of particularly loud thumps. Some plasterwork from the roof showered part of the platform with dust and debris, covering several blankets over the sheltering bodies. Startled, those who had been hit hastily moved themselves to another part of the platform. The girl screamed on, not seeming to belong to any particular group of people. An old lady was trying to make her stop the noise, fearing she would set off a general panic.

Although not in full uniform, I wore, for warmth and practicality, my health visitor's coat and hat and the black lace-up shoes and stockings I often wore on my rounds among London's poor. These and my no-nonsense manner, which proclaimed my status, together with no fear of being recognised as such in public, made me instantly recognisable to the girl and those around her. This in itself may have done the trick in pacifying her but at that point the thuds and muffled explosions from above began again with renewed fervour. The girl again looked around her helplessly, her eyes widened and her mouth opened in a large O. I lifted my right arm and slapped her cheek peremptorily, seeing the scarlet outline of my fingers develop on her white skin. The girl, blonde haired and blue eyed, opened them wide in intense surprise, forgetting in her acute shock the reason for her panic.

Although, regrettably, remembering a feeling akin to enjoyment after I had performed my "first aid" on this girl, it had done the trick. I asked around the bystanders for a blanket and a hot cup of sweet tea. The old lady who had taken on the task of trying to pacify her obliged by producing a battered thermos.

"Never go anywhere without it!" she proclaimed triumphantly, pouring the dark brown mixture into a plastic cup. "Are you nurse, dear?" she asked me when I had cocooned my patient in a layer of grey army blanket and had sat her comfortably in a corner in the charge of her elderly carer.

"Yes," I replied, as I crouched down in front of them on the platform. "It seems my duties have started early tonight!"

I assessed the girl and guessed that with any luck, she would last out until the "all clear" without further incident. "Do you know this girl? Does she live near you?" I asked of the old lady. She nodded.

"Her place was bombed," she said, pouring a little more tea into the cup. The girl was sipping it appreciatively. "Poor thing, she's only fourteen. Her family were caught in the house right at the beginning and they died – her mother and father and little brother."

I listened in a rising horror and increasing sympathy.

"Who is looking after her?" I asked, knowing that this was an all-too-familiar story, now that the Blitz as they were calling it, had mounted its attack on London for several weeks.

"She was taken in at the hostel," said the old lady, whose name I now learned was June. "But it's affected her something dreadful. Now she's terrified. That night they were all taken was a bad one like this and it brings it all back to her."

I didn't answer, not knowing what I could say and sat with my head bowed quietly in my crouched position, waiting for that "all clear".

Through talking to the girl and June, I hadn't noticed the blessed quiet descend tens of feet below the surface of the earth. There were a few snores, as people fell asleep in the new peace. Then, starting as a low groan, the siren began, rising through the scale to its crescendo and maintaining its pitch while all around us there was a sudden bustle of activity. A queue started to form in front of the exit, and I realised that we had better get into our places for the general exodus.

I looked at June and the girl. I had better get her name and the address at the hostel, I thought, and check up on her in a few days.

"It's Mavis, Nurse," she whispered, holding the mug in front of her face, her voice so low it was barely audible, her blonde hair falling into her eyes.

"Well Mavis," I said. "Go back to the hostel and get some sleep. I will come out and see you soon."

I made sure that June would accompany her as I left the station in the melee for my connection to Northolt. On reaching the town in the London Borough of Ealing about ten miles to the north-west, yet more destruction wrought by the Luftwaffe during their evening's work appeared. Concentrating their efforts on bombing the RAF Northolt airbase, they had made a one-off raid in an attempt to paralyse the RAF into severely limiting their forays during the Battle of Britain. In so doing, they had destroyed many buildings and homes around the airbase but fortunately failed in destroying the base itself.

Living and working in such a strategically vital area of London, I repeatedly placed myself in danger, and yet the work itself I recorded in my later articles as extremely dull. I do not think I attempted deliberate insouciance in my attitude, perhaps through bravado, although it might have seemed so, after the war. We did not pose as war heroines, as we witnessed day after day the empty clinics. While lesser-qualified nurses battled daily in the hospitals to care for the wounded in raids, a handful of us had our hands empty, as we prepared our clinics for patients who missed their appointments through the sheer difficulties of crossing a rubble-strewn London, or fear of daytime raids. During the afternoons we made house calls for the more urgent cases and kept scrupulous records of the missed appointments for future follow-up. This stage of the war could not last forever. Hitler was becoming too ambitious and opening up too many fronts. Even the Nazi war machine could not be invincible, surely. At the moment, the British Isles were on the defensive, but if only we could hold out and survive, sooner or later he would turn his attention elsewhere and the tide would turn....

These days, in Southborough in 1989, I hardly noticed the passage of time or the descent into the dark days of mid-winter as Christmas approached. Now, as in 1940, a strong leader grasped the reins at Downing Street – a woman held control for the first time for the past ten years and had claimed victory over both Argentina and unemployment. Unimpressed with the present, I spent my days immersed in the past. I realised that I hadn't ventured out for weeks. I was unable to walk far these days and was obliged to use a wheel chair, usually parked in the hall. Janet would step up if the need arose but I hated the thing and my loss of independence. There again, I had no need to go out. Either Janet or Bill ran my errands and saw to my needs in every way. I had the occasional visitor - Dorrie had phoned yesterday and said that she would come over before Christmas. I felt more inclined these days to think about that Christmas of forty-nine years ago and what led up to it.

I picked up an article I had written in the 1970's and would use this in the longer work I was planning of my life. I had carried on in this way with the empty clinics which caused me "utter boredom" through the lack of work, hearing about the horrors of war-ridden Europe and experiencing the dangers of crossing London on my weekend journeys or in raids over London or Kent. I never came across another Mavis when I passed through Bank Station. Sometimes it all seemed normal, with commuters in their hats and coats getting on and off the trains, which more or less ran according to schedule. Until one went upstairs, one could almost persuade oneself that peace had miraculously come upon us.

My digs lay close to Ealing Hospital, where our maternity clinics operated. Today, this busy general hospital offers the people of north London a wide range of clinical services. I walked over to the hospital every morning, one day barely distinct from the next. One morning I trod lighter than usual as I approached the impressive façade and walked through the spacious entrance foyer. It was shortly after eight and a dull, overcast day with a pale sun barely risen over the horizon. I nodded and smiled my greetings to a number of acquaintances who bustled past purposefully. Seeing my face with a smile on it prompted a similar response in those whom I encountered that morning. I felt sorry for them, thinking that usually I had an air of gloom about me but on this particular day I was too happy to care very much.

I had had a phone call that changed my whole existence. I had just got out of the bath and hurried back to my room to dress. I removed my dressing gown, looking at my Ealing Hospital uniform, laid out ready on the made bed. My sister's cap with its proliferation of frills I left until I reached the clinic to assemble. I heard a knock, and, thinking it would be the landlady for the rent, I opened, rather impatiently, with a repressed sigh. I peered out into the gloom of the hallway. The boarding house mainly accommodated nurses working at the hospital, and Alicia, a staff nurse who worked in paediatrics, stood there in her dressing gown and pyjamas, her fair hair dishevelled, repressing a yawn.

"Phone call for you, Val!" she imparted indistinctly, and, suppressing another yawn, took herself off down the staircase to one of the lower rooms to complete her sleep-in before her afternoon shift.

I muttered my thanks to the departing back of Alicia, took my keys and went down to the dingy hallway. The phone mouthpiece dangled from the hook, dropped by the sleepy girl. Even before I picked it up, I heard the faint tones of a female voice, high pitched through the line.

"Hello?" I ventured.

The unknown caller conversed with somebody at the other end and didn't hear.

"*Hello?*" I said again, louder.

I refrained with difficulty from slamming the phone down with impatience. Fortune favoured my restraint.

"Val!"

Margaret's familiar, wide-awake tones penetrated loud and clear from her WREN barracks and I held the earpiece six inches away from my ear.

"Where have you been?"

"I came as fast as I could!" I answered indignantly.

Really, Margaret was the limit sometimes. It was a good thing she had not caught me still in the bath!

Margaret dismissed my explanation impatiently.

"Listen," she said. "I had to tell you. Wake up. Someone from the QA's passed it on and I thought of you. There's an advert in this week's Nursing Mirror about health sisters being urgently required in Malaya and Kenya by the Crown Agents! Look dear, it would do you the world of good to apply, and I'm sure you'd get it. Give it a go, love!"

I jolted, every fibre of my being becoming alive in an instant. I didn't answer Margaret immediately, but tried to assimilate what she told me and to believe it was real and not a dream. I had dreamed such dreams before. From the age of ten it had been my fervent desire to go to Malaya. I remembered the stamps in the puddle, the films of doctors in the jungle and their nurses fighting rare diseases. My years of real nursing experience had not caused me to see these private dreams as mere Hollywood. The height of my ambition, although my colleagues would have laughed at my naivete, was to assist a doctor in this most worthy cause, right in the heart of the jungle. Somewhere along the road I had taken a wrong turn, and world events had conspired to work against me. Until today, it seemed that my present position as health visitor in a north London suburb was far removed from my dreams. Before the war, in order to get to Malaya, one's qualifications should have included specialising in surgery and belonging to the Queen Alexandra's Nursing Service, but now it seemed that my luck had turned. The war had begun to work for me now.

"But," I thought, "let's not get too carried away. There may be hidden requirements, snags."

I had become so lost in my thoughts that I had failed to hear Margaret's repeated attempts to bring me down to earth.

"Val!" she exclaimed. "Are you alright? You haven't said a word!"

"Sorry, Madge dear," I said finally. "That's wonderful news. I'll get hold of a copy today. This week, you say?"

"Yes, just come out! Hurry up and send in your application! Got to dash now, dear! Don't forget!"

The line went dead.

To my joy, they accepted me for interview at this most dignified institution, the London Office of the Crown Agents, an administrative body of the British Empire. I had climbed a winding marble staircase to the first floor, and waited in a plush ante-room with one other nervous-looking woman in a black costume who constantly clasped and unclasped the catch on her handbag. She smiled at me as I sat down. Strangely enough, a suited gentleman called me in first, but looking behind me as I entered the interview room, I saw a secretary from downstairs come in to speak to her and assumed the woman had mistaken the time of her interview.

As I entered the panelled room, several severe, unsmiling men were ensconced at a long mahogany table with some papers in front of them. One by one, they introduced themselves - all had gained distinction in the medical field and one or two seemed faintly familiar, but I could not place them. There were two positions on offer and at that moment I did not hold out much hope of getting either.

"Miss Coates," the dignified-looking gentleman at the head of the table began.

He wore a navy blue, pin-stripe three-piece suit with a watch chain and sported a bushy, tobacco-stained moustache. He reminded me, in build and demeanour, of our former prime minister Neville Chamberlain, but had introduced himself as Henry Watson, a consultant in tropical medicine at St Thomas's.

"Miss Coates," Watson continued. "What has prompted you to

apply for a position of health sister in the tropics?"

I had prepared for the possibility of this question. Leaving out all reference to tigers on stamps, I controlled the tremor in my voice which threatened to break through and stressed to the dignified gentleman my long-held ambition to nurse in foreign parts. At the end of my little speech, I hoped that everyone in the room had now become convinced that from an early age my whole life had been dedicated and directed to this end. I cited my training courses in midwifery, health visiting and childcare and pointed to my applications to the three services as an example of my burning desire to serve in an overseas capacity.

The questions continued for about three-quarters of an hour, then Watson glanced around the table.

"Well gentlemen, if you have completed your questions for Miss Coates?"

There was a general murmur of assent. Watson turned to me.

"Thank you, Miss Coates. If you could please wait outside a moment?"

They all stood politely as I rose and advanced towards the door. A couple of them smiled. The gentleman sitting at the bottom of the table hastily rose to open the door for me to pass through. I returned to my former seat in the now empty ante-room.

Twenty minutes later, I walked out of the Crown Agents building and into the busy London thoroughfare. I stepped sedately down the stairs, but once out in the street I defied my high heels and broke out into a run, barely restraining myself from whooping for joy.

At last, I had broken free, offered there and then, the position in Ipoh, the heart of Malaya. Now I only had to convince my parents and obtain their permission to travel, as a woman had to do then. As for myself, thinking of spending years of my life in empty clinics, I had no doubt that I was doing the right thing. In the coming weeks my resolve would bear the brunt of the negative views of others to the limit as I fended off all opposition.

I had set out on my way and I would not, could not, go back.

Chapter 5

The Colour of Water

I remember the euphoria of achievement as I skipped and ran down the Kingsway that autumn afternoon, my pace slowing to a fast walk as breathlessness ensued. I gave way to my feelings, which I knew I deserved to enjoy in full. No doubt, problems lay ahead over the next few weeks but for the moment, I allowed myself the luxury of pure joy. I felt that the straight-faced men back there in the panelled room had recognised my worth and had placed their faith in me. I almost felt like offering up a prayer of gratitude for my deliverance from Ealing, and nearing Trafalgar Square, passed the church of St Martin's in the Fields wondering whether to go in. As the suited men behind me had represented Crown Agents and Crown Agents represented the Empire, I felt determined at that moment to utilise every ability I possessed in its service.

It was a Friday afternoon and as usual I set my course for Charing Cross. I recall every detail of that showery afternoon in London. Every now and then, the sun made its glorious appearance from behind a purple cloud, heavy with moisture, and the drab scene became transformed to colour. The afternoon light reflected off raindrops from a recent shower. The weekend crowds around Trafalgar

Square seemed cheerful too, reflecting my joy as I made for the station, the brown and yellow autumn leaves wet on the pavement under my city-smart shoes. I looked at my watch. I would just get the four-fifteen if I hurried. I wanted to reach home before dark. I would phone from Tonbridge Station to ask Father to pick me up with the car.

Only when I sat in the train, settled with a copy of the Evening News, did I begin to think about the challenges I faced. I tried to predict my parents' questions and reaction when I told them the news. I decided not to mention anything to Father before we got home. I would wait until I had them both together, sitting down. I would pour Mother a sherry and Father would have his beer. I started to feel slightly nervous as I imagined the scene - Mother tearful and Father worried for both of us. I knew I had to stay strong and firm because I would probably never get another chance like this again and would spend the rest of my life not having lived.

Father waited outside the station with the old Morris. He kissed me as I got in and I smelled his familiar, clean scent of Lifebuoy soap and Brilliantine hair oil, mixed with the car smell of leather and petrol. As we chugged up the High Street towards the London Road we chatted about minor things, avoiding any discussion on the war. We had to treasure every odd moment that offered some escape from the perpetual awareness of living in wartime.

"How's Mother?" I asked quietly, bracing myself for new revelations about her permanently delicate health.

"She has been better lately. She often talks of you. She was talking about a position in Tunbridge Wells she wants to show you in the paper."

I did not speak for a moment. This would not be easy.

"Father...."

I did not say any more. Percy looked at me sideways in the gloom. It began to get dark. As we drove north past the town, the sky displayed a vivid pink on the western horizon. I looked down at the lap of my dark woollen costume and fussed with the newspaper I had brought from the train. Neither of us spoke for about half a minute.

Then – "Are you well, Daughter?" he said, concerned.

I remember I chuckled a little, under my breath, but smiled fondly at my father.

"Oh yes, Father. I am quite well. Never better, in fact. But I have to speak to you both about something that is making me very happy."

Percy looked at me quickly.

"You've met someone?"

"No, no. It's better than that. Let's get home first and have a drink."

I had broken the ice that had threatened to enclose me again with its imprisoning shards, but I realised that he might make things easier for me now that I had hinted at something.

Mother was standing at the front door as we drew up, her outline silhouetted against the brightly lit hallway behind her. Once out of the car, I let her hug and kiss me in her mother's unconditional love and pleasure at seeing me again.

"Here you are safe again, thank God," she murmured as I held her close.

"Yes, Mother. It will take more than a few bombs to shut me up!"

I made an attempt at light-heartedness in order to neutralise some of the emotion which my mother innocently created around her. With one parent on each side and my arms around them both, we walked into the house.

That night, I lay in bed in my old room overlooking the darkened garden, thinking back over the evening. Percy had introduced the subject when we had finished dinner. He had chosen his time well. I knew he would – that was why I had left it to him. He had drawn his chair close to his wife.

"Florence – I think our dear daughter has some news for us."

Florence had looked joyfully expectant for a moment, then, seeing that my face did not reflect a similar joy, started to look anxious.

"What is it, Lavinia? Have you got another job?"

"Well, yes, Mother. I have. I have been for an interview today with the Crown Agents for the Colonies and - I have been selected." I paused.

"Selected? For the colonies? Where?"

Florence had laid her hand on her heart. With her other hand she reached out for her husband.

"It will be safer than here, Mother," I offered desperately. "You know how I have always wanted to travel. Now I can. I have been offered the post of Health Sister in Ipoh, Malaya."

"Malaya!" Florence put a hand over the lower part of her face. "So far away!"

She looked at her husband.

"Percy, I don't think we can let her go, can we?"

Florence was grasping at straws. Percy patted her arm. He too was shocked, I could see, but he knew even then that it would be folly to try to prevent me from going. He said nothing for a moment.

"When would this be, Val?" he asked quietly.

"In about a month, I think," I said. "They're sending me the details."

I looked at my poor mother trying to assimilate all this information and got up to put my arms round her. She had started to cry quietly but I knew that she had to work through this in her own time. Thankfully for us all, the waiting period was not too long but I knew it would be a trial.

I certainly found the interim almost unbearably taxing but eventually the day came. That early November day in 1940 proved one of the few times in my life that I found my emotions nearly impossible to master. The weather didn't help. The morning of embarkation dawned cold, wet and grey, reflecting and magnifying a sense of loss at separating from Mother and Father. I could feel their grief and worry as surely as if I had taken their place and acute guilt because of it. At the same time, another well of excitement and anticipation lay deep in my consciousness, ready to emerge when the last moment of parting was over. I finally separated from them at Euston after a last-minute dash to change platforms with two suitcases and a heavy trunk, borne by a porter who appeared just as confused as the passengers. I reflected later that the lack of clarity over the Liverpool "boat train" which took passengers to Canada Dock and the ship, the SS *Narkunda*, may have been intentional to confound the enemy as the sailing details were issued secretly after heavy shipping losses over the past few weeks.

The three of us sat having a relaxing drink in Platform 1's buffet with, we imagined, at least twenty minutes to spare, when an announcement came over the tannoy.

"Would all passengers for the ten-twenty express to Liverpool please go immediately to Platform 15. The train is ready to depart".

We listened in perturbation and distress. I had not wished for this to happen. I had planned, for the sake of Mother particularly, not to have any last-minute rushes which could prove stressful for her delicate constitution. I tried not to panic, but Platform 15, little used except for local trains, stood on the other side of the station. Father rose to the occasion heroically and immediately summoned a porter outside, slipping a hastily prepared note into his hand.

"Where to, Guv?" said the man, grabbing the handles of the trolley and waiting for hasty directions.

"Platform 15, and be as quick as you like. That announcement was about our train. It's ready to depart."

Percy turned back to Florence, just beginning to feel the relaxing effects of her sherry. He regretted her coming now. They would all have to run for the train and he worried for her heart.

"Come on, Mother dear," I said, helping her to her feet and finding her hat and handbag. "We have to go now, quickly."

We were not the only passengers caught unawares. The way through the station over to Platform 15 heaved with people - families with children in the arms of their mothers who panicked to the point of tears, porters with heavy loads of luggage and men trying vainly to locate their families and keep them together in the rush. The shrieks of the trains, repetitive tannoy announcements and shouts from the crowd mingled together in the chaos. Florence openly cried now, with Percy desperately trying to hurry her.

"You go on, Lavinia!" he shouted at last. "Keep up with your luggage! There may be time to say goodbye from the platform!"

I knew Father had a point. I would have to try to make amends later, in letters. I quickly checked that I had everything. No, Father had my coat. Hurriedly, I grabbed the wool coat from Percy. I blew kisses to poor Mother, now beside herself. Strangely, at that point I don't remember feeling any emotion. A numbness had taken over, which would, I knew even then, give way to sadness but an utter relief once I sat alone on the train.

"I love you both! I will write soon!"

I turned and ran after the porter and, while the man loaded my luggage into the guard's van, boarded into a nearby carriage at last, panting with exertion and emotion. The train heaved with people, more and more boarding behind me with children of all ages, coats and bags. Against the odds, exercising no small degree of manipulation in the process, I bagged myself a window seat and stayed in it for a few minutes while the rest of the carriage settled themselves. I gazed through the smut-stained glass, searching for Mother and Father.

At first, I could not spot them, then saw them behind the train, at the barrier. Of course, they would not have been able to come onto the platform without a platform ticket. Yet more restrictions.

Everyone in the carriage had taken seats. I stood up and forced down the window, pulling frantically on the frayed leather strap, and put my head out. As I did so, a rush of noise and the acrid smell of smoke and steam assailed my senses, overpowering the damp freshness of the cold November morning. A small crowd of people stood at the barrier, all craning to see the departure of loved ones. Mother and Father stood at the front, in danger of getting squashed, I remember thinking. Both seemed bewildered, not knowing where to look. At that moment, the guard blew the whistle for the train to leave, answered by a shriek from the locomotive and the hissing build-up of steam power.

Usually saved for a departing ship, I pulled my handkerchief from my coat pocket. Luckily it was clean and folded, and I leaned as far out of the window as I could, waving it vigorously towards the barrier. I saw Father nudge Mother and point in my direction. She saw me at last and managed a watery smile, blowing kisses as the train chuffed slowly out, billowing clouds of steam, towards the criss-crossing of lines in the direction of Liverpool. I watched Mother's face until I could no longer see it and both forms faded to a blur before my eyes.

Until then, I had concentrated my attention on Mother, and with Father's support, had held myself strong. The worst had passed now but I did not seem able to feel anything as I thought I should have done. The situation seemed surreal. I had embarked on the journey of a lifetime to a tropical country and yet everything was mundane: the crowded, fusty carriage, the lowering, threatening sky and the drizzling rain. I assessed my fellow passengers: two couples with young children, two young men and a girl, apart from myself. None of them looked particularly sociable and I left them to their own devices, alternating gazing out of the window at the sodden, featureless countryside of the Midlands with looking over that morning's newspaper. Percy had shoved it into my hand at the last minute, I remembered, with a pang of sadness and love for his thoughtfulness. As I read the front-page news of the night-time raid of Coventry with its devastation, I felt both relief that I left a war-torn country and worry for my parents and friends who had no choice but to stay.

The journey that should only have taken three hours took much longer that day. We advanced slowly, the crowded train seeming to lumber clumsily under its own weight, from station to station. Towards midday we limped into Crewe. As I relaxed, I had begun to feel hungry, on cue, for lunch and delved into my carry-all for the greaseproof package of sandwiches, biscuits and chocolate which Florence had packed that morning. I hesitated and gazed round at my companions. I felt glad that there was plenty to offer.

"Excuse me," I ventured at the apparently impenetrable faces around me. "Would anyone care for a sandwich? The children perhaps?"

It broke the ice. The couples smiled and shook their heads, saying that they had brought their own, but one of the little boys took one anyway, and was scolded thoroughly for his presumption by his father. I smiled at him and settled into my corner with my lunch, duty performed.

It was a lonely journey, made worse by the constant threats we faced from the air and, after lunch, the dourness of my travelling companions. We had finally left Crewe after an hour's delay, hearing that there had been damage to the line which had had to be repaired. It was around four when we reached the outskirts of the city of Liver-pool. Suddenly feeling that I needed some air from the stuffy carriage, I had climbed over the feet and sundry bags and slid the door open into the corridor. I was glad I had. From the windows, which I lowered for air, the huge, blue expanse of the Mersey estuary lapped at the base of the shoreline below the raised track. Beyond, on the opposite shore, stood the city buildings, some of which I could see even from the train had been reduced to rubble. Through the window wafted the scent of the sea from beyond the estuary. There had been some fitful sunshine in the past half hour, which cast a semi-golden late afternoon light over my first sight of the city.

One of the occupants of the carriage had emerged earlier and stood at a neighbouring window.

"It's quite a sight, isn't it?"

It was one of the young men who was taking some respite from his confined position between two of the children from the families.

"Yes, it is. Have you been here before?"

I thought his manner spoke of familiarity with the scene. I glanced at him sideways. He wore neatly pressed slacks with a dark blue Guernsey over a well-muscled torso. His bearing appeared erect and military.

"Many times," said my companion. "Backwards and forwards to Bombay. Canada Dock is my second home."

"Are you familiar with the *"Narkunda?"*

"Yes, I've done a couple of trips in her. She's a good ship. Fast. Where are you bound?"

"Ipoh, Malaya, although I probably should not be imparting my travel plans to a complete stranger on a train!"

"Well, we can fix that. I'm Alec Soames, of the Royal Marines at your service, Ma'am!"

I wondered why an officer of the Royal Marines was travelling alone in plain clothes. Perhaps I could find out later.

"Val Coates," I reciprocated. "How long before we get to Canada Dock, Alec?'

"We should just be coming in now. You should be able to see the ship from here."

I thought to myself that I should really be collecting my belongings together but that I would just wait a moment to see the view. It did not disappoint.

As we came through a low tunnel, the train suddenly emerged into dazzling brightness.

The *Narkunda*, long and low in the water, rode at anchor by the wharf – P&O's largest ship built twenty years before. Her three funnels, shining black, towered over her bulk, vapour escaping from one as she stood taking her cargo onboard. Large crates were being lifted on in nets suspended from the cranes which surrounded her. All around the ship, dockworkers scurried like ants, loading, climbing on board – working against the clock. Less than two hours remained until sunset and another night of vulnerability - the sheer size of the ship gave her away. Seeing the *Narkunda* in this way, preparing for her voyage, gave me a feeling akin to pride and awe. My first glimpse of a large passenger liner up close, I had not prepared for the magnificence of the vessel. I would have loved to watch her sail out to the estuary bound for the ocean, but of course, I would be onboard and a part of her.

"I'll see you on board!"

I had barely noticed that Alec Soames had left his post at the corridor window and had gone back to the carriage to collect his hand luggage. I must have waved my hand in acknowledgment and later thought that I should have shown more interest in his friendly advances. I did not fully appreciate then what a small world shipboard life was and how confined we would all be for the next few weeks. The kindlier people felt towards one, the better. I nevertheless resolved that I would try to make amends when I saw him on the ship.

Within five minutes, the train pulled into Canada Dock Station. Perhaps the fitful sunshine gleaming off the glass roof of the terminus building encouraged it or the hints of blue estuary beyond, or the general feeling of relief on another safe arrival - but passengers who had tensely endured the previous hours on the train were galvanised into action. The station changed from inactivity into a bustling, cheerful tangle, as people disgorged themselves from the train and fought their way towards the guard's van to claim their luggage and pass through the customs office. I caught the general atmosphere and my spirits lifted perceptibly. I began to feel the thrill of excitement which had been absent during the long ordeal of the train journey, when I had still felt the ties to home and the memory of my mother's face at the barrier.

At Canada Dock nobody appeared sure of the procedure and

there seemed a dearth of porters. Trunks and suitcases began to pile up on the platform at the back of the train. The guard, standing by a customs official in a semi-military uniform, blew a whistle for silence and attention.

"Can I have your attention please, ladies and gentlemen," he began. "We have a very full train and I need you to wait for your name to be called before you approach for your luggage. Please have your tickets and passports ready." He consulted his list. "Atkins, Miss C."

Atkins, Miss C, a small, plump, rosy cheeked young woman in an emerald green mohair coat which showed off her dark glossy curls to perfection, approached at a trot and smiled gaily at the two officials, jubilant at being first. I watched curiously. If they were doing this in alphabetical order, they should call me soon. My analysis proved correct. Only two more passengers had collected their luggage and, with a porter in tow, headed for customs, before my turn arrived. It turned out that the "porters", diverted to port duties from their usual identity as sailors, had turned their hand to loading the vessel. They had appeared out of nowhere – probably, as I surmised, from the bowels of the ship.

"How many pieces, Miss?"

Close up, the guard looked younger than I had imagined from a distance. He was of a sandy, freckled complexion with auburn hair. His beard had barely begun to grow on a baby-white skin. Remembering now how the war had taken its course, being in the first stages he as yet remained unconscripted. I hoped Providence had seen fit to spare his life.

"Three – two large suitcases and a trunk," I spoke to him adult to adult. He seemed conscientious and good at his job. He deftly found my pieces and, in a flash, a burly sailor manhandled them onto a trolley. In the meantime, the customs official examined my passport.

"Safe journey, Miss Coates." He smiled, and nodded his head briefly.

I passed through to the cavernous customs shed, where a row of officials, men and women, sat at tables making a search of the luggage. The first woman waved me through to the end of the line. The last official, a woman, had opened one of my cases and made a cursory search. She refastened the case and placed it back on the trolley. She showed none of the politeness of the previous man, who had wished me a "safe journey" and without a word, held out her hand for my passport.

"What is the purpose of your voyage to Malaya?" She asked me abruptly.

I told her.

"Are you carrying anything for another person?"

I replied in the negative.

Five minutes later, I walked behind my "porter" out of the customs shed and towards the ship's gangway. *Narkunda* stood firm against the wharf, her bulk forbidding all but a slight movement in the green-grey water below her port side. My luggage separated at the ship's side, and the trunk remained standing on the wharf for loading into the hold, while the cases came with us up the gangway to the passenger entrance.

After a cursory examination of my ticket at the bottom of the gangway, I followed the sailor up and along the narrow passage, climbing at a thirty-degree angle and using a fragile metal handrail for support. As I did so, I looked down, deep into the water. This – I thought, and this flimsy vessel, would carry me away to the places I had dreamed of – would merge like mercury into oceans of a deeper blue and depth than I could imagine. The moment passed and I walked onto the ship.

A small table stood on my right, behind which sat a girl of about my own age, smartly dressed in a purser's uniform. She smiled and asked me my name. I smiled back at the girl, only dimly aware that we stood in a small, rather dark entrance lobby with a low ceiling. According to my estimation, this gave access into the ship about half way down the port side. I noticed a sign in the corner notifying me that I was on "C" deck which confirmed my estimation.

"Lavinia Florence Coates," I announced to the girl, whom, I could see, had the long, slim legs I had always craved, crossed elegantly under the table. She smiled even more brightly.

"Welcome aboard, Miss Coates. I'm Kathleen Addison, one of the pursers. You have been allocated a shared cabin on 'B' Deck. It's a nice one, with a porthole. If you have any questions, come to our office on 'A' Deck. We are a full ship this voyage but we'll try our best to help."

She gave me a small, gold-coloured key on a leather tag inscribed with the words: SS *Narkunda* and the cabin number.

"The stairs are over there in the corner. Turn right at the top. 'B' Deck is the next one up."

My bags were entrusted to a steward and it remained for me to follow the directions Kathleen had provided. I turned the golden key in the lock of the cabin at the end of a long, narrow, corridor and opened the door. A young woman, probably a few years younger than I, was already ensconced - unpacking in light streaming through a porthole into the small cabin, which held just two bunks on the interior bulkhead.

Many years later, I remembered Molly as a Duger substitute and in a sense, that was how she appeared to me. She lived her life as I would have liked myself, which became clear from shipboard days onwards. At this moment, though, I thought only that she looked rather fun.

Molly was a pretty girl. She stood looking at me in the centre of the cabin, slender and taller than I - in her slim-fitting, knee-length grey skirt and short-sleeved sweater. Her shoulder-length fair hair was drawn back from an oval, regular-featured face and fastened with bobby pins, allowing bouncing curls to cascade to her shoulders. She stepped forward with a bright, sweet smile and held out her hand.

"Are you Lavinia?" she asked in a pleasant, open manner.

I guessed at that moment that, like me, she had trained as a nurse.

"I checked with the purser and she gave me your name, though she probably shouldn't have! I'm Molly, by the way."

"Lavinia Coates, but please call me Val!"

I thought we had better start as we meant to go on. I liked the look of Molly. I hoped for some fun onboard and I felt sure that Molly would attract some attention with her looks. Although I could hold my own, it would not hurt to tag along with someone attractive as the opposite numbers usually came in twos anyway.

"Let me help you with your bags. I thought I would wait until you came to ask you if you have any preferences about bunks. I really don't mind which I have."

By the cocktail hour, which, according to an announcement over the public address system, would be held in the Ocean Room, we had formed the basis of a solid acquaintance. Like me, Molly had been recruited by the Crown Agents for her posting of ward sister. By coincidence, or perhaps some design on the part of the purser's office, we both headed for the same city in Malaya – Ipoh. Her post awaited her at the nearby Batu Gajah Hospital, the main medical centre for the district, whereas mine I would occupy in line with my experience, at a nearby maternity clinic. Like me, she had despaired of escaping from a dead-end job as a staff nurse at St Bartholemew's, where she had suffered incarceration since qualification. Her parents had been even more reluctant than mine to allow their spirited daughter to travel – perhaps with good reason – but she had finally talked them round.

Sipping our drinks in the upper-deck Ocean Room and sizing up our travelling companions, we had a good view of the loading operations. We sensed the frantic activity which surrounded us on all sides of the ship as the *Narkunda* filled to capacity, reflecting the dwindling availability of passenger ships. Later, I gradually got to know the composition of the passengers: rubber planters and government officials returning from leave; wives and children returning to their husbands in Malaya or India; a large group of

Marines (I had not yet spotted Alec Soames, although I looked out for him and told Molly about our meeting on the train). Some VIP's travelled as first-class passengers, among them a cousin of the Duke of Gloucester, but I hesitated to meet him. Probably unfairly, I guessed that he may be in the "stuffed shirt" category and I preferred a rugged planter type, with suntanned skin and shorts to his tropical fatigues.

That first night at dinner, Molly and I shared our table with three other nursing sisters, two bound for Singapore and one to mainland Malaya. We guessed more nurses would join them later. The sisters proved a lively trio and brightened up the table with cheerful chit-chat. We feared that at least until we reached more southerly waters, little in the way of organised entertainment was likely, and felt confirmed in our expectations by the sight of several vast lounges, unoccupied except for a few elderly gentlemen sunk into deep armchairs with their after-dinner cigarettes or cigars and newspapers. A grand piano stood in the corner of one of them and another boasted a bar, as yet unmanned.

"Did you hear?" whispered Molly, as she went over to the piano and began to pick out a tune, softly. The atmosphere at present in the dismal, smoky lounge discouraged making too much noise. "We won't be allowed off the ship until we reach Africa!" she continued. "Imagine! I hope things get a bit more lively!"

They did, but not in the way she meant.

We had just settled into our bunks – early, through both fatigue and boredom, when I suddenly jerked, awakened from a doze by a dreaded sound and thought for an instant I dreamed it. A siren, sounding distant and muffled through the structure of the ship had begun its all-too-familiar ascent through the musical scale. At the same time, an announcement, beginning with a sudden chime for attention, must have woken everyone onboard.

"Ladies and gentlemen, for your own safety, please make your way to your nearest lounge and report to the officer on duty. I repeat......"

I climbed down the ladder and nudged Molly, who seemed dead to the world.

"We've got to go to the lounge, Molly! Air raid!"

Molly gave a long groan and pressed her face more firmly in her pillow. I tried again and this time she sat up. I helpfully handed her dressing gown to her.

The lounge which we had left only an hour before, filled rapidly with people – some, like us, in their night attire with coats or dressing gowns slung hastily over pyjamas. Others, like the smoking gentlemen we had seen in their armchairs before, were still there, filling the ashtrays and resembling statues. Still others appeared in evening dress and carried drinks in their hands. Through the windows to the deck, I saw that the rain had returned. The drops slanted on the panes as they fell, indicating the beginnings of a storm.

The officer – second only to the captain, who stood by the piano was trying to get everyone's attention. In the end, he brought a small whistle out of his uniform pocket and blew it. The hubbub gradually subsided.

"Ladies and gentlemen, could you kindly form a queue for roll-call."

He held a clip-board with a list of the name of every passenger on that side of the ship. A passenger piped up.

"When are we sailing, officer?'

Everyone turned to look at the member of the evening dress contingent who spoke.

"We will not be able to sail until the weather improves, sir. Unfortunately, it may not be for a few days. The captain will be making daily announcements."

A pulsating roar drowned out any further words from the second officer as the German bombers delivered their deadly cargo on the City of Liverpool. In return, our anti-aircraft gunners valiantly defended the docks -and us. I sent up a wish and a prayer that we would get away before we lay dead in the water.

The higher power to whom I prayed seemed to answer. The raids continued nightly but we, the ship and all those onboard, survived. On the third day, the *Narkunda* was pulled out into the estuary by tugs and waited, while a convoy of destroyers assembled, until at dusk at last she sailed alone, heading for the high seas.

On the night she sailed, Molly and I stood looking over the side. The moon had risen, and shone a silver path across the becalmed sea. We headed north west to the mid-Atlantic, over water almost sinister in the blackness of its depths.

Chapter 6

In Suspension

On the dining room wall I had hung a painting. It held no particular pride of place – I had seen it as an obscure apology for its almost amateurish depiction of a ship, and one that no longer exists to carry out the purpose for which it was built. For it exists now, if anything remains, only as a wreck in shallow waters off the coast of Algeria, sunk by German aircraft attack in 1942. The *Narkunda* had just offloaded troops for the North Africa campaign and had begun her return journey. Thirty-one lives were lost. The voyage which had taken me to Malaya had been her last before her conversion to a troop ship.

You might miss the painting, walking into the dining room, if you didn't know it hung there. At odds with the muted beige and flesh tones mingling with the walnut and glass cabinets, the mahogany and the heavy velvets, it hangs on the right side of the chimney breast where shadows obscure the vibrant colours painted with the sensibilities of an artist bred of the East. I can't now remember how long I had worked on the archives when I had placed it there. Looking out of the window, I had seen people unloading Christmas trees from their cars, or walking by carrying rolls of Christmas wrapping paper protruding from shopping bags. I should be doing the same, I had thought but I knew from past years when I had tried, with my heart not in it, that the same routine, year after year, of putting up decorations and taking them down again eventually became pointless for oneself alone.

Sometimes these days I kept to my bed when Janet arrived, sometimes not. The routine at 7, Somerhill Road continued, unvaried, like the years, like Christmas. Janet had become used to seeing me now, day after day, either dressed or in a dressing gown, sitting at the dining room table with the ever-growing piles of various kinds of paper in front of me. Sometimes it was the newsprint of cuttings; pages torn from exercise books or notebooks; different styles of letter-paper. Nowadays few of these styles survive except printer paper, as the written word has evolved to electronics. I felt myself nearly ready for the typewriter. In recent years many people in the business world had begun using computers for word processing but I did not think I either needed or wanted this challenge at my age.

In the evenings, after sitting in on an uncomfortable dining room chair for many hours working on my papers, I felt stiff and weary. I would have dinner shortly after Janet left with a glass or two of wine, then relax in front of the television with a cigarette. Smoking had been a lifelong habit, and one I couldn't break.

"Oh, all nurses smoke," it was often said then. "It's the stress of the job, you know."

Malaya had done nothing to free me from these twin habits, neither had George. I almost felt that I did it now in his memory... Janet would privately shake her head or "tut-tut" under her breath when she saw the stubs in the ashtray or the empty wine bottles in the kitchen tidy. I often barely felt the effort of climbing the stairs after a glass or two....occasionally, indeed, I had fallen asleep in my chair and woken up at dawn with the birdsong, and had only then, for appearances sake, climbed the stairs to my room. The fear haunted me that if I were considered incapable, my doctor would recommend that I go into a home for my own safety. Janet acted as my watchdog. She did not come at weekends and at these times I became, no doubt in her eyes, my most outrageous self – not washing, not dressing – just living in my own world, of dreams, fantasies and memories. Why not? I thought. I didn't have long.

There were not many notes about the *Narkunda*. Compared to other times of my life, I had only sketchy scraps to work from. It seemed almost as if during this voyage I was beside myself, living so intensely that I could not organise my thoughts fast enough to interpret events into words. Did I even know where I was? One of my letters to my mother begins: "Somewhere at sea....."

Now, to stretch my legs, which visibly swelled to an even more misshapen condition through sitting for such long periods, I shuffled stiffly and painfully over to the painting. I had bought it in Bombay on that voyage, from a street artist with whom I had bartered and knocked down the price to only a few rupees. It depicted the *Narkunda* alright, identifiable from her three funnels, steaming along just offshore in blue tropical waters in front of a rowboat containing a group, or perhaps a family, of Indians. The patriarch stood up in the boat, gazing at her as she steamed past, perhaps envious of those within, who occupied a world unknown to him. The women sit in the boat alongside him, veiled and circumspect. They inhabited a world previously alien to me: the air warm as it gently caressed the skin, the light coaxing vivid colours from the living canvas before their eyes.

I had stood on the cusp of change. The ship had carried me towards the peaceful, blue waters in its own contained world. We were cut off from all news of the war by radio silence. The security of the daily routine replaced the activities of our former lives so that they in themselves became unreal. Loving the unfamiliarity of the experience, I, unlike some, had no expectations and did not feel lonely or bored, even with little to look forward to each day except reading the daily log or participating in a sweepstake to guess the mileage covered the previous day. I accepted the ship as my home – its security, sights, sounds, smells and routines lulled my senses and new friends occupied my mind. The further I travelled, the further seemed my home and family. I relished my new-found freedom.

Remembering my duty, I wrote hasty letters home in spare moments, ready to post from some unknown, future port. Later, when I lived in Malaya, I found it difficult to forget the shipboard life and the feeling of a temporary suspension from the world, never before experienced. The *Narkunda* sailed on, dwarfed under a boundless sea and sky, towards the shores of Africa.

Molly and I slept soundly in our bunks that Tuesday morning in November. It dawned like no other Tuesday I ever had, and no other November. At home, chill dankness would penetrate to the bone and wet leaves would stick to the pavement, while here, as I woke, the steamy heat of Sierra Leone penetrated the cabin and made me throw off all my bedclothes. All was eerily quiet, for the first time since we had sailed. I listened for a moment. The giant engines had stopped. A slight, almost imperceptible rocking indicated that we rode at anchor. I climbed down past the somnolent Molly, blissfully asleep with her face turned trustingly towards the morning light streaming through the porthole. I gazed out, then turned back to the bunks.

"Wake up, my girl!"

I shook her on the shoulder, knowing that her calm temperament would not result in a display of bad temper at being so unceremoniously awakened. I tried again.

"Molly! You've got to see this. We're in AFRICA!"

The last word had the desired result. Molly woke up suddenly with a grunt which sounded like a question and opened her eyes, looking at me as if she had never seen me before in her life. At first, she looked as if she thought she was dreaming. Still half asleep, she groggily made her way across the cabin to the porthole and gazed out at the scene.

The ship stood gently rocking at anchor about half a mile off the coast of Freetown, Sierra Leone. The palm clad outline of the shore appeared as if in a haze, the colours of the leaves on the trees a dusty grey-green. Before the shoreline, the sea sparkled a bright blue around the ship, almost too bright for the naked eye, so that we became blinded for a moment. The port in front of us appeared a hive of activity and we could just make out some long canoe-shaped boats being put out to sea from the harbour.

We passed a memorable day, one in which we finally realised that we had already travelled out of the main war zone into one which did not have to live out the daily realities of war. The sisters had all unpacked their summer tropical clothes, and while I wore a fairly demure cotton dress and sandals, some appeared at breakfast in short shorts and sleeveless blouses "to start our tans!" Molly had donned such an outfit that morning. She had a bold, cheerful confidence in her appearance which struck me as hardly surprising. I watched her now, as she chatted brightly to her future colleagues, spreading marmalade on her toast. Her well-exercised, slim legs were obscured from view under the tablecloth. The sisters formed a sorority common to nurses the world over – a bond born of shared experiences and unparalleled knowledge of the human condition. They sat at their own table in the "Atlantic" dining room, while other passengers sat in smaller groups or pairs at the other tables. The sisters' table, which seated about ten of them, dominated the room and other passengers often looked over, interested, to pick up on their conversations or to smile with them as they laughed at some obscure hospital joke. Their vivacity and wholesome attractiveness acted as a magnet towards which most eyes were drawn. I felt proud to be a part of this group.

On this particular morning, a vacant place announced the absence of one of us. At that moment a banging door leading out onto the starboard deck signalled the whirlwind approach of Irene Moore, late as usual. She looked somewhat dishevelled, as if she had just got out of bed – hastily dressed in slacks and a crumpled shirt, dark hair escaping in wisps from its confinement of bobby pins on the top of her head. We all felt a little protective about Irene. A tall, lanky girl, a little short sighted, she peered blearily now at the group around the dining table through thick lenses. She looked excited about something.

"Girls, there are dozens of canoes coming all around the ship!"

she imparted breathlessly. "I've just come from my cabin. Didn't you see them?"

Irene took her place at the table. The waiter approached, bearing her plate of cooked food. She started to eat hungrily.

"We saw some boats putting out from the harbour earlier," I said. "What are they doing?"

"I think they're trying to sell something or other," Irene mumbled, washing down a mouthful of bacon with tepid coffee. "They're natives, and they look quite mad!"

At that moment, the captain entered the dining room, looking much more relaxed than when I had last seen him at the start of the voyage. A middle-aged man with a mane of greying hair, I felt sure that he had lost more hair colour since leaving Liverpool. A waiter banged on a plate to summon attention.

"Ladies," he began, "and gentlemen, (seeing some of that gender dotted around the dining room) we are now anchored off the coast of Freetown, Sierra Leone. Now, I'm sure you are very eager to go ashore but I regret to inform you that the ship will not be docking for disembarkation until we reach Cape Town."

A few general groans were forthcoming at this news, especially from among the nurses. After being cooped up in smoky lounges for the past ten days, they could not wait to stretch their legs and explore the port city that beckoned enticingly from across a sparkling sea.

"I regret that we have been receiving reports of bandits in the area targeting travellers, especially women."

Some protests rippled round the room from among his female audience and the hapless captain held up his hand for silence. He could see he was dealing with a spirited bunch.

"Now I know that you can all look after yourselves very well but I'm sure I don't need to tell you that while you are a passenger on board this ship, you remain under my authority and you are my ultimate responsibility. As such, ladies and gentlemen, I consider it too great a risk to visit this port. However..."

At this point the captain, not an unkind man and knowing full well the stress his passengers had endured, smiled.

"...I believe that we have an impromptu performance from some of the inhabitants of Freetown if you would care to make your way to the Centre Deck after you have finished breakfast."

Captain James gave a slight half-bow towards the breakfasters and prepared to cross the ship to the other dining rooms to repeat his unwelcome news.

"Well!" Molly looked round the table. "That's a shame. I so wanted to look at their basket work in the markets! It's supposed to be world famous!"

A few of the other girls, the blood sisters Helen and Hannah Reid among them, and myself, agreed vehemently. Most of us had dressed for a shore excursion and were disappointed to be thwarted in our shopping and sightseeing aims. The waiter attending our table had begun to clear away the breakfast things.

"Now, does anyone want any more coffee or are we all done?" said Helen. She and her sister were fraternal twins, but while they did not bear a striking physical resemblance to each other, they did most things together.

"No let's go and see what's going on," said Molly. "Buck up, Irene!"

Irene hastily buttered a piece of toast and took it with her over to the deck. Even from within the dining room, they had been aware of the faint sound of music, of laughter and deep, throaty shouts rising from the ocean. Coming from the comparative dimness of the dining room, emerging into the tropical atmosphere and heat of the morning, already climbing towards eighty degrees, felt overwhelming. Even though I relished being with my fellow-nurses, I wanted to experience this atmosphere alone. I went over to the deck rail and leaned on it for a moment looking across at the port while the others peered over, gazing at the revellers below.

The African sun beat down mercilessly, burning my unaccustomed skin as I stood looking at Freetown. Even from this distance, I sensed the vibrancy of the place, seeing distant flashes of bright colour from the vivid headdresses and sarongs of the women against gleaming black skin, under the intense light. Behind the immediate shoreline of white sand, palm trees bordered the beach and the low red-rooved buildings of the town behind rose on a shallow gradient – the foothills of a low mountainous range which dominated the lower skyline, grey-green with native vegetation. The morning haze lifted before my eyes and voices and song travelled on the clear air. At that moment I counted myself as lucky to be alive: a survivor of the London Blitz, unspeakable monotony and dealing with the fallout from the war – London's poor. I lifted my face to the sun with gratitude and smiled.

"Val! Laviniaaa! What's she doing?"

As if from a great distance, I slowly became aware of Molly bringing me back to earth. She came over to me, grinning.

"Val, old thing! You must come and see these crazy people! Ask them to sing a song! They're quite good!"

Along the side of the ship, I could just glimpse a small fleet of canoes thronging the ship, some very close to the side. Their occupants all appeared in high spirits, and laughed and flirted with the group of nurses above them, now joined by a crowd of passengers. Most of those looking down upon the strange assortment of people in the canoes were women and the visitors from the port appeared to address them rather than the men. Some of the male passengers turned away with a superior and disparaging look and took themselves off to their deckchairs in a shady corner of the deck. The women ignored them.

Below, the west Africans thronged the ship in assorted vessels defying description, all vying for the privileged position against the hull of the *Narkunda*. They wore a strange assortment of bizarre clothing, presumably designed to entertain and lighten the mood of the passengers but their tomfoolery had another motive. I watched, fascinated, at some bartering being conducted by a tall African who stood up precariously in the stern of his canoe while his confederate sat in the bow keeping the boat steady with oars, supplies of fresh bananas, oranges and baskets surrounding his feet. Both wore an attempt at western-style dress but purposely caricatured. The former stood holding a huge bunch of bananas and grinning up at one of the women passengers not of our group of nurses and sisters. He showed magnificent white teeth in a broad smile and clearly charmed the somewhat elderly passenger. In the eighty-degree heat with a merciless sun beating down, he stood with beads of perspiration standing out on his forehead in a Harris tweed jacket and "old school" tie complete with pullover. The passenger appeared much the cooler of the two in her white cotton summer dress.

"Now what is it you want in exchange?" she was saying. "Aren't these wonderful? And some oranges please. I haven't seen such lovely fruit since before the war. Old clothes? Well wait a minute. I may have something....." She disappeared for a moment towards one of the first-class cabins.

Further up the hull, some boys dived off their boats down into the depths of the clear, blue water. They called up to the passengers.

"Dive for English penny, Miss, Mister! Dive for penny!"

One or two of the older male passengers appeared to be very interested in watching the boys, I thought - slim and nimble, diving off the boat and swimming towards the copper-coloured pennies as they lay on the shallow sea bed. As they succeeded in picking them up, they rose triumphant with the coins between their teeth and waved joyfully. One of them, having made what was to him a small fortune with his diving displays, got back in the boat and picked up a small banjo, starting an approximation of a popular song.

Soon, the occupants of the other canoes picked up the refrain and to the accompaniment of banjos and the odd fiddle, finished that song and several others besides, taking requests from the passengers.

The captain on the bridge smiled to himself as he heard the hubbub. I caught a glimpse of him looking out of the window, as I stood watching the scene.

It was 30th November and St. Andrew's Day. As I returned to my
bunk that night, slightly tipsy from the whiskey and full from a somewhat indigestible haggis which the *Narkunda's* chef had concocted
for the sake of the Scottish travellers who had performed the sword
dance in national dress, I committed the day to memory, thinking it
must have been one of the happiest of my life. I looked again at the
painting in the alcove. Yes, the *Narkunda* had brought happiness to
her many passengers during those years, taking them towards paradis-
ical lands before she foundered. The day after St. Andrew's Day
1940 she had steamed away from Freetown. I never went back there.
As we passed the lighthouse shortly after noon, we saw two wrecks,
their funnels and mainmasts showing above the water. Surely, if the
Narkunda had had sensibilities, she would have felt a shiver of
premonition at that sight.

Once more, we the passengers all settled down again to life on
board, to deck quoits and tennis and "Housey Housey" in the
evenings - a forerunner of the ubiquitous Bingo, that, twenty years
later, filled the sad and unused cinemas in every town and city in
England. Radio contact resumed and war news now filtered through
of Germany's air activity over England and occupation of more territory in this early stage of the war. The ship steamed southwards
towards the Cape but, through the intrusiveness of radio contact, I no
longer felt as unconnected. The feeling of being in suspension faded
and a familiar worry started to surface. Now, my mind dwelt partly
on events at home. Whereas I had previously imagined that everything had remained as I had left it in early November, now regular
reporting of news cruelly reminded me that my mother and father
and everyone else I knew were in peril. When would the Germans
stop? It seemed apparent from Churchill's speeches that they would
not. Churchill knew that a tolerable end could only come about by a
fight to the death.

We had crossed the equator. Everyone had to do that at some

time or other at least once, or face the ducking I was obliged to submit to in the ship's tiny swimming pool, filled for the occasion. A week later, Table Mountain and the Lion Peaks of Cape Town appeared through the morning mists. We had sailed continuously for twenty-five days and when we woke that morning to the sight of land, we knew for certain that a shore excursion beckoned enticingly. We were in a high state of excitement, having heard that Cape Town had the reputation of a cool and invigorating city, one where we would feel welcome and safe. Walking onto dry land for me that morning seemed a peculiar experience, I remembered. The ground appeared to sway and move as if I were still onboard, and I regretted wearing sandals with a heel. We had decided to go ashore as a group of four, remembering the captain's warnings about Freetown. There would be safety in numbers.....later I had second thoughts about acquiescing in this arrangement, as constantly rounding up four curious people could be frustrating and time consuming. The twins, who had accompanied Molly and me, kept wandering off, captivated by the colourful market displays and brightly lit streets, in contrast to the blackout at home. It felt as if we had crossed the sea to another, unrelated world, where war had never come. We stayed at Cape Town two days. The following day, Molly and I decided to go out alone.

Heights did not pose a particular problem for me. If they had, I would have found the ascent of Table Mountain challenging. Molly, of course, accepted them as breezily as she did everything else - she seemed to skim over the surface of life like a high-speed skier, never questioning her nerve or abilities to cope. I could not by any means be called by any means a shrinking violet, but I stopped short of her headlong rush into every experience. Nevertheless, she made a stimulating companion. We ascended the foothills of Table Mountain by bus, in order to reach the cable railway which would take us to the summit. A group of engineers from the ship, ultimately bound for the Colonial Service in Penang, had come along. I had met a few of them onboard. They made a welcome change from the constant company of nurses, although mostly they looked younger than us. A young engineer called Samuel Bailey was among them – he had told me that he was writing a diary about the voyage. Perhaps he published his work and described that day on Table Mountain and other details about that voyage which I could not. I never knew.

The swinging cage of the cable car had carried us to a height of four thousand feet that morning, bringing back to me that same feeling of weightlessness I had on the ship. I could not help looking at the flimsy wooden floor of the car and thinking of all that space below me - all that kept us from falling thousands of feet a few metal ropes and a series of pulleys. Molly did not appear to think of anything but taking pleasure in the opening up of the vast landscape beneath us. Bailey, in the car with us, was something of a reliable presence, commenting on the engineering feats involved. I wondered, on that short ride to the top whether he actually noticed the views. From the peak, those vistas over the city, the bay beneath and the plains of South Africa reaching to distant foothills blue in the distance, banished everything else from my mind.

That morning in Cape Town had dawned perfect and cloudless, with a cool breeze which gently ruffled our skirts as we walked over the plateau of the summit. Bailey accompanied us, pointing far below to the harbour, where the *Narkunda* stood moored, awaiting our return. I would have preferred solitude, and thought that I had become quite reclusive. Molly's chatter distracted me by breaking frequently into my thoughts but I had time to reflect that in all likelihood, I would never come here again.

"Look, ladies," Bailey was saying. "Over there you can see the highest point on the mountain." He pointed to the eastern end of the plateau towards a stone construction. "It's called Maclear's Beacon, used for surveys. Built by an astronomer to measure the curvature of the earth!"

We followed his gaze, interested. I would have liked to climb up to see it, but just then the crew member who had accompanied us called over.

"Ten minutes, ladies and gentleman!"

The ship was due to set sail at sunset and I could see that the sun had already begun its descent towards the horizon.

I remember that ascent up the east coast of Africa towards Mombasa, Kenya, as hot and airless. For some reason – perhaps the risk of large waves - the captain had ordered the portholes closed at night, making sleep difficult. There were other inconveniences too, such as the ship's laundry unable to cope because of overcrowding, but this did not pose too much difficulty with us nurses. We promptly washed our own clothes and strung them up round our cabins to dry, adding to the humid atmosphere.

Bailey became a frequent partner for me, on those airless nights, as we danced on deck in the moonlight with the other younger passengers. He seemed thoughtful and kind, and I grew fond of him. I noticed, however, that as the climate had become hotter, the outfits he wore had not varied very much since leaving home.

"Is this your first time in the tropics?" I ventured one night, as we careered around the deck avoiding the other passengers in a foxtrot.

We only had a wind-up gramophone to provide the music, but one of the lower-rank crew members filled in as what we would now call a "disc jockey". As long as the music continued, we did not really care.

"Yes, why do you ask?" he said, steering me away from a rather drunk couple performing the most extraordinary dance moves.

"I just wondered. I heard you saying that you had worked with a city firm before the war."

"Yes, if it hadn't been for the war, I probably would have stayed there, but it has given me the opportunity to travel and gain experience. I wish I had known it would be this hot though! I suppose one doesn't realise."

I agreed, thinking that if I had not had such an obsession with the possibilities of travelling to Malaya for most of my life, I may not have thought of it, either. I looked over towards the other girls of my table. Although women outnumbered the men on this voyage, none of us appeared to lack dancing partners. The twins danced quite close to each other with their escorts and even Irene had been appropriated, partnered, as I saw in surprise and pleasure, with a titled lord to whom we had all been introduced. But I couldn't see Molly. Then I did. In a corner of the deck, she stood with a drink in her hand in deep conversation with one of the crew members. I felt concerned, thinking that she went too far. Fraternising with members of the crew was frowned upon and that night marked the first time I had seen it.

Late that night, I heard Molly come into the cabin. I had slept soundly but suddenly woke to hear the soft closing of the cabin door, then felt a slight shaking of the bunk frame as she got into bed. I heard her sigh as she settled to sleep. It was some time before I managed to sleep again. I knew it was ridiculous, but I felt somehow betrayed and not a little jealous.

The next morning, we spoke very little with each other. The easy camaraderie had dissolved. Molly had, I knew, gone beyond me into a world of which I had only scant experience – and had, we both knew, broken the rigid boundaries of class and propriety. For the rest of the voyage, we dealt politely with each other but scarcely spoke beyond the essentials, unless in company with our own group. But I missed her and one evening after dinner I tried to speak to her.

"Look here, old thing. It's not my business what you do or who you see in the evenings. I'd just like everything to be the same with us as it used to be. Let's go and have a drink and a laugh like old times, shall we?"

So, we did, and it felt a little better. I started to realise that not having known her before, I had not known of the differences between us. I could never form a close friendship with her because this was Molly and she could not help herself. She would betray a woman friend time and again because she did not value them as I did and would put, like Duger would, the whims of a casual boyfriend over a rendezvous with a bosom friend such as I could have been.

Christmas approached. On the morning of the 15th December, the ship docked in Mombasa for the day and we passengers had permission to go ashore for a few hours to walk to the shops and post office. The scene before us was one of military activity, as several British troop ships had just arrived and shortly afterwards launched the successful Abyssinian campaign. We sailed that evening, beginning the normally ten-day crossing of the Indian Ocean to Bombay, and arrived just before Christmas in record time, the *Narkunda* well known in the marine world as a fast ship.

Dawn on Christmas Eve revealed the distant coastline of India, the shores of the sub-continent gradually becoming clearer before the eyes of some wakeful passengers. If I had read, many years later, my erstwhile dance partner Sam Bailey's reminiscences and comparisons, I would have agreed with him. He compared this gradual unfolding of a scene in a voyage by ship with the sudden and jolting arrival afforded by air travel today ..."the slow arrival of a misted horizon and the gradual disclosure of unknown shores" by which the passengers of the *Narkunda* during that wartime Christmas of 1940 approached India.

Chapter 7

Briar in the Crown

I had often thought of Alec Soames. I had seen him around the ship, apparently occupied, and although he had glanced at me and given a half-smile of recognition, he had not sought me out. Occasionally, I had seen him in the company of one or two of the young female aristocratic set, or, as we liked to call them, the "evening dress contingent" which I remembered from that very first evening – the night of the onboard bombing raid. I had puzzled over what had hindered us getting to know each other during the voyage, then I knew. Shipboard life was a microcosm of life at home – rigid with class structure. Like mingled with like onboard, and occasionally I had felt these differentiations acutely, as I did with Alec Soames. I was curious about Alec. In those days "who people were" was essential knowledge. Once having it, one could ignore or act on it at will. I had assumed Alec was a gentleman, from his speech, manners and bearing, and felt myself somewhat put in my place as a working woman merely from the middle class.

Because of this, I felt somewhat taken aback that first morning in Bombay. Still on board, I mingled with a crush of passengers near the C Deck portal. For some, like me, eager to disembark, it was their first experience of the sub-continent while others, many with hand luggage, left the ship for the last time. I had nearly arrived at the gangway, the softened sunlight of the winter morning feeling warm on my bare arms.

I felt the soft touch of another's hand on the sensitive underside of my upper arm where it emerged from my short-sleeved dress. Alec stood at my elbow, still gently holding me, as if to escort me from the ship. In his other hand he held a brown leather attaché case. A light raincoat was folded over his arm. I looked up at his face, startled, and close enough now to see the changes the voyage had made since we had last spoken on the train pulling into Liverpool. The tanned skin contrasted with sun-bleached blond hair and the crisp white shirt he wore over his pressed uniform trousers. I surmised that, like me, the task of laundering one's own clothes held no horrors for him. I felt glad that, under his close scrutiny, my own well-fitting cotton dress was as neatly pressed by my own hands.

"Forgive the intrusion, Miss Coates. I wondered if you had plans for today? I have to join my battalion later but I have a few hours to spare. I wondered if I could show you the sights of Bombay?"

I did not answer immediately but looked around me, somewhat perplexed. I had indeed arranged to meet Molly and Irene near the portal with a morning of sightseeing the intention, but could see no sign of them. Alec looked at me with concern.

"Well – I had arranged to meet two of my friends but they don't seem to be here yet."

I felt anxious, not liking just to walk off and leave my friends in the lurch. At the same time, Alec posed an attractive offer and I was interested in getting to know him better. Even though he disembarked, one never knew. The world grew smaller by the day.....

Just then, I caught a glimpse of Irene's cream linen skirt through the legs of the crowd and, rather spitefully I suppose, thought that for once she had taken trouble with her appearance. She stood in a corner of the lobby, near the gangway. My eyes travelled upwards, encompassing a white muslin blouse and wide-brimmed hat and then noticed her flannel-trousered companion, who stood close to her. They seemed oblivious to their surroundings as they connected with each other, deep in discussion. Irene looked vaguely over to the portal. I waved, thinking to attract her attention but her short-sighted eyes passed over me as if I were invisible. I recognised her companion as the aristocrat she had befriended. As I watched, both passed through the portal, down the gangway and onto the quay, in a few seconds lost in the morass of humankind that was Bombay.

"Well," I thought, "that's one of them taken care of! Now, where's the other one?"

To Alec, I said, "Just let me look for my friend Molly, and I'll be with you. If I can't find her, I'm all yours!"

Alec smiled mischievously. "Miss Coates, we have only just become acquainted, so I won't take you up on that, but I would be delighted to get to know you better over coffee before we head up to Malabar Hill!"

As we had crossed the Indian Ocean from the east coast of Africa, I had taken advantage of the ship's library and had researched our next port of call. Malabar Hill was one of the richest and most exclusive residential districts in India, and rated highly among the most desirable suburbs in the world. Up there brooded the Towers of Silence of the Parsis with the odd temple or two, and hanging gardens. I had asked Samuel Bailey if he would be visiting this macabre burial ground of the Zoroastrian descendants but his intent seemed just to go ashore for a few hours into the streets with some fellow-engineers. I had a good idea that they meant to target the local hotels and "colour" and hoped he would take due care. Bombay's brothels were reputably some of the most notorious in the world.

We had stood here waiting long enough. Around us, the crowd had thinned to only a handful of passengers. I never knew what Molly got up to these days. I looked at Alec and shrugged, holding out my hands in a helpless gesture.

"Let's go, shall we? Obviously, my friend has had a better offer. It's just as well you turned up! Where to, Mr Soames?"

Alec grinned, taking my teasing remarks in the spirit I intended.

"Firstly, we'll go to my sober coffee house. It's where I go either to sober up or get over a hangover. This only applies to myself, of course! Present company excepted!"

I laughed and joined in his banter.

"Well, I'm not so sure. Those deck dances can get a little out of hand!"

As we walked onto solid ground and left the side of the ship, Alec tucked my hand through his arm. I felt reassured and protected in the foreignness of the city, aware of the muscular firmness of his bicep under the thin material of his shirt. I picked my way over uneven road surfaces in my flimsy footwear towards a waiting cycle rickshaw. The driver stood beside it, smiling and gesturing us to get on.

"Now, this pedal power -" Alec pointed at the rickshaw - "is the latest improvement on shanks's pony!"

I gathered, as I climbed in, that he meant the unfortunate driver's shanks, rather than our own. It proceeded slowly, and I could see, even on the flat, that propelling us along the crowded streets towards the Gateway of India caused him considerable effort, although neither of us carried surplus pounds. I felt gratitude towards this stranger for his goodwill. Through him, I had my first sights of India – breathed in the warm humidity of the air, laden with peculiar scents of the east – spices, human bodies and sweat and the heady incense of the frangipanni flower. I gazed around, unable to make sense of the chaos of people, vehicles and animals, yet everyone seemed to know where they were heading and their intentions once they got there. My senses soon became overwhelmed.

"We'll be free of all this in a minute. We're just about to pass close to the Gateway. Just as well we're not on foot or we would be surrounded with photographers and hawkers."

As we crawled past the gigantic monument, constructed to commemorate the visit of King George V in 1911, I fished inside my handbag for my little Kodak camera, a vast improvement, I thought, on my old BoxBrownie. I would never have fitted that in my handbag.

Having plenty of time to focus, I snapped the Gateway of India twice, thinking to send one of the snaps to Father. He would be fascinated. Alec obligingly leant backwards out of the way. The monument's placing against a backdrop of sea and sky showed it off to perfection. It was separated from the teeming city streets by the open space which surrounded it, as if to endow it with peace and dignity. Through the arch I caught a glimpse of the azure blue of the harbour waters and said so to Alec.

"Yes, that's right. We are almost at the mouth of the harbour here, overlooking the Arabian Sea. Over there you can see the Taj Mahal Hotel, opened I believe around the turn of the century. Wait a minute."

Alec tapped the driver on the shoulder and said something in very rapid Marathi, the foremost language spoken in Bombay. The driver nodded and with effort, turned the vehicle towards the rear of the hotel, the front of which spectacular edifice overlooked the sea.

"I hope you don't mind. They have an excellent bar here but they also serve coffee if you like."

I felt rather thirsty in the heat and dust and acquiesced. As Alec paid the driver, I climbed down and looked around. Immediately, at least five or six eager-looking dark-skinned men surrounded me, gesturing and speaking rapidly. Everyone appeared to be on a different mission – wanting to take my photograph; selling souvenirs of the Gateway and the hotel, or the real Taj Mahal, or gesturing me to follow them into the hotel or to a waiting taxi. I felt bewildered and a little faint, surrounded by the grinning faces. I looked round for Alec.

To my relief, he appeared out of nowhere and bustled me off towards the hotel bar, giving the pressing, hectoring residents of Bombay short shrift as he spoke to them sternly in their own language. Gradually, they drifted off. I felt annoyed with myself for displaying weakness. Good heavens, I thought, Val old girl, pull yourself together. This is not the woman who braved the bombs of the Blitz to reach her patients. But I recognised in this situation something I had never dealt with before – a foreign country which did not play by the rules at home. Here, I sensed danger of a different kind, almost a primitive force. It was nothing to do with the people. I started to warm to their humanity, the empathy they showed, as if everything I felt they already knew, through wisdom accumulated by living among so many. As we entered the bar, several waiters, rather than one, attended to our every need. With the utmost respect and courtesy, they seated us comfortably and took our drinks order, each waiter in charge of one minute task. I reflected that at home, even before the war, one waiter could easily have taken the place of the half-dozen who fussed around us.

"I've ordered you a gin and tonic," Alec murmured, looking at the menu. "I hope I was right? You looked as if you needed it a moment ago."

"Well, I could certainly choke one down!"

I made an attempt at nonchalance to save face, unsure that I wanted to allow Alec to take control in this way. I decided to adopt a watch and wait strategy. In the meantime, I examined my surroundings.

We were seated in the window, overlooking the sea. The bar we occupied bore that description in the loosest possible way. It was the most luxurious bar I had ever visited and at the moment we seemed to have it all to ourselves. It seemed a different, more intimate world from the bright, sunlit square outside. Suffused lighting reflected red off the wine-coloured leather club chairs and glinted in the myriad glasses and many-coloured bottles behind the bar. A piano tinkled softly in the corner, while the light, clear ring of the glassware handled by soft-footed waiters mingled in their muted sounds. I looked over at my companion while I sipped my drink.

Why is he doing this today? I thought, as I took in the exactitude of his toilette – the close shave, the meticulous tying of the knot of the regimental tie, the set of his collar. *Is he trying to make amends for ignoring me? Is he feeling guilty?* I sat with my back to the window. Alec sat calmly, gazing past my shoulder out to sea, at the small craft chugging in and out of the harbour, the larger ships anchored offshore and the brightness of the sea and sky outside this red, intimate, womb-like room.

He answered as if he if he heard my silent question.

"I'm glad I ran into you today. I've been meaning to speak to you but you know what shipboard life is like," Alec made a helpless gesture. "I gather you're bound for Penang? I'm guessing you're a nurse, right?"

I nodded. "Health visiting, rather than sick nursing. I'll be based at the Ipoh clinic, actually."

"Malaya is a small colony. Everyone knows everyone else. I know. I was based there myself a few months ago until I got a transfer to Bombay. This is my first mission in India. So, you'll be working with Sister Howard?"

"Howard!" I nearly swallowed my gin down the wrong way. "But she used to be at Ealing!"

"Not any more. She works closely with the doctors Drew – married couple. You'll be meeting Clarissa Drew at the Ipoh clinic fairly soon after you arrive, I should think. I knew them all well. Socialising is the life-force of Malaya, so I hope you're the gregarious sort!"

I felt a little indignant. I rather resented Alec's confident, breezy approach to life and his neat categorising and disposal of all my hopes and dreams. They occupied a sacred place in my mind and to have a stranger knowing all one's business felt beyond the pale.

It seemed uncanny the way he always seemed to know what I thought. Before I had a chance to make a retort voicing some of my thoughts, he chuckled suddenly. His face, which had previously looked morose, now lit up charmingly and he appeared boyish and mischievous.

"Miss Coates - may I call you Val?" I nodded, somewhat mollified by his changed manner. "I can tell you disapprove of me so let me try to set that straight so that you take at least a few favourable impressions of me to Malaya with you. Have you finished?"

I nodded, draining the last of my gin and tonic, and stood up. At once, we became surrounded by the waiting fraternity - pulling back our chairs, brushing imaginary crumbs off the surface of the table and bowing, as we passed through their ranks. Alec passed over some bank notes to the head waiter.

"I hope that will cover it," he murmured. With some difficulty, we tore ourselves free. "Now, how do you feel about taking the bus to Malabar? Strangely enough, it's the best way to go. You're up higher and you get a better view."

"Fine by me," I said, enjoying the emergence into sunshine and stretching my legs.

"The bus stop is over here. Let's hope it won't be too crowded."

The bus overflowed with Bombay's citizens but I relaxed into the experience. Inside the well- weathered vehicle, assorted, nearly over-powering odours of humanity, perfume and petrol mingled into a humid entity as we mounted the stairs. This route mainly served the household staff of the mansions of Malabar. Looking around me from my window seat next to Alec I gazed admiringly at the young Indian women immaculately dressed and swaying in their seats with the movement of the bus - some in a kind of uniform sari or tunic, called a *kurta* with loose, baggy matching trousers. Others carried containers of food and I saw a woman cradling a clutch of brown eggs in a box on her lap. As the bus groaned up the hill in bottom gear, it gradually lost its passenger load. By the time we reached the top, with the vista over Bombay beneath us, I began to feel the benefit of some air wafting through the open window vent above my head and could breathe more easily. I glanced over the view and Alec leant over me, pointing downwards. As he did so, coming close to me, I caught the scent of his hair oil – subtle yet distinct.

I could see the natural curvature of a bay below me, sweeping the Arabian Sea in the shape of a C. At the edge of the bay, land side, massive construction work was in operation along its entire length.

"That," said Alec, jabbing his finger at the work in progress,"is one of Bombay's major projects at the moment. It'll be called Marine

Drive and link the two halves of Bombay – the business district, Nariman Point, with the rest of the city. A lot easier to get up here, too, by a connecting road. Imagine what it'll look like at night from up here!"

"I don't suppose I'll ever get to see that!" I said, thinking that although Bombay could show her tourists sights that could rival any modern city, it still had something of a social problem. Even from my brief experience, I had seen the beggars in the street, the dirty children begging for food and the crowded hovels bordering the city's roads. By contrast, we had passed several huge mansions, most gated and barred, belonging, Alec had informed me, to moguls, film stars or celebrities, and the oldest and wealthiest families in the land.

We approached a large wooded area near the summit of the hill and the bus groaned to a halt. Looking around, I could see that only we remained, the last two people left on the bus. Silence fell as the driver extinguished the engine, then a bell tinkled below.

"Last stop! Towers of Silence! All change, all change!" called a heavily accented male voice from the lower deck.

Hastily, we climbed down the curving staircase and out onto the road. I looked around me and tried to get a sense of direction. I could see nothing except dense foliage ahead of the dead-end where the bus had drawn to a halt. Behind and below lay the city, and beyond, the blue of ocean and sky spread out to the horizon like a mural.

"Where are they?" I asked Alec, bewildered.

The bus fired up its engine once more and in a cloud of fumes and dust, started back along the road towards the city. Alec said nothing but pointed up towards the sky over the thicket of trees. Several large birds were circling directly over the centre of the thicket. They looked huge and menacing and as I watched, one or two swooped down suddenly to something, or someone beneath. I looked at Alec questioningly, trying to understand. I had only read sketchy descriptions of the Towers in my researches and had imagined that they were a kind of giant tomb for the followers of the Parsi faith.

Alec led the way over towards the thicket and a path opened up before us. As we walked, Alec explained gently - rather unnecessarily, I thought, in deference to my sex. The wood through which we passed bore no clues of its sombre purpose – the camouflage of the Towers of Silence of the Parsis. Life abounded as if in defiance of the proximity of death – several brightly coloured parakeets fluttered and called in the canopy above, while below in the bushes and low trees surrounding us, crickets, invisible to our eyes, chirped almost deafeningly in the heat of the winter afternoon. The air in the wood hung close and heavy with the scent of aromatic timber and flowering shrubs.

Alec looked at my legs and feet in their impractical sandals. "We should watch out for snakes," he warned.

I nodded, keeping my eyes lowered, but remained silent. What Alec had told me had both shocked and made me feel foolish in my innocence. A large stone circular structure came into view ahead of us, rather like the turret of a castle or water tower. At first glance, it seemed as if there was no access or door, but then as we followed the track around the tower, we saw a narrow entrance with a wooden door set deep into the stone, approached by worn stone steps. I stopped.

"Alec, what are we going to do? We're surely not going to go inside and see..."

"Well, now that we've come so far, I thought we could get an idea of the interior," said Alec, poised at the top of the steps.

We both saw that the door was slightly ajar. Alec gave the heavy slab of ancient wood a push and it opened further, a dense blackness beyond. My palms began to sweat with anxiety. Surely, the Towers' authorities did not allow sightseers, which in a sense described us, macabre and ghoulish though it sounded. Something did not feel right. The whole area seemed sinister – the dense wood, the circling creatures high above, the silence. Now that we had come so close to the tower, I saw another turret close by, and another, just visible through the trees. An oppressive atmosphere exuded the place – a sense of death and decay.

"How many of these things are there?" I asked, wishing we had got back on the bus while we could.

"Five. There's been a large Parsi community in Bombay for nearly a thousand years. They came from Persia fleeing persecution from Moslems."

Alec's voice sounded hollow as he had disappeared from view. At that moment, a dark figure appeared round the curve of the tower. It materialised into that of a man in late middle-age dressed in a black tunic and trousers, a round, black hat reminiscent of an Egyptian fez atop the outfit. He spoke to me in excellent English, mildly accented, looking concerned.

"Madam, are you alone? Oh dear, it's common knowledge that the towers are closed to non-believers."

He looked me up and down, taking in my short summer dress, sheer-stockinged legs and sandals and clearly took me for a non-believer. I wished at that moment that I had not exposed my decolletage that morning when I had dressed. I had not wanted to be outdone by Molly. I called to Alec, who had climbed well up the stairs inside.

"We have had so many break-ins and thefts lately that we have had to be strict. My name is Ishvat. I belong to a management committee who look after the Towers of Silence."

Alec had re-appeared in the doorway and came down to stand beside me. He darted forward and held out his hand to the Parsi.

"Alec Soames, Mr?...."

"Just Ishvat."

The Parsi only met his eyes briefly and refused the proffered hand, bowing instead with his hands together in the prayer gesture of greeting.

"Excuse me for invading your domain," Alec continued, unfazed. "The door was unlocked and I had no idea it was closed to visitors."

The Parsi bowed again.

"Some of the committee's duties consist of conducting tours around the towers. We have just such a party coming from a ship docked in the harbour tomorrow. The *Narunda* or some such."

"Oh, the *Narkunda!* That is our ship. I had no idea there was going to be a tour tomorrow, on Christmas Day!"

"Yes, Madam, but for us there is no holiday," Ishvat reminded me. "Now, I can take you for a very personal tour, just yourselves. You would like this? Please remember that you will not be able to see the interiors."

This sounded interesting, but part of me still yearned for escape. I felt uneasy and out of place. Ishvat ushered us round the other towers and explained to us the origins, beliefs and persecutions of his people, their history in India and other countries of the East and their manner of burial after death. Alec whispered to me behind the Parsi's back as we threaded our way through the undergrowth between the towers.

"I got to see something of the inside!" he said gleefully.

I looked at him in slight alarm, surprised at his apparent ghoulishness.

"There are some in there, quite fresh." He looked up at the circling birds above, fewer in numbers than before. "Perhaps they are sated. They should have made short work of them by now."

"It is considered a final act of charity. One that does not defile the sacred elements of earth, fire and water."

The Parsi had heard Alec's whispers. I shivered in the heat and felt ice-cold. Since we had arrived, I had felt the oppression of the silent towers, now embodied in the black figure in front of us, gliding through the trees.

Alec had escorted me back to the ship later that afternoon, before joining his battalion. We had taken our leave beside the huge hull of the *Narkunda*. With one foot on the base of the gangway, I looked up at him. He put his fingertips under my chin, held my face in position and kissed me lingeringly on the lips.

"Goodbye and good luck, Sister Lavinia Coates. I'll look you up if

I come to Malaya. Give my regards to Howie."

I nodded, unable to form words. Out of the corner of my eye I saw Samuel Bailey approach the ship, looking somewhat the worse for wear. My heart sank, fearing the worst as he and Alec exchanged glances, but Samuel walked straight past with barely a nod in my direction and mounted the gangway unsteadily. Alec followed my eyes to Samuel, then looked back at me in one last, long, penetrating glance. He grinned suddenly, as seemed his wont, then, just as suddenly patted me on the shoulder, turned on his heel, and walked quickly over to the taxi rank. I looked after him, seeing him lean into the cab to speak to the driver, before the car sped off towards the city centre. He didn't look back.

I made my way up to the cabin in a trance. There was no doubting the man's charm which I found myself responding to in spite of misgivings. I could not read him– he must have adopted his apparent insouciance throughout the voyage deliberately – but why should he have troubled to seek me out that morning? And the kiss.... I caught my reflection in the dressing table mirror – noted the heightened colour on the cheek, the complexion reflecting a glow and a sparkle in the eyes. Samuel had only attempted a nervous peck about an inch to the left of my lips when we said goodnight. I had never taken poor Samuel seriously, I realised now, as, from my dining room chair, I glanced up again at the painting of the *Narkunda* in the alcove, lit by a rare shaft of sunlight. No spark existed between us.

They had all congregated in the Pacific Lounge, where afternoon tea awaited them – except Samuel, no doubt sprawled on his bunk below; and Irene, doubtless with her lordling, taking advantage of the two-day sojourn in port to deepen their acquaintance. I would have to wait until breakfast to hear their impressions of Bombay. The pure tourists among the sisters – the twins and Molly, who had appeared at the tea urn trolley professing starvation through missing lunch, had experienced quite a different city to the Bombay I had seen. For them, the sights and smells of poverty overpowered the senses and provoked homesickness and depression. Molly gave me no explanation for "standing me up" that morning, and I made sure that she knew it had been to my advantage. The twins had even thought they had seen me in the distance in the rickshaw.

"Val, you dark horse! I saw you in a bicycle rickshaw with that marine – what's his name? The one who used to hang around with Lady Titchmarsh," enthused Hannah, heaping jam on her bread and butter and holding out her cup to be filled with tea by the on-duty tea steward. Afternoon tea was always an informal affair in "steerage" as the twins jokingly called their second-class cabins.

"Alec Soames," I offered casually. "Yes, we had a good day. He's not a bad sort but he's left the ship now. Joined his platoon or something."

"Oh, did you go up Malabar Hill?" interposed Molly. "We're doing that tomorrow in the tour. Why didn't you book? What's it like up there?"

I told them, omitting the details about the Towers and our unique experience with the Parsi, knowing that their tour would be rehearsed and tailor made for the tourist.

"You know what we did? A group of us went to the Asiatic quarter shops, then took a taxi to the European ones. My dear! What a contrast."

Molly did not have to concern herself with keeping her naturally svelte form, I thought enviously. I had always had to struggle with my weight. She had heaped several iced finger buns on her plate.

"Don't ruin your appetite," said Helen, looking at her watch.

"We're only having a light buffet supper on deck tonight," said her twin. "They're having a special do tomorrow, Christmas Day!"

"Oh, really? Yes, now I come to think of it, I saw them doing something with flags in our dining room. But do go on about your shopping trip, Molly."

I usually called her "Molls" like the others, but since we had become rather strained, we were more formal with each other. Molly naturally excelled at storytelling and her observation skills which served her well as a nurse expanded to general humanity in her portrayal of detail. Looking out over Bombay Harbour in that late afternoon of Christmas Eve 1940, we all experienced through her the bazaars and eating houses of the Asiatic quarter, its pavements dotted by the red patches of spat juice from the betel-nut chews beloved by residents of the city, and smelled the pervading and competing aromas of dung and incense. The suffocating dust filled our eyes and nostrils. We saw the vivid colours of the saris and bajus worn by the women who, unlike their Moslem counterparts, exposed their curved brown midriffs with pride.

"I tried on a sari in one of the shops!" said Molly. We nodded, held entranced. She described how the shop women had fussed around her, tweaking the voluminous material into position and admiring her beauty as they did so.

I had been quite envious of Molly's sari, of a soft apricot coloured silk with intricate silver thread embroidery and a matching brassiere top. She had worn it to that Christmas day lunch which I remember to this day, so well, Molly generally admired in pride of place at the table, in the sari. We had even done her hair and makeup like an Indian woman, the red spot of my lipstick which I placed carefully between the eyebrows, known as a *bindi*.

"We should have read this up a bit more, Molls!" joked Helen, as we had stood back to admire our efforts. "That mark is meant to indicate that you're a married woman in the Hindu culture!"

"She doesn't look married, with that figure," I remarked.

The waiters, some of whom had themselves been born in India, looked admiringly at Molly, saying that she looked like a Kashmiri woman because of her pale skin. I said nothing, but smiled with the others, bearing Molly no malice or ill will. It was as if I stood outside the scene watching, in my own thoughts. I remembered last Christmas, at home with my mother and father and thought of them now sharing a meal reduced by food shortages. I thought of the next one and wondered how and where I would celebrate it. Now, I know what happened and that if I had known, looking at my merry companions in 1940, I could have changed the future.

Chapter 8

Scent of the East

It was the last morning. I felt sheer disbelief that we were finally so close – Penang Island, off the Malayan mainland – just across the water, almost within touching distance as we approached the emerging landscape of green mists, slowly rising from a calm sea. I reached out my hand as if to try. Excitement welled within me yet underneath it all lay sadness too, at leaving the safe routines of the ship and those with whom I had travelled for all these weeks. Few now remained to journey so far east. The departing passengers had all but taken the life and spirit from the ship. Those that stayed, such as myself and a few of the sisters, just wanted to reach our destination. After Bombay, Colombo, in Ceylon, our last port of call, had contrasted with the Indian city as an oasis of calm cleanliness and orderliness but had seemed, I thought, rather dull. It reminded me of any modernised metropolis in the world.

I had risen early to complete the last of my packing. Molly, I had left in bed after a riotous last night which I had, perhaps primly, managed to avoid. I now stood on deck as far in the bow as I could, as if this would make the approach of the tantalising shoreline speedier. I saw very few passengers about – at this pre-breakfast hour, most early risers busied themselves with last-minute packing in their cabins. I felt butterflies in my stomach and didn't think I could eat much anyway. I took stock of myself. Because it meant so much to me, I had saved my best clothes for this day and now checked down my body at the neat linen skirt and navy-blue blouse, at the white peep-toe sandals and freshly-pedicured feet. My hand valise lay ready in the cabin on my neatly made bed and my main luggage already awaited disembarkation, taken to the loading bay by our steward. From this moment what I made of the future was up to me alone.

A soft footfall, barely audible, sounded to the rear and I looked around, startled. I had not expected to see a soul at this hour. Samuel Bailey came to stand beside me, mirroring my position at the handrail. We both leaned over it together, looking across the calm water at Penang. A deep tranquillity, broken only by the mewing of gulls high in the dawn sky marked the last moment of calm before the bustle of arrival began. I did not suppose that I would ever see him again. It had not even ranked as a shipboard romance. I have no mementoes, no letters from Samuel. Just a few hazy, somewhat intoxicated memories of a brotherly companion.

If, many years later I had lived to see the general use of the world wide web and become expert in searching it, I would have seen his account of this voyage for the world to know, but I never had.

"It's a strange feeling, isn't it, journey's end. I may not have the chance to say goodbye later..."

I turned and smiled at him. He looked crestfallen and sad. I held out my hand, then changed my mind and leaned over to kiss him. This time, I kissed him on the lips, which in his bashfulness he had never managed. He said nothing, but looked down at the deck, then turned away from me and walked back along it to the stairwell.

The ship docked, clanking and banging the side of the wharf as it dropped anchor. A rushed last breakfast had passed, eaten amid last-minute exchanges of addresses and phone numbers and hasty reiterations of promises to meet among the sisters. Molly I would see very soon, when we had both settled ourselves at our destinations. She would stay the night with relatives in Penang and go straight to Batu Gajah tomorrow. This general hospital, a few miles from Ipoh, looked set to be a centre for both of us and I felt sure that we would see as much of each other as we wanted. I had gone below for my hand luggage and took a last look round at the cabin we had shared as if to imprint it on my memory. I left my key on the dressing table and walked over the narrow doorway, through the ship and down the gangway for the last time, to see my luggage ashore. The arrival instructions I had brought with me from Crown Agents had implied that a driver wearing Crown Agents insignia would meet me but first I had to go through customs.

A Malay customs officer greeted me on the wharf and it soon became apparent that he spoke not a word of English. During the voyage, I had tried, with the help of a Malay grammar, to come to grips with the complex language but still had only a very rudimentary grasp. I hoped that with use, my knowledge and pronunciation would improve. The officer spoke rapidly and with an unexpected intonation that caught me off-guard. With exasperation, he waved a long list at me apparently itemising objects liable for duty from which I recognised a few odd words. At last, patience exhausted and convinced that I had nothing to declare, he waved me past. I walked through the shed to the outside, breathing in the humid, foreign air, heavy with the strange scents of the East - the freshness of the sea nearby but inland the aroma of spices and palm, and as yet unknown tropical flowering plants.

I glanced around me on the wharf, standing on tiptoe trying vainly to see beyond the direct proximity of the ship through the chaos of passengers looking for the same thing. Some stood around helplessly, while others had friends and relatives waiting for them whom they greeted joyfully. The sweating porter bearing my suitcases around his person paused behind me. At last, I spotted an Indian driver in khaki standing beside a large, black saloon car of a model which I did not recognise. He held aloft a card bearing my name, and as I and my small entourage approached, greeted me with a head bow.

"Sister Lavinia?" he enquired, in good, although heavily accented English.

At my affirmation, he began loading my luggage into the boot of the car and then opened the back door for me to climb in. I hastily tipped the porter and in relief, entered the cool interior. It smelt of expensive leather and a hint of petrol. I hoped that I would not feel nauseous, as I sometimes did in cars. I would have to get used to being driven about in back seats, I could see. As the automobile started with a barely perceptible vibration and glided forward to exit the quayside, I felt quite lost in the spacious interior and glanced around at the luxurious leather seats and arm rests, at the plush matching beige material of the headliner above.

Although I felt utter relief to be on my way, the driver had obviously received instructions not to speak until compelled to respond to any commands I might give. This resulted, to me, in an almost deafening silence. After the shipboard camaraderie, I (perhaps unreasonably) had expected him to initiate conversation but he continued to weave in and out of the streets in silent concentration. As we drove through George Town, Penang's capital, which I had heard from experienced travellers had a reputation for beauty and elegance, I had looked forward to exchanging impressions of my first experiences in Malaya. At last, I spoke, hazarding a remark about the imposing street along which we passed. I raised my voice, so that I would not distract the silent figure in front from his task.

"What a beautiful street!" I exclaimed. "What is its name?"

The driver, without taking his eyes off the road, inclined his head sideways towards me.

"This is Beach Street, Madam. We are in the centre of George Town in one of the oldest streets. Here you can see one of your great London banks."

He pointed to a huge monolith of a building to the left, showing the familiar sign of the black horse. Immediately, I felt myself transported home to London, comforting yet surreal in the tropical heat. Here, I thought, yes - I can see the influence of the British – our influence - echoed in building after building along this old George Town street. It bears the wear and tear of over a century and a half of occupation. I did not feel sure if I approved or not, then - I only noticed the incongruity. It seemed like home and yet as we progressed along the street it did not. As the car moved silently along, I wondered how the other road-users heard us in the ambient noise, through the hooting of car horns and miscellaneous vehicles and the jostle of pedestrians. It narrowed, and became more obviously Asian in character. Chinese shops, offering a bewildering array of unfamiliar food and merchandise, stood cheek by jowl with temples and shrines - old Chinese men and women sat outside their shops in the sun, sucking their pipes or drinking two-handed from ornate Chinese bowls.

"How long will it take to get to Ipoh?" I asked the driver. "What is your name, by the way? I can't very well say 'hey you!'"

My attempt at a joke fell a little flat. Apparently, I did not behave in the way an "English Miss" should. I felt a little uncomfortable in my role and could see that I would have to keep my distance with the inhabitants of Malaya.

"Thank you, Madam, my name is Dev."

"And you work for the Crown Agents, Dev?'

"Indirectly, Madam. The Agents sub-contract my company for their business. To answer your question Madam, it would take about two or three hours, but I am only taking you to the station at Prai, on the mainland. We will have to catch a ferry over the Strait. You will take a train from there."

I had opened my mouth to ask Dev questions about whether he enjoyed living here, in this elegant city, but I answered my own question in my head, before the words left my lips. The future of Penang, where elderly ex-pat British pensioners found a more affordable living than at home, the equatorial climate being an added attraction, lay far in the future. In 1941 it existed as an imitation of a British system, or as close as they could get it. If I were to attempt a life independent of this system, no doubt I would fall foul of marauders on these streets, expressing their resentment of the foreign rulers. I thought of Bombay and remembered blank, questioning glances from those Indians who had no axe to grind with their colonial masters.

Nevertheless, I began to relax and enjoy the journey and marvelled at the organisation involved in ferrying me from the Port of Penang to my destination at Ipoh. Everything seemed taken care of. I hoped that the "senior nurses" whom the Agents had arranged to meet me at Ipoh Station would not have long to wait but no doubt they would have been informed exactly what time to expect me. I did not relish the idea of another sea crossing, however short, but the drive-on-and-off system, reminding me of the Dover-Calais ferries, operated surprisingly efficiently on the twenty-minute crossing.

Dev deposited me on the station platform at Prai somewhat unceremoniously, his duty performed. I felt oddly disappointed that he had not let slip his guard for a moment and as he carefully placed my luggage on the platform near a wooden seat and left, acknowledging his tip with a little bow, I felt momentarily lost, looking at the pile of luggage. I hoped that I would manage to get everything onto the train. So far, the terminus had seemed almost abandoned, like a ghost station. Everything baked in the sun and I had seen no sign of a train. The midday heat shimmered off the railway line and a large clock with Roman numerals, hanging from one of the wrought-iron roof supports, ticked loudly in the silence. The raucous call of a lone myna bird accentuated the quiet. I hoped that the train would arrive soon. I began to feel light-headed and unreal with the heat as the sun climbed in the sky towards its zenith and I could see very little shade on the platform. Although I had prepared myself well clothes-wise for the tropics and felt initiated by the heat and dust of Africa and India on the voyage, I wondered how I would cope with working every day in this climate with its high humidity – so humid that I could see the moisture collecting on my sunglasses. The thin fabric of my blouse was wet with perspiration and clung uncomfortably to the tops of my arms and chest.

Looking back, it struck me as strange that I had stood there alone on that day when at almost all other times then, people surrounded me. But my solitude did not last long. The confident tones of strident English voices long preceded the appearance of a large group of girls and men from the ship, the girls giggling, tottering on their heels, muscles standing out on their calves as they pulled their luggage behind them, and the men opining on the general unreliability of Malayan trains. The peace of the station evaporated.

"....be surprised if it left Taiping on time. Waits for the miners... should be here waiting by now.." (from one of passengers with whom Alec Soames had been acquainted and not now in the best of tempers at having to fend for himself.)

"...where are these porters? I thought this was one of the better stations...."

"...slow down darling, it's not here yet. These damned cobbles! I've just laddered my nylons again..."

"Rafe! Wait for me. You promised to help me with this heavy one...."

Hearing the clank and chuff of a steam locomotive was a relief, as it wheezed pneumatically up to its buffer stop and disgorged its passengers who had travelled from as far as Singapore. The station immediately transformed itself into one of noise and rush. As the black bulk of the Federated Malay States locomotive let off steam with a sudden, ear-splitting hiss, those on the platform made way for the sudden surge of passengers who alighted. Not for the first time, I looked around for a porter and spied one, just receiving a tip from an overdressed, blowsy woman in a feathered hat. I knew we had a few minutes before the train started out on its return journey but I felt afraid of being stranded with no help. I took my chance and called over the young Malay porter who wore traditional dress, making a mental note to study the customs and costume of these people and of the other nationalities who had settled here. The young Malay, dusky skinned and lithe against the whiteness of his *baju*, smiling and bowing courteously, wasted no time in stowing my luggage into the guard compartment. It had proved a productive day for him, I surmised, seeing him gleefully bite the coin I gave him, showing white, even teeth.

The train began to move. I settled back into my upholstered seat to take in the route we travelled. I sat alone in a second-class carriage - I wanted to drink in this first journey greedily and not miss anything – the strange sounds of unknown, gaudily coloured birds calling in the trees, the foreignness of the scents drifting through the open window. The track initially wound among dense jungle foliage, filtering winking sunlight through its leaves. It came up nearly to the track so that I could almost lean out to touch it and release its euca-lyptus scent. The train travelled slowly at first. Gradually, the foliage thinned, and I could make out wooden houses, some on stilts, dotted among trees, and some in groups with clearings and dirt roads sepa-rating them. I knew, from my investigations in the onboard library of the *Narkunda* that these were the *kampongs* mostly of Malay families and felt a great curiosity about them. How had they come there? I wanted to learn their ways and customs and gain their trust. I felt convinced, in my arrogance, that I could help them to live a better, healthier life, they and their children, several of whom I could see scampering in and out of the houses, some running down to the railway line to watch the train pass, and along the track, as if they could outrun the locomotive. A few waved, and I waved back, smiling with joy at their wonder and at their little brown, wiry, naked bodies.

What right had I to think that I had authority to change them, I thought now in 1989. Janet and Bill took me over to Weekes' depart-ment store just before Christmas. Put the wheelchair in the car. We had met up with Dorrie for lunch and talked about how we were. Oh yes, she had said. We were full of ourselves then.

The journey to Ipoh took nearly three hours. The train had followed the coast road along and then swung inland, stopping briefly at the tin-mining town of Taiping, industrious with its heavy machinery carving scars into the landscape, not sparing this virgin land for the European war. On down to Ipoh it went, chuntering finally into the colonial grandeur of Ipoh Station. I don't think I had any premonition that day of the importance these train journeys between Ipoh and Taiping would have in my life over the coming months. I just braced myself for the reception committee I knew awaited me. I gathered my hand luggage and stood waiting at the door.

The train stopped with a jerk and a long-drawn-out exhalation of steam. As I pulled at the lever, clouds of acrid, grit-filled smoke and steam billowed in through the open window. Undeterred, I flung open the door, as others were doing along the length of the train. As I stepped down onto the platform to join the throng, three figures stood a little way off out of the melee, like ethereal ghosts emerging from the steam, alone. In the moment before they saw me, their expressions were morose and straight, like old Victorian photographs I had seen. Two women and a man, moustached, slightly taller, stood there close together, like statues. I thought I recognised one of them. Clutching my vanity case, I approached them cautiously, doubtfully, almost afraid they might not be human after all. Then the steam dispersed, and a tall, slim woman of about forty in tropical sister's uniform, white with blue epaulettes and starched cap, came forward at once, the spell broken. She smiled now, thinner and more tanned than I remembered from Ealing. More lines had formed around her eyes, from squinting in the bright sunlight and the frown-lines between her ruthlessly plucked eyebrows had accentuated with worry and responsibility.

"Why, Lavinia dear!" she exclaimed as she advanced to embrace me. "I had absolutely no idea it was you! We were given no names through the Crown Agents. I suppose they're used to maintaining secrecy! What a wonderful surprise. Let me introduce you to the doctors."

All this came forth in a torrent of words, although the manner stayed controlled and cool, while I succumbed to "Howie's" hug and a wet kiss in the region of my left cheek. The "doctors" came forward, arranging their faces into pleasant expressions while Howie performed rapid introductions. Then I remembered my luggage in the guard's van.

"...Doctor Clarissa Drew and her husband Dennis.....Clarissa will be working with you in Ipoh Clinic.....your luggage Val? Oh, is this it?"

Through all this I had managed to respond to Howie and acknowledge the doctors' greetings as well as I could, while attempting to locate my luggage and thank and tip the guard who had overseen its safe delivery onto the platform and into my hands. I barely had time to take in my surroundings save a dim impression of another colonial station, its timber buildings adorned with wrought iron. Flowers in tubs had been arranged at intervals and their strong musky scent almost overpowered a pervading residue of sulphur and ash from the train, which now disappeared along the track south in the direction of Kuala Lumpur.

I did not tell Margaret Howard, whom I had last seen authoritatively tramping the wards of the Prince Edward Hospital in Ealing, that I already knew of her position here through Alec Soames. I feigned surprise, but privately wondered why she had suddenly taken it into her head to come. I had heard nothing before I had left England, and assumed she still worked at Ealing. *This, I thought, warranted further investigation. Did it have anything to do with Alec Soames?*

It was all exactly as Alec had predicted. I felt somewhat annoyed with him because he had taken away the surprise and freshness of the first hours of being in my future home and workplace through his world-weary account of what I could expect.

Alec could not detract from the warmth of the doctors' welcome. A middle-aged couple from the Home Counties, their external personae reflected the British in the tropics. I later discovered that Dennis worked as a specialist in tropical diseases and that the pair had devoted themselves to the welfare of the inhabitants of Malaya, particularly the Malays, since several main nationalities constituted the population and their cultures and need for western intervention varied. They looked thrilled to welcome a new recruit to their cause but I guessed that they would not spare my energies any more than they spared their own. I felt honoured that they had found the time to come and meet me. For the time being I allowed myself the luxury of soaking up the atmosphere as we left the station to find the doctors' car, leaving a boy to struggle with my luggage. The doctors took no notice of him. England and the war faded fast, like a dream. The next half hour seemed equally unreal, as we drove through the old town, busy with lunchtime traffic - bicycle rickshaws wove round motor cars and pedestrians and stalls and street hawkers sold rice, noodles, meat on skewers and pancakes to serve to the passer-by as a quick snack - all against a background of colonial buildings mingled with smaller shops. Outside the spacious confines of Dennis Drew's limousine, the street noise seemed muted. Inside the car it felt cool with its own peculiar car smell. Apart from the need to make hand signals, the driver's window remained firmly closed against the humid heat. In my place in the middle of the back seat along with Howie and Clarissa Drew, I caught an occasional whiff of Howie's scent and remembered it from Ealing days.

Nobody seems to do a thing for themselves in this place, I thought, as I watched the doctors' Malay driver skilfully avoiding fast-moving traffic and occasionally shouting out of the window at the many conveyances blocking our way. I realised that much of what he shouted was probably untranslatable and thought of the London cabbies using the English-speaking version back home. The doctors and Howie merely smiled and began to talk about my future home.

"Lavinia," said Howie, "you would not believe the trouble we had trying to find a boy and an *amah* for you! The quality of household staff in Malaya these days is very poor."

"Oh, I can do everything for myself!" I protested, innocently and in vain. "I really don't need waiting on, but thank you all the same."

"My dear girl," said Dr Drew, "that's simply not done at all. You would be exhausted in this climate in no time. Besides, we expect you at the clinic bright and early every day! How on earth would you manage?"

"Well..." I began. "I've always.... In London..." I tailed off.

I knew what my companions said about the climate had a basis in truth. Since getting off the ship I had constantly craved to escape the heat by crawling into somewhere cool. Although by keeping the windows closed the worst of the sun's rays could not penetrate, the interior seemed unbearably stuffy and I longed for some air. My clothes clung, damp with sweat and beads of perspiration constantly trickled from my forehead and into my eyes. Clarissa nodded in sympathetic understanding.

"Yes," she said, seeing my discomfiture. "You're in Malaya now, God forsaken place!"

Her husband looked at her in surprise, then turned to me.

"You've only just arrived my dear, but there will be times when you long to be back in Blighty and the thought of a snowy day will seem like the next thing to heaven. Romance is all very well and the young must travel to see the world but believe it or not, we're a temperate race and can't survive for long outside our natural habitat."

"Yes, luckily we have *them* to help us, and sometimes I think they hold the power and not us!" Clarissa went on. "They know the best places to shop and bargain for goods in their own language. They expect to do everything. After all, it's their country and we could not manage without them."

A silence fell – a contemplative pause in the car. It seemed all to be much more complicated than I had thought. My romantic notions, held dear since my youth, began to show cracks in the face of stark reality. I looked out of the window at the constant motion of the city streets – the human population of all nations, rulers and ruled, jostling together.

Howie brought me back from my reverie. We had just turned off the main highway and into a quiet side street with low red-rooved bungalows nestling deep in the trees and foliage of their own grounds. I had noticed the street sign: *Windsor Road* and the house number 4. I had not liked the idea of being so isolated in a separate house but at the sight of it, I changed my mind. Later I had tried to paint it, for Mother and Father, so that the colours of the trees and flowering shrubs would be brought to life, but my skills did not match my enthusiasm. What a pity they did not, I thought now. Such a little painting would have looked good in that alcove underneath the one of the *Narkunda*.

"It stood, like the others, in its own ground, surrounded by trees and flowering shrubs, not a bungalow on the ground but supported on three-foot pillars. It was made of wood, painted white, with a black and white roof. A veranda surrounded the building on three sides, approached by a little staircase. A white painted gate opened off the street."

I looked at the others, speechless.

"Tomorrow morning you will be expected in clinic ("So soon!" I thought). And I've arranged for a rickshaw to pick you up at seven-thirty. It's an early start in Clinic to see the bulk of mothers and babies until midday, then it's out to the *kampongs* in the afternoon, but you will have an hour's siesta as it's the hottest time of the day."

I began to feel a little apprehensive. I did not feel ready to be thrown in the deep end and had a lingering nausea from weaving in and out of the city traffic. While the driver unloaded the luggage, the four of us climbed out of the car and walked up the path, under the shade of a large jacaranda tree near my front door. With some cere-mony, Howie handed me the keys. I walked into the most spacious bungalow I had ever seen. I wrote to Mother later:

"The front door opens directly into a lounge and dining room combined, about twice the size of our lounge at home. Across a narrow passage, two colossal bedrooms open out one from the other, with a bathroom allocated for each one. High ceilings and polished floors dominate throughout and the whole is tastefully furnished."

"This certainly beats my digs in Ealing!"

Howie smiled. We shared many of the same memories but there the similarity ended. Now she looked cool in the heat of the day and at home in these alien surroundings while I still had a feeling of disconnectedness. I wished I could remove all my clothes and lie motionless under one of the ceiling fans I had noticed, silently revolving above. I heard a sound from the back quarters, where I assumed lay the kitchen and wash house. Howie strode off to investigate in her brisk manner and returned between two figures, a Malay "boy" who looked to be about thirty-five and an older Indian woman with a dour expression. These then appeared to be my "staff", the only previous experience of "staff" I had remotely had being our daily "helps". Both stood mutely, dressed in traditional cotton clothing which, to my relief, perhaps unreasonably, looked clean. Howie motioned them to come forward, somewhat impatiently, I imagined, but perhaps she had her reasons. The Drews were looking into the other rooms with a critical eye.

Perhaps not as good as theirs by Malayan standards, I thought.

Howie enunciated clearly as she addressed the hapless servants. I felt as if her patronising manner towards them placed me in an awkward position, afraid of getting off on the wrong foot in my relationships with them.

"Now, this is Sister Lavinia. You will take your orders from her every day. Val, this is your houseboy, Tam. He's a good cook and can prepare most English dishes as long as you explain exactly what it is you want."

I privately thought that if I had to explain everything in such detail it would probably be quicker to cook for myself, but in doing so I would go against the unspoken rules of Malayan colonial custom.

"Now, this, Val, is Mary."

Sister Howard turned to the dusky figure beside Tam, who had kept her eyes firmly on the ground throughout these introductions.

"Her own Hindi name is unpronounceable, so it makes life simple. She will take care of your laundry and buy your personal items from the market but I'm afraid she speaks no English. I hope you managed to learn some Malay during the voyage? It will make things much easier for you here. I'm afraid..." (this to me in a low aside) ..."Mary can be rather cunning, so keep an eye on her and let me know if you notice anything"....To the servants:...."You may go and resume your duties and Sister will come and inspect the kitchen presently."

Mary, without taking her eyes from the parquet, studiously wiped her eyes with a corner of her *dupatta*. Both bowed and backed from the room. I wondered what Howie had meant. Was Mary suspected of being a thief?

Although I had prepared for a very different way of life, the prospect of sharing my home with strangers and having everything done for me felt alien to my independent nature. Certainly, Mother employed a woman from the village to undertake our rough house-work but she had always done the cooking herself unless she was ill, and whenever I came home, I had invariably helped with the washing up. Now, it seemed that whether I liked it or not, a rigid and ingrained system controlled me - of keeping up appearances in front of the "natives," as imprisoning for the rulers as it attempted to domi-nate the ruled. I wondered, fleetingly, whether I would fail in keeping up the façade.

"Boy is preparing tea for you," Howie continued, glancing at her fob watch -"and we will leave you until later. I didn't think you would feel up to a big party tonight but I'm having a few friends round this evening for dinner and hoped you would feel equal to joining us. Everyone is dying to meet you! You will be able to rest for a few hours while Mary unpacks for you. My driver will fetch you at eight."

With Sister Howard's words ringing in my ears, she and the Drews took their leave and left me alone with my staff of two in the bungalow. The heat and excitement had drained my energy and I badly needed some time alone, to reflect, rest and most of all, bathe.

Chapter 9

Northolt Transposed

So began my life in Malaya. Like most British colonials, a vibrant social life occupied an equally important place with work. Perhaps we lived with greater intensity and passion than we did at home to reinforce and justify our unity and place in the world as a foreign power, our tenure at best fragile. Or perhaps it served as an antidote to homesickness and the yearning for news. As a nurse, I filled a unique position to gain insight into the country and although I had long imagined it, the reality differed completely. Whilst I had grown accustomed to London's poor, I found the heat, flies and squalor of the *kampongs* challenging. My romantic notions of "natives" living in charming rural villages could not long survive.

I had slept late that first morning, exhausted after a late night at Howie's, several glasses of champagne and a large meal in excellent company. Despite her assurance of an informal dinner for a few close friends, ten souls seated themselves around the dining table, including the Drews and several medical staff from Batu Gajah. In addition, a misunderstanding had arisen with my staff concerning what time they should wake me. So it was that my first awareness of the new working day was an insistent ringing of a bicycle bell on the road outside. After several weeks of travelling, duty called me again. At that moment, I had doubts about my ability to cope without the stimulating effects of coffee or tea.

I peered through the mosquito net and down the front garden, seeing a bicycle rickshaw waiting on the road. A thin Chinese stood patiently beside the contraption, gazing towards the bungalow. As I watched, he reached over to the handlebars and pulled the handle of a shiny silver bell. I waved vigorously in his direction to let him know my state of consciousness and not to leave without me. I dressed hurriedly in my newly acquired uniform, thankful that I had already folded and pinned the starched cap so that the white gauzy material cascaded to my shoulders, nun-like. Howie had given me several grey uniform dresses last night, needing daily laundering in the oppressive climate. The material felt stiff and new, but once dressed, I felt more equal to meeting the day. I picked up my nurse's bag containing my midwifery instruments and hurried to the door. At that moment, Tam appeared in the kitchen doorway looking alarmed.

"You want breakfast, Sis' Lavinia?" he asked, looking quite distraught. "I have ready."

"No time!" I snapped at him in my agitation. "Please have it ready on time tomorrow and have Mary wake me by seven!"

"One minute Sis," he said, disappearing into the kitchen quarters. "I will pack for you. Very quick."

I waited impatiently, but reflected, once my initial panic had subsided, that in Malaya, as I had learned last night at the dinner party, nobody ever rushed anywhere. The rules about timekeeping that we had at home simply did not apply here. Besides, I knew I needed something to sustain me until the midday dinner. I would have to learn about a suitable pace for the sake of my health otherwise I would exhaust myself in a very short time.

Tam duly returned rustling a brown paper bag carrying my portable breakfast, which he handed over with a little bow.

"Your lunch will be ready at twelve, Sis," he grinned, trying to curry favour, showing white, even teeth. "No hurry, I will wait for you."

I merely nodded at him, not quite ready to let him off the hook. With as much dignified haste as I could manage at that moment, I made my way down through the front garden, past the jacaranda, past the frangipani bush and the lilies fragrantly in flower in the early morning, Sister Lavinia Coates of the Colonial Service, to my waiting conveyance. The bronzed, thin Chinese driver gave a little bow and helped me into the back seat, then took his place at the pedals. As the rickshaw gained momentum, pulling out into the street and shortly afterwards making a right turn into the busy main road, I realised that I would have suffered acute embarrassment had my driver struggled on account of my weight. Even so, he was obliged to stand on the pedals in order to climb the slight inclines on the short route to the clinic. Perhaps, I reflected grimly, I had not yet the proper mindset of a fully-fledged colonial, who surely would not worry about such things – yet empathy for others had become second nature to me.

The ten-minute drive through morning traffic gave me the opportunity to take advantage of Tam's packed breakfast, but I needed coffee. Perhaps there would be an opportunity at the clinic. As we approached the long, low building of the Ipoh Old Town Clinic, I could already see the queues of dark-skinned women and children spilling outside, chattering together. Many of the women appeared too old to be mothers, I thought. Climbing down from the rickshaw, I wondered how I would penetrate the throng, but on seeing me, it parted mutely. Not wanting to appear like a distant, god-like figure, I smiled right and left, patting one or two young children on their black curls. Here I felt at ease, in my element. I knew instinctively that children were children the world over, regardless of race, colour or language. Some of the women smiled back, gratifyingly, and the tension eased.

Inside the close, stuffy building complete chaos reigned. It seemed packed with people in apparent confusion. The close air was rank with the smell of human bodies mixed with a faint tinge of antiseptic, as even at eight o'clock in the morning, the temperature inside the building climbed rapidly, the ceiling fans in their laboured circuits making little impression. Indian and Chinese nurses in plain white uniform dresses and starched caps resembling wings, moved among the crowd, sorting the patients into some kind of order in a primitive form of triage. Babies screamed and the general hubbub of raised human voices assaulted the ear.

I gradually became aware that within the clinic, mainly comprising a large hall, cubicles for different tasks and purposes had been set up. In one of them, I recognised Howard, already bending over one of the babies and questioning the mother (or grandmother), with an Indian nurse standing nearby. She looked up and saw me. I started to apologise for my lateness, but she waved this aside and motioned me to a chair on the other side of the cubicle. I watched her as she took the child into her arms in her deft, yet gentle manner, carefully examining the emaciated, shrivelled limbs and bloated abdomen. We both recognised the signs of malnutrition, though thankfully a case so severe was fairly uncommon these days. Howie gave back the child and instructed the Indian nurse to put her in the doctors' queue. The child had become trapped in a downward spiral and needed considerable rehydration before she could properly digest enough food to enable her to gain weight. She no longer had even sufficient strength to suck at the breast, and bottle feeding would be too hazardous in her current condition because of inadequate sterilisation procedures in the *kampongs*. Howard went over to the sink to wash her hands, then turned to me.

"Unfortunately, a too-common sight," she said, nodding in the direction of the departed patient, "although more advanced than usual. When you go out to the *kampongs* this afternoon you will catch them further down the road, hopefully on the way to recovery. It's the same old story. The mother's milk fails, often because of leaving the child with the grandmother while she works on the plantation, the babies are started on bottles and with the unsanitary conditions...well... you know the rest. Poor mites get a nasty gastro-enteritis and dehydration sets in. Now!"

Howie sat back at her desk and motioned the Indian nurse, who had returned, not to bring in any more patients for a few minutes. She gave her full attention to me.

"It's good to see you here, Val. Now, I'm always here a little early on Tuesdays." (Here it came again, I thought, that adherence to routine, which I thought I had escaped. Mondays, Tuesdays, Wednesdays....) "It's just to give us a fighting chance of seeing as many babies as possible. Today is our health visitor's clinic and you will be following up many of them in their *kampongs*. Nurse Kapoor will take you to your station and direct the patients to you and will also act as interpreter for you. It's all basic stuff, mainly failure to thrive, caused by living standards in most cases. If you have any questions, don't hesitate to ask. We have two doctors here this morning, Cameron and Holloway, and they're wonderful with the mothers of the really sick children, like that little one I just saw. You won't be seeing many of those but don't hesitate to refer if you have any concerns."

I wondered where Clarissa Drew worked on this particular morning, then remembered that she had said last night that she had a stretch at Batu Gajah in theatres. Howie went straight back to her notes, preparing for the next patient. I hesitated. I had just remembered that I had left my stethoscope packed in my luggage back at the bungalow. I felt annoyed with myself. It showed a level of incompetence, I thought, unforgiving of my own shortcomings. I remembered now that I had unpacked it on the ship as Molly and I had been practising our heart sounds and I had not returned it to where I had packed all my other instruments. I did not suppose for a moment that Mary had unpacked it yet and foresaw that I would have to spend a considerable time looking for it this evening.

"Howie....." I began, hesitatingly.

"Yes Val?" Howie barely looked up from the notes.

"I seem to have forgotten my stethoscope. Would you have a spare one I could borrow by any chance?"

I tried not to sound too apologetic and feeble, but, ridiculously, I felt intimidated by Howie. Only too clearly, I could see myself through other's eyes and even though she knew me from old, desperately wanted to make a good impression. I knew so well the scope of Howard's experience and intelligence and that I could hide nothing from her.

Howie smiled.

"Yes, of course. You will find one on your desk along with all the other equipment you may need. It will be old, and it is advisable to bring your own and look after it!"

For the next two hours, before a much-needed coffee break, during which I was formally introduced to the doctors, I must have seen at least ten cases, taking the little mites onto my lap from the arms of their trusting mothers, or, if they screamed too loudly, examining them as best I could in whatever position they presented themselves. I listened to little emaciated chests, peered into already open mouths and down throats, examined bottoms for the most appalling nappy rashes I had witnessed and watched as babies pulled up their little legs in pain with colic.

I can still see some of their beautiful little brown faces today as I look back over the years – so many years. They survived – I am sure they did, as it was my will, my life and my work. Now they would be grandparents themselves, in a changed world in a south east Asian country, the foreign rulers and health workers long gone. Perhaps the legacy remains. I like to think it does and that the work I did that first day and all the days afterwards was the groundwork for all that came later. How I wish I were still young. The desire is still there, but my old body is tired. The young, strong nurses – British, Australian, American, full of confidence, sign up to work in foreign parts – no longer the Empire - with MSF, the UN. We are still out there, but under different names; the same doctors and nurses but under different names....

That morning, I listened to accounts via Kapoor of lack of appetite, diarrhoea, constant crying or wakefulness. Many of the children presented for inoculations against polio, diphtheria and tetanus which slowly gained acceptance, against, as always, much initial mistrust. We carried on until lunchtime, regretfully leaving the local nurses to explain to the remaining mothers still waiting either to return the next day as the clinic would soon close, or to provide their names for a home visit. This was to be my task for the afternoon after a short siesta - a Chinese or Malay nurse would accompany me into the jungle.

It hardly seemed worth the rickshaw ride back to the bungalow for lunch. Tam had everything ready as promised, and afterwards I thankfully took my uniform off and lay down for an hour on my cool bed with its cotton sheets, shrouded by the ubiquitous mosquito nets. I tried hard to doze but my mind obstinately remained a mass of pictures and impressions, like a film constantly re-running in my head with the accompanying soundtrack. The voices of foreign languages pierced my half-doze. I thought about the people I had met that morning – the quiet, unsung efficiency of the local nurses, the cheerful young doctors, seeming to relish a comparatively stressless morning away from their usual hospital duties. The medical staff consisted mainly of young graduates expanding their paediatric experience but their presence added a welcome dimension of expertise to the nurses and midwives in the clinic. With Holloway, particularly, I had felt an immediate rapport and resolved to add him to my list of prospective dinner guests at Windsor Road. He still looked young, but from his breadth of knowledge, compassion and technical ability, I predicted a bright future for him. We lived as if the present was the future and forever, never dreaming that within a year many of our finest doctors and nurses would perish in the camps or on the Burma railway.

Hadji, the Indian syce or chauffeur, already waited beside the car at the clinic. One of the Chinese nurses I remembered from the morning, looking neat and slim in a spotless white uniform dress and winged cap, sat inside. I entered the rear of the roomy, black hospital personnel vehicle, old but serviceable, smelling of fumes through baking, stationery, in the midday sun. The interior was almost as large inside as a London taxi, and the nurse and I seemed lost in the space.

"Good afternoon," I greeted the nurse, who acknowledged my greeting with a smile.

"Good afternoon, Sister. I hope you're feeling rested?"

"Yes, although I didn't sleep. Where are we bound this afternoon, nurse?"

Her name, as I later found out, was June, or to use the Chinese spelling, Jun. I liked it when the names had similarity to ours as it made them so much easier to remember.

"A long way in the jungle, Sister. It will take about half an hour to get there. We will have to continue from there on foot and leave the car as the jungle is too dense. I know the way but we will have a guide too."

Hadji had ensconced himself behind the wheel, having removed his sandals, grinning with relief, and proceeded to operate the pedals barefoot. He wore a khaki uniform and an Army and Navy forage cap, or *songko,* as I later learned. He set off at a brisk pace towards the outskirts of the town.

"You seen jungle before, Ma'am?" he asked me, giving a sideways glance towards the back seat.

"Only from the train, Hadji," I replied, wishing that he would concentrate on his driving.

We started to career off the main road and onto one that more resembled a track, penetrating deeper into dense foliage. The very density of the jungle forced Hadji to slow down. The jolting was starting to throw Jun and me around in the back seat, and I held onto one of the straps above my head. A rich profusion of many different trees and plants combined around us and way above our heads as we pushed through the jungle. Although we could hear little noise inside, I could imagine that outside the car would be a plethora of sound – here nature had won over the feeble intrusions of man, left further and further behind us. Without, the sun could not penetrate, and we became immersed in a green shaded gloom. A non-initiated person would quickly become disorientated and lost here. It felt an unfriendly place and yet one could equally become lulled into a sense of security amid the encircling, embracing fronds.

At last, Hadji stopped the car near a group of attap huts, dotted about in a large clearing. Obviously, this had been hewn from the jungle and the dirt track down which we had come serviced this *kampong*. Beyond, the track petered out, and any further progress would have to be done on foot. We climbed out, as several Malay children approached the car curiously. Hadji shooed them away but they took no notice of him and continued to gaze open-mouthed. A couple of the bolder ones touched the headlights or the door handles, shiny in the subdued light.

"In most families the mothers work either in the rice fields or the rubber plantations and the grandmothers look after the children," explained Jun as we approached the nearest of the huts. It had a wooden ladder accessing a kind of balcony which ran around the base of the hut.

Jun climbed the ladder first and called out in Malay. I could just understand the words "sister" and "nurse" which announced our identity and purpose. A middle-aged woman of about fifty years of age, but old and wrinkled beyond her years, came to the narrow doorway, carrying a young baby, who grizzled with the moaning cry typical of a sick child. I had heard this cry many times before, and as I, with some difficulty, reached the wooden landing and greeted the woman with a *salaam* and a handshake, asked Jun if she would allow us to go inside to examine the baby.

The interior of the hut presented to our eyes as dark and airless, although fairly clean and almost bereft of furnishings. Although the permanently open doorway admitted the mingled sounds and scents of the surrounding jungle, the air inside smelled stale. Without hesitation, I sat on a cushion on the floor and gently examined the child as she held it. The woman allowed me to take her (for the child was a little girl) onto my lap and I assessed her weight as well under the centile average for her age of about six months. I asked Jun to question the grandmother (as I took the woman to be) about the child's feeding routines. The older woman spoke in rapid Malay, which was beyond my struggles with the language on the ship, showing toothless gums as she spoke.

"She is now being bottle fed," explained Jun. "Her daughter, the child's mother, walks many miles through the jungle to work on the plantations to buy food to feed her family. She is away all day. Lately, the baby has been vomiting up all her feeds and has gradually been losing weight."

I nodded at Jun and looked sympathetically at the woman. I completed my examination of the little girl, noting that if the feeding issue could be solved, she was basically healthy and strong. She should survive into adulthood with proper care and attention to hygiene.

"Jun, could you please explain to this lady that her grand-daughter has gastro-enteritis and malnutrition, brought about by inadequate hygiene and sterilisation of the feeding bottles. Please try to explain that if the bottles are not boiled after each feed, bacteria will form on them and cause sickness in the child. The milk must be boiled too, and the hands kept clean by washing with soap and clean water."

With about another five minutes of talking and exchange, my directions were relayed to the grandmother.

"Sister, she says that they have no soap for washing."

"Let her know that it can be obtained from the clinic free of charge but in the meantime, they can have this."

I reached into my bag and drew out two bars of the precious commodity, having previously been forewarned by Howie that it might be needed. The woman smiled and her eyes filled with tears.

"You have to remember, Val, that these people have nothing. Do

not imagine that this is like London," Howie had said. "There, even the poorest have access to more than they do."

I knew, even as I spoke, that finding adequate supplies of clean water became a daily battle and often involved travelling miles on foot. In the case of this *kampong*, I learned that the nearest water supply, a nearby stream, often dried to a trickle in the driest months of the year. Its source sprang from a mountainous region many miles away. I had heard in the clinic that morning that many of the villagers thought that if mountain water appeared clear, it was safe to drink. I had not imagined, before coming to Malaya that my work would encroach into the area of public health. Here, everything seemed reduced to absolute basics of survival. The knowledge I could pass on to these *kampong* dwellers owed more to my membership of the Girl Guides than to my years of nurse training.

An older boy came into the hut of about eight or nine years old, wearing a sarong, or *sampin* tied loosely around his hips, with a *baju* over baggy trousers. The older woman addressed him sharply and he bowed to me, holding his hands together in front of him in the prayer position. The boy sat down on the floor opposite me as I sat holding the child and more three-way conversation took place, between Jun, the grandmother and the young boy. After a few minutes, Jun turned to me.

"Sister, this is the little girl's older brother. He will help with the boiling of the water and milk and the fire for heating. I have explained everything to them that you have instructed."

I carefully handed back the little girl to her grandmother's safe keeping and rose from my cushion. I felt somewhat stiff from sitting for so long but also felt a peculiar sort of satisfaction from this family encounter. It struck me as one thing to administer care to the rich who had everything but quite another to start from scratch and involve all family members.

"Give the child plenty of boiled water to combat the dehydration and don't forget, you must sterilise all bottles and teats after every use. The clinic supplies bottles very cheaply if you need them."

As we climbed down the ladder under the eye of the grandmother, who bowed and smiled her thanks as well as she could holding the little girl, I continued giving instructions to Jun.

"I'll return in a few days to see how they're getting on. Could you make a note of that, please Jun?"

When we were on the ground, surrounded by the brothers and sisters of my little patient, Jun pulled out a diary from her uniform pocket and made a note of my intention to return. It would appear on the list of visits for later in the week.

The attentive family of my first kampong patient escorted us a good way further into the jungle, their support and gratitude almost overwhelming. I chucked a couple of the little boys under the chin and ruffled their black hair, making them grin with pleasure. They were a charming, warm people, I thought and I felt a warmth akin to love for humankind grow inside me. I reflected as I walked along, ever faster, in Jun's wake in the broiling heat of the afternoon, that this seemed as far removed from Northolt as I could imagine, yet essentially human beings were the same the world over, and ignorance and folklore as common in the London slums as the Malayan jungle. I felt a sense of familiarity, of confidence, as many of my feelings of trepidation dispersed. I also knew that I had the support of the Colonial administrative and social system, ready to speak for its British subjects in His Majesty's dominions overseas in any emergency. I felt the power behind me – my training, knowledge. Everything I knew.

That first afternoon, I had seen two more patients in a large *kampong* deep in the jungle, before we had retraced our steps back to Hadji and the car. I had only had a chance to take a quick assessment of them that morning but they had aroused my concern and I had mentioned them to the doctors before leaving for lunch. If my suspicions proved correct, I would have to arrange for their immediate admission into the Batu Gajah hospital but knew I faced reluctance and shyness on the part of the mothers, both of whom cared for their babies themselves. They had gone that morning before the doctors had had a chance to see them but the clinic nurses, by speaking their language, had managed to extricate from them where they could be located. They had attended the clinic together and were neighbours. The babies seemed about the same age and the mothers friends, often going in and out of each other's houses holding their babies in their arms.

That morning, in the chaos of the Ipoh Old town Clinic, I had witnessed the tell-tale signs of bacterial meningitis.

The trees and bushes had gradually thinned, admitting more daylight onto our path. All along our route, the stillness of the afternoon had been profound, and the noise of our tramping footsteps had sounded loud in the ambient silence, broken only by the echoing, persistent call of a laughing thrush high in the trees, who appeared to follow us along. Our young guides from the previous *kampong* had left us some ten minutes back and Jun and I had continued alone. I walked doggedly in Jun's footsteps, thankful that she seemed as at home in the jungle as she did on the streets of Ipoh. I kept my gaze on her slim white-uniformed back and black-stockinged legs, feeling a little disorientated and "at sea".

Only a few days ago, free of care, I had travelled aboard a liner in the middle of the Indian Ocean, and now tramped along a jungle track to see a patient I suspected as suffering from a contagious disease. Although I had abandoned my white voile nurse's hat and replaced it with a small navy blue felt model, my uniform dress chafed and clung to me and I was sure that I stank of stale perspiration.

The second *kampong* appeared much larger than the first, as we gradually became clear of the trees and bushes of the jungle. The area occupied by the wooden stilted houses spread out to cover more cleared ground and, occupying a separate piece of land which seemed dedicated to its purpose, I recognised a mosque or *masjid*, its dark red roof tiered and quite unlike the domed rooves of mosques I had seen in India. I assumed that this building might serve the inhabitants of other *kampong* settlements. Beyond the buildings, a large area of cleared land appeared to be under cultivation.

"Jun," I panted, coming up behind her. "This is a much larger settlement. Is there another road for access? And is that a paddy field?"

"Yes, there is a more direct route with a wider road from Ipoh," agreed Jun. "You are right, Sister. This *kampong* has more for the villagers and is more....."

"Self-sufficient?" I suggested. The nurse nodded and checked her notebook.

"The patient is in the house over here, Sister," said Jun, gesturing to a hut slightly separate from the others.

Although the *kampong* appeared larger, less evidence of life showed here than its neighbour. Few children played under the huts and no throng of curious youngsters greeted us as before. It seemed eerily quiet.

"They know there is sickness here," said Jun, looking around her thoughtfully, as if sensing the fear the villagers felt. True to her word, I glimpsed several faces peering out at us from the open windows of the huts, hurriedly controlled by an adult within.

I produced two white cotton face masks from my bag and gave one to Jun. We assisted each other with tying them behind our heads before we approached the hut Jun had indicated. Like before, Jun called out as we climbed the rickety ladder and a young woman appeared in the doorway, the expression on her almost childlike face fearful and, I thought, furtive. She stood aside without a word to allow us to enter the dark interior, but the atmosphere felt very different from the previous one.

As we entered, I heard sounds coming from a cot in a corner of the room and went over to look. The same baby I had seen in the clinic that morning lay there, fitfully arching its back and whimpering with a high-pitched cry. It looked about three or four months old but, like so many others I had seen that morning, undergrown for its age. I did not attempt to pick up the child but examined it where it lay. It was immediately apparent to me from its apathetic appearance that fever raged in the child's body and I did not need to undertake the "glass" test to notice that on the child's abdomen, the tiny red rash typical of the highly infectious disease was present. In the meantime, Jun had spoken to the young Malay woman and came over to me.

"Sister, the mother says that the *bomoh* has been here and left talismans. Her mother believes in this traditional medicine and was angry that she came to the clinic this morning. She lives in the other *kampong* but she comes to look after the baby. The mother did not go to her work today."

Not the first time, I felt frustrated and angry with myself for not being able to speak the language. I needed to impress on the mother the urgent need to take the child to the hospital. I suddenly had an idea.

"Jun, we can take them to Batu Gajah in our car. Tell the mother, please, and we'll leave now." The mother seemed to understand and be relieved that we had provided an easy solution. She gathered together some things in a basket for the baby, whom she picked up lovingly and held close.

"She must be worried sick. She does not need conflicting advice now. Take some boiled water for the baby," I directed Jun, wondering how I would have managed without the intelligent efficiency of the nurse.

As we were leaving, I heard raised Malay voices from outside. I went out and stood on the balcony atop the steps. An older woman stood below, arguing with one or two older boys who appeared to have just returned from a jungle expedition. The baby's mother adeptly managed to navigate the steps to the ground holding her baby and we followed. To my surprise, she said nothing to the older woman but walked past her without a word, heading for the jungle track down which we had come. Jun and I followed her and walked past the group standing at the base of the ladder without altercation. As we began entering the jungle, leaving the village behind, I heard more raised voices from behind.

"All is well, Sister," said Jun. "Of course, that older woman was the child's grandmother. It was lucky that the baby's uncles arrived at that moment, otherwise it would have been hard to leave. They were controlling the grandmother. She believes in the ways of the old times but the young people, they understand the western medicine and believe in it. This young girl wants her baby to live and knows the right thing to do."

I had had to return to the *kampong* to see the other child while Jun escorted the first mother and baby back to the car. I told them to wait, that I would not take long. The second baby's illness had not advanced to the same extent and the grandmother had some rudimentary English. I left instructions that the baby should be presented to the hospital the following day, as I had no doubt that the disease would progress. Then followed a lonely walk through the jungle. The late afternoon sun was beginning to descend in the sky as I followed the jungle path alone, hearing the unfamiliar sounds encroaching from both sides.

Later that afternoon as Hadji finally pulled up outside 4, Windsor Road, I reflected that it had not amounted to a bad start in "kamponging", with the young mother and baby safely delivered to the infectious diseases ward of the hospital under my supervision. As I gave my report to the receiving nurse, I did not fail to mention the near-miss with traditional medicine and the appearance of the grandmother. Yet another example of the fight against misinformation and ignorance, I thought to myself as I let myself into the bungalow to the ministrations of my staff.

Chapter 10

Between Two Worlds

It was marvellous to put an address at the top of my letters home after all the time spent "somewhere at sea". I wrote to my mother that I had so much to say that I hardly knew where to begin. It all seemed so dreamlike. My English eyes, used to the gloom, saw everything transformed to colour, like an exaggerated reality. I tried, rather inadequately, to describe the difference.

"Everything is so beautiful, the sun shining all day and refreshing rain just to cool things off".

For the first few weeks, I did not hear from home. Dependent on ships traversing the same treacherous route I had, it often took months for letters to get through and sometimes they never arrived. Reports of heavy German bombing in London, a mere twenty-five miles from my parents' home in Kent, made me worry more than I ever thought I would. Before I had left home, I could reassure myself every weekend in visits and by regular phone calls, that they remained well and unharmed. Telegrams, or "wires" as we called them, provided a solution, which, in a few sparse words, brought the relief and comfort of instant communication.

During the endless long, hot nights inside my mosquito net in an airless room I despaired.

"If only I could get a letter from you!" I wrote, and spoke out loud in the unforgiving silence of the night. Nobody heard. I tossed and turned on my damp sheets, kicking off the thin counterpane angrily. I took my pyjama jacket off, not being able to bear the chafing cotton material so close to the skin, then put it back on again, imagining Mary shocked at chancing upon a half-naked woman lying in a position of abandon in the morning.

I could not understand why I had not had a letter since I had arrived in Malaya. Surely, if they had written regularly and had timed the letters to when they knew I would arrive, no break should have occurred. In desperation I had visited the Ipoh Post Office.

"I have arranged now to hear by wire from you every two weeks. You don't have to pay your end. I pay when I receive the wire." I wrote, fearing that it was cost which had caused this inexplicable silence.

Why, I wondered, did they not consider telegrams themselves? Did they not realise that I suffered agonies, picturing my beloved home rubble?

They must think I have gone from them, I concluded. Disappeared into the ether like one dead. In that case, what grief they must suffer now on my account. I tried to take my mind off the relentless images of destruction as best I could. The newspapers did not help ease my mind, although I had Tam buy me several of the English-speaking dailies regularly, which I devoured with my tea as soon as I got home. Having all but given up on receiving reliable news from home, I concentrated instead on getting the bungalow straight with the reluctant and sometimes puzzled help of my staff. They could not see why the settee was in a better position under the lounge window for example, rather than where it had always sat, opposite the fireplace. But I wanted everything just right for my entertaining schedule. This meant having one of the two bedrooms with adjoining bathroom guest-ready at a moment's notice and the dining room and lounge arranged exactly according to my notions of congenial hospitality.

I had learned very early on that entertaining was expected and reflected that if I had been the shy sort, I might have found this expectation challenging - but I could have consoled myself by remembering that as a social environment, Malaya bore no comparison to middle-class and conservative Kent. It resembled a vast club, where members played by the rules and up to their role as guests, contributing as much to the party ambience as the hosts who provided the food, alcohol and premises. Having accepted Malaya on its own terms, I willingly complied so in early February I gave my first dinner party for Molly and two of the doctors from the clinic. Already, Molly had been a frequent guest at the bungalow on an informal basis. The first weekend we spent in the colony she had turned up at the door like a waif, asking if she could stay for dinner, as she had run out of food and awaited her first pay. I had, luckily for her, happily welcomed a familiar face. Having shared a cabin for so many weeks it felt like putting on an old glove, so easily did we resume our former camaraderie.

"Oh Val!" She had said, pushing past me into my newly-arranged lounge. "I love what you've done with this room. It looks so much bigger!"

Molly had popped in one evening before, as she could not wait to see the grand accommodation Crown Agents had provided for her contemporary. As I explained to her, before she became consumed with envy, it went with the job. I had gestured to Tam, who had appeared from the kitchen looking as if I had usurped his position. It usually fell to him to open the door as the "man of the house" and in lieu of a butler.

"Thank you, Tam, everything's fine. One more to dinner please."

Tam had opened his mouth as if to say that there wasn't enough but shut it again. A few minutes later I saw him walk around the side of the house swinging his shopping bag and looking rather mutinous, a face which he would never have dared show to me. Later that evening, when Molly had admired everything from the back terrace to the delightful view over the garden in the guest bedroom, we had sat one each end of the dining table and enjoyed a bottle of wine from the Windsor Road "cellar" with Tam's passable chicken and rice. Molly regaled me with stories about her new ward at Batu Gajah.

"Oh Val, you're so lucky! I've just got a room in the hospital! To have all this!" She waved her hand around the room vaguely, narrowly missing the half-empty bottle. "Now here's a bit of gossip for you, old thing! You know that snooty chap you went out with at Bombay... Alex someone?"

"Alec Soames?' I supplied helpfully. I thought I knew what was coming next.

"Yes, Soames. Well, it seems that he and Howard were an item! They kept it quiet though because he's got a wife in New Zealand. Really passionate affair, apparently. Poor old Howie, she took it quite hard when he shot through suddenly to India. I mean, just look at her. She was crazy about him. Never got over it!"

I had made no comment. This sounded like the embellishment of gossip. To me, Howie had looked as self-contained and dignified as ever. She kept her personal life private and commanded respect for doing so. How could such a person to abandon herself in this way? But there was no smoke without fire, and in affairs of the heart.....

I had briefed Tam minutely before the dinner party, but he reassured me with a broad grin that he had "much experience" with parties so I relaxed somewhat and left it to him. What appeared that evening, for an overall cost of $8, bore a resemblance to a chicken curry, a dish that I was fast becoming fond of, although somewhat tepid and rather sweet. Tam did not wholly disgrace me and I gave him credit for waiting well at table and for the general presentation. Conversation that night flowed, helped immeasurably by the ever-vivacious and flirtatious Molly, and I have to say that the evening achieved a fair measure of success. It felt like pure luxury to be able to concentrate on entertaining one's guests without concerning oneself with the chores of cooking and clearing away, like at home, or the burden incumbent on guests to offer to help.

As a new arrival, I fully appreciated the privileges I experienced. That night we chatted as only people can who work together, about colleagues, our different backgrounds and what had brought us to Malaya, and the war news – ever more worrying. In this, we had a common bond, being exiles and finding in daily work forgetfulness – at least for a while. The war at this stage seemed purely a European one and we counted ourselves fortunate to have escaped it even though we went through the motions of concern for those who had not. Part of my worry about my parents and friends I could identify now as guilt. When I began at last to receive letters from home, my mother's as usual filled with woes and self-pity, I felt considerably relieved - but once I had reassured myself of their wellbeing, I returned to the business of loving life and sitting out the war from the sidelines, convinced, like most, that nothing fundamental would ever change.

It lay incumbent upon me one morning to turn my attentions once more to my little household. I felt that my relationship with my *amah* would have been more satisfactory with better communication. She could speak no English and only very bad Malay, and I described my own Malay as "very funny". I began to think that I would have to complain about Mary to my employers. Although she would not have dared to behave badly in front of me, in spite of my efforts at insouciance *vis a vis* an unfamiliar culture I found her habits, such as the un-English way she had of blowing her nose through her fingers or using her *dupatta* as a handkerchief for nose-wiping or brow-mopping, offensive. Several times, I had heard heated arguments between her and Tam, which puzzled me. Her generally disagreeable behaviour led me to wonder about her background. I knew that Tam had worked as a houseboy for the previous inhabitants of my bungalow. Perhaps he looked upon Mary as an intruder on his territory, although none could deny that in Malayan terms, I did need a personal maid. I knew that both had been difficult to find and I wondered how an almost middle-aged Indian woman came in need of employment. Her obvious attitude and demeanour suggested a turbulent past about which only Crown Agents would know.

As these things tend to do, everything came to a head, in this case early one morning. A sound of breaking crockery and shouting from the kitchen quarters penetrated my consciousness and awakened me from a deep sleep which got the day off to a bad start. Later on, I had reflected that the melodrama reminded me of a slapstick film of the silent era. Regretting my inexperience with servants, I felt nevertheless that I could not let this pass. I had shown lenience for too long and my anger mounted in me – not least because of disturbance from much needed rest. Taking on the mantle of a *pukka memsahib* which I felt was long overdue, I threw on my dressing gown, tying the belt as tightly as if I wished it wound around the throat of the wretched *amah* and marched somewhat groggily into the kitchen.

The *amah*, her dusky face contorted with rage, her long, black hair in wild disarray like an escapee from a Victorian lunatic asylum, stood dangerously close to the knife block. I thought she looked capable of anything at that moment. I still felt too sleepy to think of possible reasons for her passion and acted on instinct. With the concentrated stare and purpose of the murderer, she looked about to launch herself at the boy. If I had not intervened quickly, he would have been obliged to defend himself, perhaps his life, regardless of her gender. He stood backed up against the wall, his hands defending his face like a boxer.

At that moment, both became aware of my presence, but Mary's rage was too consuming to stop immediately. I even thought for one split second that she may turn on me - she gave me a look of such hatred and resentment. Not for the first time, I felt placed in the position of being one of a ruling class and judged accordingly, as a reverse prejudice.

Why did it have to be like this, I wondered. I had not asked for servants.

Looking back, I thought I had handled the drama rather well.

"What has been going on here, Tam?" I asked the boy, appealing to the apparently sensible and responsible side of the duo.

We had managed to restrain the deranged woman between us until she had calmed down, eventually realising, probably with something like horror, what she had done.

"Miss Sister, I don't know," Tam held up his hands helplessly and shrugged his shoulders. "Maybe she like me."

I did not delve deeper. We both looked at the now crumpled, tearful figure in its green silk sari sitting on one of the kitchen chairs at the table. At that moment I felt something akin to compassion for the woman but knew that I could no longer keep her as staff. I rang up the Crown Agents that afternoon feeling like a traitor. Like my father, I would be a fair employer, I realised, given the chance. One owed a little loyalty and solidarity to other members of one's household. If Mary had not given me several previous examples of an unhinged individual, I would have given her the benefit of the doubt. She left that very afternoon for her *kampong,* her future employment prospects looking bleak. I waited some time for a replacement, I remember, but in the meantime, Tam took over the laundry and I foraged in the markets myself for my personal needs. It proved good training for what came later, for what could not have been foreseen.

There it came again. That reference to "X". I had delved deep into the archives, into unknown territory. These papers I had not seen for fifty years, written and then stored and forgotten. Who was "X"? I mention him only to illustrate the turmoil of my social life in those early weeks.

I had become a socialite. How trite that sounded, how unoriginal. How could I have become the superficial party-goer which seems to emerge from these pages, shrill and empty-headed as a rich man's mistress. One side of me did not fit the other, for in my care of mothers and babies I had to throw off this mantle - somewhat insincere and adopted as a social façade. Underneath it all, I knew that I looked for something deeper, for lasting love. I could not boast beauty but I had cultivated a vivacity and quickness both fashionable and attractive then. I possessed a sweet smile, refined through twelve years of nursing the sick and infirm – my armour and presentation to the world. I felt flattered and overwhelmed by the male attention single girls commanded in Malaya. Men vastly outnumbered women in the colony and I found most of my evenings accounted for and men competing for my attention. The insistence of the would-be gallants caused me to be at risk of losing my head, often living as I did in a state of happy confusion at their onslaught from all sides.

By the end of January 1941, I regularly "dated" someone I took care to refer to only as "X" in my diary. Looking back through the pages, I can see that I saw him every day around that time, until a much more forceful and determined personality came into my life. With "X" I danced at the Jubilee, dined at the Rex and went to the swimming pool, where we listened, one sublime Sunday evening, to unaccompanied Bach from a makeshift stage, courtesy of the Perak Chinese Amateur Dramatic Association's orchestra.

Was "X" married? A minor aristocrat perhaps, connected to one of the great families of England who would have closed ranks to avert a scandal? Or was he an official of the colonial regime? I am not at liberty to say, so even after all these long years, he must remain simply "X", another of those unexplained mysteries which have followed in the wake of the English royalty and aristocracy since the beginning of time. In any case, it hardly matters. In just a few weeks, my integrity barely stood firm, tested to the limit as I battled to preserve a vestige of self-respect and dignity against a merciless onslaught on my senses and, if truth be told, my deepest desires. Although I had travelled to Malaya out of a longstanding natural curiosity and desire to see the world, the possibilities of romance had remained at the back of my mind but love and loyalty for my parents – perhaps because of Tommy – had made me feel that no husband could take their place. Deep inside me, I preserved an inner kernel of self. Later in life, perhaps this gave me strength to endure what I had to.

I wanted my mother and father to share what I experienced to a small degree and sent drawings of people I had seen and descriptions of most of what I experienced. In those last days of colonial rule, we lived alongside the many nationalities which fascinated me in their variety. Perhaps I encountered foreignness for the first time with a kind of youthful innocence but I responded to its variation from our ways with eager enthusiasm and wonder and a hunger for knowledge and experience. Like a curator from a museum collating a collection belonging to some ancient and forgotten tribe, my instinct was to record, draw and "snap" the living wonders and curiosities I saw around me. I wanted to enter their existence, understand their mores and their *raison d'etre*.

In such richness, I wrote, not knowing what I wrote, even poverty was picturesque.

"Work is going on quite well. The babies are lovely. I'm afraid they're much prettier than ours. The routine is very much the same as at home except that I have more responsibility and there is less red tape. The kampongs are much more interesting for health visiting than streets. It's such a huge district that no place ever looks the same. Sometimes it's right out in the jungle, another time in the caves and it may even be in the Chinese palaces, which are absolutely marvellous. Often, especially in the crowded morning clinics, we are very busy, but as you know, it doesn't matter in health work, one's evenings are always free."

One afternoon towards the end of January, I gave, as part of my role, some lectures in home nursing to the married women. I felt very nervous as I thought I had forgotten everything from the wards. In the dusty old Ipoh Red Cross Hall I had set up a bandaging and first aid station in one corner, and on the other side of the hall I had managed to acquire an old hospital bed complete with sheets and blankets. I addressed the assembled wives much more confidently than I felt.

"Good afternoon, ladies. Welcome to my home nursing course. We will have six weekly hour-long sessions followed by an exam.

Then you will be presented with a certificate at a special afternoon tea! You may bring along a guest."

One or two of the women looked rather frightened at the prospect of an exam but cheered up again at the mention of the afternoon tea.

I stood on the raised platform at one end of the hall in my uniform, staring back at the dozen or so women seated on folding iron chairs opposite me. Many smiled and looked interested. I knew some of them already from social events as the wives of administrators. No military wives came but I saw with pleasure that Mrs Murray Ainsley, the district judge's wife, had put in an appearance.

"We will start with bandaging. Now, you will work in twos and take turns being a patient and a nurse. If I could have a volunteer, please?"

Several women put up their hands. I felt grateful that the group as a whole seemed supportive of my efforts and played their part well.

Mrs Murray Ainsley acted as my "patient" on whom I demonstrated my first bandage. She had a child-like prettiness with a near-perfect figure, a devastating French accent and a temperament inclined to be anxious and dithery in a crisis. Today she wore a crisp white and rust-coloured cotton dress with cap sleeves, perfect for bandage demonstration purposes. When her turn came to bandage on another of the women, freeing me to circulate and correct, her hands trembled visibly. I felt surprised. Surely, as a wife and mother, she would have soothed and bandaged the minor childhood injuries of her young brood and acted as first aider and nurse for grazes, cuts, bruises and general aches and pains for her family? Or had she always left this privilege to hired *amahs* and nannies? Slowly and deliberately, eventually Odette Murray Ainsley had managed to produce something resembling a hand bandage.

"Sister Lavinia, could you please check that this is correct?" she called over to me as I was directing another of the "pairs" in the intricacy of bandaging a foot and ankle. "Oh dear, I'm sure this part around the thumb is wrong."

I went over to see. One could not keep a judge's wife waiting and the wife of a cousin of a viscount to boot.

Her partner, the plump wife of the manager of the Chartered Bank in Ipoh, helpfully held up her hand to be examined. I could see immediately that the bandage was too loose and would never have held a dressing in place on a real wound.

"No, you've done it quite well," I said encouragingly. "Perhaps slightly tighter though. Have one more try then change over!"

When it came to bedmaking with a patient in situ, Odette's state of nerves with everyone looking on made her even worse. She became so nervous that she seemed literally frozen, and could not remember how I had demonstrated tucking in the corners like "envelopes" or the width of the fold of the top sheet. The poor patient would have been numb with cold before she had finished, adding to the discomfort of his other ailments. In the end, Mrs Murray Ainsley's nervousness about the prospective exam caused her to refuse to take it. Afraid to bring disgrace on her illustrious family, she had worked herself up into a state of panic weeks beforehand, all to no avail. I would have passed her in all likelihood and her husband's indulgence of his attractive wife prevented him from caring very much. The next weekend I dined with them in their bungalow on the outskirts of the town, tasting real colonial luxury and privilege, followed by an invitation to spend a whole weekend with them. As an independent, professional woman I held a certain status admired by the wives, whose sole role revolved around their duties as hostess and as a support to their husbands.

The administration granted the European wives magnificent residences in which to conduct their entertaining. The weekend of Chinese New Year saw me invited out for a dinner and dance. I had little knowledge of the hosts – they were something big in hospital management and I had heard of the event through one of the sisters at Batu Gajah. I used this event as a description in a letter home – the house typically vast but similar to others I came to know.

"Downstairs there is usually a huge lounge with the dining room

to one side and the servant's quarters leading off from that. There is also a little study on the other side. Upstairs there is another large cocktail lounge where the cocktail parties take place which in this country are called "pait" parties, meaning "bitters". Then the bedrooms branch off from this room, and they are colossal. Each bed has a mosquito net and a bathroom and lavatory are attached to each room. I've never seen such spacious rooms except in hotels and country houses[1]."

I lived in a whirl of activity, dances, impressions, meeting new people and new experiences as if I frantically strived to fit as much into life as I could, before I no longer could. Letters home had a breathless tone, full of superlatives and enthusiasm. I almost gave up on trying to decide which accounts to include in any autobiography I wrote. How did I manage to squeeze in so much? My diary had a similar quality.

"One Saturday at the commencement of the Chinese year of the Snake, we went en partie *to the Ipoh Club to dance".* (The club culture held an important place paramount in Malayan society through introductions by an existing member. Most colonials had membership of at least one.)

"I met three people who I don't like, two who need watching. I had two other invites for this evening including the army, which I would have liked much better. The following day I went to the Ipoh swimming club dance – we danced to the radio and had a very enjoyable evening. The day after that, a group of us went to the Kinta Club swimming pool (Chinese). The Chinese are very good swimmers with their small, lithe, muscular bodies and fast movement. They beat us up – 9-3 in water polo".

And:

"Yesterday I went to the races. I lost money, but it was a marvellous meeting. It's all under cover to avoid the glare of the sun. In the evening we went dancing. I had every dance, I just couldn't believe it. The race was in aid of the Spitfire Fund so one was almost glad to lose. In spite of all this the people are thinking a lot about the war and trying to support wherever they can."

"Although it's rather too hot for energetic sports, I do play golf in the coolest time after I leave work, until sundown. This is celebrated at 6 o'clock by a drink known as a "stingah", which consists of a tot of whiskey filled up with soda and ice.

"Just as one imagines all is quiet the Punjabi regiment comes into light, and a certain Captain Brown received the OBE for forestry and gives a marvellous party, champagne, etc. We danced and had a lovely time. We went out again the following day. Unfortunately they are gone now. We hope to have some more soon."

And:

"On 13th February, "X." The next day, I went to dinner with a Miss James, who was a hairdresser for two years in Tonbridge and we went to the flicks. Saw "He Stayed for Breakfast" with Loretta Young and Melvyn Douglas. Very good indeed!

The following day, I had an invite for dinner at the Burgesses. Mr B is Art Director for Perak. Very interesting evening, decide I like Mrs B, only snag I fell from top to bottom of the stairs! Also at dinner was an American missionary.

Then, sombrely, perhaps a sinister premonition of things to come, is the following brief entry.

"Five unknown bombers fly over Singapore encountered by our planes but two are missing."

One glorious day around that time I had gone with a party of "fellows" to Pangkor Island in the Malacca Strait. I described it in a casual way and the tropical paradise in which I found myself does not seem to have made the main impression. I seem more concerned with light-heartedness and fun. In this diary entry, intended to reveal my most intimate thoughts about whom I liked or did not like, my tone comes across as blasé, fashionably insouciant and careless, as if I had been visiting tropical islands all my life and found them a bit of a bore.

"Great fun and went all day. Bathed and got burned up. Travelled in a noisy launch to island and then in a derelict Crossley fit to shake the organs from one's bones. All day the lazy Malays stared at us. It is

reached by Lumut, Sitiawan, a beautiful spot by the sea with trees going down to the water's edge. The sea is a wonderful blue. In the distance there are green trees but to add a serious note to the scene a leper colony can be seen although I believe there are few patients. Leprosy is nevertheless on the increase."

I thought that I now lived in a noisy country, on the whole. The decorous way of life I had grown accustomed to in Kent did not exist in Malaya. Here, a life force unencumbered by enforced modes and manners or puritan ethics had free rein.

"They always seem to be getting ready for different feasts. Tomorrow is All Soul's Day, which commemorates the birthday of Mohammet which is rather like our Christmas Day. If there aren't feasts then there are funerals which need a terrific amount of preparation. They are frightfully decorative these funerals, attended by heaps of people and accompanied by a band."

I must have felt an obligation incumbent upon me to turn my experiences into an educational advantage to instruct my parents and anyone to whom I happened to write (but especially them). Perhaps because I had left them behind in a country at war I tried to compensate, and not to write about my innermost thoughts and feelings, which I may not have even analysed at that time. I may have hoped that it would divert them in a positive sense, especially Mother. If only I could encourage her to think beyond herself and be happy for me in my new experiences, seeing them through my eyes as I wanted her to.

In later years, I remembered those early weeks of 1941 as a transitional period before my life changed completely, in more ways than one. I had begun to keep a journal, in actual fact pages from an old ledger, in which I recorded thoughts and feelings in a kind of code, perhaps knowing that afterwards, in later life, I could recreate the people, places and events I experienced. I tried to cram as much into my life as possible, perhaps aware on a subconscious level that time, mine and everyone's, posed its own limitations. How could such an idyll continue to exist? I was enough of a woman of the

world to know that heaven cannot exist in this life without a price
to pay.

---

1. This employment of a huge amount of space is seen in the cities in Malaysia
    today, in hotel lobbies, entrances, public rooms and hotel bedrooms – a luxury in
    itself and redolent of these times.

Chapter 11

The Roaring Tin Dredger from Taiping

It had rained for several days, a steady deluge that pattered heavily on jungle ferns and hissed in the tall trees. In the *kampongs*, a thick yellow mud surrounded the huts and invaded everything, including the mouths and faces of the children. Nothing suggested a day different from any other in my new normal existence. It was 17th February 1941 and I had *"kamponged"* the entire day. Despite the rain, a serenity always pervaded the jungle which I had grown to love, so welcome after the intensity and stress of the busy clinics.

Hadji and his big black car had trailed us all day, the automobile's front quarters emerging from tangled vegetation at the edge of clearings – a mechanical monster at odds with virgin forest. That afternoon we had arrived at a Chinese village deeper in the jungle than I had ever ventured. The roads had dwindled almost to tracks, impassable for any but the most robust of vehicles. Hadji took pride in the fact that the car rivalled any jeep in durability, although several times Jun and I had had to get out and push it out of puddles or deep ruts, while Hadji sat behind the wheel revving the engine. I felt that this exercise was a little undignified and said so to the syce.

"Hadji," I said breathlessly to the driver after one of these episodes, "When are you going to be provided with a proper *jeep*?"

I looked ruefully at my shoes, which had been cleaned by the new *amah* only last night. They and my black stockings were spattered with the glutinous yellow mud, which I would have thought in most other scenarios but deep in the Malayan jungle to show a less than fully professional image.

"Crown Agents say soon, Miss Sister," replied Hadji with his usual grin, more a courtesy than as a response to something amusing. "Red tape! Un'stand Ma'am?"

I understood only too well. Crown Agents represented a mere cog in the great colonial wheel, which turned laboriously slowly. My post had been newly created and speedily filled, although I had spent many weeks *en route*. I sighed, realising that I would probably get through many more pairs of stockings before the faceless bureaucrats saw fit to fill the order for a utility vehicle. Adding to Crown Agents' customarily majestic pace, the war complicated matters further and I knew the armed services would have first pickings over such supplies.

I turned my attention to the *kampong* before me and looked out again at the rain, falling steadily upon the surrounding jungle. I wore a gabardine, really too warm in this climate but it helped to keep one's uniform dry. The huts which came into view were little more than hovels. It was to the credit of the colonial service that no sick person in need ever missed out in favour of those wealthy enough to pay, or lay beneath our attention. This principle held true in Batu Gajah and other district hospitals, and like the National Health Service which came into being only a few years hence, worked on the principle of providing professional expertise to all. The only difference between the care given to rich or poor was the setting.

I looked up at the sky and seeing no break in the heavy clouds, decided to make a run for it. Jun got out of the other side of the car simultaneously and preceded me towards the nearest hut. I managed to avoid a puddle so huge that it appeared as a muddy pond in the centre of the clearing. Outside the car the rain had released the sharp scents of damp soil and decay, mingled with sandalwood and forest plants, some in a profusion of flower and turning their half-closed faces to the abundant moisture.

It took several seconds to accustom our eyes to the interior of the hut. I felt as if my senses were being assailed, all five at the same time. The inside seemed illuminated solely by a dirty paned window on one wall, by which light I gradually made out the interior. At the same time, I noticed a strong, sickly smell, which I could not place. Jun whispered to me, virtually inaudibly.

"Opium," was all she said, and gestured slightly to a corner.

I just made out a thin figure on a dirty mattress in a corner of the room, reclining and staring up at me where I still stood in the door-way. I saw a man of about forty, yet looking old beyond his years, holding a pipe with a long, thin stem. I had thought the practice of opium smoking illegal by then but was not naive enough to think that its practice would not take many years to eradicate.

I began to feel a little intimidated by the scene which appeared somewhat sinister with the eyes of the reclining man upon us, appearing to glitter in the pervading gloom, until a young woman emerged from the shadows holding a little boy by the hand, dressed in a wide-sleeved tunic and trousers. Another, older child stood nearby, looking at me shyly. As we watched, the smaller child stumbled, looking dazed, and his mother scooped him up into her arms. I smiled encouragingly as Jun and the woman entered into conversation. The young Chinese woman had laid the sick boy onto a nearby rickety table, and lifted up the front of his shirt which showed several raised, angry red spots.

In a few moments, with the aid of Jun's interpreter service, I had diagnosed chicken pox and set up a treatment plan. The child had only a mild fever and I did not feel greatly concerned. I took out some aspirin from my bag and instructed the mother, through Jun, to obtain some calamine lotion from the clinic. She expected her husband home at any moment, she explained, and he could fetch it. I made sure the woman understood and then turned to leave, but to my surprise, the little boy's older brother waylaid us.

On the way in, I had heard some porcine-sounding grunts and squeals from a tumbledown shed which stood precariously against the side of the hut but had dismissed them. The sounds had blended in with other jungle noises – the calls of unknown birds in the trees, the barking of feral dogs, which I had not yet identified. Now, to my surprise and pleasure, the child took me by the hand and led me outside to the outhouse. Jun smiled – it was probably the first time I had seen her do so – and followed us. The mother, holding the boy's little brother, looked on indulgently. Apparently, whatever we would do or see, met with her approbation.

I spoke to my new companion in English but of course, he did not understand. He was a boy of about six or seven years old – and considering the disadvantages evident from within, his clothes looked clean and his demeanour appeared bright and observant. His intelligent face, framed by straight black hair carefully combed, looked up at me with trust and curiosity. He pulled at my hand impatiently as if he could not wait to show me what lay within the shed and unfastened the catch on the wooden door. The rain fell steadily onto my hair and clothes and I quickly draped my gabardine around my head as protection.

As the door opened, a wall of scents, almost overpowering, greeted me – of the warmth of animal flesh mingled with that of excrement and hay and the smell of birth which I knew so well. On a bed of dried grass and straw, exuding the natural summer fragrance of open fields, lay a mother pig, huge and recumbent, with several newborn piglets blindly clambering over each other or squirming around her distended teats. Some had managed to latch on with hungry mouths, and were sucking voraciously. From her continuous grunting, the mother pig looked to be about to add to her litter.

Jun came up behind me.

"The sow often has around fourteen piglets," she explained.

I counted the piglets already wriggling in the straw and came up with nine. The little boy broke his grip on my hand and went up to stroke the sow's rump.

"Who is looking after the sow?" I asked. "Can she manage it all by herself?"

"Usually, yes, unless there are problems. The cord stays attached and will eventually come off as the piglet tries to walk. Each piglet is independent of the others by having its own placenta. Look, here it comes."

As I watched, feeling a sense of having seen it all before and yet not quite the same thing, an object recognisable as a piglet's head appeared in the nether region of the animal, followed quickly by a dark-coloured body. The little Chinese boy watched carefully from the sow's side, as if ready to help the family livestock. I knew this counted as an important day for the family and would ensure their food supply for some time to come, in terms of meat or sales. Jun and I crouched down beside the family of piglets but did not attempt to touch them. I knew instinctively that a new mother of any species, including human, could become fiercely protective of her offspring.

The family had been my last call of the day. As we prepared to leave the *kampong* having taken our leave of my little Chinese friend and his new family of piglets, we passed a hut on the edge of the rain-soaked settlement. Despite its obvious poverty, there appeared to be enterprise in this community. First the pigs and now pottery, I thought. I had heard a whirring sound as I approached, and peered in through the doorway. On a stone circular rotating wheel, the potter, Chinese and wiry, capped with the greying hair of the fifty-year old, threw a lump of clay in the centre of the wheel and formed a circular mound. His deft and sensitive hands seemed to caress the clay into shape as it grew taller under his cupped palms, his fingers probing and teasing the top of the mound into the cup shape of a vessel. I watched, mesmerised, not able to take my eyes away from his skilled shaping. The potter seemed completely absorbed in his work like one hypnotised and did not look up as we stood there. Jun, who, irritatingly, I thought, seemed to know everything, pointed to the sky.

"Usually, Sister, the pots are put outside in the sun to dry. This man must know that the rain will stop soon, perhaps tomorrow, and he can put them outside."

We made our way back to the car and found Hadji taking a nap in the front seat. He jerked awake when we opened the back door.

"I'm sorry, Hadji, we were longer than expected," I explained. "I have just seen the first pig of my life being delivered and a little Chinese boy who seemed to be more competent than some midwives I have known!"

Jun gave me a look, as if to say that my comments ranked as unprofessional behaviour. I ignored her and settled into the back seat for the drive back through the jungle and home to change. Really, I thought, she had become over-confident in her relations with me, although I could not deny her efficiency and interpreting skills were vital.

Ah yes, midwives..........I recall now a particular day only a few weeks later when I visited another *kampong*: Satri Jadi, again in the middle of the jungle, where, I wrote later in my "code", the altitude was "*anything but vital.*" I thought and wrote as my thirty-year old self in March 1941.

"*The midwife appeared to be the vaguest person in the community, so what took place when she had lucid intervals is best not thought about. To make investigations as to birth rate, death rate or any other rate is definitely that of a detective sniffing out crime.*"

That particular Monday evening in February, I had agreed to go to the swimming club dance at the *Celestial*, which with the *Jubilee*, hosted most of the local dances and events. I nearly sent my excuses, feigning a headache, but Tam brought in a *stingah* on a silver tray on my return to the bungalow (I had trained him) and I perked up considerably. Besides, Pete, one of the junior doctors I had worked with at the clinic, had arranged a party of us to go and I foresaw the awkwardness that might ensue later.

The dance looked well underway and the early, sedate part of the evening had passed with a few foxtrots and quick steps. Howie and

Clarissa Drew had put in an appearance to support the event held in aid of war widows, but had not yet joined in the dancing. Howie had obviously taken care with her appearance tonight but had not had any offers yet, and the pair sat at one of the tables in the corner. The band was good, I thought. You could always trust the swimming club social committee to put on a good do. The party had not yet warmed up enough to branch out into rumbas, sambas or swing, and the slow waltzes would be saved for last – for the benefit of those who had paired up – or if one hadn't, as an accompaniment to fetching one's wrap from the cloakroom. The hall was on the large side with plenty of room to encourage our creativity with dancing moves. I had sat a few out and perched at the bar before joining Howie and Clarissa, feeling the champagne, bought for me by Pete who had set up a tab for the group, ease all the stresses of the day. Molly circulated among the group at the bar, a glass in her hand. She had beaten me in the clothing stakes tonight. While I wore a simple floral cotton dress, albeit on the short side, dressed up with some jewellery and makeup, Molly seemed to have gone all out in a slinky black lame number with a deep decolletage. I vowed to try out this look at the next dance. Tonight, Molly did not lack for prospective partners but after all, one could only dance with one man at a time.

A sudden burst of noise, as a whirlwind might make on approach, assailed my ears. I read this diary entry over and over and stood at the door of the French windows, looking out over the garden. It was an early spring day in Southborough. Although the prevailing colours of nature were the soft browns and greens of winter, minute buds were just visible on the branches of trees and pushing their way through the earth, so recently rock hard with frosts. I slid open the door and let the cold February air mingle with the overheated stuffiness of the room, sniffing the damp earthy scents of an English garden. Pale sunshine lent the hope of spring and the newly formed buds seemed to respond with raised faces. A robin opened his throat in song, mingling with the cheeps of the sparrow. My mind had wandered, but I forced it back to that dance hall fifty years ago, the stifling heat of central Malaya, the band, my lithe young cotton-clad body. I looked down and read my notes.

Serenity and a certain sedateness had held sway until the entry of the Roaring Tin Dredger from Taiping. From that moment, I must admit, despite my reservations about men sweeping me off my feet, the most marvellous evening ensued. I danced practically every dance with George, the best-looking man I have ever known - tall, dark and very handsome, to vary a cliché. I had saved a picture of him – perhaps he would not have been thought as handsome today – he presented as too lean for modern tastes and the slicked down black hair went out of fashion a good twenty-five years ago. Although we had met before, I had not expected to see him again as he had told me he would be in volunteer's camp for two months, but, in answer to my queries, he told me that he had "escaped" from the confines of the camp, tedious in the extreme, to come over tonight. He had had a suspicion that I would be at the dance, he explained.

My first impressions mainly involved his directness – refreshing after the almost bumbling manner some of my male contemporaries went about their courtships. George went straight to the point in his pursuit, and I felt drawn to his unapologetic masculinity. How would one control a man like this? Yet, in spite of his lack of education beyond compulsory schooling, or culture, or perhaps because of these things, I felt attracted to him as someone deprived of air in the stifling social norms of the colony. He had much experience as a naval man, and had brought with him into that dance hall some of the danger of the high seas and the strength and energy needed to survive that environment. His voice emerged loud and booming, his manner uncompromising and as wide with largesse as the sails he had so often seen above. When we danced, I felt the hardness of his body and the control of his energy as he held me, perhaps a little too closely for a new acquaintance. But I did not care. Quite unlike me, I shouted my phone number into his ear. Perhaps it was the champagne or the *stingahs,* or perhaps it was the beginnings of a love affair.

I chuckled as I walked back into the dining room, where Janet had served my coffee. Mills and Boon could not write more cornily, I thought. I had better tone it down a bit when I tried to recapture how I felt that first night.

Yet I was still seeing "X" and the following evening it seemed almost as if the swimming club dance had never happened. I had stayed in, expecting him to call but he did not arrive.

"Much fuming and fretting. "Kamponged" and rained the next day. What, I wondered, would the poor potter do about his pots? But "X" came and everything in the garden was just fine".

Perhaps after all it proved fortuitous that I had met and renewed my acquaintance with George, as "X" fast faded out of the picture, perhaps miffed with my attention to George that Monday. Not to turn up until it became too late for anything reached, I thought, the height of bad manners, of which George, at least, could not be held responsible. What did these aristocrats learn from their nannies and public schools? While I puzzled, the answer came to me, and it halted me in my tracks as far from flattering. "X" expected a "night-cap" after his evening with friends, to whom he did not see fit to introduce me. But then, perhaps I only had myself to blame for his appraisal of my morals.

After the middle of March, I exclusively saw the Tin Dredger, but the affair of "X" took a long time to fade out. Each knew of the other's existence but with George it caused moods and tantrums, fuelled by liquor. "X" became, for a while, more ardent and conciliatory, so that I overlooked his occasional unreliability and almost began to reconsider continuing the relationship. One evening in early March I had intended to spend in meditation, hoping to clear my mind of confusion. I had felt fairly certain that I would be left in peace but "X" turned up at the door about seven when I had just changed into my oldest and most comfortable clothes. There never seemed a moment to myself.

"I was staying in to wash my hair tonight!" I greeted him – perhaps not the most welcoming. "I won't stay long," he said hastily, while Tam stood uncertain of whether to bring him in or not.

I looked furtively around outside and up and down the road, in fear and trepidation lest TD should enter on the scene. He had said something about dropping by later.

"I'm on my way to a dinner, but just wanted to bring you this," said "X". "A peace offering and an apology for the other night."

He sported a dinner jacket and black tie, his fair hair slicked down with a large amount of aromatic hair oil - as always immaculate, with accent and manners to match. He drew a large parcel from behind his back and gave it to me with a kiss on my hand and a small bow. Inside was a bouquet of the most exquisite pink orchids and a box of candied fruits. I had to ask him in and hope for the best.

"Come in for a drink," I offered, feeling I could do nothing less. He could really be a gem if he tried, which did not help the confused state of my mind at that time.

I had not completely forgiven him, but his charm almost defeated me in spite of myself. Class always won me over and I usually, probably naively, failed to see the faults which lay behind the façade. By the time George appeared two hours later, he had gone. That night, my intentions of a quiet evening during which I had hoped to recoup my energies vanished. We went for a drink at a certain hotel where I had the dubious honour of being the only woman present. We drank and danced until at least midnight – the alcohol masking my fatigue and the stimulation of George's presence and energy passing from him like an electric current.

But he knew about "X" through gossip. The colony in relative terms ranked as one of the smaller in the Empire and he had his spies out, sharing a bungalow in Taiping with two colleagues who had in turn their own spies. On the weekend of 15th March, although I had invited George to tea on the Saturday, I inexplicably (perhaps pleased that at last "X" did not appear averse to a public appearance) allowed "X" to take me to the swimming club dance, resulting in a fight with George - a "fight royal", as I described it in my diary, which raged all the next day, through a swimming pool engagement, tiffin with two acquaintances and Pahits at the Barrington's, mutual friends of both George and me. Again inexplicably, that evening I allowed "X" to take me to the "flicks". When we were in company with our friends, undoubtedly the fight took on a more passive character. The following day, George rang, a "changed character."

"Any time, the zenith of his passivity will be reached, I'm sure, and a reaction of beer swilling orgies will ensue. However, until that time comes, life is grand, absolutely grand!

On the 16th, I decided to terminate my Musical Comedy Act 1, and to close the Theatre, but owing to a previous promise, altered the whole course of my secret strength," I wrote, cryptic as the Times crossword. *"TD took me out and played a very clever act planning to finish our musical comedy pact. Under the deluge of self-inflicted liquor peace was maintained and another period of hectic virtuoso ensued."*

This had brought about the loveliest day I had spent in Malaya. We had been bound for Taiping, the work place of TD. In the evening just before sunset we had found Heaven in the form of a swimming pool. One climbed up a winding path of wooden steps bordered by shady trees with no idea of what was in store. Then quite suddenly there were two translucent pools fed by cascades of water from two waterfalls almost touching the sky. The pools were surrounded almost entirely by rocks covered by climbing plants and many varied types of trees. The waterfalls radiated a wonderful coolness and the pools were almost cold. I thought that this spot was almost too wonderful to describe and I shall never forget the effect it had on me.

But colonial Malaya was not all heaven, far from it. If I had had nothing to do but enjoy the privileges associated with the rulers, like the pampered wives of the administrators and petty officials, I might have imagined that as the extent of the status quo. My work kept my feet on the ground with glimpses of the underprivileged, the suppressed and the sick, both physically and mentally, the latter kept out of sight with the lepers as an affront to the delicate senses of the elite. I visited such a place that March. It had a balancing effect, much needed, to counteract the headiness and euphoria of realising that two men loved and wanted me. Of these, I never really considered "X" a lasting candidate, but as a means of encouraging George's ardour in the beginning, he proved invaluable.

On the Ipoh to Butterworth railway line lies the small town of Tanjung Rambutan in the Kinta district of Perak, famed still for its psychiatric hospital, the Ulu Kinta, the oldest in Malaya and opened in 1911. In my capacity of health visitor, I visited this hospital that March to carry out some basic examinations on the inmates. It seemed an acutely depressing place, apparently without hope. Few recovered enough to leave.

"We were given one small room, a pair of suicidal scales and an environment consisting of faces at the window who have lost face with this world."

I did not think the general atmosphere of the place conducive to recovery or that the authorities did anything to make the lives of these poor creatures bearable. I felt sad as I left this "arena of the dead" and thought how futile health work could be in certain parts of this beautiful island. I knew that the hospital had, at best, employed my services to assure the authorities that at least the inmates received basic care. I proceeded gently with the poor creatures as I assisted them onto the scales and set my stethoscope onto their bony chests. If they had a few moments of diversion through me and my team, I would have paid a small portion of my dues for my life in this world.

Later that day, feeling the need for fresh air and exercise, I went to golf, proud to use my new clubs accompanied by the smallest Tamil acting as a caddie. I saw him through a benign colonial's eyes - categorising, patronising. These Tamils, I thought then, have the most expressive mellow brown eyes and are especially lovable as children. This particular one asked me in very quaint Malay if he could be my caddie every time. Thereafter, as soon as he spotted me coming up the drive, he beat all the bigger caddies to it like a flash of grease lightening. I coughed as I played the course, though I ignored it and resolved to add a little ginger to my evening *stingah.*

In actual fact, my health began to cause me some concern. From babyhood, I had never attained robustness in physical health, always subject to chest infections. I had hoped that the tropical climate would have benefited this tendency but this did not occur. The long hours of work together with equally long hours of partying, late nights and early mornings, began to take their toll and I became prey to infection. My cough became progressively worse, so that by the end of the month, Howard had noticed it. One morning in clinic she asked me into her office.

"Lavinia dear," she began. "How are you settling in? Is everything alright at the bungalow now? Did Crown get another *amah* for you?"

"Yes indeed, Mary's replacement is exemplary, Howie, thank you!" I spoke breezily, but in the pit of my stomach an uneasy anxiety arose unbidden.

Would they, could they, send me home? I tried to suppress another cough but it exploded out of me while I produced a neatly pressed handkerchief to cover my face. I continued, while Howie paused.

"Rose does not provide me with the same diversions as Mary's rather colourful behaviour did," I paused and smiled, hoping to elicit a similar light-hearted response from Howard, who continued to look serious, "but she looks after me well. However," I added, foolishly as it turned out, "I'm hardly ever at home these days! My working and social life is so hectic!"

"Yes," went on Howie, and I knew that I had walked straight into it, not thinking. "Perhaps you may be overdoing it? I know you don't mind me noticing these things, Val. You are effectively under my care while you are here and I always make a point of looking after our sisters. I know you had a stringent medical exam in London but what is not realised is how demanding the work is here and how exhausting it is working in this heat day after day. Disease is rife in the *kampongs,* as you know, and tuberculosis is always a threat. We put ourselves at risk all the time."

She stopped for a moment and gave me a penetrating look.

"I feel that you would benefit from a thorough assessment and a short rest, Lavinia," she went on, while her words sank in. I felt a cold hand clutch at my heart. I was right, I thought. Heaven cannot go on forever, but I can pretend for a while.

"I have arranged for you to be admitted to Batu Gajah next week for some tests, and perhaps we can get to the bottom of what's causing that troublesome cough of yours. Don't worry, it's probably quite harmless. You will be on full pay, of course."

Howie stopped again, and smiled, while I assimilated her words and their possible consequences.

"All our best wishes go with you, Val. It's been a joy and privilege to have you among us and we all benefit from your experience in London. Get well and come back to us soon!"

I had lived and worked in the colony a little less than two months and I felt as if my life had ended. It felt hard to hide my disappointment, frustration and grief but I had to put a brave face on it. Perhaps, as Howie said, it would turn out as something harmless, but in my heart, I had a bad feeling about it. I decided not to mention it to my parents, who would be almost beside themselves with worry and so increase my burden. But it felt hard to make my letters sound as effervescent as usual for their sake and in so doing I felt like a fraud.

"The boyfriend is just as marvellous," I would gush. *" I'm always saying that, I know, but if only you could see him. If you've had all my letters, you will have heard all about him. As time goes on, I like him better than ever. The only thing is that he's so good looking everybody looks at him but luckily he isn't very conceited so it doesn't matter. At the moment he's very keen so I'm not worrying. It's so lovely to have someone who's fond of you and somebody you don't have to keep making excuses for all the time."*

As I wrote the trivia my eyes filled with tears - longing for the comfort they could give me and yet obstinate in my decision not to worry them.

"I'm glad you found your ring it's funny I told you I thought you

would. I'm sure the garden looks lovely it's such a very pretty garden I wish I could have had a snap of it perhaps you could send me one. Yes I think Reg is rather a problem. I hope the girl he marries knows about the asthma. I don't think it's fair not to tell her. I hope by the time you get this Christine will be better, let me know how she is."

A rogue teardrop splashed unbidden from my eye and onto the page as I wrote. It wouldn't show if I left it out to dry.

For only a few days after my chat with Howie, my test results had come back, fast-tracked through the hospital system. As the doctors showed me, on the X-Rays the lesions on my lungs appeared very obvious. They gave me a diagnosis of bacterial pulmonary tuberculosis and admitted me, without further ado, into the infectious diseases ward under the care of Dr Shelley.

Chapter 12

George's Malaya

There was no doubt about it, I thought. Meeting Val in early 1941 turned out to be one of the best things that had ever happened to me. Once we had met, everything seemed to progress very quickly. I have no pretensions about my life before the war as a marine engineer and once my marriage started to go wrong I just stopped caring about standards and morals. My life with Madge was a mistake from the start for which I blamed myself, probably wrongly, for tying myself up yet again to a particular type of woman. I really believe Madge hated men and many times I felt as a cockroach must feel, crushed beneath her elegant stiletto heel.

But Val was different, or was she?

The war had opened up many opportunities. Very early on, whilst on leave from my ship in 1940, I read a newspaper advertisement for tin dredgers in Taiping, Malaya, with a London-based agent. The wartime demand for tin was colossal, and the supply of experienced labour fast becoming short. The autumn of that year saw me ensconced in a bungalow with a couple of fellow workers employed by a company called Tekka Taiping as an engineer on a dredge. Tekka specialised in working the colossal dredging machines and we rotated shifts around the clock, so that the relentless production of the silvery metal never stopped, except for repairs. The work could be monotonous, but not hard, as long as one kept the coolies going and punished any misdemeanours promptly with the sack. On days off and weekends, I took myself off to Penang or Ipoh and enjoyed the social life of the colony, or the club. The nurses attached to Batu Gajah hospital near Ipoh could always be relied upon for a good time although if they lived in, a curfew usually operated which discouraged late hours.

I first met Val properly on the night of the Ipoh Swimming Club dance in February 1941. We had met briefly before and I liked what I had seen. The dance in February promised to provide the usual sort of entertainment with the same crowd, but new arrivals added some diversion and often excitement. I'd heard from Jock and Ian in the bungalow that the new nursing sister had taken up residence in town and felt curious to get to know her better, although I knew she probably lay well beyond my reach. There seemed no harm in looking though. I got there late – the syce maddeningly slow on the drive from Taiping, and when Pete and I walked into the Club it had already warmed up, the swing music blaring out from the gramophone to give the band a break. The dance floor had become crowded with couples enthusiastically trying out the latest moves. Others stood around in groups with drinks in their hands. Still more, mostly in an older age group, danced more sedately around the edges of the hall. I made my way to the bar and ordered a couple of *stingahs*, then looked around trying to see a familiar face. I didn't have to wait long. I downed the first drink in one, both refreshing in the sultry heat and calming. Several of the Tekka people were there and I found a group of acquaintances forming around me. The dance ended and the breathless and perspiring participants – those not waiting for the music to begin again, crowded to the bar. I recognised Dr Drew among the ex-dancers, whom I had consulted on the rare occasions when I'd suffered anything worse than a head cold, buying drinks for his wife and Sister Howard, both sitting at a side table. With them was the vivacious-looking young woman in a floral dress whom I recognised from before but looking, I thought, even better than I remembered.

The doctor saw me and raised his hand in recognition.

"Well sailor," he said, "it's not often we see you in Ipoh these days. What brings you here? Come over to our table when you've got a minute. I've got someone you must meet."

I downed my second *stingah* in five seconds, excused myself from the group and made my way across the dance floor. I fleetingly wondered at the doc's familiarity but then I had always got on with him well and we adopted a kind of bantering tone whenever we met, which professionally had not happened often, thankfully.

"My wife Clarissa you know - Margaret Howard (presenting the sister), "and I'd like you to meet Val Coates, our latest addition to the clinic. Val's taken over the health sister's post. This is the healthiest man in the colony, Val."

"George Powell," I enlightened the young woman in the floral dress who had risen to shake hands and stood before me. Her dress seemed on the short side, I now saw, showing white shapely legs in peep-toe shoes. She looked slender with a neat, curvy figure kept toned, I guessed, by years of tramping hospital wards. I took the white, warm hand she offered and held it gently, bowing slightly over it before looking into her eyes. In that split second, up close, I thought her rather pretty. A playful smile, promising fun but compassion, lit them and made them shine. "Delighted."

"Happy to meet you, Mr Powell," she said. "I can see you won't be calling at the clinic then."

Drew chuckled. "Sit down, Powell, join us for a few minutes. I will have to leave you all soon – serious case I will have to check on. Not been out long, first baby. You know the one, Val. But you enjoy yourselves."

As a miner, I felt a little out of my depth at first conversing with the health professionals but I reflected that the same rules of social hierarchy did not apply as at home. Wartime had acted as a great leveller too. After all, we fought in this together, in our various ways. The Drews and Howard enquired politely but with genuine interest about the tin workings at Tekka and my life on the dredge, while Val looked on, listened and spoke little. I noticed her intent gaze upon me. After a few minutes, the doctor took his leave, and the band struck up a foxtrot. I took the opportunity of asking Val to dance, and led her out to the dance floor. As we gave ourselves to the mood of the music and the dance, Val felt pliable in my arms, moving in perfect rhythm. She came up to my shoulder, and for the first time in many months, I felt as if I held something intrinsically valuable or precious.

One dance led into another and as we danced, Val became more and more vivacious. Once or twice I glanced over at our table and saw that Clarissa Drew and Margaret Howard had both found dance partners. I suggested sitting the next one out and having a drink at our now empty table, but Val insisted on just one more dance. Halfway through a swing routine, which I executed as well as I could, she surprised me by pulling down my head and kissing me full on the lips. I guess, I thought, that one never knew what women were going to do and she had seemed demure. I can't remember exactly how I responded - I think I was too bemused, but shortly after that the announcement for the last dance came over the microphone and we were again caught up in the rhythm of the slow waltz, gliding through the remaining couples on the floor.

In the general bustle, with the band packing up and the dancers standing around in clusters taking their leave of friends or retrieving coats and wraps from the cloakroom, I glanced around for my acquaintances and found most of them had gone. I helped Val into her wrap, even though the night was close, and asked if I could take her home, then stood by the car at the bottom of the steps with the chauffeur Kempy and waited. I remember vividly the tropical night, the call of the nightjars and the scents of jasmine and flowering tobacco plant heavy in the air. The steps of the club rose before me, and I could see Val at the top in her white silk wrap, talking to a group of friends. I know that several thoughts went through my mind at that moment.

"She looks about thirty," a small voice inside my head went, "quite a nice height - she talks nice and is just the sort of person I've always wanted to meet. But I suppose she is above me and I've not got a chance, for I'm only a miner, not a planter and my salary is just over three hundred, I'm married and it's no good."

Ten minutes later, we drew up outside Val's Windsor Road bungalow. The lights still shone out from within and as we watched, her boy emerged and came down to the car to see her in.

"Call me," Val whispered as she turned to go inside. "Ipoh 437".

I turned back to my syce. The two-hour drive back to Taiping lay ahead of us and as we drove along the darkened and deserted roads, I reflected on the evening and the significance of Val's behaviour. I had no doubt that I would see her again and soon. The relatively small British population in Malaya made it difficult to avoid people, even if one wanted to. Although, being many miles from Blighty and wartime to boot, one had licence to behave with greater freedom than one would within the class-bound constraints of home, I had retained enough social awareness to know that Val, as a middle-class girl, seemed determined to let her hair down and enjoy herself. I wondered when and how I should come to know the real Val.

I must have dozed to the drone of the Ford sedan car and the seemingly endless road winding through rubber trees either side which, grey in the yellow headlights, loomed eerily as we passed through. When I awoke, we had come close to the Tekka bungalows on the outskirts of Taiping. I saw an electric light still burning dimly in the third one from the left. Boy must have left it on for me and retired to his quarters. Looking at my watch I saw with surprise that it was nearly one o'clock but fortunately I did not have to report to the dredge until the afternoon for the late shift.

I did meet Val after that as often as our demanding schedules and distance allowed. Val seemed to prefer the safety of the crowd around us at first and I concurred, though I knew she held me at arm's length.

She also saw one or two other men. One of these I knew of as a rich man, an aristocrat who, I found out, nominally worked for the Civil Service but in practice had many free hours to pursue his fancies, including Val. I realised that in her capacity, from her earliest days in the colony, introductions to the cream of colonial society would be performed. This would have included the Governor's circle and the Murray Ainsleys, who held frequent soirees in their spacious bungalows. Part of me felt proud that a girl who had noticed me was so well connected wherever she went, while another, negative side told me that I was a fool, that even if we married, I would forever feel her inferior. But these were early days for me to feel jealous about rival suitors, and in any event, I knew that an unknown, primitive force would compel me to continue the chase.

On most weekends throughout February and March 1941, I travelled down to the Ipoh bungalow, on some occasions narrowly missing the aristocrat, as I later found out from my spies in the Tekka industry via the efficient colonial grapevine. Val seemed to have an insatiable appetite for the hedonistic life of work and pleasure in the society known as British Malaya and had thrown herself into it, making up for lost, dreary wartime years at home. I patiently waited. Val's irrepressible, bubbly personality, intelligence and quick repartee made her rewarding as well as great fun to be with, and I quickly realised that a treasure lay within my reach. Her awareness about world events pertaining to the war particularly, put her well beyond the kind of woman I had known hitherto, and I relished the experience. For the first time for many years, I began to dream of a bright future, one that for a change did not threaten to drown me in a morass of unbridled decadence.

Day to day life undoubtedly became enriched by her society, and we went to dances, took picnics, visited temples and swam in the glorious natural pools of the Ipoh and Taiping swimming clubs. She loved mixing with the crowd, and over the weeks we gained more acceptance as a couple. I entered into her world more than the reverse, although my fellow workers or housemates occasionally accompanied me to an evening do. Sometimes she came up to the bungalow for tea, travelling by train, with Jock and Ian tactfully making themselves scarce, and this gave Boy a chance to show off his culinary skills, of which he had become inordinately proud. To his immense gratification, Val praised his efforts even to his satisfaction, ate everything including his best cucumber sandwiches and was altogether a perfect guest. He grinned from ear to ear and asked continually when Miss would grace us with her presence again, as he wanted to make her a Battenburg cake.

It happened that on one of these visits around the middle of March Val became more than a friend. True, we had kissed, but there was seldom an opportunity for privacy among friends. Perhaps Val engineered it that way, but I had begun to think that I had thought wrongly in my initial assessment of her character. Perhaps she really was as demure as she had appeared the first night before the kiss.

That night lingered long in my memory.

I thought she would get the train back to Ipoh after we'd been to the club but it got late and we returned to the bungalow for a night cap. We were both a little tight, and for the first time, when I kissed her, I felt her body relax completely, so that when I lifted her in my arms and carried her to my bed, she was utterly compliant. I later wrote to her.

"You were so small darling laying in my arms, and although you were a teeny-weeny bit tight, you were still a little bit shy and when I looked at you, you lowered your eyes. It was a wonderful feeling holding you like I would my own daughter – I think that picture will live in my memory forever. Yes I undressed you and put your pyjamas on – unknown to me you had brought them – a pretty pink silky pair, and I couldn't help looking at your white body, such a small flat tummy, small breasts – the loveliest I've ever seen and what I've always heard talked of and read about – they were pink, the first time I've ever seen anything so sweetly pretty. Please darling don't say I'm unkind to remind you of that night because I live for that and all my hopes are that one day I shall be able to say it's all mine."

I used to get so wrapped up in what I wrote to her that I felt I relived these scenes, and began to perspire and shake, so that I'd have to get up and walk around the room, listening to the radio. Our letters, which by the beginning of April passed between us daily, became the only thing that kept me going. I have never been secretive, and I poured myself and my feelings out: thoughts, dreams and hopes, while Val's letters still seemed full of social chat about mutual acquaintances and her family at home, struggling in the early years of the war. I had only taken her out for a couple of months and I don't know what I expected but I am not a patient man and wanted her for my own.

But the microcosm that called itself British Malaya remained a small, inward-looking society and gossip spread up through its tendrils from Ipoh to Taiping and back again as I wondered if she knew what she did. She had been seen hitting the high spots but I reasoned that no promises had passed between us and she remained free to enjoy herself. Heaven knows, it would not be for long if I had anything to do with it. Although even now we had become accepted as a couple, Val seemed disconcertingly determined to lead her own life, writing of starting a home nursing class for the local women while I on the other hand wrote to her of my plans after the war to enable me to support a wife and family.

"I have to keep dredging, here, or Siam, South China, Australia, South America, Philippines or South Africa. If I remain in steam 3 years I can sit for a ticket to run a dredge, but that only counts in Malaya, anyway Val, you can see what I am up against after this war. Why do I tell you this? Because you have only known me a short time and have more than once proved you are happy with me, you have never said you loved me, it's true, but you have said if I were free you would marry me, which is, and does, mean something, so I have told you my future as far ahead as I can see..."

If I had a spare twenty-four hours or so at the weekend, I grabbed my syce and motored down to Ipoh as if my life depended on it. On these occasions we hired a room at the rest house, away from the curious eyes of Val's boy and amah, where we could relax as ourselves and do as we pleased. If Val faked her feelings she could have fooled anyone, and at these times, holding her sweet body, I felt as strong as a lion, yet afterwards shaken as if I had poured out the very essence of my soul.

After one such meeting I left it so late for the return journey, I had to get the syce to put his foot down hard so that I would not be late for my night shift. I made it on time with the syce doing just on fifty all the way.

"Val darling my hand is not very steady sweetheart - I wrote the next day. I cannot make it out as I didn't drink a lot over the weekend as you know, but my nerves are a bit jumpy and I think I know the reason why, don't you? I came back full of beans roaring like a lion, ready to sack my "Boy" and half the crew on the dredge."

After that, I talked shop in my letter for several pages, even though I knew it bored Val, but I wanted her to know every moment of my life and live it with me. Her return letter to me caused me to worry but her evasiveness disturbed me more. Her letter told me that she had to go into hospital, but not the reason, and I could not understand why she was being so cagey. I started to panic. Had I hurt her in some way in my passionate need for her? She had not complained at the time but had seemed to welcome me to her, which only made me lose control more.

Val had told me that she had had an X-ray a couple of weeks back, but selfishly, in my all-absorbing obsession, I had forgotten about it. Now she was telling me that her admission had nothing to do with this but did not enlighten me further. I felt puzzled and worried but at breakfast, Jock said something that made me think that Val had not fully opened up to me about her illness. I began the conversation by saying that I hoped to get a letter from Mrs Powell today, and Jock answered, "Yes, I suppose you should, it's two days since you saw her." I enjoyed my breakfast up to a point, until he said, "When did your young lady start to get ill?" and I without thinking said, "Oh, about Tuesday." He replied that it didn't stop her going out with her boyfriend on Wednesday night.

Jock's words, though well meaning, came as a profound shock and immediately, the food tasted like bitter acid in my mouth and I had difficulty swallowing my food through sudden nausea. I felt as if my world crumbled around me but I managed to reply to him that Val was free and could please herself who she went out with, or when she went out, saying that I did not expect her to sit in a bungalow all by herself. Jock replied, "You do, don't you, and what's good for one should be good for two, in a case like yours, anyway."

Jock's warning words had undeniably cooled me and had a sobering influence, but perhaps it had been for the best. I did not let on to Val that I knew of the others but it made me want to be more cautious. I thought of the risk we took every time we lay together, although we had exercised due care so far – but I knew that it had come very close several times, and Val risked her career, reputation and disownment from her family. I knew too that my conscience would ensure that I would have to support her and her child if anything happened.

But Val lay in hospital, her delicate body succumbing to her own demands from it, all too soon. The most information I managed to get from her for some time concerned a persistent cough, but I was no fool and knew that this did not amount to sufficient reason to keep her there. By the beginning of April everything still stayed uncertain. I felt that if only I could get down to Batu Gajah, I would learn more, but for now I could only keep going to work every day (I worked a run of nights at this time) and write to her in spite of the difficulties caused by the vibrations of the dredge. I kept my letters positive, trying to keep up her spirits. I did not know what she might face down there in the hospital and I felt protective.

"One of these days I want to bring you on board the dredge and show you this table, and how hard it is to write, then you will see what a good fellow I am to try and keep my promise... I do hope you will under-

stand sweet, and not say I was a little tight when I wrote to you... Gee, sweet, it's hot, and I'm sweating like blazes, as a matter of fact I'm sitting 3 feet above the main engines and the time is ten minutes after midnight - you are asleep I suppose – how I'd love to sneak into the hospital and see you, you could rest your head on my chest and go to sleep and I would cuddle you close all night. Darling, I don't like to talk shop but I'll have to walk round now as I've got 3 men short, a greaser, bucket cooly and a fireman, so I've got to be everywhere tonight, but I'll be back in a few minutes. It's so hard to write and at the same time keep an eye on these fools.....Val what do you think will happen, will you have to leave the country, go home, a month's holiday with an examination after it, or will you be able to go back to your work, I sincerely hope you will darling because I want to take my leave when you do, so try hard to make a complete recovery and when we leave the country we leave it for good.... Val, I have never asked you before, but is there a man at home you are in love with, or anywhere in the world, if so, please tell me darling, don't let me keep telling you of my love if it makes you unhappy......I have a window open behind me, and as I look out I can see No 2 dredge headlight about a mile away over the trees and bushes, I wonder what Jock is doing, reading or writing I suppose.... "

Although Val in her letters remained inexplicit about her illness, I knew after a few weeks that her recovery would not be rapid. She described the investigations she had undergone and I wrote back in a chiding tone, jealous of the doctor who examined her chest. I knew that Val would not take me seriously and I also knew that she put a brave face on it not only to keep the truth from me to stop me worrying too much, but also because she felt less of a woman than others and not fit for marriage. I did not care. To me, Val remained, as I knew when I first met her, more special and different from other women I had known, even her contemporaries. In spite of her lack of robustness, she possessed spirit and intelligence in compensation. I made up my mind, observing her courage, that I too, would play my part and contribute to building an unshaken love between us.

"Val," I wrote, *"If you want any shopping done and you can wait a*

little while tell me what it is, I can most probably get it in Taiping, you know I'm not fussy and I don't care a damn who knows, I'd just as soon walk into a shop and buy a pair of knickers, stockings, or brazier as a packet of cigarettes. Don't blush, darling, its true, and what's more I'd love doing it after all, who's belongings do they cover and am I proud of them? I'll tell the world you're a lovely little bundle of love, just enough to fill my arms and heart, and I've no room left after that."

Yet I yearned for her to attain full health once more - working, paying me visits in Taiping, planning with me our future together and me watching her busy at some ordinary task in the bungalow with her customary quickness and deftness.

"I've never told you before, but I do love the way you walk, so upright, and such a short snappy step, as if you're going someplace all the time and cannot linger. That's something you didn't know sweetheart, isn't it, that a little thing like that was a joy to me, well Val I cannot explain the feeling but I watch you and it brings back my old yearning for a nurse or sister, so clean, upright and smart, it's a thing I love, and puts other women in the shade with all their beauty... I went up to the swimming club yesterday morning just to pay a cheque in and I thought of every step up with you and I looked up at the top of the chute and at a certain table in the corner and I must say, I bit my bottom lip very hard."

More than once though, Val's letters from the hospital threw me into fits of morbidity so that I felt convinced that she wanted to end our affair. Living for her letters, I existed from one letter to the next imagining a future without her. In the middle of May I heard on the radio an announcement asking for seamen to bring our ships from America and started yearning for an escape, from the tedium of life on the dredge, and for the freedom of the seas, to prove my worth at sea as a sailor – so that I could say to my future child, if he or she should ask me what I did in the war, that I made a real contribution, and not "mining tin". I don't know whether I did it to frighten Val but sometimes I behaved as perversely brutal to her as I did to my coolies, swearing at the poor devils who didn't understand English and threatening to break their necks. I put these fits of morbidity down to frustration at the long absences from Val, worry about the course of the war and our future. I longed for action of some kind and decided to begin divorce proceedings from Madge, so that whatever the outcome of our affair, I would at least become free of a past burden.

At last, on a weekend at the end of May, Val had permission to spend a weekend away from hospital, and our customary Ipoh rest house witnessed our reunion, details of which made me blush to recall, but nevertheless, in spite of Val's illness, renewed our passion for each other. On my return to Taiping, I found among the letters waiting for me one from my London solicitors which I sent to Val for her approval.

"I hope you like the solicitor's letter," I wrote immediately to Val, *"it is very plain, and to the point I think, and I am sure you will see it as I have, so Mrs Powell hurry and get better and don't worry your sweet self about anything. I do hope that your next X-Ray will show an improvement darling, also that you will soon be on your holiday.....darling, please do not be angry, but it was nice to come home and have some really nice food, cooked by my "Boy" just how I like it, at the same time I could have eaten rest house food forever as long as I could see you, sweetheart."*

I knew we were in for a long haul to get where we wanted. Divorce constituted only the first step. After that I would become free to remarry, but this in turn raised many more questions that I did not want to face just then. I had set in motion a course of action that I had no idea where it would lead. And I in turn had no idea that in reality we had no control over cosmic events, try as we might. The futility of the actions of we insignificant creatures would in the end come clear, but I was still compelled to fulfil whatever destiny the gods ordained.

Chapter 13

Weak Flesh

I awoke and lay with closed eyes, allowing the morning sounds of the hospital to intrude on my consciousness, still half dreaming. My dream had become a nightmare, and in it some faceless person had taken me somewhere sinister against my will, only I did not feel ready – I did not have something and they hurried me. I tried to reorient myself but the atmosphere of the dream lingered. Reality, I appreciated, after emerging from the abyss, felt normal, dull, but blessed, if anything could be so in a place so foreign to an Englishwoman as Malaya. Over the months it had indeed become normal to me, its sounds, scents, customs and heat slowly replacing the familiarity of home.

I made a rapid physical assessment of myself. Over the preceding months I had lost the weight typical of tuberculosis and the unyielding hospital issue mattress pressed against my protruding hip bones. I felt a new affinity with patients enduring weeks of strict bedrest, as I now had, under the care of Dr Shelley. The left side of my chest was painful too, after the doctors had performed the procedure to collapse the lung. This would allow the affected organ to rest and hopefully heal, but it was a lengthy process and that brought its own problems. Nature refused to be hurried or deviated – one could only provide the most favourable conditions, and in the case of my illness, I had had to confront my own limits, having forced my never-robust body for too long to obey my will. But even though my strength had ebbed even further during the weeks of inactivity, I felt desperately disappointed and angry in my helplessness.

Painfully, I eased myself into a sitting position just as, after a cursory knock, one of the isolation ward sisters, her hair pulled back severely under the confines of her cap, put her head round the door of my room. Her lips formed into a smile, but her eyes remained as cold and grey as the English Channel. Since my arrival at Batu Gajah Hospital three weeks ago, the European nurses had treated me with a strict correctness in protocol and a deference to my status as Health Sister, but a certain distance. This now seemed evident with Sister Williams as, seeing me awake and struggling, wished me a cheerful "good morning, Sister" and, bustling into the room, proceeded to adjust my pillows. With her large, compact body leaning over me in its grey-blue sister's uniform, I caught her faint aroma of scented talcum powder. I felt sure that I cannot have smelled as good, as even baths were forbidden in the doctors' ruling of complete rest.

"Now Dr Shelley has just started making his round, Sister," she informed me. "I'll have your breakfast brought in. Doctor said he wanted to see you today to let you know the results of your Xray."

I felt a faint twinge of excitement. Depending on the results, and my progress, I could be allowed up for short periods every day, which would be gradually increased. As Sister Williams bustled out of the room and I waited for the appearance of both doctor and breakfast tray, I automatically turned my head towards the light of the French windows, parallel to my bed. These gave me access to the balcony which stretched continuously around the upper floor of the European hospital but up until now I had only been able to gaze longingly at the outside world. With the curtains drawn back and the doors standing partially open for coolness leaving only the fly screens in place, sun streamed into the room, its rays covering part of the counterpane. The curtains fluttered in a slight breeze. I could see the ornate wooden cream-painted rails of the balcony and beyond that, the tops of the taller palm trees in the grounds of the hospital against a cloudless sky. Lying here week after week I had become accustomed to the various sounds of a busy hospital, both inside and out. Now, for the time being, there came a lull, and as I had often done lately, lying here, I gave my thoughts and memories free rein.

I was my father's daughter. Percy Coates was a practical, no-nonsense businessman with a calculating mind and good head for maths, who had made all the right moves at the right time. He had succeeded in helping to build up the best leather goods factory in the Home Counties, even though some might say that he had had a good start with his family background. This had undoubtedly helped to set him up in the beginning, but he had kept the momentum going with a strong Puritan work ethic. He had passed on his values to me and Tommy. During my school days at the Tonbridge "County School" in those momentous years of the early 1920's, my contemporaries, the middle-class, exuberant daughters of the local bourgeoisie who "owned" the town, had ragged me as a "bluestocking". I considered the epithet rather misplaced, as I thought of myself as neither over-serious nor particularly intellectual, but I had a head for figures and facts and a reliable memory which proved useful for exams, at which I excelled. Quite often, when I allowed myself, I was just one of the girls, finding everything hysterically funny and dashing round the town and countryside on my bicycle. We were the first generation of girls able to experience the comparative freedom for women which had come with the Great War, the natural vivacity of youth amplified by the hope and promise of the generation. Our parents, subdued by the horrors they had experienced only a few years before, let us go, perhaps through a fond indulgence, seeing us live the youth they had sacrificed, or perhaps because they felt powerless to control an unstoppable force.

At twenty-two, I had entered nursing, not because of any altruistic notions of doing good – considered a natural attribute for young women in any case - but because I had a competent, retentive, organ-ised mind and a personable and discreet demeanour. I had, indeed, no trouble getting a place at St Stephen's Hospital in London in the autumn of 1930 on my excellent School Certificate grades, especially in biology. By the 1920's, girls from our social background were expected to work at a useful career even though the choices had remained limited for them, unlike their brothers, who were only limited by themselves. I knew, although I had not admitted this to myself, that I had always in my heart resented the pride my parents had in Tommy and his academic prowess. He lived without, as he would have continued to do had he lived, restraints similar to those I faced, and free to pursue a professional life without the responsibili-ties and expectations incumbent on me, particularly with regard to my parents and their circle. Without doubt, I loved my parents dearly, but this only served to entrap me more. Their hold on me showed through my ingrained sense of duty and love and through them, to their wider social circle which encompassed all I had ever known, and which held me even now, so far away. I knew that I did not have long, that my escape could not last forever and that I would have to go home soon. Poor dear Mother's letters had become increas-ingly explicit in her need for me and often held a pleading quality, asking me outright when I would come home. And Father – never, as I wrote to him, had the two of us exchanged so many letters in the thirty-odd years I had been on this earth, and although I knew I must seem a poor substitute for Tommy, for a man whose emotions made as difficult reading as Percy Coates, I had felt his love through his letters more than any other time.

Duger always said that I kept my feelings under too tight a control and never let myself be swept away by desire or inclination and that in this way I denied myself the pinnacles of excitement and pleasure which she had known and wanted me to know too. Certainly, in the past I had kept my head around men, even though I enjoyed their company, but until meeting George, although I could no longer claim the category of young girl, I had not seriously thought of marriage or children. Perhaps my job compensated me in part for that – I had qualified in midwifery early on in my career and had seen a plethora of babies in my time which I adored – and still did as Health Sister – and now George accused me in his letters of controlling myself too much – but perhaps it had become a part of me now and too late to address.

A rattle of crockery heralded the arrival of the breakfast trolley in the corridor, and a young Malay nurse appeared, carrying a large tray. Behind her, a tawny head topped a white coat, and, hastening to open the door wider to accommodate the nurse, Dr Shelley came through ahead of her to my bedside, thoughtfully placing the bed table in front of me. Shelley, a thin, energetic man with Caledonian good looks, a British doctor in his forties and an infectious disease consultant specialising in pulmonology, spared himself nothing for his patients. I felt fortunate indeed to have secured his services, as during the seven years he had looked after the Europeans in Batu Gajah, his reputation had placed him among the best doctors in Malaya. He had become a pioneer of one of the most advanced treatments for pulmonary tuberculosis. Now, he took an Xray plate from its cover and held it up against the light to show me. The nurse, having deposited the tray on the table, had quietly left the room.

"Well Val, I think we've got it."

I let out a little squeal of pleasure as I followed the doctor's perusal of the plate. Even from a distance of a few feet away, I could see that there was a marked lessening of the infiltrates visible a few weeks ago. The doctor's prescription of complete rest, good food and fresh air was working. Shelley smiled at my obvious pleasure.

"We'll be continuing the air treatment for a while yet. It's early days, but I'm proud of you, Val. It's not only we doctors who can take all the credit, if patients don't play their part. As a special reward, you can get up and sit in your chair for two hours in the mornings, otherwise carry on the good work. By the way, how's that sailor of yours?" he teased, in his good- humoured way. "I thought I saw him walking up the hill just now."

I felt a little startled. It seemed very early in the day for George to visit and yesterday's letter had said nothing about making the journey from Taiping over this weekend – but giving surprises formed part of his personality. I wished, though, I had had a little time to prepare myself, both physically and mentally. I felt only too conscious of my invalid status where George was concerned and that I did not look my best. Involuntarily, even though the early morning temperature was over eighty degrees, I pulled on my wrap to disguise my thin arms and smoothed back my hair.

A hearty male voice from the main ward area down the corridor carried through the open door as Dr Shelley took his leave. George had become acquainted with many of the hospital's senior European nursing staff as part of the colony's social structure, and chaffed and joked with them whenever he saw them. Through his good looks and easy, charming manner, he enjoyed general social popularity and acceptance, particularly among women, as they felt cheered by his reassuring masculinity. His confidence in his maleness measured against his peers reinforced these qualities. He had laughed with me when, before I had come to know him well, I had coined a description of him, "The Roaring Tin Dredger of Taiping" which suited his social style to a T. Only when I knew him better, did I see the reverse side of the man – one might almost have said the feminine side – uncertain, self-critical and slightly lost. But now, as he appeared in the doorway, grinning at me like a mischievous schoolboy, whatever social graces he may have lacked, I felt almost overwhelmed by his physical presence and beauty.

"Val, darling, how are you?"

George came into the room, bent down over the bed to kiss me (perhaps riskily but he would not have cared) on the lips and pulled up a chair to the bedside before I could catch my breath. A pomaded lock of black hair came down over his brow as he bent over me, and I could feel the coarse bristles on his chin and smelled the faint scent of soap, hair oil and sweat which characterised him. He took my hand and held it tightly in his own. I could feel the callouses on his palms, testimony to his manual work on the dredge.

"George, how wonderful to see you, but it's such a surprise!"

"Yes darling, I know, and I'm sorry if I startled you. I only knew at the last minute and wanted to surprise you. They're dismantling the boiler on Number 1 dredge over the weekend and I've got a furlough. I came down with Jock and stayed at the Rest House last night but I wanted to come in early to make the most of our time together. You're looking better, Sweet. What did Shelley say?"

"Marvellous news, George! The X-rays show an improvement and I can get up this morning. Here, do you want a slice of toast? They must think they're feeding an army!"

"Absolutely not, I insist you eat every scrap yourself. No getting up until you've eaten all your breakfast, then I will help you, darling."

"I think they're taking me for a bath first, George and they'll probably make you wait outside until I'm ready. We're not married yet, dear!"

"We would be if I had my way," answered George soberly. "You're my wife in all but deed, Mrs Powell."

I changed the subject, thinking over the impediments which stood in the way of our marriage. George had recently written to his solicitors, Banks and Braithwaite, or "B&B" as he liked to call them, to start the divorce process from Madge on the grounds of her adultery, although as they both knew, George could not claim complete innocence. But he always insisted that he had remained faithful until her behaviour with other men had forced him to concede that their marriage had failed. It had depressed him beyond measure, he told her, and this had revealed to her that vulnerable side to his character which his bluff, easy manner kept well hidden.

I turned to the topic which, indirectly, was the cause of the delays in communication and hence the delay to the progress of the divorce – the war, which lengthened the time it took to receive letters from England to weeks, sometimes months. News of the war depended on the often-inaccurate broadcasts from Radio Malaya and the newspapers which frequently did not appear in the hospital for days. I diligently followed the progress of the European situation and took press cuttings of amusing snippets of Malayan life. Sometimes the antics of the various races of indigenous Malays provoked hilarity and I saved the stories of their civil court cases - of love affairs or minor misdemeanours (often conducted by Judge Murray Ainsley and so of particular interest to me) and the trivial gossip of Malayan social life. It acted as light relief from war news, which at the moment had become dominated by the German campaign in Russia.

"George dear, have you heard anything more about your next camp?"

George took part in weekend military camps and manoeuvres as an army volunteer. The part- time soldiers, besides preparing to face the Japanese Imperial Army on the Thai border and practising various military exercises, drills and weapons training, spent a good part of their time hunting down the night life and taking the opportunity to spend most of the night drinking in local bars. Although the British acknowledged the threat of invasion, especially as they understood that Japan had particular interests in Malaya's tin and rubber reserves, the confidence in the strength of our defences against the enemy, both in Singapore and on the Thai border, remained all-encompassing. British society in Malaya remained complacent in their supreme superiority.

"No darling, but I expect to, shortly. Honestly, Val, I resent having to spend a whole weekend at camp drilling with a lot of half-wits when I'd much rather come down to see you. Let's not talk about all that. It's more important to get you back on your feet."

As I had finished what breakfast I could manage with my delicate appetite these days, he took the tray from me and moved the bed table away, preparatory to my getting out of bed.

"Now," he continued, "we have to get you up, my beauty. Where's that girl?"

George went off down the corridor, shouting "nurse!" in booming tones. Having reassured the sisters and nurses who responded in alarm that no immediate emergency threatened but that Sister Coates would like to have her bath, the little Malay nurse in her white dress and cap followed him back to the room. He remained to oversee my first unsteady steps from the bed into the bathroom, then went back into the ward. With the doctors' rounds in full swing, he found nobody there to pass the time with, so started down the stairs to the gardens.

The enforced rest occasioned by my illness provided the time needed to focus on my relationship with George. As the weeks passed and I grew gradually stronger, I graduated from spending all my time in my room to daily walks in the lovely grounds of Batu Gajah, where I sat with my letters and diary in a shady alcove and wrote my daily missive to George. Tensions had emerged between us which were evident before my illness from time to time but I had laughed them off. My attention had then been divided between my emotionally absorbing work and a hectic social life and I had fooled myself into thinking that George really didn't matter to me as much as I liked to think I mattered to him. At least it now seemed that way. I wrote to my mother about it and told her not to pin too many hopes on our romance.

Like many sailors, George liked his drink and had once written to me that as our first meeting had been conducted through the rosy glow of alcohol, it only seemed right that subsequent meetings should have the same enhancement, which explained our usual downing of a few *stingahs* at the Club before (depending on whether we were in Taiping or Ipoh) he took me home - to the Ipoh Rest House or to his bungalow. As a precursor to passion and a celebration of it, this seemed all well and good, but on other occasions when either alone or with his colleagues, he had the inclination to drink for reasons unknown to me, which resulted in what he termed "morbid" moods. Although not usually with him at these times, I received the brunt of them through his letters. Several times during the course of our affair he wrote of calling the whole thing off, which hurt me dreadfully, but I forced calmness on myself and waited for his next letter, which had invariably returned to portraying his old optimistic self and felt beyond wonderful. One of his darker missives seemed sparked by worry about the cost of my treatment going into the future.

On the down times, only my self-discipline allowed me to concentrate on anything else but my pain and grief, but I continued my war diary, cut clippings and wrote to my parents in the same cheerful vein as ever, keeping my illness secret from them. I don't think George realised that he had become an unconscious manipulator of my heart and mind. He possessed a naturally exuberant, energetic personality with a fertile brain and ideas constantly occurred to him, filling him with excitement about particular projects about which he wrote to me passionately, hoping to convince me of the feasibility of his schemes. One of these materialised as a manuscript of a short book entitled *"The Sea Tramp"* – not autobiographical but a seafaring fictional story full of fantastic characters encountered in foreign lands and on the high seas drawn from his naval experiences which I offered to type for him. This kept him occupied for several weeks. I kept the manuscript and still have it somewhere among my things... I have it now, seeming even more fantastic and out of place in the relentless gloom and monotony of England.

George's abounding energies often drove his impulses, and I could see that being a frequent attendant at my bedside became very trying for him, although he stoically and sweetly endured his role of honorary family member in the absence of my folks. They remained in blissful ignorance of my illness and even had they known, could not have done anything. I knew that my mother, particularly, would have become ill with worry, giving my father more to cope with than he already had. I had fabricated, in answer to their questions about my job, some concoction that it continued much the same as before but that I was unable to say much about it as many government posts existed anonymously these days. In so satisfying them by adding a mystique which lent a certain amount of glamour to my job, I kept calm myself and concentrated on my recovery and keeping George happy. At first, I could not do much except return his kisses, when I was no longer infectious, and try to look as cheerful as I could. Later, he wrote to me that he could not have endured it if I had had to return to bed. If we ever parted, he said, he would always remember me -

"I did not put much faith in you at first, you were just another woman and to me all women were the same – when you were ill it struck me how much you meant to me – yes I may marry, but I should always see your face before me, hear your cough that seemed to choke me, your face pale and your little thin arms, but always a smile on your lips –"

Surely, I thought, because this seemed the roughest affair I have ever experienced, it must amount to true love. What did "love" mean, then? I did not feel the same control I had felt with the others, and yet George had often complained that I put up a barrier between us. Did I fear loving him? he asked. I had no awareness of any barrier, only perhaps, a kernel of doubt amid the euphoria, when sometimes I wondered about my identity or what I did here, that small feeling of drowning or suffocation in his all-consuming sexual power. As for my own desire, it battled against that stern presence that prevailed, always watching, always seeing, a merging of God and Miss Barden my form teacher in a tweed skirt - conditioning for a nice girl born in the time of Edward VII which I had learned too well.

By mid-August, I was allowed out of the hospital for the day, but always under strict curfew. It took me a while before I could build up the courage to travel up to Taiping on the train, so most weekends George travelled down. The first time I walked out of those hospital gates into the world again with George beside me I could have shouted for joy. We got a car from the gatekeeper's lodge, drove into Ipoh and went shopping – bliss, as it enabled me to buy the personal things I needed. George was a dear – he was not at all embarrassed by my purchases and claimed that he would have been just as happy to walk into a ladies' underwear shop and buy a brassiere for me. I laughed and kissed him openly while the shopkeeper tied up my parcel with string and brown paper. Later, when I got tired, we went to the club and had lunch, then repaired to the Rest House, where, on procuring a room for the afternoon, George wanted me to try on my recent purchase "for size" but I laughed again and drew him into my arms, feeling his hard body under the cotton twill shirt close to mine. I relived this day later as one of our happiest. They were not always so.

When we could not meet, letters passed between us daily. Occasionally, George could not get away because of extra shifts on the dredge or through hastily organised camps or parades. These seemed to increase as the year went on. Several times, George could not account for his time (and I did not press him to). Later I received a very contrite letter from him and a confession of infidelity. The bungalow he shared, owned by Crown Agents, stood next door to some lived in by Europeans – families, the heads of which worked in rubber or tin, or held administrative posts. The eighteen-year-old daughter of one of these families by the name of Webster, had been attending boarding school in England but had returned home temporarily, pending her dispatch to "finish" her education at an elite Swiss school, where in any case, in spite of the expense, her father considered it advisable to have her out of harm's way. Gladys had grown a pretty child with an already voluptuous body, which she liked to show off in the new short skirts and shaped blouses of the of the season. Contrary to her father's wishes, the naughty girl applied her make up in the telephone box down the road prior to shopping trips or tea dances and such like in Taiping, where she had got to know some young people of her own age through the "network".

George had first encountered Gladys when coming back from telephoning me in the Club late one evening, and thinking that the young European girl wandered the streets too late alone, approached her and (as he later told me) asked her if she needed assistance to find her way home. He headed, he had said, towards the Tekka bungalows and could walk with her. According to George, Gladys had led him on from the start and as he constantly missed me, after an initial attempt at propriety he could not resist. She showed no objection to him accompanying her that night. He realised that he had seen her around the neighbourhood but because of his frequent morose moods, had paid no attention. They had chatted and he had found her mature beyond her years. Already, he knew, with the instincts of the sailor and man of the world, that she had learned many of the arts of flirtation and was far from innocent.

According to his "confession" which comprised a separate piece of paper slipped between the sheets of one of his normal letters, they would meet "accidentally" around the neighbourhood and take walks along the jungle tracks at the back of the bungalows. Gladys had expressed an interest in botany, and George had offered to show her an interesting species of tropical fern he had seen out there. In any case, he loved the relative peace of the jungle and during those few weeks of insanity until she went away, wanted to impress the girl who had given him a temporary diversion from his frustrations. There, amid the sounds of jungle life in the deep, deep bracken and the heat of the day, they had created their own primeval paradise.

Once the heat had begun to subside in him, feelings of shame and contrition compounded his moods and he knew that he would have to get this off his chest somehow. Writing it all down in the "confession" brought immediate relief as, like a naughty schoolboy, he transferred his guilty burden to me – in so doing endowing me with the false position of a "mistress" figure - and sought forgiveness. By our next meeting, I had thought through the affair and somewhat contrary to my own expectations, did not feel the hurt I experienced at those times when George had wanted to end things between us. Now I felt stronger and had benefited from the long rest, I felt more able to deal with the intensity of our relationship and saw the Gladys affair for what it amounted to – a dalliance, though knowing George I felt sure that much passion was involved – testament in a way to my fiancé's manhood and virility. I knew the girl and had previously sized her up as a hussy. Although I appeared, for form's sake, not to forgive him straight away, that first time we made love after the affair I felt more aroused than ever before and, losing control of ourselves, we feared the worst. But we felt so happy, we were past caring for conventions. For the first time, George wrote from the bungalow later that night, at last I had given myself naked to him, not as the prim and proper Miss Lavinia Coates but as an equal in creation.

There followed almost a honeymoon period, when everything seemed to go so right that realistically, I knew it could not last. It coincided with a steady improvement in my health and although I still spent my nights in the hospital, my days remained free to do as I chose. Technically, I maintained the status of employee of the Hospital Board and still received my regular salary for the time being, but the Board expected conformity to the decisions of the doctors about my treatment and progress. There had been some discussion recently about a few months' holiday in Australia to finalise my convalescence, after which, if my health permitted, they would expect me to return to normal duties.

In the meantime, between our meetings, sometimes in Taiping when I would surprise him by a visit, George wrote almost daily – letters filled with ideas and plans for a post war future together which he seemed convinced would come. He would get his divorce papers, we would marry and, when it became safe to do so, we would go home to England, perhaps with a baby in tow. Our life in Malaya would seem a distant memory in time.

"I often think of when we are old, about 55 –" he wrote, *"I shall see you standing in the garden, or by the window, watching the sun set, how I shall walk up behind you and put my arm round your waist and say, 'Think back twenty long years dear wife, of our lives in Malaya', then together we shall re-live these months together."*

Through his letters, George betrayed his sense of living in a momentous period of history and the uncertainty that brought – a sense of losing control, of being victims of fate or the puppets of some great, unknown puppeteer. Perhaps this awareness at times induced his moroseness and moods, yet at others filled him with optimism and hope. I also was not immune to these feelings of living on a precipice but he expressed it better.

"*Tonight in the west there is a bright star, a very bright one, and its rays stream out across the water, to me it is a token of something what I cannot say, but I'm sure it has a meaning and if I sit and look at it for a long time, I am sure it would have a meaning for me, so darling note the date 9-9-41 and we shall see what letters are written to us on this day, and what big meaning in world history it has.*"

In less than two months, our idyll would shatter, destroyed by a stronger power- for in a time of world war, against a seen or an unseen foe, who can truly claim mastery of their lives.

Chapter 14

Last Days

Paradoxically, the Gladys affair brought about a deeper understanding between us. I never saw her again. Fortunately, she left for Switzerland only a week or so later. George and I briefly met her parents in the Taiping Social Club where they told us that the Japanese threat had hastened her departure.

"She's better off out of the way," Tom Webster rumbled into his drink. He brushed cigar ash off the front of his dark blue blazer. "You never know with those little blighters. Could be tomorrow and wouldn't want to leave her exposed - innocent young girl.....They're supposed to be a decent lot but all's fair, what?"

Tom wandered off the point as he cited several instances of rape and pillage in his former military experience, his face becoming a mottled red. His mousey wife, standing quietly beside him, stirred the cocktail stick in her champagne glass and nodded emphatically in agreement.

"Yes, it wouldn't have been easy, even though they say it won't happen. I'm still worried for her though. It's so dangerous crossing the seas in these times."

I felt almost conspiratorial with George, as we stood there

together listening to the foolish, doting parents. We could utter nothing except platitudes. Agnes Webster obviously thought me remiss for not praising Gladys's attractions as her friends did – which had probably resulted in her becoming even more conceited. Clearly, the Websters had always viewed their only child through rose-coloured spectacles and we did not disillusion them. George didn't say much but I knew he would have conflicting thoughts. He felt as I did, that parents never really knew the capacities of their children and that Gladys had a level of maturity well beyond her years. This combination of emotional maturity and physical youth had attracted him.

We had talked, in the privacy of the Rest House or the bungalow, and I had felt like a parent myself. The role seemed natural for a short while but I believed George knew that my tolerance had a limit. If he had not shown remorse, I would probably have reconsidered my options. George also realised that if he had been with Madge, she would have been violently angry and would in all likelihood have thrown him out of the house, even if only temporarily. He seemed to feel for a while an almost humble gratitude and perversely, I enjoyed the change - while it lasted. He had taken a gamble with the confession – I could have ended things and with good reason, for a mere chit of a girl. I wondered, when he had too willingly accompanied Gladys into the jungle, what he had imagined the outcome might be. Had he perhaps thought, even for one brief moment, that they could have made a go of it together? Possibly, his heightened senses, temporarily deranged, had imagined some blissful future in a kind of Arcadian bubble. In the moment, this may have seemed entirely feasible. I fully understood this, and sighed. For George had, at times, imagined me in a similar place - that Never-Never land where wars did not exist, along with the usual need to earn a living. There lay the difference between us.

As he started on the road to psychological recovery, his spirits rose, along with some self-justification. He was not a naturally self-effacing man. I would not have expected him to remain contrite forever, as I loved him as he was. In some ways he hated himself for his lack of self-control, but what the devil could a fellow do – my incarceration for months in that damned hospital, watched over by the "B.G. Sisters" as we called them - whom we felt sure took a great deal of pleasure in spoiling our fun, had rendered me an invalid in all senses. Molly, I did not classify as a "B.G. Sister" in the strictest sense, wrapped up in her many affairs as we in our one. I often wished she had had the assignation of my personal nurse instead of Williams. I felt sure my recovery would have progressed more rapidly, or at the very least, more enjoyably. Now that I had felt the awakening of pleasure, we might have had more in common since our shipboard days on the *Narkunda*.

That first time after the affair, we experienced each other more profoundly than we had ever done before, and had been abandoned to pleasure and our love. It was strange the way imagining him with Gladys had affected me in this way. Perhaps a perversity, as I had heard men had pleasure from seeing women together – forbidden lust or the taboo, slowly, bit by bit, revealing a *demi-monde* that I could barely imagine.

I chuckled to myself, accidentally dribbling tea on my dressing gown. It didn't matter. Janet could wash it next time she did the laundry. How the world changed! Women from a middle-class background had barely heard of these things then and men had to keep it under their hats, prolonging the delusion that they did not exist. What hypocrites we all were...

As the days and weeks passed, I had a growing sense of unease.

"When do you expect to be rather under the weather, Sweet?" George asked me, one drowsy Friday afternoon in September in the Rest House in Batu Gajah village. We lay together in the spartan room which contained only the minimum of furniture: the old-fashioned double bed, a washstand equipped with an ornate Chinese jug and basin (cracked) and a carved bamboo-seated chair on which our hastily removed clothes lay.

After a moment, I moved my head from his shoulder and looked up at the dark chin stubble on the angular jaw and full, sensitive mouth above.

"Three days ago. I was going to tell you soon, George dear, but I was afraid of what you would say. I was going to wait a few more days."

George grew still but he still held me close.

"What shall we do, George? If..."

He patted my bottom, meaning to convey reassurance, but I knew his mind was far from easy. We also knew he was in no position to marry, both legally and financially. I had already had time to think it through. The best thing to do if the worst had happened would be to conceal it for as long as possible, then concur with or encourage any plans of the Board for a convalescence in Australia. I would not be able to work, of course, but Dorrie lived in Sydney – married now and with a baby of her own. I might be able to stay with her for a while – I had predicted how George would feel – guilt and concern for my health. Had I the strength to bear a child? I did feel a little different, the way I had, numerous times, heard newly pregnant mothers describe it. My breasts felt full and tender and a strange sensuous feeling of heavy languor encompassed my abdomen and loins.

"Sweet, wait a few more days. We won't worry now. Just remember, darling, that whatever happens and whatever you choose to do, you have my support."

He bent his head down to my level and kissed me gently, and quite differently from the way he usually did, sweetly restraining himself. In return, I kissed him with more passion and felt the response from him, which he quickly controlled.

George was, and he knew it, helpless to do anything, and this made him angry and frustrated. With Lavinia safe back in the hospital that evening, he paced the room restlessly and finally went down to the bar. He needed a drink badly, but whilst it afforded some relief at first, the cumulative effect felt far from relaxing, and a feeling of unreasonable resentment grew inside him, which railed against the damnable luck that was his, George Powell's. With an effort, he stirred himself and started looking around him at the other Rest House visitors. Only a few patronised the bar tonight but the time had not yet advanced to the usual hour for a drink - a couple of Australian officers *en route* for Singapore sat smoking over their beers deep in discussion, and a young couple quietly shared the corner seat, holding hands. Suddenly, he downed the dregs of his drink, bade old Joe the Chinese barman goodnight and started for the staircase. Joe looked startled.

"Goodnight, Mr Powell sir!" he called after him. Never had he known George to leave the bar before closing time. "Everything alright, sir?"

George waved his hand for answer. He had to be alone to put his thoughts on paper, then he knew he would sleep more easily. First, though, he took a detour to the lounge, where he had seen headed writing paper laid out on the desk for the Rest House patrons, and helped himself to a few sheets, while he patted the breast pocket of his shirt where he kept his fountain pen.

Alone in the sparsely furnished room, he looked at the side of the bed on which Val had lain, saw the imprint of her head on the pillow and the hastily thrown back sheet. He lay down for a moment and, catching the faint residue of her perfume, closed his eyes and breathed deeply. In a few minutes he realised that he was falling asleep and forced himself to sit up, resting his back on the wooden headboard. Leaning on an old copy of *Vogue* that someone had left in the room, he began a letter to Lavinia. After a few lines, he looked at his watch. It was seven-thirty and he suddenly realised that he hadn't had any dinner. If he wrote what he wanted to say to Lavinia now, he could send it up to Batu Gajah tonight with the courier - the young boy he had seen this afternoon around the House waiting for orders. Then he could relax and order a meal, knowing that Val would read it before she went to sleep.

George wrote in light of the news that he had heard that day - it seemed to him like a kind of vow which stated the way he felt and how things stood between them at that moment in time.

Nobody could blame him for getting a girl into trouble if Val had this.

He wrote that he wanted them to live together as husband and wife, not in the future but now. Weary of the way they lived their separate lives, he had written this to her before, but now it seemed even more appropriate. If she had succumbed to a delicate condition, he would take care of her as he should – of them both - he owed this much to her. But he wanted this, too, he knew. He would find some-where for them to live (there must be somewhere away from prying eyes! Perhaps on a plantation, if he made use of their contacts to secure a post) and they had a few months to think things through. Deep down, although he did not write this, he hated the thought of Val going away to Australia. He reiterated that he would not desert her whatever happened. So darling, he wrote, sleep easy and all may be well tomorrow. It had hit him as a profound shock at first but after all, Sweet, we have dreamed of a baby of our own one day!

Sitting there on the old bed with the tropical dusk falling outside the Rest House window, open to the heavy scents of the humid night and the rhythmic sounds of the cicadas, George wrote of other dreams of their future together. Of how, when they finally went back to England, they could hire a boat and explore the Norfolk Broads, all three of them (it was a theme they had often dreamed of together) or walk in the green hills and picnic, as he had often imagined while gazing on the "big foreign hills" he could see from the dredge. While they still lived in Malaya, they could go for a jungle expedition and take photographs of all the exotic animals and plants they saw. Indeed, they could start with the crocodiles George had often seen from the dredge and had described to her in his letters. He compared the blissful married life they would have with the "living hell" of a life he had experienced with Madge. She had effectively driven him to sea, where he had lived a devil-may-care existence on board his merchant navy vessel in the South China Sea. In ports he had his pick of women, and men too, if he had been interested. Well, he had started life in a foster home while his mother had worried herself to a shadow and a fully white head of hair by the time she reached forty-three. He had, nevertheless, made something of a success of naval school where he went at thirteen and became, in due course, a sailor, policeman, soldier and miner.

"Well, my darling, I have a wealth of experience of the world to protect you and our children – the idea of planting is not a fad and I have often thought of it."

Lavinia knew the wife of one of the big noises in local planting, - Cheney – could she put in a good word for him before he applied, if they decided it would be for the best?

"You have talked about your family- their position and your superior education when we have been at odds with each other – but I, my dearest, have learned the other way round from you in my lessons from life. I know I do not speak as well as you do and sometimes feel inferior but I am a fast learner, Val, and I'm sure I could improve with a more gentlemanly career such as planting if you teach me. I would, for example, like to learn algebra, but there are so many things. I don't want my son to have a beginning like mine, Val. I want him to be a gentleman and a sportsman and be proud of his father, and my daughter to be a lady, at ease anywhere."

From almost the beginning of their correspondence, they had signed their letters with a secret sign, mysterious and unfathomable to the uninitiated. Now he joked, while he signed it, that she should be careful not to show this to anyone, otherwise they would be suspected of being Fifth Columnists! He signed the letter with all his love, the secret sign and a myriad kisses, sealed it and went downstairs to find the boy.

The following morning at breakfast the boy returned with a telegram:

ALL WELL STOP FAMILY DELAYED STOP SEE
YOU LATER STOP LAVINIA

George felt almost disappointed, although he knew that this reaction was ridiculous and unreasonable. How could one grieve for something or someone that did not yet exist? Yet they did grieve, and this experience seemed, to him, proof of his love, if he had needed it.

That October 1941 became for me a month of gains, in terms of health and strength. My latest X-ray, which I had to attend myself unescorted in a little clinic in Ipoh, showed my lesions to have all but cleared, and these days I coughed very rarely. I had gained a little weight, which I had desperately needed to do, and this meant that I no longer felt ashamed to put on my swimsuit and accompany George to the swimming pool. It felt so good to practice my strokes again in the cool, deep water of the rock formation pool with George fussing over me in case I became tired or developed a cramp. A little brown Malay boy threw new pennies for us and we dived to retrieve them, emerging at the surface breathless and triumphant. My swimming cap had become loosened with the underwater swimming, and George attentively smoothed back the wet strands from my face as I laughed up at him, spitting water. The sun shone steadily above, reflected a thousand times in droplets of water on the whiteness of our semi-naked bodies, while George gazed at me anxiously.

"You're just like an old mother hen, George!" I panted, swimming across to the rock-formed steps. "You worry too much!"

"I have to, darling!" answered George, protesting. "I don't want you having to go back to bed because you did too much. I had quite enough of sitting by a sick bed!"

Avoiding the steps, he lithely clambered over one of the sides of the pool and held down a hand to me to help me out. The pool on that late Saturday afternoon was quiet as most people were at home changing for the evening socials, and there was that air of peace which often occurs just before dusk which gave us the privacy we needed. As we sat at our old corner table drying our bodies in the golden twilight, George ordered a couple of *stingahs* from the hovering waiter.

"Darling, I think you've earned it," he said in answer to my weak protests. I gave in all too easily.

"My first drink since I became ill!" I said, somewhat redundantly. "Oh George, it's so wonderful to be out in the world again!"

"I know, my Sweet and we have to celebrate that." He held up his drink so that the liquid glowed golden in the evening sun. "Here's to you, my love and your health."

I sipped my drink and watched the working of the Adam's apple in his tanned throat as he swallowed half of his glass. The alcohol, after so long, made me feel fuzzy and warm. I hoped that Sister Williams would not accuse me of being drunk while I was still a patient.

"My darling, we'll remember this day in years to come," said George, enjoying seeing my pleasure in this private moment.

The rays of the dying sun glimmered on the now-still water of the pool. The waiters hovered silently. I did remember, and the so-typical idyllic scene remained forever printed on my mind, adding to my sadness.

Life in Batu Gajah continued with its comings and goings and its rigid routines for the rest of that month. With my lifelong love of order, I too, had my routines on weekdays, while at weekends George always visited. I had progressed to the point where the hospital almost felt like an hotel, and I became free to arrange my own amusements, only limited by my nurse's common sense and my determination for a permanent recovery. I had visitors, too. Molly, still in uniform, often called in on her way back to the nurse's home. During our voyage out in January we had become fast friends, although Molly's love life shocked even me, changed as I had become by George. In fact, Molly risked being disciplined for her behaviour. She had recently become engaged to a serious, bookish British doctor who was currently based at Penang Hospital in George Town and like George and me, they could only spend time together at weekends.

Even then, Angus remained on call and their time often became truncated. As I had known on the ship, Molly's philandering bordered on the incurable and despite my own lively social life, I had often suddenly awakened disturbed in the early hours when Molly had returned to the cabin after a rendezvous. Once in Malaya, she became one of the "fast set" of nurses whose off-duty hours were spent enlivening every party or social event they could. The entire colony had raised its eyebrows when Molly had become engaged and could only assume that there lay hidden depths of passion and open-mindedness in the quiet doctor. Molly's physical attractions in her dark curling hair and eyes and enviable figure were obvious, but her indiscretions became the talk of Ipoh. It seemed that everyone knew but her hapless fiancé...

Although Molly's infectious energy and love for life made her a lively companion and cheered me up, I felt duty bound not to openly encourage her most outrageous escapades. The ward sister's flirting seemed almost pathological sometimes. George and I met her one evening towards the end of October in the Rotary Club in Ipoh, on the arm of a planter who seemed particularly enamoured with his new escort. Molly played a dangerous game but the claustrophobic, humid atmosphere of the colony itself seemed to encourage overheated liaisons, as I knew from my own experience. I had done my share of two-timing.

Improving health and a narrow escape, coupled with a restlessness brought about by George's uncertain moods (often these days stimulated by the delays of B&B and their demands for fees), sometimes led to a resurgence of my independent spirit. One Friday afternoon well on in October, George had become angry when I arrived ten minutes late to meet him at the station, but to avoid a prolonged argument, I had adopted a carefree persona and kissed him and made a fuss of him so that he forgot his grievance and we left the platform with our arms around each other. He had been a week either cooped up in the bungalow with Jock and Ian or on the dredge working a spell of nights that had left him exhausted, full of nervous tension and longing for me. When I had not arrived on time to meet him, he had tried to hide his disappointment and sense of betrayal. We went back to the hospital, found a quiet spot in the gardens and chatted about my latest escapade which probably did little to quieten his mind.

I had seen an advertisement in the *Times of Malaya* for nurses to work in Australia. They were not sister's posts but lower status, ward-based jobs, and I had decided to send in an application. Looking back, I often wondered what feelings had prompted my actions. Did I love George less than I thought? My health had very much improved, although there would always remain a propensity for a weakness in my chest. Staying here much longer would not change anything and there seemed a good chance in any case that the Board at this moment discussed an Australian convalescence. I had felt an uncontrollable urge to take matters into my own hands, to reclaim mastery of my life once more. I'd had my fill of being a patient. I felt confident that George would wait for me while his divorce came through, even though the separation could make or break our relationship. When a favourable reply came from the Royal Melbourne Hospital, I knew I had to tell him, which I had done in one of my daily letters, but George's very definite veto of the idea stopped me in my tracks. He appeared baffled as to why I should have done such a thing and proved eloquent in his argument against going to work in such an inferior position in Australia.

"...You have never told me you had written for a position down there – what's more, Val, my rotten selfish, jealous nature and love, won't let me think clearly, but I'll say this, if you go down there to stay I feel sure it is goodbye for us and our future. Yes we shall be miserable for a couple of months then I shall take to the "Boys" and drink which will take your place, I know it for sure that I cannot wait until after the war with you down there. I have thought 6 months a life-time but 18 months to 2 years well it's hopeless, I cannot wait that long..... I have tried to make you see that the government are responsible for you and if you leave it to them you would have been OK but when you

volunteer to nurse in Australia well they only have to wash their hands of you and say, that's one fare less to pay home..... Australians have no time for us English or pommies as they call us..... What is a "pommie"? It's an Englishman who goes to Australia to find work, gets a job and when asked to do so, does it and smiles, but an Australian would not do the job himself and hates the other for doing it, he tells his friends that the Englishman is a creeper and crawler a pommie in other words.....Darling of course I'm angry – how can I be otherwise when you jump out of a nice comfortable position into a slave-driving job. I won't have it. – you do as the "Board" say and demand to come back here after 6 months, then you can think about work or marrying me.....you are not going as a nurse to a crowd of roughs for anybody so just forget it."

George had, as he said, the confidence of both Dr Shelley and Dr Drew who had both told him to try to get me to stay in Malaya or at the very least, go south for a holiday for six months to regain my fitness in a cooler climate and clear, fresh air. I could then have my chest tested and if the results were favourable, I would be in a position to come back and take up my normal duties as Health Sister. George seemed adamant that my place remained with him, and effectively, I found, the way forward had become clear. But despite my love for George, I began to have a feeling of being trapped in his all-consuming passion. The power of his strong character and nature, focussed in his possession of me – magnified since my pregnancy scare - encompassed me and left me few choices.

While we tried to shape our futures, without our world, outside forces continued their momentum. For the time being submitting to George's firm views, I remained in my solitary hospital haven, read the English language papers and continued the clippings. The German Russian campaign continued but at great cost, leaving Germany vulnerable on two fronts and paving the way for the invasion of the Allied forces on D-Day. However, silently and stealthily, a new threat emerged in the east which began barely perceptibly, although I noticed some early signs.

At the beginning of November, a grainy, yellowed press photograph depicts the evacuation of Japanese civilians from Malaya, queuing as they mount the gangway to their vessel carrying suitcases, coats over arms and holding on to their children – slim women in costumes and smart hats being evacuated on intelligence received, ostensibly for their own safety and going to a home they perhaps only dimly remembered. Although mostly unnoticed, two Japanese staff officers leave their posts in Pearl Harbour and return to Japan. On another fragile piece of newspaper dated that November, the faded forms of soldiers are seen. If one looks closer, one sees that these soldiers are wearing their tropical battledress with an army "bush" or "slouch" hat with the rising sun emblem on the upturn: Australian troops on guard in the Malayan jungle waiting on the border with Thailand, their rifles slung over their shoulders. Hard on the heels of these signs, Sister Williams' hat made another appearance around my door, one early November evening. The plump face underneath looked flushed and flustered, signalling an unusual busyness in Isolation Ward that evening.

"Telephone for you, Sister," she panted, and disappeared again.

I felt relief that I could walk well by myself these days, for I was sure that Sister Williams would not have stayed to help me that evening.

"Thank you, Sister," I answered to the back of the door, left ajar by the busy nurse and through which I could hear the hum of voices from the ward.

I heard the deep male tones of the senior registrar whom I knew, and the almost inaudible, higher pitched replies from his female patient.

I hurried to put down my book and left the room as I was. These days I dressed every day but wore slippers in my room. The main ward area felt hot and stuffy as I passed through, despite the open louvres down one side of the room and the constantly rotating ceiling fans. I barely noticed the row of women occupying the beds in the long ward, each one with its white coverlet having a wooden chair placed at the foot where the patients sat during the day. Most stared as I walked through, curious of catching a glimpse of the recluse in the side ward.

The black dial-faced telephone sat in pride of place at the end of the room in a cubicle, forbidden to all but recovering, non-infectious patients. The receiver lay placed on its side and, knowing that George must wait at the other end I lifted it somewhat nervously and spoke into it, wondering what I was about to hear. I knew intuitively that after having heard it, things would never be the same.

"George?"

"Val darling, I didn't want to worry you but I had to phone straight away. I'm in the Club."

He sounded unlike himself, distraught, in tones that I had never heard from him. Although coming from a distance of little more than fifty miles, the reception was poor, sounding like waves on a beach, as I strained to hear him.

"I have to go away with the boys, darling. I can't say more now but I don't have much time – a few days. I'm so sorry Val. I have to see you – I'll be down tomorrow."

His voice grew more distant as it was overwhelmed with the interference. Never before had we seemed so far away from each other. It was as if something or someone pulled George from me, under the sea. Later that evening, I wrote to my mother.

"Mother dear, George phoned this evening which marks the beginning of a parting. I can't tell you much as I don't know myself, but he is going away and we don't have long together. I can't tell you how upset I am, but it is to a better job with twice the salary, so I should not complain."

Shortly after his arrival in Malaya and posting to the tin mines in Taiping, George had, as he often put it, "played at soldiers" with the Perak division of the Federated Malay States Volunteer Forces, formed at the outbreak of war in 1939. Through all the camaraderie and dissipation of his platoon, there underlay serious intentions but somehow it had never seemed so real before. Now, the military authorities called George for duty near the Thai border as part of Malaya Command under the overall leadership of Lieutenant-General Arthur Percival against the silent enemy, wherever he may strike. Thailand was standing by her neutrality, denying any involvement with either Japan or Britain.

The following morning, Mrs Murray-Ainsley phoned, extending an invitation to George and me for dinner that evening on what we thought would be our last day together. Later, after George had gone, I finished the letter to Mother, begun on the night George had phoned. I described the evening and made much of the little details that I knew would interest her.

"I know I have mentioned the Murray-Ainsley's to you before, Mother. He is the Chief Justice of Perak and a cousin of the King, if you remember. I have saved cuttings of some of his court cases. We had a lovely evening. Mrs Murray-Ainsley is very fond of George because he is handsome."

We had a little more time than George had previously thought. Before leaving Taiping, he had, at this time of all times, received notice that his divorce petition had arrived in Singapore and awaited his collection. On the fourteenth of November, he went alone to Singapore and collected it from the Colonial Office, returning to Batu Gajah on the same day. He had checked into the Rest House for three nights before his departure for the north via Taiping to finalise matters at the bungalow, then was to travel on to Penang, where he had orders to present to Headquarters.

I remember the time we spent alone together during these last days as snatched and dreamlike. George had already gone from me. I often caught him looking at the familiar scenes, walking on the main street of Batu Gajah Village, with the little two-storey houses and shops downstairs, shaded from the fierce equatorial sun by the blinds covering the front windows. The palm trees cast their shadows on the opposite side of the street, with the little grassy park behind. I could always visualise what I wore that last day - the white full-skirted dress with a tiny yellow flower print and pretty white sandals – I had dressed for him. George did not see these things as I looked at him but maybe a foreign battleground in the jungle, far from home. In his mind's eye perhaps he saw a clearing, with men carrying weapons.

We called into the tiny post office together and posted the petition to B&B. Surely, I thought, this must be a sign from heaven. Inside the musty, dim interior of the store which sold all manner of miscellaneous items, stood the statutory glass-fronted counter at one end, behind which worked the tiny Indian woman who mainly dealt with the needs of patients and staff of the nearby hospital. Adjusting her silk dupatta scarf over her jet-black hair and with a chink of golden bangles she accepted the precious package under the glass screen and filled out the form for its urgent category. Our hopes and prayers went with it. We watched as she deposited it in the foreign mail sack behind her and looked at each other.

"Well, I don't know about you, darling, but I think this calls for a celebration."

George turned back to the woman. She had a quiet, dignified demeanour according to custom but also a sympathetic air and our hopes rose a little.

"I say, Madam, would you happen to have any champagne?" We had seen some crates of beer, bottles of whiskey and the like in a dusty corner on the way into the gloom.

Without a word, she disappeared into a little back room from where she could be heard speaking Tamil. A male voice answered in the same language and she reappeared after a few seconds holding a large green bottle embellished with a gold label and gold wrapping over the cork.

"It is our last one," she explained, giving it to George with a little bow." It is for you."

Later that night, after George's departure, I wrote an entry in my diary. The ink is fading on the page now, the paper grey and discoloured.

"My room in isolation in the hospital up the hill has been witness to a champagne duet as we toasted our future."

Chapter 15

Wartime at Home

Percy Coates tidied his office desk meticulously. It was a fine Saturday lunchtime in April 1941 as he closed his leather goods factory for the weekend and prepared to face the humdrum journey home. Percy habitually travelled from Paddock Wood to Hildenborough by bus. Since the start of petrol rationing in 1939, the running of private cars such as his had become a luxury, and now he saved the precious essence for his habitual runs out on Sundays. He would take Florence and often a long-standing Tonbridge friend, who appreciated this weekend diversion from the daily tedium of their wartime lives. They would traverse the Kentish lanes on a summer Sunday to villages such as Goudhurst or Plaxtol - horn honking as they rounded each narrow bend, dropping into a pub or teashop on their way home. He supposed that eventually he would have to stop running the car altogether and put it up on blocks for the duration but for the time being, he felt determined to hold out against the inevitable. The shortages, after two years of war, did not as yet feel crippling but began to make themselves felt. Leather, the raw material on which his father had based the business, became increasingly hard to obtain for the small, luxury items in which the factory specialised, the outlet being the shop in Tonbridge High Street.

The bell for the half-day closure sounded out across the floor and penetrated the glass doors of the office. Percy locked his door, made his way across the mezzanine and clattered down the staircase onto the cutting room floor where his manager and foreman, Tom Bridges, was waiting for last minute instructions for Monday morning. He touched his cap as his boss approached.

"How did those bespoke orders go, Tom?" he asked. "That last batch of material was shoddy stuff. What did you make of it?"

"It will show in the wear, sir," the foreman responded. "The girls have done their best and the customer knows there's a war on."

He picked up a beautifully crafted object from a nearby work bench and held it out to his boss for scrutiny. Percy, putting his thirty years' experience into the examination, did not miss a delicate curve, a bevelled corner or an exquisite row of stitching and finally, satisfied that the reputation of Coates' Leather remained intact for the peaceful future he had no doubt would eventually come, nodded his approval and without comment, handed it back.

"Just leave it all tidy and drop off the keys to me, Tom," was his parting shot.

The foreman assented with a salute-like gesture and turned to the job of shutting up the factory for the weekend. He felt content for now. Percy had shown himself a good if exacting boss and Tom had no complaints. Both were veterans and survivors of the Great War and had reached an age too advanced to be called for any special war duties - for the time being, but if hostilities continued beyond another year or so, it might be a different story.

As Percy donned his long tweed overcoat and made his way towards the nearest bus stop opposite the church, he paid no attention to the beauty of an April deep in the heart of Kentish hop country. He remained oblivious to the weak sunshine drying the red clay-tiled rooves of the houses in the village and the light green traceries beginning to shroud the branches of the willow overhanging the pond. He stood deep in thought. His ruminations resumed, not for the first time, the train the examination of the leather work had set in motion. He knew the standard of his goods to be second to none in the area, unless one compared his work with Northamptonshire factories, the centres of excellence where he had first trained as an apprentice back in the days when Victoria still reigned. Working hours were so long that by the end of the day he would be dropping from exhaustion. He had been shown no concessions by his bosses, despite being born into a well-to-do Kentish family descended from county gentry, but then Percy had expected no favours. His outlook had been essentially pragmatic, perhaps limited, but to him application and hard work yielded its own rewards, helped along with family contacts and a certain financial lubrication at times. A young middle-aged man of 39 when the Great War broke out, he had joined his father's old regiment in 1915 as a first lieutenant in the Sherwood Foresters. He signed up unquestioningly, ready to do his duty by his country, as he knew his parents expected of him, leaving his business - his shop in Tonbridge with workshop attached, in the care of his ageing father. He had left dear little Tommy a tiny babe in Florence's arms when he had gone to war, and Lavinia a cheeky little thing of seven, never robust but making up for it with her boundless curiosity and quick wit.

He heard the wheezing of the green Maidstone and District country bus well before it rounded the bend in the centre of the village, and raised his hand to stop it when it finally hove into view. As he climbed aboard, with the unnaturally blonde conductress in her forest-green military style uniform casually leaning against the vertical rail running from the mounting platform, he saw that the bus had become fairly full as usual, with youngsters undertaking their weekly jaunt to Tonbridge for shopping or the pictures, their mood high with the Saturday freedom, housewives bound for last minute weekend grocery shopping or older married couples, their demeanour weary, sad. The air felt fusty and smoky, mixed with the petrol fumes of the outdated contraption, as it lurched away from the stop and turned from the village into open countryside. With Percy on the window side of a double seat, the conductress sauntered up to him with a lighted cigarette protruding from one side of glossy, crimson lips. Her pancake makeup, he now saw, shiny in the spring sunshine, ran into creases around her lips and forehead.

"What'll it be, love?" she mumbled, adjusting her ticket machine in front of her in readiness for his fare.

"A ninepenny one please," said Percy, without looking at her. "Watts Cross."

"It's tenpence ha'penny now love," said the conductress belligerently. "It's gawn up."

Percy would not have described himself as an argumentative man, especially towards the female sex, with whom he usually maintained the utmost courtesy and gentlemanly behaviour, but a certain insolence in this woman's demeanour outraged him, almost as a betrayal of her sex. He stared at the woman.

"I travelled on this bus only yesterday," he protested, "and it was ninepence then!"

"Yeah, went up this mornin'," was the rejoinder. "Sorry love, them's the fares now."

"Oh, very well. Here."

Percy produced a shilling and received a penny-halfpenny in exchange from the conductress's worn leather satchel, which she wore with the strap criss-crossed on her ample chest with that of the ticket machine. A green ticket produced with a metal handle on the side which made a ratchet sound when wound, concluded the transaction and Percy sat back in his seat and sighed heavily. As the conductress returned to her former pose on the front platform, the bus continued to rattle its way round the bends of the lanes, its gears labouring and branches from overhanging trees audibly scraping the roof. Percy, in the absence of the newspaper he usually remembered to pack in his briefcase in the mornings but had today forgotten, fell once more to thought. Today, April 12th had been Tommy's birthday.

The death of their only son in 1930 at the age of 15 had struck

Percy and Florence an almost unbearable blow of grief. He would have been 26 today and more than likely serving now in the family regiment if he had lived - a higher ranking officer than his plodding father could prove capable of, Percy felt sure. Tommy had shown himself a bright boy, winning a scholarship to the Kings School in Canterbury at the age of ten, gaining the highest marks of all the candidates from the Skinner's School in Tunbridge Wells, where he had profited academically from the age of seven. As Percy traversed the Kentish lanes in the number 7 bus, his thoughts roamed far from its atmosphere of wartime stoic endurance and in his mind's eye he relived the scenes of Tommy's life – as a babe in a long lace christening gown during another war, the ceremony brought forward to within a few days of the child's birth because Percy had to join his regiment – as a toddler, like Lavinia not robust but described as "wiry" and inquisitive – as a schoolboy and finally as Percy last remembered him, in the surgical ward of the Kent and Sussex Hospital, where the nurses had brought him from theatre that nightmarish day after his "minor surgery" and laid his young body in a side room. Percy, summoned from the factory after a call from the hospital informed him of the unimaginable - his son's death under anaesthetic during a tonsillectomy – had felt numb with shock. As he sat in the cold, clinical room beside the bed, he thought only that Tommy had died alone.

Percy's focus gradually returned to the present, to the slow procession of brown and green verges passing his window and hedges rising above them to the powder-blue April sky. With chagrin, he noticed that his cheeks had become unaccountably wet and saw the conductress glance at him. Turning his head away towards the back of the bus, he drew out his handkerchief from a trouser pocket, neatly folded by the woman who did the washing, and, opening the folds, surreptitiously wiped his face, clearing his throat noisily as he did so. He made a show of getting something from his briefcase to distract himself and drew out a sheaf of work papers showing the minutes of yesterday's general meeting of staff. That, he thought, should bring me back to earth. No amount of regret, of endless questions, of reliving that inquest about why it should happen - why a healthy youth like Tommy Coates should just stop breathing during a perfectly routine procedure, would bring him back. He had to carry this burden alone. Florence shared his grief but for her sake he adopted a stoic modus vivendi.

The worst of it was, in spite of the stiff upper lip, the perseverance and sheer determination it took to keep going day after day. Everything would end with him. Everything he had worked for, dreamed of for his family in perpetuity, would be gone. Lavinia might marry yet (her letters lately had brimmed with news about this mining fellow in Malaya who worked in tin) and although Percy did not doubt her full capacity to understand the way the business worked, from his knowledge of women bosses, they had a hard time keeping the staff in order and it took longer to gain their respect. He didn't want that for his daughter. No, always in his vision of the future he had imagined his son would succeed him in the business. He would not have to work directly with staff all the time but the steadying male presence and control would ensure that everything he had built up stayed in safe and steady hands.

With a start, Percy realised that he had passed his stop and had to carry on to the one outside the "Flying Dutchman", which would mean walking back along the London Road to the Edwardian house he and Florence called home. The house stood alone, set back from the busy roadside amongst its gardens and small paddock on the side, which they shared and to which he hoped Lavinia would return one day. He had bought this house back in 1926, from the proceeds of selling his previous one in Tonbridge to the Raymonds, for the sake of the gardens. Florence loved gardening, although in recent years her frail health had prevented her. Percy pressed the bell and the bus swayed, rattled and wheezed itself to a standstill outside the pub known as the "Flying Dutchman" and with a curt "thank you" to the conductress, alighted into the welcome, fresh, cool April air. The forecourt of the old pub greeted him, alive with daffodils, the front door open to the crisp spring sunshine. Percy resisted the temptation to enter the dim but convivial interior of the Tudor building to see if anyone he knew was there having a pre-lunch drink and decided to press on. Florence would be waiting and probably anxious, on this day of all days.

Ten minutes later, Percy turned his key in the lock of his front door, calling out as he did so. The cool interior of the hall, smelling of wax polish mingled with the fresh scent of a vase of narcissi arranged on the hall stand, greeted him with an air of peace and timelessness, as it always did. As he took off his overcoat, he caught a glimpse of himself in the hall mirror. He had never claimed good looks - his face was too long and narrow, with its pointed chin and long thin nose, the eyes above it piercing and rather stern. At sixty-six years old, he had passed the age when he should have handed over the reins of his business to an heir, but he held on simply because he knew nobody he could trust to carry on as he would wish. His relationship with his brother Victor, the only possible successor, continued fragile to say the least. Luckily, he remained healthy enough for now and he had for several years delayed the decision to sell. Perhaps when the war was over – perhaps - he trusted he would know when the right time came but not yet. Not yet.....Although he always kept regular mealtimes, his slight frame maintained a boyishness despite his age, perhaps due to his strict teetotal habits and insistence on regular exercise in the form of "constitutionals" and games of golf. Now, he smoothed down his thinning white hair and went through the house in search of his wife.

He found Florence in the kitchen at the back of the house, putting the final touches to a simple Saturday lunch. She had not heard her husband come in and looked a little startled. On seeing Percy, her expression changed to surprised pleasure. Four years younger than her husband, she appeared the senior, her greying hair caught in an approximation of a fashionable half up, half down style, but altogether too wispy and unmanageable. She had attempted to make up, putting on bright red lipstick and eyebrow pencil, so that the effect was startling on her otherwise pale face. She had a homely, round and open face topping a small, compact figure – although now thinner than usual, otherwise one would have known from where Lavinia had inherited hers - making her instantly likeable. Although they had been married for nearly 35 years, Percy loved his wife dearly for her simple sincerity and devotion to her family and friends. Percy crossed the large kitchen and tenderly kissed his wife on the cheek, enquiring about her morning. She still rested in bed when he had thoughtfully made his own breakfast that early morning and left for the factory, as she had complained to him that she did not generally sleep well. Although the raids had thankfully lessened in recent weeks, the aerial bombardments had, she claimed, destroyed her nerves completely, and she lay in bed hour after hour, waiting for the siren to send them down to the garden to take refuge in their Anderson shelter.

"Isn't it lovely, Percy," she smiled up at him, a slightly trembling hand putting a wisp of unruly hair behind an ear. "Mrs Bristow brought me some spring greens from her garden and we've got some for lunch. The chickens have laid again this morning, too! We can have an egg for our tea later and I saved you some celery."

She looked anxiously at her husband. She always knew whether he had had a good day and she thought he looked sad. Her life seemed bound by worry and fear – about her daughter so far away and about them both, for whatever would become of them?

"It all looks delicious, my dear," soothed Percy, trying to reassure her. He knew what she must be thinking and realised that his face must still bear the sadness of the mood that had overtaken him on the bus. He needed some fresh air and his mind turned with something like pleasure on the prospect of a game of golf this afternoon. The weather seemed perfect for it. He sat down at the kitchen table at which they ate these days. Florence had laid it at each end as impeccably and formally as if they were entertaining. There were just the two of them and it did not seem worthwhile pressing the more formal dining room opposite to use.

"Didn't you tell me you were going out to tea this afternoon?" he enquired in a gentle tone. "Who was it now? Ah yes, Mrs Raymond I believe. Don't you usually meet her over at the Wells?"

He brought out his family heirloom of a gold pocket watch to check the time.

"You'd better make haste, my dear. There's a bus in about half an hour. Don't worry about the washing up. Mrs Bristow can do it in the morning."

Florence frowned slightly but acquiesced. She never liked leaving things like that for her daily help that she could do herself but she was in a hurry. Although she would not have dreamed of reproaching him, Percy had arrived home later than usual. As they sat down to eat, she ventured a question.

"How is everything at the factory, Percy?" she asked. "Did you get that order out?"

"Yes dear, Tom made sure of that. Oh, by the way, he's dropping in the keys on his way through but I'll wait for him. I'll get up to the links later on but I'll be back by the time you get home. It's lucky it's lighter now in the evenings and the rain has held off again."

"Alright dear." Florence concentrated on eating her lunch for a few minutes and a silence fell in the kitchen, broken only by the ticking of the grandfather clock in the hall. The memories lay between them like a wall, impenetrable and insurmountable. Through the open window a blackbird sang from the branch of the budding apple tree in the garden and then flew off suddenly, perhaps startled by a cat stalking below the tree.

Finally, Percy asked, "Has the post come yet? Is there anything from Lavinia?"

Yet as he spoke, he knew that if anything had arrived, he would have known about it before now. An unnecessary question, trying to breach the unbreachable. Lavinia's letters usually arrived in twos and threes, after long silences sometimes lasting as long as two months, and their arrival on the front door mat transformed an ordinary day. Florence would usually wait until Percy got home to open them and would read them out loud, if Lavinia had addressed them to her, otherwise she would lay the letter beside Percy's plate, so that he would take the feather-light envelope into his study to read privately and show it to Florence later. They wrote weekly, too, usually taking turns, although Florence's letters were usually more frequent and filled with gossip - about people they both knew and whom Lavinia would remember – she did not disguise the fact that she missed her daughter terribly and wanted her back. She also felt secretly worried, and that her daughter was hiding something from her. Lavinia's letters of late had been more hurried and the news scanty, although she still enthused about the new man in her life, but Florence's maternal instincts had become aroused. She hoped that Lavinia was looking after herself properly as her life out there did seem so hectic.

"No, dear. I did hope there would be today after so long but there was nothing. Don't worry dear, I'm sure we would have heard on the wireless if anything was happening there."

The grandfather clock struck two, the resonant chimes reverberating through the house bringing them, almost with relief, back to the present reality.

"There, just listen to the time," said Florence, laying down her knife and fork and getting hurriedly to her feet. "I was meeting Mrs Raymond at three. I hope she's heard from Dorrie. It's been just as bad getting letters from Australia, from what she's said."

"You'll just get that bus if you hurry now," said Percy. "I'll clear everything up."

Florence hurried to put on her coat and hat, adjusting the navy-blue felt pre-war model in the same mirror that had reflected Percy's face half an hour before. Well, she thought, she would have to do, although Mrs Raymond always looked so smart. Percy appeared in the hall to see her off and she went to him to kiss him on the cheek.

"I should be back by six, dear," she said, putting on her black leather gloves which had been specially made for her as a Christmas present from Percy in the factory a few months before. "I'll bring back a pie from the Cadena. I think I have enough coupons."

"Hurry my dear, never mind the pie. You'll miss your bus."

Percy looked at his wife with exasperated affection and opened the front door for her, otherwise he knew that she would never leave. In reality, Florence felt slightly guilty that she left Percy to his own devices, but she knew that she could not disappoint Mrs Raymond. Besides, she needed an outing and the stimulation of talking to an old friend.

The distant rumbling of the bus could be heard several seconds before it appeared, and Florence waved to it from the other side of the road. The driver saw her and slowed the vehicle to a halt at the bus stop conveniently situated opposite the house. Florence crossed over, thinking fleetingly that before the war, many more cars would have been evident on the London Road that Saturday afternoon. Percy waited long enough to see his wife safely aboard the bus and waved as it drove off. He lingered a moment in the front of the house and looked up at the sky, relishing the emptiness and peace of the washed blue vista. Late during the previous summer of 1940, he had witnessed the Luftwaffe in successive and relentless formation, flying low overhead bound for Kentish airfields and the defending attacks and subsequent dog fights with the RAF. Lavinia had worked in London then but at weekends had come down to the country to be with them. Then the late summer sky had been obscured by haze and smoke, the tranquillity of the ancient weald shattered by the deafening sounds of combat. After that had come the Blitz, with the sinister black shapes of the German bombers droning overhead towards their London targets, night after night. Many neighbouring towns had suffered too, and Tonbridge had had its share, but for the time being a reprieve held sway and the night time raids had lessened. But the tension of waiting and the dread induced by the wailing siren never seemed far away.

Percy turned back towards the house and tried to imagine it a pile of rubble but quickly dismissed it from his mind. He heard a loud "hollo!" from behind him as he reached his front door and turned abruptly to see his foreman approaching on the footpath coming from the direction of Tonbridge. Tom had changed from the long brown protective overall he wore in the factory and had donned a smart, grey, sports jacket and flannel trousers, his still-dark hair neatly pomaded over a crisp white shirt. He raised his hand in greeting while Percy undid the latch of the front gate again.

"Off out somewhere, Tom?" said Percy, surprised at the foreman's smart appearance, in contrast to his workaday overalls.

Tom gave a cursory glance downward at himself while he thought of an answer, but whatever he may have said he checked, while the two men glanced at each other, rooted to the spot and listening. From somewhere, it seemed, or nowhere yet everywhere, a familiar yet dreaded two-toned sound gradually ascended, apparently from the bowels of the earth, to encroach on their consciousness with the first tendrils of fear. The siren increased in sound, spurring Percy to action as he gestured to Tom to come into the house. Simultaneously, his thoughts flew to Florence's bus, which would by now have reached Tonbridge town centre, and he unconsciously made a prayer that the bus driver would have the foresight and training to head out of the centre of town and make towards the countryside.

Strategic bombing, he thought. The planes would be making for the railway and the south end of the town, with the aim of obliterating the junction so vital for services between the capital and the south coast – it struck him as unnerving how accurately the Germans knew the geography of his beloved home county – and through his fear, a kernel of white-hot anger grew within him and emboldened him.

Trying to appear calm, although his face had grown ashen and his heart pounded, Percy made a quick decision to head straight round to the Anderson shelter at the back of the house and guided Tom towards the garden gate. With any luck, no planes would come over this far to the north of the town, but it always remained on the cards in wartime that the direction may be misjudged or the aim of the raid would include some of the fine old Elizabethan buildings in the north of the town or generally to demoralise the population. As the two men hastened through the green painted gate with the sound of the siren fading gradually to silence on its lowest, deepest notes, the sunny garden with its lawns and Florence's flower beds so recently turned over to vegetables struck an innocent, incongruous note in the face of the menacing threat approaching from the Channel.

Percy rarely smoked cigarettes these days as Florence didn't like it and complained that it left a lingering smell in the house, but he pulled out the packet of Players navy cut he had in his sports jacket, took one out and lit it with slightly trembling fingers, belatedly offering one to Tom. They had reached the shelter at the bottom of the garden and stood outside, smoking and waiting for any warning sounds, knowing they could duck into the shelter quickly if necessary. Both men gazed at the sky in the direction of Tonbridge and strained their ears for the drone of low flying aircraft.

Tom produced the keys to the factory, handing them to Percy, who looked at them as if he had no idea what they were. Then he shook off his trance and took them, putting them in his pocket.

"I'm sorry, Tom," he said. "I'm just thinking about Florence. Her nerves are bad at the best of times, and this would have to happen. It's been quite a while since we had a raid and I suppose I thought they were over, at least for now."

"Don't worry, sir," Tom was a reassuring presence. "I remember them saying on the wireless about this strategic bombing now but you're a good way from the railway here and the town too. I hope your good lady is alright sir," he added. "They should've come by now if they was going to, I reckon."

"I hope you're right, Tom."

Percy was just about to offer some explanation for his concern about his wife and her anxiety attacks when just at that moment, the all-clear siren sounded and both men grinned at each other in relief.

"There, sir. False alarm." Tom ground his spent cigarette into the garden path, then picked it up and put in in the compost heap. "I reckon it's a round up at the links you need then a pint at the local."

Percy looked at his watch and thought quickly. The hands stood at two forty-five and by seven-thirty, darkness would have fallen. Just enough time remained if they walked quickly and played the short course. Florence knew to reach him at the Golf Club, where he had maintained a regular membership since just after the Great War.

He slapped his foreman on the back, remembering, after the stress of the moment passed, the relationship they had shared over many years. The relative inequality of their positions and background prohibited close friendship, but Tom's steady, unobtrusive loyalty had proved a valuable support to the Coates family and he was amply repaid.

"Care to join me, Tom? I've heard you play the odd round yourself."

They walked off up the garden amicably together in the undisturbed peace of the afternoon, pausing every now and then while Percy pointed out this and that vegetable crop, planted for a summer harvest.

Chapter 16

Invasion

Just three weeks remained to the outbreak of war. Tensions grew in Far Eastern Command and the British population waited. Troops of the Malayan forces, George among them, took up their positions along the north east coast and over the border in neutral Thailand. For me, incarcerated in Batu Gajah Hospital, the wait for news was almost unbearable, but I disciplined my mind into a strict daily routine and forced myself, drawing on long-held conditioning, to maintain a cheerful demeanour and retain a sense of humour. Not for one moment, despite the anxiety about George, did I or anyone I knew, seriously doubt that we would pull through. The British community at large believed unquestioningly what their governors and military commanders had told them– that the colony was invincible. Unperturbed, they carried on dancing and drinking tea on their verandas as usual. Even If they had private doubts, they would not have dreamed of undermining the spirit and morale of their compatriots.

On the sixth of December, I received two letters from George posted in Hat Yai in southern Thailand, not far from the Malayan border, where he stayed in a rest house after two days travelling.

From their tone, he might, I thought, have just been away for a rollicking weekend at camp with the boys as he had been many times before, instead of preparing to take part in the defence of Malaya. I lifted the densely written pages and sniffed the scent of the paper and ink, before carefully placing them in my diary, knowing that he had been the last person to touch them. I turned to a third letter, from Mrs Murray Ainsley, thoughtfully inviting me to stay with them for the weekend.

"You must be missing your handsome fiancé," wrote the judge's wife, "and we are a little dull here at the moment with all the boys involved in the manoeuvres."

The prospect of a sojourn with the Murray Ainsleys in their spacious bungalow in the hills seemed a welcome distraction from my thoughts. As usual, the entertainment attained its usual lavish proportions with every consideration for my comfort, and Odette had allocated me a suite of rooms with a tranquil outlook over the garden from a private balcony. As the last weekend of peace, in retrospect it had an even more magical aura. For around midnight on the Sunday, eighth of December, Japanese troops landed at Kota Bharu in north east Malaya and by noon the next day, despite vigorous defences by the British Indian Army and Australian air attacks, made headway into the surrounding area, causing Allied forces to begin a retreat south down the peninsula. At the same time, enemy forces had invaded Thailand to the north, which capitulated after five hours of fighting, joining the Axis powers by signing a treaty with their invaders.

I returned to hospital to find yet another letter from George but by now I felt desperately worried and bewildered. The rapidity by which the enemy had gained the upper hand seemed almost incomprehensible and in the chaos of war, his whereabouts were very uncertain. He had written the letter the day before the Japanese sightings off the coast of Kota Bharu and if he had enjoined in battle, he could have had no idea of its imminence then. As a patient, I had no choice but submission to the directions of those caring for me and again fell to waiting. I did not have long. On the ninth of December, although as irrelevant as George's divorce papers arriving on the eve of his departure, I received my papers for Australia.

I still remember the pain I felt at being parted from George. Reading through the account of the Battle for Malaya as I did now, through all the chaos it permeates my writing. At the same time, my determination to "keep faith" with him revealed a stubborn but persistent hope for a future.

"Dates are very vague at this point as I feel the going of George so much that it almost stifles me to write about it at all but I had a marvellous letter from him on this day of all days which makes me believe that through all this chaos everything will be alright."

That last letter, almost like an epitaph and written before the landings, marked the end of our long correspondence, although I had no idea of it then. Or did I?

Adding to my distress, bewilderment grew within me at the strength of the Japanese thrusts as town after town fell and individual accounts of experiences from many acquaintances in the Health Service filtered through. At Kota Bharu, I had written, Sister Allen stayed with her staff at the hospital treating the wounded for as long as she could until events forced her to evacuate – and because the enemy had machined gunned her car, fought her way through dense jungle guided by Malays until she and a couple of colleagues reached a village where they boarded a bus for Kuala Lumpur. I happened to see them a week or so later, outside the station insouciantly eating ice cream. If their experiences had scarred them, there appeared little sign of it but then perhaps they exercised the proverbial British "stiff upper lip."

"In two days," my diary account ran, *"the Japanese had done this to our powerful, or said to be powerful, defences in north Malaya. Whatever could be the reason? The whole Peninsula since I have been here has bristled with troops. The Punjabis were said to be in full force at Sungai Petani, Kota Bharu was supposed to be impregnable as Australians were massed there and even films showed encampments*

of soldiers to prove a menace to the enemy in guerrilla warfare. Officers came on leave from the north talking about tanks and howitzers in full swing and all this, and more too, is the result of our "powerful defence". We read later that no Australians took part in the conflict. Where had they gone?"

I had, I remember, strong reason to believe that a lack of coordination existed in the administration of the army and the RAF which resulted in the absence of RAF defence over towns such as Sungai Petani. Perhaps I had gleaned this from the press or used pure deduction. In this northern Malayan town, the largest in the state of Kedah in the north east, no warning preceded the attack and no siren sounded. A woman enjoying a quiet cup of early morning tea on her veranda looked up to see about thirty planes flying overhead and thought them friendly - only to be disillusioned shortly afterwards when the bombs started dropping. In a few hours, Sungai Petani had been taken.

Over Penang itself, bombing increased in severity from the following day. As news filtered through via the newspapers and witnesses, I watched in horror as the island state which had provided me with my first experiences of Malaya less than a year before, suffered atrocities to its population in George Town. While about a hundred Japanese planes dominated the skies in broad daylight bombing the main administrative buildings, the defenceless citizens, caught completely unprepared, succumbed to machine gun fire before they had a chance to take cover. The RAF only supplied some opposition in the late stages of the attack. Reports came through that the enemy threw piles of the dead onto the grass enclosure in the centre of town. It emerged that Europeans had tried to obtain reinforcements from Singapore but military personnel there informed them that they had no back up available to supply. Many escaped on the water, spending over twenty-four hours at sea with no food, on ferries organised by sailors from the *"Repulse"* and the *"Prince of Wales"* battleships - sunk two days after the landings, also without air defence.

Throughout the methodical taking of each town or city, I heard news through the hospital grapevine of medical and nursing staff I knew – many involved in acts of personal courage, in the circumstances expected of them. In George Town, for example, a Dr Evans stayed behind with the Eurasian and Chinese doctors, but one Mr de B. received criticism on receiving the OBE for his work, as he had left Penang by plane the night before with his wife while others worked on despite the danger.

While the Japanese infiltrated more territory, soon having control of the whole of the north west coast parallel to Penang as far as Province Wellesley, the medical staff of Batu Gajah awaited the order to evacuate. They knew, from the speed with which the Japanese progressed, that it must come soon. It seemed that we were vastly outnumbered, although my own estimate of five Japanese to one British soldier was later proved an exaggeration. In addition to numbers, the Japanese also had the advantage of surprise. Their guerrilla tactics, utilised in the jungle, together with the highly organised attacks on each Malayan town or city, their quickness and their unorthodox survival methods, ensured their success.

I have since done a little of my own reading. Historians speak now of a liberal colonial regime which could have resulted in treachery, exposing the superficial control exercised. I agree with that. The exact details and extent of pre-invasion unofficial agreements between the different nationalities and even rulers of colonial Malaya and the enemy, may never come to light. I am not the only ex-colonial who believes that anti-British factions, such as the original inhabitants of the peninsula who had lost large amounts of land - the Sukai, and Malays, inhabiting for example, "Colonel Berkeley's territory" near the Thai borders in the north east, colluded with the Japanese and guided them through the jungle. The Japanese certainly appeared to support the cause of the "native" and assured them in numerous leaflets dropped on the different territories they sought to control that they had come to protect the native and "kill the Britisher".

Over each large settlement, the pattern of invasion repeated itself in a terrible monotony. First came the aerial bombardment, concentrating first on destroying any means of defence such as airfields. Next, civilians received the brunt of machine-gun fire both from the air and on the ground, and finally came fighting between the troops themselves. The battles at that stage seemed largely tactical or close quarters combat because of the geography of the land. A "front" famed by orthodox military campaigns historically beloved by British red-coats could not exist – we were caught unprepared by the irregular warfare tactics of the Japanese, impossible as they turned out to engage in direct combat. The enemy climbed rubber trees armed with tommy-guns, so that as the British tried to take up fresh positions for counter-attacking they were unceremoniously met with showers of bullets from above. The Japanese seemed able to survive in the jungle for days by stealing bicycles and, dressing up as Malays, rode into the *kampongs*, demanding all foodstuffs and valuables brought to the leaders of the units waiting in the jungle. The unfortunate Malays, their food stolen, must have thought they were *ketuas* or elders, and gave in.

Occasionally, and improbably, war can provide material for a perverse jocularity. Anecdotal accounts of some consequences of this irregular warfare gave us some light relief from our merciless humiliation. We had to take our humour where we could find it. A division of Gurkhas was captured by the Japanese who, true to their purpose of protecting the native and thinking the Gurkhas Malays, instead of taking them prisoner disarmed them and told them to cease fighting and to go and live in peace in their *kampongs*. The Gurkhas, ever loyal to the British, returned to their units to continue their fighting. Because of the difficulty of forming a proper front, Allied divisions tended to become divided and then units became split up so that the result materialised in odd men from different companies wandering about in the jungle, occasionally running into acquaintances. I, ever on the alert for news of people I knew, heard that the fiancé of my acquaintance Lucy Storch, named Fred, bumped into Noel Dyson

Rooke this way - Noel being a close friend of Molly's. Together, they found a broken-down car, which after a little manipulating, worked. On their way to re-join their respective units they encountered several Japanese. Noel wondered what to do as he was driving, and Fred answered, "Drive right through them and I'll shoot." The result of the shooting remained a mystery, as speed at that vital moment took priority over statistics.

On the 15th of December, air raids started over Ipoh and Batu Gajah prepared its beds. From the isolation of my side ward, I felt acutely involved, though I could play no actual role in the preparations to receive the wounded. They first consisted of two volunteer reserves with minor injuries, one being a former agriculture officer from the Cameron Highlands working as a cook with the reserves, who had sustained a nasty bullet wound in the buttocks when a new volunteer cleaned the rifles. I felt helpless in my enforced idleness and took a keen interest in prospective arrivals, expecting ambulances and stretchers to line up outside the hospital. Instead, I saw a Ford VS underneath my window from where I stood on the balcony. Out stepped the other Federated Malay States volunteer looking as fit as a fiddle, about whom I later learned that he had "irritated feet". In my lonely state, I felt glad of the company of these men and had my meals with them, bestowing upon them the benefit of my frustrated but genuine human interest and empathy.

On the following morning, a Tuesday, at eleven o'clock, orders came from the military to begin the evacuation procedures which came as a bombshell in itself. We had heard nothing about evacuations in the north, although this had occurred since the fateful Monday of the invasion. I heard a commotion from the ward as I sipped my morning coffee and hurried out to see the isolation sisters talking earnestly with a group of doctors. Some of the patients stood around among themselves in groups at the bottom of the beds, looking frightened. Seeing me, Sister Williams came up to me.

"There's no cause for alarm, Sister," she said, the slight tremble in her voice betraying the opposite. "We've been given orders by the military to evacuate by early tomorrow morning. You will need to get your things together, but I believe we can only take two suitcases each. Matron is talking to the senior doctors now."

I didn't waste time talking to Williams, whom I considered too prone to becoming flustered for a nurse. I made for the staircase in a state of disbelief. Although news of a rapid Japanese advance had reached us, we had had little sense of imminent danger from the invaders. Several seconds before I reached Matron's little office off the spacious tiled entrance hall, I heard raised voices. On my approach, the little Pekinese dog which Matron kept with her when she did not make her ward rounds, ran out to greet me, uttering short, sharp, yapping barks. Dr Shelley and several of the other senior doctors stood around the office as I looked in. Notwithstanding my patient status, they greeted me as an equal but maintained their serious composure. Matron looked furious as she sat at her desk looking through some papers in front of her - typically ramrod-backed, small and neat in her grey uniform dress.

"Dr Shelley," she was saying, "You know the situation as well as I do. We have some seriously ill patients here and goodness knows how many more wounded will be admitted. All the ward sisters have told me that they are not going, orders or no orders. They cannot imagine leaving their patients and I support them in that. Then there's all the Asiatic staff I simply couldn't walk out on. I'm going to ring the military Head Office now."

With a determined appearance of purpose that few in the past had challenged, Matron Holmes picked up the telephone receiver on her desk, consulting her papers as she waited for an answer.

"Give me Colonel Astley, please. Matron Holmes from Batu Gajah."

There was a five second delay.

"Colonel? Matron Holmes here. We can't possibly leave, Colonel. There are very sick patients in our wards."

A slightly high-pitched male voice could clearly be heard by all in the room.

"Matron," said the voice, in its distinctively Etonian accents, now conveying a sense of urgency. "I'm glad you rang but you must take these orders seriously. We've had reports of severe attacks on civilians in the north and now we know what we're up against we're evacuating all the European women and nurses to Kuala Lumpur. Tomorrow morning, Matron. You must be ready to leave by car. This is a military order. Good morning."

The line clicked and the dialling tone commenced. Matron put down the receiver thoughtfully and gazed at it for a moment before looking at Dr Shelley. Briefly looking at me, she gestured to a chair in front of her desk and I sat down gratefully, my legs feeling less than steady. Dr Shelley in that moment surprised me. Often when I had seen him with Matron his resolve had been less than certain as he met with her supreme confidence in the handling of the running of the hospital. Now, he looked straight at her and uttered three words. "You must go!"

Shelley's usually approachable demeanour vanished, as he towered above her, his freckled face white and deadly serious.

Matron knew she faced defeat, looking as I had never seen her. She appeared heartbroken, as she silently prepared to follow the sad orders, and carry out a final round of the hospital, staff and patients. She knew that it was her duty to obey the orders of the military and the medical staff in the last resort. I left the scene and went to find my volunteers to impart the news. I found them in the kitchens. They both expressed their approval of the nurse's plans to depart.

"Well, that's a relief, by God, Sister," said Lowe, the agricultural officer. "You would all have got raped if you'd stayed."

I hugged them both. We had all shared our stories and experiences in the brief time we had known each other and no-one could say what lay ahead for the two brave men. I could only hope that the Japanese would treat them with the respect they deserved. I left them to each other and went to begin my packing.

The following morning, the 17th of December at seven o'clock, ten sisters left with their luggage in five cars. We left Dr Shelley in charge of the hospital with the Asian and Malay staff. Luckily at that time we had no bedridden patients or newly wounded soldiers.

"I shall never forget this day as long as I live," I later wrote in my diary. *"The day we made our strange exit from Batu Gajah. Memories of this little village will live with me until I die. Had the cause of our retreat been non-existent it might have looked as if ten women had quarrelled with their boyfriends and decided to all have a holiday to forget it. The day was glorious. The sun shone on the little mining pools transforming them to iridescent lakes with deep red shores, the hills pre-eminently static defeating us entirely, those everlasting hills enthroned in misty white foam early in the morning with the deep blue peeping through as the day crept on. Perhaps it was a good idea to shut off one's brain, and imagine one was touring Devon."*

Sister Denyer drove the car in which I travelled. A nurse who had lived and worked in Malaya for more years than most of us could remember, she was a supremely practical, competent and yet unassuming woman in her late forties. Nobody had ever known her romantically involved with anyone. She occupied the position of Matron's right-hand woman and as deputy matron, fulfilled her role with a thoroughness and kindliness which carried over into her managership of the men's surgical ward. With her slight, wiry frame, Joyce Denyer believed in a hands-on approach and worked harder than anyone in her ward. When her men came round from their anaesthetic, she was often the first person they saw, busy round their bedside or waiting for them to regain consciousness with an appraising gaze, ready to speak to them as they opened their eyes. When she had heard of the call to evacuate yesterday, her first reaction had been one of denial and rejection of the orders. Like all of the European sisters without exception, she at first refused to countenance the prospect and carried on with her duties. When it had emerged that the orders had originated from military HQ and that the doctors had arranged to stay assisted by the Asian nurses and orderlies, she had to agree under duress. Now, having Molly and me as passengers with her in her car on this beautiful morning, Denyer's spirits lifted. She loved driving and now that she had accepted the inevitable, she enjoyed the presence of her two companions.

The road remained comparatively clear until we caught up with a convoy of soldiers with several gun carriages, most without the customary sarong on the end of the guns in order for motorists to assess their length. Denyer had successfully passed several lorries and gun carriages until one of the drivers ahead refused to let us pass, despite Denyer's repeated pressing of her horn. Having finally passed the huge vehicle, an officer on the side of the road waved us down and, notwithstanding her obvious senior status, severely reprimanded Denyer. On finding out that we filled the description of refugees, his annoyance that the British Army should encounter obstruction in this way appeared very evident. Denyer responded with dignity and explained that she in no way wished to stand in the way of the Army carrying out its duties but she also had a duty to deliver these nursing sisters to the Bungsar Hospital in Kuala Lumpur. The convoy drivers waved us through after this, and Molly threw chocolates among the troops as we drew alongside, having got the idea from an officer in a car which had previously passed. He had thrown bananas. The soldiers, although looking exhausted after fighting in the north, looked up and waved and grinned cheerfully at us, while I waved back and Molly blew kisses.

The remainder of the road journey to Tanjong Malim, where we had planned to stop at the Rest House, passed uneventfully apart from Molly producing a bottle of warm champagne which we shared with two sisters whom we passed sitting on the side of the road. Their car had departed from it and plunged a little way down, only coming to rest when it came into contact with a large rubber tree. They seemed unhurt, if a little shaken, and awaited a car from Tanjong Malim. These sisters, one of whom was recently married, hailed from Kedah in the north west, near the Thai border and had only evacuated by chance, when one of the sisters, hearing the sound of vehicles passing, looked out of her window and saw staff from Alor Setar hospital passing by with equipment and ambulance. Only after she phoned the hospital to try to find out what was happening, were they advised to evacuate as soon as possible. Hearing that the newly married sister, Mrs Boxhall, had left behind most of her wedding presents and all her silver, I felt almost ashamed, as I had, by comparison, left very little at Batu Gajah, although I had acutely regretted leaving behind a fox fur coat which I had bought under fire during the Blitz in London in September 1940.

The Rest House at Tanjong Malim, on the border of Perak and Selangor, bustled with refugees, from the oldest to the youngest. As I entered the stuffy, smoke-filled bar with Molly and Denyer, a cacophony of chatter and laughter hit us with the warm, fermented smell of beer like a barrage. A woman sat at a table feeding her baby from a feeding bottle, an elderly man sat at another smoking an aromatic tobacco blend in a pipe, and several sailors from the *"Repulse"* lounged over the bar in the corner over their pints. Denyer found an empty table in another corner and went to the bar to see if she could order food. Meanwhile, Sister Smith, or "Smithie" as she had become better known by everyone, came into the room, followed closely by Matron holding Duchesse, her little Peke. Sister Try had driven her car closely behind Denyer and had encountered the same obstructions with the Army convoy and the officer. On arrival at the corner table, Smithie looked breathless.

"Do you know what I saw on the road?" she began as if imparting a tale of great tragedy. "Two sisters from Kedah almost passing out, looking as white as a sheet, both of them. I gave them some of my brandy then they looked a lot better. Oh, you ought to have heard what the officer said about Try's driving, he said it was awful."

Smithie gazed all around as she said this, lest Try should suddenly arrive.

Amid the laughter and camaraderie, I detached myself for a moment and though I smiled, my exasperation must have shown on my face. Anyone would have thought that we enjoyed a firm outing, instead of fleeing for our lives. I gazed fondly at my colleagues and around the room. I wondered if I would ever come here again. Every mile we covered took me further away from George and from the places we had shared together, carried along against my will with the mass instinct for survival. I laughed now as if I had not a care in the world but at my core the empty loneliness waited.

We entered the city of Kuala Lumpur just after four, as the late afternoon sun made the heat inside Denyer's car almost unbearable. The traffic had increased, with the military dominating the road in their dust-covered khaki jeeps and lorries. Jungle and rubber trees had given way to first the occasional roadside shack, then side-streets branching off the main highway. Denyer seemed to know exactly where she was going and we drew up at a large bungalow set back from the main road amid well-kept grounds, the first of similar houses along its section. A woman of Denyer's own age and build in mufti appeared on her front veranda as we approached and parked on the front drive. Longing for some air, we, Denyer's passengers, almost fell out of the car and straightened our rumpled clothing, damp with sweat. With relief, we stretched our legs on the gravel. The two women embraced, then Denyer introduced her travelling companions.

"Good to see you again, Pappy." This was Sister Eileen Pape's nickname in the nursing sorority and to her friends. "This is Lavinia Coates, Pappy, and Molly Cooper."

We stepped forward. We knew most of the nursing sisters in the colony, but we had had only a passing acquaintance with Eileen Pape. The KL Hospital district health sister nodded and smiled, but soon became serious.

"I'm sorry to be the bearer of bad news, ladies," she said.

We travellers nervously awaited what she would say next and I felt as if I would collapse if I didn't sit down soon. I must have looked pale because Pappy soon noticed.

"This can wait, damn it. You're not well, Lavinia. Let's all go inside and have a cool drink."

I nodded thankfully and followed Pappy into the cool reception rooms of the bungalow. The spacious interior with its polished wood floors, Persian rugs and comfortable chintz-covered armchairs arranged here and there in conversation groups, exuded the calmness and faint lavender scent which reflected the confidence and timelessness of the Raj itself. Pappy gestured for us to seat ourselves and a few seconds later, a Malay boy appeared with a tray of lemonade and tall glasses.

"My husband has been urgently called away this afternoon," Pappy explained, as the travellers thankfully settled themselves.

One of the hard-working wives of military men in the colony, she, having valuable qualifications, had felt herself compelled through personal compunction, to use them among the poor of the city.

"Now, that news I was going to tell you," Pappy continued, pouring out long drinks of the ice- cold cordial. "You see, all orders from the military need authorisation from the Resident-General's office before they can be implemented, and the orders for your evacuation were not authorised. I have to tell you, ladies, that you are to return to Perak."

There was a general groan. Denyer thought Pappy somewhat pedantic, but understood her being in a difficult position.

"That may be," she said, "but if they think I'm going to return another two hundred miles in one day and most of that under blackout conditions, they are mistaken."

Our hostess had delivered her message and now left us civilly to decide our course of action. While we three travellers consulted each other closely, two other women of the European community joined us - Brenda Macduff, recently married, and Daisy Clark, an older nurse who was due for retirement. The same message, delivered to them, resulted in their decision to return the way they had come. The results of our own deliberations were that as we belonged to the government, we had no choice but to proceed to the Bungsar Hospital. Thus, an hour later, weary and puzzled, we arrived in the hospital's sister's quarters to await their disposal.

The central block of the hospital had been evacuated and became our headquarters. I shared a room with Denyer, and the rest of the

Batu Gajah crowd arranged themselves much as they saw fit. Most of the other sisters with whom I had travelled down paired off, either to see their respective boyfriends or to meet other people who had come down from the north. For the first time for many months, I experienced the bitter pangs of loneliness which had at intervals in my life covered me like a grey shroud. For the past ten months, George had banished this to the outer recesses of my consciousness but it had remained there waiting. Just one letter from him or the scantiest information as to his whereabouts would have served to fill my mind with sunshine.

In the hospital, my new companions did not help my mental condition as I found them insensitive and, in my fragile state, selfish. Fortunately, however, I found myself a job, while the others set to work among the patients. I became Home Sister, which meant that I had responsibility for the supplies and cooking, aided by the Malay orderlies. The most problematic issue, sugar, always seemed in short supply. Livingstone, from the Theatres crowd, definitely ranked as the worst offender as she had a sweet tooth, but at that time the sugar always had to be hidden from view because of the "boys". It fell to my lot to hide it and so to Livingstone, who adored sugar, I felt that I amounted to nothing more than a sugar cane. I had even heard my colleagues address me as "Sugar." I felt almost popular, but then reasoned that most of my newfound popularity could be put down to cupboard love.

I remained in Kuala Lumpur for exactly ten days. After a week, the enemy had advanced nearly half way down the Malay peninsula and battle after battle ended in retreat for the British Commonwealth Army units. The residents of the colony retreated before them, closer to Singapore.

Chapter 17

Singapore

If I had allowed myself to think about it, I would hardly have believed all that happened around me. We fled before an enemy whose methods of warfare seemed cruelly efficient and deadly. I lived for each day, concentrating on the tasks in hand and resolutely blocked off any thoughts of the future. I went out daily on shopping forays and forced myself to look around, to admire the city of Kuala Lumpur and its buildings as a tourist might do. They had an air of permanence which reassured me.

"Whether the city is in enemy hands or ours, one feels that buildings like those must live forever disdainful and impervious to petty men," I had written, for some unknown reader.

Two of them, the Post Office and the Chartered Bank, sustained hits and about twenty civilians suffered wounds in the daytime raids which had commenced over the city. Molly and her fiancé happened to be undertaking business in the bank during the raid but as usual, I noted somewhat spitefully, the "devil looks after his own" and both survived unscathed apart from Molly's black dress suffering bleaching and her fiancé's hair standing on end. The humour seemed desperate, determined, I now thought, reading through *"The Battle for Malaya."*

My role as Home Sister at the hospital required daily expeditions, impeded by a lack of wholesale supplies to the stores and "wholesale panic" by the populace. It also involved a very early morning start before the usual siren heralded the daily raids. Sister Barbara, one of the Batu Gajah crowd, thoughtfully stepped up to the breach with her car. Liking the odd tipple, she seemed not, as I noted appreciatively, under the influence of alcohol for these drives. We penetrated the early morning mist (which I enjoyed as it reminded me of England) to our first stop, Cold Storage – a warehouse for perishable goods set up by the authorities after the closure of the Chinese and Indian shops which had previously met the population's supply needs. After the war, I wrote an article for a local Kentish newspaper describing battling my way to the front of the various queues for different goods such as butter and milk. I have the article before me now, the cheap paper yellowed and limp, smelling of damp. The incompetent manager, having no duplicate keys and whose native staff constantly ran off into the jungle during raids out of sheer terror, often could not access the refrigerators. This made obtaining supplies a matter of chance before the doors finally slammed shut in the faces of the shoppers. At the market a similar story occurred and I often had to resort to bribery to obtain fresh fruit and vegetables.

Through all the daily hardship which living in wartime involved and continual worry about George, I remembered these days as a comparatively happy interlude. Despite constant news of the atrocities from the north, I felt that I contributed to the wellbeing of the Batu Gajah nurses and for the first time for many months felt of some use. I recognised that as long as I could interact with my fellow beings, hardships were bearable. The Station Hotel served as a favourite meeting place for the refugees and one evening there I met one of George's best friends from the army camps, Bill James, traumatised by losing his home in the north and the distress to his wife and baby son. Bill stayed in my memory long afterwards because of his encouragement to me about George, saying that any information might take months to come through but that I must "just have faith."

"I know Bill thinks George is lucky to have me and wants me to stand by George which I intend to do with all the strength I have in me," I vowed in a diary entry.

I never allowed myself to believe that George continued in any way but alive and well. The alternative would have instigated in me a hopeless feeling from which I would have been unable to rouse myself. From Bill, I heard much about the north. He and Tom Kellway, another volunteer soldier present that evening, had been employed in blowing up key sites to prevent the Japanese using them to their advantage and to slow their advance. They had returned to Ipoh to blow up the aerodrome, with the enemy now about thirty miles from Ipoh.

That same evening, I heard what had happened at Batu Gajah after we left, through Sister Brenda, who had returned to Perak from Sister Pape's with Daisy Clark. After sleeping the night at Gopeng, they described the chaos at the hospital the following morning, with the two senior doctors, Mr Chitty and Dr Shelley, working there alone apart from one male Asiatic nurse. As well as managing to undertake surgery and post-surgical nursing, the doctors had had no choice but to wash clothes, give out bed pans and undertake other menial work, as most of the Asiatic staff had not come into work. Daisy, knowing the staff, scoured the nurse's homes and *kampongs* and rallied the nurses so that their morale improved and they returned to assist the exhausted doctors. No sooner had order returned to the hospital, however, than the military ordered another move and I heard no more. Other sources record that after the European staff left, military medical personnel took over the running of the hospital.

Although the authorities at that time seemed to have little idea about what was going on state by state, the informal communication system lived and worked well. I had a good awareness of how the colony operated through acquaintances. The planters appeared the worst hit economically, as having abandoned their land and houses, they had arrived penniless in the southern cities, many not even possessing cars. While still in KL, I met the daughter of one of the richest planters in Malaya, Diana Evans, who informed me that she and her father were looking for jobs in the railway offices as they had no money. At that time, sailors from the two sunk battleships, the *Prince of Wales* and the *Repulse,* drove the engines and generally ran the railway.

I had spent a week in KL when the fighting reached as far as Ipoh and Batu Gajah.

"I cannot believe that fighting is actually taking place perhaps at this very moment between those two beloved landmarks, Ipoh and BG. When I think of that narrow twisting road winding its way under those everlasting hills with the sun setting behind the coconut palms and George singing "Down Mexico Way" it all seems a terrible nightmare. I only hope that George will return and we will be able to impress yet another country with our spirit and it will not fall into the hands of the enemy. If we have enough faith, we may even see Ipoh and Batu Gajah resurrected again."

Taiping had suffered a similar fate, with the lovely swimming pool laid waste by fighting and anarchy reigning, citizens unable to walk the streets for fear of being stabbed. Distressing as these stories undoubtedly were, I felt compelled to allocate them to the back of my mind as once more, I was forced south through the intervention of destiny.

I had spent ten days in KL, when, try as I might to maintain a low profile, someone found me out and brought me to the attention of the medical staff. My wretched lungs needed their next refill of air which could only be given at Singapore General Hospital. Granted a pass by Dr Young, my senior doctor, he ordered me on the 10 pm train to Singapore. Denyer and Cogan, another nursing refugee, gave me a send-off and bought me dinner at the Station Hotel, which I thought kind of them. I had booked an air-conditioned coach on the train on account of my condition, and having said goodbye to my friends, boarded during the blackout. Partings these days had taken on added poignancy as we left each other to an uncertain fate.

The coach felt hot, crowded and without a breath of air, the air-conditioning having apparently broken down. It seemed full of RAF ground staff, one of whom, a long, lean individual, gave me his seat as few empty ones remained, and then proceeded to try to chat me up. I had to play into his hands eventually and went to stand in the passage with him, as I badly needed air, but afterwards managed to discourage him with the magic word "marriage". On finding out his happily married state, I managed to return to the carriage unscathed.

After unsuccessfully trying to sleep, I started, rudely awakened by an officer's loud voice as we were stopped at a country station.

"All you men get out of here! Twenty Australian sisters want the carriage!"

"Where are we to go?" piped up a meek voice.

"I don't know!" was the curt reply.

I thought it was about time I said something.

"If there's nowhere for these men to go, I'm sure the Australian sisters would hate to turn them out if there's enough room," I said.

The sisters poured in, and to their delight, the men stayed. The Australians, a nice, cheerful crowd, livened the atmosphere as we settled down for the remainder of the journey. We felt brighter after that, until within two miles of Singapore when track workers discovered a time bomb on the line, calling for the removal of railway lines and a two-hour wait. I had managed to pass some of the time with a middle-aged planter who, having lost his job, journeyed to try his luck with the Singapore-based police. He very kindly gave me whiskey ayer and biscuits and all but revealed to me his tin-plated abdomen, a legacy of the last war. After another hour, news came through that a lorry would take anybody who wanted to go, to Singapore.

I arrived by bus in the early hours of the morning of 31st December at the Grand General Hospital of Singapore and was admitted to a ward. I knew, when I entered the hospital, that I would take up my role as a patient again and cease to live. I spent a few moments in weeping and then made preparations to put my house in order. During the next few days, I settled my passage to Australia, (chosen because I had to draft my money somewhere and I wanted to see Dorrie) my money and my passport. My X-ray showed a very unkind result, revealing that some trouble had developed on the right side as well. I wasn't terribly surprised, although very disappointed, as it meant eternal hours of bed again. In my diary, I stopped recounting my personal life because: *"It's absolutely nebulous and very lonely. I shall deal solely with the Battle of Malaya and war news."*

I lay in my hospital bed at the General gathering news, while the Japanese crept closer to Singapore. I heard about the scorched earth policy adopted by the British as they retreated and which rendered most of the tin produce unavailable to either side and only half of the rubber available to the Japanese. I heard of roads darkened with the smoke from burning rubber trees. I heard of the women driving the ambulances during the Blitz in Ipoh, the Chinese army on its way to Burma and the Australians engaging in jungle warfare behind Japanese lines. The Japanese did not win without a fight. On the 11th January, news came through that Allied submarines had sunk enemy shipping and on the 13th, Singapore had beaten off 125 enemy raiders. On this day too, Kuala Lumpur, the capital of the Federated Malay States fell, lost to the enemy. London reported that *"The scene in Malaya tries the patience sorely."*

The Siege of Singapore commenced early in the morning of 31st January, heralded by the Argyll Regiment, who played the bagpipes as they crossed the Johore Causeway. The subsequent blowing up of the Causeway behind the retreat was heard in the "ward" as several massive explosions at about 4 am. By this stage, I and two other patients had tolerated upheaval, moved from the Singapore General to St Andrew's School, to make way for war casualties. I and another patient suffering from a similar complaint were assigned a school-room completely open on one side, forming a veranda, which exposed us to the full view of passers-by. After the final retreat, the noise from the guns, booming from both sides day and night, increased. Air raids became more intense, answered by deafening anti-aircraft fire which shook the building like matchwood. During these raids I lay under my bed while my friend in the next bed gave a "running commentary" on the progress of the raids. I took my cues from the natives, however, who scrambled under the trees during overhead raids, about how they progressed. These same "natives" marched around the *kampong* every evening offering up prayers for their deliverance, while the children laughed and played and ran in and out of the marchers.

An amiable Tamil doctor of diminutive size had been put in charge of the two patients in the schoolroom and had come to introduce himself, small and neat in his immaculate white coat covering a shirt and tie and neatly pressed trousers.

"Good morning, ladies," he said on the first morning. "My name is Dr Chanker, and I will be looking after you."

My companion and I smiled to ourselves at the unusual name and the keenness of his manner.

"I will be coming later with Matron Waugh to examine you and take a history, but first I would like to know, please, what nature of diet you require?"

I cast a sidelong glance at my friend. I decided to play a little joke on the poor doctor, who seemed somewhat at a loss.

"Doctor, our condition requires a high protein dairy diet. We need as much cream, milk, butter and eggs as you can get. This is very important."

I heard my friend in the next bed stifle a giggle.

During the Siege of Singapore, it was very unlikely that this "requirement" could be granted. The doctor stared at us helplessly and muttered something about "seeing what he could do" but retired to his other patients with a crestfallen look. To his credit though, our meals did contain one or two of these ingredients occasionally.

For us, the days passed far from dully as we watched the world pass by our open veranda. In the next schoolroom were about a dozen women of several ethnic groups. I recorded their bravery in my diary as they convalesced from raid injuries and described the way they continually stared at us, strangely saying "*Add makan*" each morning instead of the usual "*Tabek*". One old Sikh woman always used to go under one of our beds when the raids were on, although I wondered what she thought we could do. Through her apparent extreme age and eccentric manner, she put the fear of God into us. She had a young Sikh to visit her – perhaps her son or grandson, as I thought.

The Battle for Singapore edged closer, with the guns booming more consistently each day and bombs indiscriminately, so it seemed, dropping everywhere. Out of the window could be seen colossal mounds of grey, curling smoke with deep red jets of flame darting up from the ruined buildings. One building survived the onslaught, the Cathay Building, the highest building in Singapore. Rumours reached me that this building served as an enclave of Fifth Columnists protected by the Japanese, and later became a housing place for Allied prisoners. As time went on, we grew accustomed to the noise, from the boom of the guns and the galvanic reactions of the building in which the authorities had housed us, to the sinister, gentle thud of the bombs. Life even became almost bearable once I had made up my mind to adapt myself to existing circumstances. It seemed quite possible to feel, however, that at any time we might hear the quick march of the enemy.

Actually, the nearest Japanese mustered only about five miles away.

The process of adapting to existing circumstances involved the execution of my evacuation plan to Australia. Every morning, I would either phone the P&O office or trek up there, which in my state of health required a singular effort of will. I used Matron's office downstairs for my calls, sitting there with Matron's assistants, a Bengali on one side and a "rather cynical" Chinese on the other but received nothing but a "no reply" signal or a terse clerk answering with the inevitable "no ship." Desperate for results in the little time that remained, I rallied what strength I had left to overcome what seemed endless obstructions. The whole project of securing transport to the other end of the city had developed into a "work of art" but I managed to obtain room in a car by taking some soldiers to the General Hospital for X-ray. This enabled me to get into town, but it was quite another matter to drive five miles to the other side of Singapore to the evacuated P&O office, as the petrol shortage had become so acute that even taxis could no longer operate.

"After considerable strategy, one did manage to reach the P&O signboard only to discover that a long, winding hill awaited with a terrific gradient, which one had to climb. When at last after risking one's very poor lungs one reached the top of this celestial palace, one faced confrontation by about half a dozen strong, tall, broad-looking men attired in full military uniform with anything but affable expressions on their faces - rather like men called to do a job nobody wanted. They obviously made the worst of a bad job."

"No ship today, madam," ran the constant reply.

"After one or two jaunts of this description I decided to tell the MOH that I did not wish to take part in any more of these joy rides. We tried to forget our woes by community singing with the troops but since the doctors told us that singing did not benefit our lungs, it took some of the glamour away."

Unusually for me, I only made two friends from among the troops, one an Australian whom I knew previously, and the other a man from Kuala Lumpur. Despite the seemingly hopeless position in which I and everyone else found ourselves, I saw and recorded the humour in a bathroom story, brought about by the fact that we patients boarded in a previous boy's school.

"There was no distinction of bathrooms, except that the different sexes were instructed to use one on either side of the quadrangle. Although satisfactory for those familiar with the layout of the building, for newcomers it proved different. As a result of this somewhat haphazard method, I found myself washing down to my waist beside a

man in an equal state of undress. Not a word passed between us and when I looked up again he had gone".

There seemed no way of escape. We became almost persuaded that to stay put was the best policy. I made no further attempt to climb to the "celestial palaces" of the P&O offices on the hill, as another shipping office near Collyer Quay had taken over arrangements for departing vessels at this late stage. I spent many hours in the school's office trying to get through to Collyer Quay with little success. I also received calls through my persistence in the office and on one of these the caller instructed me to give a message to one of the Australians to be at Collyer Quay by 3 pm.

This was, I later wrote, rather too much for me to swallow.

"Would it be alright if I came along as well?" I tentatively asked the faceless one on the other end of the line, whose voice sounded somewhat uncertain.

"The person dealing with the situation apparently only dealt with a certain section of the community and would have nothing to do with me. I did not think this was a time when there was one law for the Medes and another for the Persians."

I tried a "spot of autocracy" and won through. They switched me to another man who was probably *"looking after the Medes."* The second person, altogether more positive with a voice to match, was all on my side and told me to go to the quay.

In the early afternoon, I, with the fortunate Australian and my "confederate" Jones (the patient in the next bed to mine) piled into the hospital administrator Mr Forester's car with our luggage, driven by a Chinese syce. As we drove out of the school gates in the direction of the quayside, I looked back at the little group standing at the front portico who had gathered to wave us goodbye, Matron Waugh and Dr Chanker among them. They smiled cheerfully, but I wondered through the bustle and hurry of this departure what fate awaited them They had all acted so kindly to me and Jones, the two oddballs in the open-veranda'd schoolroom, perhaps the biggest white elephants to take part in a campaign. Later, it seemed that we should have taken a list of names to relieve the minds of their relatives and friends, but at that moment I knew how cruel it would have seemed to suggest their position was hopeless. Even at this late stage, I and my companions did not face up to reality. The nearer danger loomed, it seemed, the keener is one's sense of humour and eagerness to live. Our brief sojourn at St Andrew's School had passed sweetly at times despite nearly being killed by the shells, one of which only just missed us as it whizzed through the roof and on to the interior veranda only a few yards away from our beds.

There were about fifty people already at Collyer Quay as the syce abruptly deposited us and our luggage on the quayside, then departed promptly the way he had come, gazing fearfully at the sky as he did so. The little group had ascertained from a military policeman who seemed in charge and was writing on a clipboard, that they had yet to obtain transport to another quay three miles further down. There was barely any time to review the situation, however, before the wail of the siren started again and bombs started falling dangerously near.

I grabbed Jones's arm. An arcade stood across the road near a bank, which might afford some shelter.

"Quick, Jonesy," I said urgently as Jones, her hat askew in the panic, seemed to hesitate. "In the bank over there!"

We left our luggage where it stood on the quay as others did, scattering in various directions as we tried to find some shelter from the hail of missiles. Over in the bank, it seemed that hundreds of people of all colours, nationalities and creeds had had similar ideas. My skirt was pulled by someone underneath a shelf by which I stood among the mixture of sweating, praying humanity which turned out to be a young Chinese man anxious for me to take cover. His insistent pulling gave me no option as I looked around for Jones and saw her a little way further in the building, between a young Tamil woman holding a baby and a large Australian. Relieved, I squatted under the shelf between the Chinese and a Tamil, the latter engrossed in his prayers to Allah and furiously quoting the Koran. As he raised his eyes to heaven, I felt even more startled to see the whites of his eyes gleaming in the darkness.

As I mused much later as I relived the chaos, danger really did not seem so bad until someone starts to pray outwardly, then I am almost finished, even though I certainly did some praying myself, silently. In my later recollections, of all the memories I took away with me, the scene in the bank was the most vivid with the activity going on in the confined space far outdoing the activity the Japanese undertook in the sky above.

While I squatted under the shelf under the threat of being trampled to death, I became aware of a very inebriated Australian nearby, with his six odd feet towering above the squatting crowd around him. By this time, Jones, not wanting us to be separated in the melee, had joined me in my refuge, and we both observed the Aussie in his cups, lurching and swaying above us as he gathered together a new army, equipping them with imaginary weapons. I vividly remember the look on a nearby Chinese guard's face, fathomless in its depth of meaning, not an eye or a feature flickering. Of the Australian, some of the crowd laughed, and some were disgusted. Yet others, like myself and Jones, felt more afraid of him than the bombs, his ludicrous and crazy antics unreal, dreamlike and almost from another, more sinister half-world.

It happened that the Australian's unpredictable behaviour at length persuaded us fugitives to flee our hiding place and face whatever lay outside on the quayside. The raid seemed diminishing in its force. I pulled at Jones's sleeve again and yelled at her in the half-light of the refuge.

"Let's make a run for it," I mouthed urgently. "We'll get our luggage and flag down a car."

Running behind the inebriated Aussie while his back was turned, Jones and I found a path through the mass of humanity, noting that luckily nobody appeared injured, although I noticed some obvious cases of shock However, we felt aware at that moment of experiencing a rare situation of life and death and did not stop. We stood on the side of the road, waiting to dash across the boulevard.

Once more in retrospect, I reflected that if anyone believed in the hand of fate, here was an example from life. As we stood there on the kerbside, we saw Mr Forrester's car with Mr Forrester driving, pass by. Perhaps he had come back looking for us, annoyed by the way the Chinese syce had unceremoniously dumped us on the quayside. We waved frantically, nearly running in front of the car as we did so. Forrester pulled up across the road and we ran over to him, narrowly avoiding the traffic as it congested by the quay. The chaos resulting from the raid surrounded us, plumes of smoke rising from bombed buildings behind the quay and many houses and shops alight. We did not stop to look more closely. I knew subconsciously that if I would survive to find George, everything depended on my actions in the next few minutes. Forrester put his grey head out of the driving window, his face with its military moustache wearing an expression of alarm mixed with rapt attention and urgency.

"Do you have luggage?"

"It's over there, where I left it, I hope!" I shouted, "I'll bring it over! We have to go to Boat Quay!"

Forrester nodded. "I know it."

Seeing a pile of three or four suitcases and coats near the railings by the quay, Forrester drove over to it, then jumped out to help us with the luggage. I noticed casually that the group of passengers we had abandoned in our flight across the road to the bank at the start of the raid had dispersed, and I assumed that they had all gone to Boat Quay. The official with the clipboard no longer stood at his post either.

Forrester covered the three miles across the city as if all the demons of hell followed us, zig-zagging to avoid burnt out cars and abandoned vehicles. I looked at my watch. It showed twenty minutes past three and keeping a tight check on my emotions, I managed to control the surge of panic that lay below the surface of my conscious-ness. Glancing at Jones, I saw that she had such a tight grip on her portmanteau that her knuckles showed white. A few minutes later the quayside came into view with a crowd of people and luggage almost obliterating the sight of two or three military police who appeared to take names with their backs to the harbour. I could see beyond them that the harbour appeared full of vessels of different sizes riding at anchor, with smaller tender boats taking the evacuees to and from the ships. Forrester drew up close to one of the groups.

"Ladies," he said as he deposited us with our luggage on the quay, "I must leave you and get back to the hospital before the next raid begins. May I wish you both all the luck in the world."

He hid his face from view and turned on his heel before I could thank him as he deserved. He had risked his life to get us safely to our ship and we bore him a debt of gratitude. Forrester must have realised that for himself and his wife, it fast became too late to leave and, in any case, he would not have abandoned his hospital post unless given explicit orders to evacuate. As we fought our way to the front of the queue, I turned to look back and saw Forrester's car turn back the way it had come, across the ravaged and burning city. The humid and smoke-filled air made me cough, and with my eyes watering, I tried to focus my sights on the policeman who stood at the head of steps leading down to a small launch which served as tender to one of the ships. I grabbed Jones's arm. We could not lose each other now.

"We've almost made it, Jonesy," I jollied the younger woman along. "Where are your papers?"

Jones rummaged in one of the outside pockets of her portmanteau, looking temporarily fazed but pulled them triumphantly from another pocket. Meanwhile, whether Jones looked ready or not, I took advantage of a gap in the line to approach the official.

"Coates and Jones, priority," I announced to the policeman somewhat abruptly.

Our patient status had given us a slight advantage in that almost certainly the authorities would allocate us a shared cabin. I looked the policeman directly in the eye, giving him the benefit of my steeliest Sister's gaze. The man dropped his gaze to consult his list.

"*Gorgon*," he read. "You're on this launch."

Ten minutes later, thankfully without a further raid, the little tender made its way out into the harbour, fully loaded. We approached a small passenger and cargo vessel well out, among a flotilla of similar craft, bearing the emblem of the Blue Funnel Line. On its bow I made out the words "*Gorgon*" and underneath, "Fremantle". This diminutive ship, then, was to be my means of escape to Australia and freedom.

Chapter 18

The Gorgon

The black hull loomed above our little pilot boat as it drew alongside the ship. In the overloaded launch we could see at close quarters every detail of the scars it bore from many voyages. I and a few of the other passengers huddled on wooden seats had glanced back, hardly daring. Around us and on the shore the scene resembled the hell of an underworld. As fires blazed among the dockside warehouses and oil installations on the shore, the sky filled with a black, acrid and choking smoke, obliterating the sun of a perfect day. Fires onshore reflected in smaller conflagrations on vessels dotted around the harbour, the old and tattered ship in front of us our only slender means of escape apart from death. The wail of yet another siren was heard from the shore, an urgent reminder of the imminent approach of the enemy.

Sailors, working furiously, lowered a rope ladder from a port half way up the side, causing consternation in the launch.

"If they think I'm going to climb up that in these shoes, they've got another think coming," grumbled an anxious voice behind me.

"Ooh, it's so high! I don't like heights," said another, the voice of a timid looking woman sitting beside us, clutching a large valise as if her life depended on it.

I thought I should try to allay their fears, although the prospect of navigating the ladder on the side of the swaying vessel seemed far from appealing. I rustled up a smile for the two quite elderly ladies who had voiced their disquiet.

"I'm sure there's nothing to worry about," I reassured them. "The crew here will help you and stand below, and you will get a hand up from the sailors waiting at the top."

I gestured to the faces of the men above them as they secured the ladder. There came the shouting of orders, a clanking of rope-ends on metal and a general air of controlled haste from the seamen as they made the launch fast beside the side of the ship.

"Ladies, leave your luggage here and it will be loaded into the hold," ordered the pilot captain as he stood in front of them, bewhiskered in his naval cap and tropical whites. "Let's be orderly about this, shall we? No panicking please – you will all get your turn. Now – older ladies and mothers with children first please. You, you and you…"

He pointed and waved through several of the women to where the ladder hung, his manner not unkind but firm. He looked at the sky and estimated they would just have time to load this launch. The sun descended to the horizon and in a couple of hours it would be dark – more difficult for the enemy in their fighter planes above to spot a blacked-out ship in a harbour full of vessels, many of which burned, casting palls of smoke. As he saw the first of the women under his charge start the climb with two of his men standing below to steady the ladder, he wondered how many more launch loads he would get away. Many had failed and they were running out of time…

My turn came, nearly the last to board the *Gorgon*. I had held back, perhaps through a long habit of overseeing others, although I rated, in reality, one of the weakest. I did not feel fear, in the sense that fear did not paralyse my senses and limit my actions. I know that, remembering now. Before the war, I had known of my ability to handle stress through dealing with life and death. Since then, I had experienced personal danger in the London Blitz. I had not expected further testing again in Malaya but deep within me lay a fundamental optimism that I would pull through. Now, with Singapore burning around us, I had waved Jones through before me. I could see her above, looking over the side. She waved reassuringly. Now my turn had arrived. I felt surprisingly nimble as I started up the ladder, smiling a little to myself. I could almost hear George's voice at that moment, half in fun, half serious, in the hearty, passionate way he had of speaking.

"By God, Val, I'll bet those damned sailors had a good look at those lovely legs of yours. I would have knocked 'em over the side if I'd seen them."

In truth, I thought fleetingly, a cotton summer dress, stockings and white peep-toe sandals seemed less than ideal climbing attire. The flimsy ladder which I could feel swaying with every step, held.

"Don't look down!" My own voice as a thought echoed in my ears.

But I did look down, and wished I hadn't. The little boat I had just left seemed small beneath me, the men holding the ladder looking up and foreshortened in perspective. Their disembodied white faces appeared like moons, with eyes reflecting light from the fires. Directly beneath my feet the waters of the harbour rippled an oily green. It would only take one slip...

In less than a minute, I stood on the deck of the *Gorgon*. It looked crowded with women and children and for a few moments, I could not locate Jones – then I saw her among a small group standing by a capstan, some of whom I recognised from the launch. An officer read from the inevitable list and as I approached, I heard my name and that of Jones read out. At the same time, several planes flew overhead towards the port and I grabbed Jones's hand as the officer read out the deck and number of our cabin. I realised that many of the other women were less fortunate and would be sleeping on deck on the mattresses I had seen them carry onto the launch.

"Down below, Jonesy! B Deck 14!" I shouted over the combined noise of the ship's engines and those of the aircraft.

But Jones had already heard the officer and headed for the nearest ladder below decks. We soon realised that we did not have the privilege of sole occupancy of this particular cabin. Six others of a similar age with a few carrying mattresses, made for the ladders to B Deck. By no means all of them had crossed the harbour with us on the same launch. Before the drone of the enemy planes had drowned out his voice, we had just heard the officer give orders to present ourselves back on deck in an hour for a briefing. Below deck, a confusing labyrinth of narrow passageways confronted us with ropes in place on the sides. We became aware of an almost overpowering stench as we penetrated deeper into the bowels of the ship – of stale sweat, vomit and unwashed bodies. We heard later that the *Gorgon* had not had the benefit of cleaning after it had unloaded troops for the defence of Singapore on the outward voyage – troops that had arrived too late.

"Cabin 14?" I enquired of a frightened-looking sailor who was hurrying up the passageway towards us.

He pointed silently down a passageway to the left and in a few seconds, we came to a door with that number almost illegibly painted on the door frame. I pushed the door. It hung ajar. In the gloom of a tiny cabin, we could just make out six narrow bunks against the bulkheads with a narrow space in between. Each bunk awaited us unmade, with a coarse grey hempen sheet, ticking-covered pillow and one navy-issue blanket folded at one end of each thin mattress. The atmosphere inside the cabin pressed in closely, clammy and stale with no porthole to let in light or a breath of air. I felt both dismayed and relieved to notice a large tin bucket with a lid in a corner of the cabin.

I put an arm around Jones, whose expression appeared as one of hopeless resignation.

"Bag yourself a bunk, Jonesy."

I had heard the scuffle of footsteps in the passageway. I had put my overnight bag on the bottom bunk of one of the tiers. I did not think that my lungs would stand the strain of nocturnal mountaineering. Best leave that to one of the younger women. Jones rallied herself and went for the bunk directly above, while with the arrival of the rest of the inmates, the space available in the cabin severely limited our movements. Luckily, the women with the mattresses had arrived expecting to sleep on the floor, so as I had feared, no arguments occurred. Apart from myself and Jones, I recognised several of the women as the wives of planters and the rest convalescent ex-patients from Singapore General, recently outposted to St Andrew's School.

Twenty minutes later, introductions and bunks having being made, the eight inmates of Cabin 14 climbed back on deck. The sun disappeared over the horizon but over the harbour, the darkness of night made little impression. The fires from the shoreline reflected in the night sky and the burning ships on the harbour sent trails of shimmering light along the black water. Standing a little way from the *Gorgon* another, larger passenger ship and two naval vessels rode at anchor, swaying a little on the disturbed surface, around them just visible the same activity of the boarding of civilians. Around us, launches still unloaded a never-ending stream of human cargo as we looked on nervously. How could this little ship hold so many? A hush fell, as the captain, flanked by his first and second officers, started speaking. Others of the ship's crew stood a little way off.

"Ladies, I am Captain Marriott," began the captain, neat and clean-shaven in his whites.

I thought he looked calm and business-like – he would have to be. I was struck by his mild, unassuming manner as he looked around at his passengers.

"I'll keep this very short, for obvious reasons." He gestured at the sky. His voice sounded quiet and his audience strained to hear. "We hope to be away by just after midnight, sailing under blackout. We are very full tonight – there are nearly four hundred of us and it's not going to be a pleasure cruise. This ship has been built for only eighty passengers, sturdy as she is for her size. But she has the advantage of being nimble and with a bit of luck and a following wind we'll make it to Batavia[1]."

The captain glanced out to where the other ships assembled, waiting.

"We've got company and we'll sail in convoy. *Empire Star* is almost fully loaded and *Durban* and *Kedah* will escort us for the first leg of the journey."

He looked round at us all.

"This will take all of your cooperation. After Batavia, my plan is to sail straight for Fremantle in Western Australia and I will not speak to you *en masse* again. You will need to organise yourselves into groups of eight or ten so that one or two of you collect food from the cooks at mealtimes, while others look after children and the sick and organise the use of what toilet facilities we have. The crew will help but it's up to you to get us through. Those of you with no cabin allocation can use the allotted areas on deck.

"That's all I have to say. Let's say a short prayer. May God speed."

There on the little cargo vessel amongst the sights and sounds of the fall of Singapore, nearly four hundred people bent their heads.

The captain turned on his heel and made for the bridge to make radio contact with the other vessels. He looked at his watch as he went. Almost simultaneously, queues of women, some holding children, began forming in front of the officers.

Shortly before midnight, I lay in the stuffy heat of the cabin, listening to the snores and deep breathing of the seven other women. In the dim light filtering through from the passageway, I saw a hand descend from above and grasped it warmly.

"Goodnight, Jonesy," I whispered, not knowing whether my friend could hear me. "When you wake up, we'll be well on our way to Batavia."

The hand patted mine and withdrew.

I estimated that approximately half an hour later, I felt some bumps through the ship's wall and heard the muffled tread of steps hastening up the passageway outside our door. Quietly, I pulled on my wrap and, treading carefully through the cabin, pulled open the door. There was no one in the passage. Making my way to a little-used part of the deck above, I looked over the rail into the harbour. Several small native vessels and a motor launch had pulled alongside the ship a little way along the hull. I could see several men in military shirts and shorts standing up in the boats gesturing and talking earnestly to officers on the *Gorgon*. As I watched, the captain appeared and after a few moments gave the orders to lower the ladder. I counted as the men climbed onboard. Forty-eight more men added to this chaos. I had better warn my cabin-mates in the morning.

Almost immediately, as if to deter more last-minute attempts at boarding, I felt the ship's engines rumbling in the depths of the vessel. Then quietly and in darkness, I felt movement and a gliding sensation as the ships within my view appeared to be moving backwards. As we headed towards the open sea, I could see the black bulks of the other ships of the convoy at a distance. The fires of Singapore still burned.

A silence fell over the ship. On the decks, mattresses and their occupants lay in any available space under the night sky. As we sailed south between the myriad islands of the South China Sea, the air cleared and stars became visible. I slept at last, after a fashion, a shallow, dream-filled sleep almost indistinguishable from thoughts or memories.

I woke, disturbed after what I thought a short time by the occupant of the top bunk climbing past and the framework shaking. I glanced at my watch. It was just on seven o'clock and I surmised that I had, after all, slept for longer than I thought. Just then, over the ship's loud speaker, the piercing sound of a bugle playing the *Reveille* aroused the remaining sleepers of the cabin, followed by the captain's voice requesting everyone's presence on deck in half an hour. The morning air felt cool and sweet on our faces on A Deck, as, in twos and threes, sleepy passengers emerged from the stifling heat of their cabins or appeared from the nether corners of the deck space, many appearing frowzled and unwashed. From the appearance of the surrounding scene, it seemed hard to imagine that only a few hundred miles away lay the chaos and carnage of Singapore under attack. The two naval escorting vessels, the *Durban* and the *Kedah,* sailed calmly a little distant from the *Gorgon,* while the large passenger vessel which had carried troops from Bombay to Singapore only a few weeks ago, *Empire Star,* glided majestically a little in front. A few smaller vessels which had set sail with them from Singapore were at the fringes of the convoy. At that moment, it struck me that in any attack from the skies, the *Empire Star* would likely take the brunt.

The first officer, a young, thin man in his mid-thirties, stood at one end of the deck near the ladder to the galleys with several crew members. Trestle tables were erected close by. He waited until a size-able number of the more than four hundred passengers on board assembled on deck. I, having managed little more than a splash on my face and hands from a bathroom basin near my cabin, noticed that the troops who had boarded during the night had not presented them-selves at the "roll call" and wondered at their whereabouts. Jones arrived at my side within a few minutes, breathless but looking rested.

"Good morning, everyone," the officer began, looking round at us all observantly. "I trust you slept well. The cooks below decks are about to serve breakfast. I should like you to form into groups of six. Two passengers from each group will follow these officers to the kitchens and then return to their groups to distribute the food. You should eat on deck then return to your cabins or your deck space."

The officer paused and looked serious.

"I must tell you that we have intelligence of enemy planes approaching from the north, expected to be overhead in approximately one hour. I would ask you all to finish breakfast as speedily as possible, without..." Here he smiled a faint, rueful smile... "giving yourselves indigestion, then take cover. To reassure you, both *Gorgon* and *Empire Star* are equipped with defence weapons which will be utilised in the event of an attack as is of course, our naval escort. We are about to enter the Bangka Strait and expect to reach Batavia in the Dutch East Indies late this afternoon."

The officer disappeared towards the bridge and, like the previous evening, queues formed as, with surprisingly little fuss, others sat in groups at the trestles, many looking nervous. Even though the deck did not open fully to the sky, everyone felt more exposed than they had ever done in their lives. After a few moments, it seemed apparent that the ship changed course. Dimly, to the port side of the vessel, I could see the hazy shape of a group of islands and *Gorgon* now took the lead of the convoy towards the archipelago. On the deck, not liking others to cater for my needs, I propelled Jones towards the queue even now disappearing down the ladder to the galley.

"We'll get a group together when we come back from the galley, Jonesy." Jones looked a little pale – partly from the slight rocking motion of the ship and partly from sheer fright at the prospect of once more being under attack. She had never claimed bravery despite having to battle her long illness and she felt her remaining strength weaken as the demands on her resources continued mercilessly. "You'll feel better after breakfast, dear." I looked at my companion. She had advanced further in her convalescence than I but psychologically the effects of her illness had lingered. I felt that without my support she would not have coped. As for me, I knew that when we reached safety, I would probably have a reaction from forcing myself to remain steadfast for so long. I jollied Jones along, knowing that we both needed to eat. "Come. I've always wondered what these ship's kitchens look like!"

It had edged close to nine when we made for the ladder down to our cabin. We felt reluctant to go back into the close, airless environment with our six cabin-mates and I suggested that we take our coffee to the little hideaway from where I had seen the troops boarding during the night. Although no comfortable deck chairs seemed available, piles of ropes provided alternative seating as well as built-in enclosures for equipment which formed kind of shelf conveniently at seat height. Out of the blue, at that moment of impending danger, I thought that George would be in his element in this nautical environment. From our vantage point, we looked out over the ocean at the islands, enjoying the respite. What the first officer had said about the approach of the enemy did not seem real.

A jarring sound jerked us back to the reality of war when suddenly, overhead appeared a large flight of fighter planes and bombers. They all but obliterated the morning sky with their noise and low flying presence. We both held our hands over our ears with fright and took more shelter in our corner. I felt that even now, I would rather stay here on deck than below decks in darkness, waiting to be hit and perhaps sunk. The bombs started falling, most hitting the water and exploding, making heavy waves which rocked the ship. The *Gorgon* still headed for the calm inlet formed by a nearby island. Behind us, across the water, we saw the *Empire Star* sustain a direct hit and sailors scurrying around the decks. Our anti-aircraft guns as well as theirs, retaliated the attack by taking aim and firing at the enemy planes, too numerous to count. Looking up at the dreaded red circle symbol on the body and wings of the khaki-coloured planes, I counted at least twenty. The bombing and machine-gunning continued for what seemed an eternity, with the *Empire Star* sustaining two more direct hits, from which it was doubtful she would be able to recover and continue. The *Gorgon* had not had a direct hit, but had several near-misses. The planes dive-bombed so close to the ship that we could see the pilots, frighteningly visible and trapped in their cockpits.

I finally admitted defeat after another twenty minutes of shattering noise and smoke, which filled my nostrils and lungs and provoked a severe coughing attack. We went below decks, feeling the explosions vibrate on the sides of the vessel. The muffled boom of the ship's guns continued, relentless. Shock waves from bombs hitting the water caused the vessel to rock erratically, so that we struggled to reach our cabin. We both lay on our bunks and prayed, putting our fingers in our ears. The raids continued, off and on, for four hours, while on the bridge, Captain Marriott and the crew manoeuvred the little, heavily overloaded ship in and out of the rocky outcrops of the shoreline, taking shelter from the view of the enemy aircraft in hidden coves and inlets. The convoy by this time had become scattered but later that afternoon, by some miracle, all the ships of the *Empire Star* convoy docked safely in the harbour at Batavia.

The capital of the Dutch East Indies would only remain unoccupied by the Japanese for a few more weeks but there in the safety of neutral territory the *Gorgon* received necessary repairs and the military personnel disembarked. Impatient to reach complete safety in Fremantle, Captain Marriott set sail again within a few hours. In the meantime, neither Jones nor I felt in the mood for sight-seeing, but not having had anything to eat since breakfast that morning we eventually found a restaurant on the quay which accepted the Australian currency I had prepared before leaving Singapore. I reflected during the meal, looking out over the harbour in Old Batavia, that this marked the first time I had managed to eat a meal peacefully, without being constantly on the alert for the air-raid siren, for many weeks. We gazed at the ship with the shipwrights swarming over her decks and hull in awe. Captain Marriott had been right when he had said that the ship was nimble. We may not have been nearly so fortunate in a larger ship. The *Empire Star* also received essential maintenance but her wounds, as we could see, were much more severe and she would not be sailing with us to Fremantle.

Only when we got back on board, did we hear about the deaths of fourteen people on the *Empire Star* during three direct hits that morning.

On 27th February, after a voyage of sixteen days, the *Gorgon* reached Fremantle, the port of Perth in western Australia. Despite the constant threat of mines and Axis submarines, no further incidents occurred. During the remainder of the voyage, I wrote nothing in my diary. I struggle now to remember my exact feelings all those years ago. It seemed as if, having survived to a condition of comparative safety, I hesitated to draw attention to myself from – whom? Some set of pagan gods perhaps, the Christian or Old Testament God, the god of those upon the sea or whatever or whomever I felt had protected me. The danger had not been the usual one faced by sailors. No tempest had battered the ship, no iceberg had pierced her hull. The onslaught under which the *Gorgon* had laboured had come from human power alone, concentrated into a deadly and efficient force. My own feeble human voice had been silenced and humbled at last, perhaps even my irrepressible sense of humour in the face of danger finally subdued by what seemed like the hand of the supernatural in my survival. Sailing over the endless depths of the Indian Ocean I could have wondered why I had been so chosen. Surely, I thought, it must reach the zenith of cruelty - the whole meaning and purpose of all this just for an existence, which I felt then being without George would be.

The *Gorgon* had sailed in the last convoy carrying evacuees after an official directive to clear Singapore Harbour of ships on the 11th of February and of the forty-six ships which left, only six made it to Australia.

I had experienced heartbreak, seeing my beloved Malaya overrun. After the worst of the danger of the escape had passed, I had time to reflect on my ideas about what had happened to enable the Japanese such an easy victory. Jones and I sat one evening after dinner over a *stingah* in our favourite corner of the deck of the *Gorgon*, looking out at the sunset over the ocean. Onboard, Jones and

I usually kept to ourselves during the day. At night time we saw quite enough of the other occupants of our cabin and, especially in my new more subdued mood, I had lost interest in the former colonials. My eagerness to embrace my new life had dissipated. These people, I knew, would return to dull lives in the Home Counties, spending their remaining years remembering and reliving the past.

"You see, Jonesy, it all boiled down to treachery. For one thing, our colonial policy was too trusting to the Malays and the sultans were ambitious and highly educated. They had two masters, effectively, for the Japanese were paying them."

Jones looked rather shocked. She could not imagine all this skulduggery happening behind the scenes of the tranquil colonial life she had known.

"Are you sure, Val?" she ventured. "I never heard anything about that."

"Oh yes, of course. The British would have been on their guard if they had known. And the Eurasian community! The British were trying to overthrow the race bar but they were still jealous of some of the young colonials who possessed what they never could. They supported the Japanese too, through their Fifth Column activity."

Jones looked as if she did not like to disagree. After all, I always read the newspapers. But I could see she had a niggling feeling that the "traitors" may have had a point.

"And don't," I went on, "talk to me about the Sukais. They're the aboriginals, you know. The Malays are only escapees from surrounding islands. Well, they led the Japanese through the jungle, you see."

"Do you have any proof of all this, Val? It's extraordinary."

"I don't need proof, dear. It's all about the colour of money and about being on the winning side."

"We've had our innings, I suppose," said Jones reflectively.

Now my turn came to look shocked.

"I can't understand why the British government wasn't more appreciated," I said sadly. "Everything they know we taught them and it was a benign system. I was really very fond of my dear native patients. The little babies were so pretty,,,"

I felt pensive and sad.

"Care for another *stingah* dear?" I rallied as I reached down for the half-bottle of whiskey beside my seat.

As the years have gone on, I have revised my ideas but only a little. The war was the final nail in the coffin of our demise and signalled the beginning of the end of empire.

I stood at a good vantage point on an otherwise deserted deck as in the early morning of the 27th February, the coast of Western Australia appeared distantly to the east, looking like a mirage in the rising sun. I made out more and more of the coastline as the ship progressed, seeing to the north miles of white sandy beaches, while directly in front rows of low flat buildings forming the customs and immigration sheds surrounded the entrance to the rectangular harbour. Behind stretched the town of Fremantle, its single-story houses almost lost, set low in the flat, sparsely vegetated terrain. I had packed my few remaining possessions the night before, and had made this pilgrimage to the deck in the early morning purposely. As I watched my destination approach, I saw it as a completion of my journey from England to the other side of the world. I had no high hopes of Australia and in retrospect, I knew that I approached her shores sadly.

An hour later, as the remaining passengers assembled on deck for a final breakfast, Captain Marriott appeared to wish us a safe onward journey. Somebody started the round of applause which soon became pandemonium, with utensils being beaten together and on the rough trestle tables. I wondered who had organised this as I had heard nothing about it. Or had it happened spontaneously? I recognised the woman who rose to thank the captain for our safe deliverance and joined in the applause again at the end of the speech. It was his due.

He was decorated with high naval honours, as were several members of his crew, for bringing the *Gorgon* home.

As we disembarked into the blinding clear light of the Antipodes under a sky so deeply blue that its blueness seemed reflected in the atmosphere itself, I felt almost defensive. I had not wanted this, and yet I knew that it was at least a safe haven with new possibilities. I determined on positivity and decided to make the most of it until I could return to England. After all, they spoke English, or rather, I thought, ruefully, a form of it. And Dorrie had made her home here, although four thousand miles away across this vast wilderness which I would have to cross to get to Sydney.

Unexpectedly, however, my initial encounters with the inhabitants of this vast island surprised me. A row of customs officials, neat in short-sleeved shirts and shorts, waited for us as we made our first steps onto Australian soil and safety. "Welcome to Australia, Madam." The official closest to me, young, blond and tanned, spoke politely. "Come this way please." His accent sounded soft on the ear compared with the clipped English to which I had grown accustomed since birth.

All the passengers received a similar treatment and those ahead of me and Jones had already progressed half way through the first customs shed having their papers examined. As strictly patients, holding hospital letters from our doctors at Singapore General, the officials waved us through to a separate desk apart from the main flow of passengers, where two uniformed nurses were waiting for us. They subjected us both to a brief assessment and questioning. One of the nurses examined my papers.

"Miss Coates," she said in a friendly manner.

As a female version of the first customs official, she stood tall and well-built, young, blonde and tanned under her white cap. I thought at that moment that in this dry, warm climate, the likelihood that she would succumb to tuberculosis as I myself had done so quickly, appeared slim. Here, I thought, I should make a complete recovery.

"I see you are a health sister, so I don't have to explain everything to you. But here in Australia we keep infectious diseases quarantined until the disease is stabilised. You are running a slight temperature, but I understand that you have been through an ordeal. An ambulance is standing by to take you and Miss Jones to the Royal Perth Hospital."

Jones and I acquiesced resignedly and found ourselves escorted to the waiting ambulance. In a few minutes, we travelled through the streets of Fremantle among yellow stoned colonial buildings which, ever the chronicler, I determined to explore on another occasion. Now I looked at Jones, while the drivers concentrated on the busy main road between Fremantle and Perth. I took her hand affectionately. She looked so unhappy. Another parting loomed.

"Now don't worry, this isn't goodbye, Jonesy," I said, trying to reassure the younger woman. "We may be separated now and I might not get another chance to say this." I paused. "We've been through a lot together – more than most. I – I'm glad I went through it all with you, Jones. Get well soon, but above all, write to me."

We had arrived at the Royal Perth Hospital - a huge, modern red-bricked building, whose edifice towered above us as the ambulance chugged up the drive. I sighed. Yet another hospital, another prison, awaited. The ambulance drivers escorted us both to the reception area and left us for a few moments. About five minutes later they came back with wheelchairs, into which they bade us patients sit. Considering that we had both survived climbing rope ladders and aerial bombardment, I, perhaps through relief, pent up stress and the mental strain of all I had endured during the past few weeks, began to laugh hysterically. Jones looked at me in surprise and laughed a little too. The ambulance driver, an experienced paramedic and a father of three, patted me on the shoulder. He parked the wheelchairs in a quiet area of the lobby.

"You'll be right love," he said kindly. "Carter here will get you a nice hot, sweet cuppa, won't you, Carter?" He nodded and winked meaningfully at his colleague, and gestured with his head towards the refreshments counter. Carter took the hint and came back with two steaming mugs. "Come from Singapore, have you?" he said sympathetically. "A rough business. Here, you drink this, love. The Aussies know how to make a cup of tea!"

I felt my eyes filling with tears at their kindness. If this was Australia, I knew that it would not be so bad after all.

---

1. Before 1949, Batavia was the capital of the Dutch East Indies. It is now Jakarta, Indonesia.

Chapter 19

Australia Wide

Dorrie saw the newspaper come sailing over the front fence and the tail end of the truck as it vanished down the street and round the corner. She ran out to the front garden to scan the *Sydney Morning Herald* anxiously. The last she had heard from Lavinia, she had been incarcerated in the hospital in Singapore, trying to get on a ship to Australia. Since then, she had been inundated with letters from Lavinia's friends and family, asking if she had arrived. The news from Malaya over the past few days had got progressively worse, with the enemy advancing closer to the vital port of Singapore.

The newspaper headlines confirmed what she had heard on the wireless last night. Singapore had fallen, surrendered to the Japanese. Dorrie felt sick with anxiety and took the paper inside. She ate a quiet breakfast alone at the kitchen table, in the bright, modern bungalow in Brighton-Le-Sands on Botany Bay, where she and Roe had begun married life. They had taken up residence there, glowing with happiness and the cool mountain air, directly from their honeymoon in Katoomba. Now, looking around the sunlit kitchen in the peace of the early morning, Dorrie, trying to assimilate the news, reflected on the contrast between the humdrum routine of her quiet daily life and the horrors of the warfare over the water, steadily encroaching on their bastion of Australia. As if to reflect this expectation of continued peace, the baby, fractious during the night, had only settled towards dawn and was now sleeping deeply in his cot in the bedroom, chubby arms raised above his head in surrender. Roe had left for the bakery hours ago.

Hardly bearing to look, Dorrie scanned the smaller print of the leading article. Several large passenger ships carrying evacuees had sailed from Singapore but with chaos ruling there, no passenger lists had appeared in print. News now emerged of the air attacks – machine gunning and bombing of the ships as they tried to escape through the Bangka Strait. The enemy had sunk many ships with terrible consequences. Dorrie feared the worst, if indeed Lavinia had managed to board a ship. If she had remained in Singapore and had succumbed to capture, perhaps she stood more of a chance.

Nearly two weeks had passed before the telegram arrived. Having spent the last weeks going through the motions of housework, cooking and baby minding, Dorrie stared at the envelope the telegraph boy held out to her as if she feared it might bite her. She prayed quickly that it did not contain bad news and tore open the envelope.

ARRIVED HOSPITAL PERTH YESTERDAY STOP
LETTER FOLLOWING STOP LAVINIA

Dorrie laughed for joy, at which Roe appeared from the lounge-room carrying his newspaper. The particular peace of a Sunday morning at home had prevailed until now. She tried to gather her thoughts quickly and turned back to the delivery boy.

"Send this back," she said. "Ready?"

The boy nodded and licked the end of his pencil.

SO RELIEVED DEAR STOP HAVE A WONDERFUL
REST STOP DORRIE AND ROE

As the boy disappeared down the garden path, Dorrie turned to Roe in jubilation. "It's Lavinia, Roe! She's alive and in Australia!" and threw her arms round her husband.

Roe, unaccustomed to such demonstrations of affection at this hour of the morning, looked surprised but pleased nonetheless. He put his arms around her. Now, he thought, perhaps Dorrie would feel happier. Since their marriage nearly two years before, his wife had, firstly during her pregnancy, suffered somewhat from loneliness. Then, when little Brian had arrived, a homesickness had settled on her like an enveloping shroud. Well, with the war on, nobody could go anywhere – later on he would see. He would try anything to keep her happy and anyway, he had always harboured a soft spot for England and the English people.

Lavinia was as good as her word and wrote as soon as she could, telling Dorrie everything that had happened since she had left St Andrew's School for the ship. In Brighton-Le-Sands it seemed an incredible story, yet everything in wartime was so. After Roe got home, he ruminated for a long time when Dorrie showed him the letter, shaking his head with incredulity.

"When is she coming to Sydney?" he asked her.

"I told you, Roe. She's not been well and she's got to be cleared by the hospital before she can travel. TB." She said the last word in a quiet voice. Even in these enlightened days a certain stigma accompanied the disease.

"Oh. Gee, that's no good." Roe rustled his newspaper and cleared his throat. "Will she be clear of that when she gets to Sydney, then?" He looked at his baby son, for once playing quietly in his playpen in the corner.

"I'm sure she will, dear. They're very strict about that here. They won't let her travel unless she's completely well. I hope it doesn't take too long though."

Dorrie couldn't wait to see her friend. It would sound so wonderful to hear an English voice again and hear news of everyone at home. And it would be wonderful, too, to hear all about Lavinia's adventures in Malaya, especially George..... had she heard from him yet, she wondered?

I stayed in Perth for nine long months. The trauma of the escape from Malaya had had more of an effect on my health than I realised at the time, buoyed up by the basic instinct of the desire to survive. In Perth General, the nurses cared for me well and I became very impressed with my two doctors, a Doctor Muche and a Doctor Henzel, who in my opinion came a close second to my beloved Dr Shelley. I had arrived in Perth with a letter from my consultant in Singapore which had given the Perth doctors a good idea of my condition. This had enabled them to ascertain any changes resulting from my arduous experiences. They tut-tutted over my X-rays while they stood in consultation near my bedside.

"This will take time, Miss Coates. You have had a setback, but it's not surprising considering what you have had to endure."

I remember that the doctors and especially the nurses, also had concerns about my mental condition. Trauma aside, I had an underlying melancholia which was obvious to their trained eye. I would lie for hours on my bed just staring into space. On seeing that I did not go unobserved, I would hastily pick up a book or my pen and diary, or the letter I wrote. These days after Vietnam there is more understanding of the condition known as PTSD– then, the hospital staff knew simply that my experiences must have had a profound psychological effect. They had not, however, any awareness that my fiancé was missing and, wishing to keep this very personal affair private, I did not enlighten them.

Around this time, I started writing to George. Through the daily newspapers, I had discovered that the Red Cross endeavoured to deliver letters to prisoners of war if one wrote monthly on one side of a page to the prisoner at their last known address. Determined to "keep faith" that George lived somewhere and would receive the letters, I never missed this opportunity.

In the first letter I wrote of the "wonderful news" I had heard in Singapore before I left, of his whereabouts. I had contacted Mr Weir, his former boss, who had told me that he in fact worked again on the mine, now of course under the control of the Japanese. This had given me a "spark of hope." But through the joy, niggling doubts arose, try as I might to ignore them. I knew that if this were true, somehow he would have found a way to write to me in all this time.

"I live those last two days over and over again," I wrote. *"The week after our parting was spent in a state of oblivion. I couldn't think straight at all. I just felt as if I had come away from another planet with no wars and where the sun shines all day with just enough shade to make it beautifully warm, and feeling at the same time your arms around me. I think it is that last comforting feeling that keeps me sane. Nevertheless, I was bitterly lonely."*

Nearly fifty years later, I held this wad of letters in my hand. With what hope and conviction I had sent them! I had painstakingly copied each one by hand, ever the efficient secretary.

In the warm, dry climate of Perth, my body slowly healed. I had to admit to myself that perhaps the climate and lifestyle in Malaya had not, after all, been conducive to my good health. Despite my later criticisms, I wrote to George that I liked most things about Australia. The great advantage was that they did "tell you exactly what they think of you". My great ambition, I wrote, was to get my old job back in health visiting in Australia. I failed to compare my comparatively poor physique with those of the nurses I had seen in Australia, many of whom resembled Greek goddesses – tall, perfectly formed, permanently tanned and blonde. The doctors expressed their doubt and put my enthusiasm down to lack of insight, perhaps as a result of my chronic depression. They submitted their report to the Australian High Commission advising against it.

In the late November of 1942 the doctors came to my bedside to tell me that at last, I had now recovered sufficiently well to travel to

Sydney. As I had done many times before, I took matters into my own hands to force the matter through. I had gone into the city to the Colonial Office, having "won the battle" to make an appointment with the representative there. Understanding that my mental health would benefit from seeing my old friend, the representative gave in and granted me permission to go to Sydney in December.

"The High Commission for Australia has discharged me! The tragedy is that my sincere nursing friends who would have fought for me are interned in Malaya. The Commissioner has recommended secretarial work, so Dr Henzel has provided me with a letter of recommendation to a secretarial college in Sydney," I wrote to Dorrie.

In much better spirits, I prepared to set off on my journey across Australia which began on the 2nd December. I dutifully made my last rounds of the wards and said goodbye to the patients I had supplied with toothpaste, soap or talcum powder, feeling a sense of *déjà vu* as I did so. I had said goodbye so many times during this war and it would not be the last. This distribution of stores formed part of the "Grade" work convalescent patients had to do and which in my case had involved trolley-pushing around the hospital. I realised when my recovery had progressed that it had stopped me from thinking and I had met and chatted to many women. But I had only made one real friend among my fellow TB patients with whom I had exchanged addresses – an Australian woman and ex-nurse, whose candid way of seeing the world appealed to me and under whose tutelage I became initiated into the Australian consciousness. Our friendship had blossomed in very different circumstances to those surrounding Jones and me. Dear Jonesy had made a more rapid recovery than I and had been discharged some months ago, to spend her convalescence in a nursing home in Fremantle. She had returned to nursing fit and well.

During the evening of the 2nd December, I boarded the sleeper train at East Perth Terminal known as The Westland, which would take me nearly four hundred miles on the first leg of my journey to the gold mining town of Kalgoorlie-Boulder. Considering my recent illness, the doctors had advised me to book a sleeping compartment to myself. The dining car actually operated on this train too, although often suspended during the war years, and served dinner on the outward-bound trip (the dining car uncoupled *en route* and reconnected for the purpose of serving breakfast on the return journey). I settled in for the three-day journey to Sydney, relishing my new-found freedom.

In the early morning of the following day, I stood on Kalgoorlie station, waiting for the Trans-Australian train which would take me over a thousand miles across the Nullarbor Plain to St Augusta, in South Australia. From there yet another would take me to Sydney, across New South Wales. The country's track system used different gauges only completely standardised at the beginning of the 21st century, enabling continuous journeys between the eastern cities. In December 1942, I faced the prospect of the journey with some trepidation. In the early morning light, the surrounding country of Western Australia had looked intimidating in its vastness of rust-coloured earth, dull green dusty scrubland and spindly gum trees under a wide, powder-blue sky. With the so-called wisdom of age and hindsight, I realise now that I dismissed the scene as not attaining any level of allure because I had never seen its like. I could not see the uncompromising grandeur, if not stark beauty of the country. Instead, my first impressions centred inevitably on the contrasts and comparisons with England in a strange and hostile environment. I wondered what Dorrie thought of it all.

A large blue locomotive roared into the little station. Behind it followed the carriages containing sleeper and non-sleeper cars. I had been unlucky with my booking and was unable to obtain a sleeper for this part of the journey – the worst part, I thought. I hoped, for the sake of my poor lungs, that not too many passengers would accompany me on that train today. It seemed quite sparsely occupied but several people along the carriage already puffed on cigarettes, and my heart sank. At least, I hoped, it would be air-conditioned. I had a good supply of food and drink and settled into a corner seat, primed for the journey. I had a triple seat, so unless any more passengers boarded from the tiny settlements *en route*, I would be able to put my feet up surreptitiously later on.

The Nullarbor, as I had discovered from my Australian patient friend before setting off, literally meant "no trees." Aptly named, I thought, as the blue locomotive sped along the straightest stretch of track imaginable for hundreds of miles, through the desert landscape towards Port Augusta. I looked around the carriage, since little fired my imagination outside the window. It was small but comfortable, with blue-patterned plush high-backed seats. A sliding door led out to the corridor, into which I had made up my mind to escape if the smoking gentleman in the opposite corner became overwhelmingly fumous. I felt a cough coming on and desperately tried to repress the tickle, as I knew that a loud bark would forcefully emerge when I least expected it. I stared in turn at the three coloured paintings in railway-issue frames on the opposite side of the carriage, depicting the treeless plain from several different angles. The views did not provide enough distraction and I became victim to an explosive coughing fit. In desperation, I took out my handkerchief, pressed it to my mouth and with scarlet countenance and streaming eyes got up and made a dash for the corridor, nearly falling over the feet of the fumous gentleman. He, settled comfortably in his corner with news-paper and cigarettes, looked up in consternation.

"I say, are you alright, Madam?" he inquired in an English voice with genuine concern.

He looked rather nice, I thought. In different circumstances I might have started a conversation. Occasionally, these days I began to feel the need for male company. This man, unusually for outback Australia, presented a neat appearance, smartly dressed in immacu-lately pressed slacks and open-necked shirt. He was clean shaven with light brown hair recently trimmed and slicked down in a side parting.

"Oh yes, thank you," I managed to get out. "I'm afraid that I shall have to get a little air. I have just been discharged from hospital, you know. Lung problems."

"I see," replied the stranger. "I'm sorry – my cigarettes must have exacerbated your cough. Do come back in when you're ready. If I need to smoke, I will go out to the corridor myself."

The rest of the journey passed pleasantly enough. Eventually, my travelling companion introduced himself as John Benson, who worked for a mining conglomerate based in Port Augusta but who currently supervised various operations in the rich mineral fields of Western Australia. Presently he produced some papers from a battered brown briefcase and started to work on them, while I dozed or read. Waking up to look outside at regular intervals, I noticed that the scenery barely altered. The train stopped twice at what seemed like ghost towns. Once I asked John where they were and their names.

"This is Rawlinna," explained the engineer. He too had stopped reading and was looking out at the most remote post office I had ever seen – little more than a shack by the railway siding, fronted by a small covered walkway. "There is also a lime mine here which is used in the gold production in Kalgoorlie," he continued. "Sometimes I have to stop here to get some samples. Back there about an hour ago you may have noticed we stopped at another little railway siding called Cook."

I had been dimly aware of stopping at a remote location some time ago, but I had felt so drowsy that I might almost have dreamed it.

"Only a handful of people live in these towns," John said informatively. "They were built mainly to support the railway around 1917. They're still useful as halts for the Trans-Australian line and you can request to get off if you've a mind."

I had had no thoughts of alighting somewhere hundreds of miles from civilisation. What a nightmare if the train left without you. This journey made me realise that I had not as yet attained my full robustness. As the train rattled along the sleepers in what seemed like an eternity, I felt eternally thankful that it at least represented an oasis of civilisation in a hostile landscape – a microcosm sufficient unto itself.

I must have fallen into a fitful doze, when I jumped at a nudge on my arm. John had left his seat and gazed out of my window. He smiled and pointed at some moving objects about half a mile from the train, which now travelled at much less than full speed. Bounding amongst and dodging the scrubland, a large herd of red kangaroos almost kept pace with the train, running in a parallel direction. A shimmering heat haze above the red earth distorted the observer's view. Way off in the distance, a low line of blue-green hills showed barely visible on the horizon. Intent on their flight, the creatures, with their rust-red coats barely distinguishable against the desert soil, did not appear aware of the near presence of humankind and their huge mechanical conveyance. I gazed and laughed in surprised pleasure.

"You may as well see something of the real Australia while you're in the outback! Must be dingoes around," John guessed from his experience. "There!" He pointed to an indistinct shape, minute in the distance, the colour of sand. Whatever it was worried the heels of the larger animals and appeared to want to round them up like a cattle dog.

In the railway carriage, we travellers watched the natural drama unfold, as several more dingoes joined the chase and brought down a kangaroo. At this point, I stopped looking, not liking to be reminded of the reality, if not brutality, of the natural world. I resettled myself into my seat, but a moment later again looked out of the window, fascinated. Despite the loss of one of their number, the rest of the herd continued to bound forward.

"Often," continued John, "You will see camels in this region, travelling in herds of up to forty or so."

"Camels, here!" I exclaimed, surprised. I had never heard of this before. "We're not in the Sahara or Arabia!" I continued to gaze at the kangaroo herd as they gradually gave up the chase and dropped behind the train.

"Quite so," agreed John. "That's our fault. The British imported them here in the last century for transport and construction work. They were ideal in this environment if you think about it. But now there are too many of them and they're talking about a cull."

Although I felt indifferent to domestic pets, I found the natural flora and fauna of this unique land interesting, and had I intended to stay, it would have acted as a means by which I could have begun to affiliate myself to an unfamiliar country. This would have extended to the original peoples of Australia, as I had loved those of Malaya, when I had envisaged no end to that life.

Just when I thought that I had travelled on the train for about a week (less than two days had passed), we arrived at the seaport and railway junction of Port Augusta – a small city a few hundred miles north of Adelaide. Before we said our goodbyes, John helpfully pointed out to me a hotel where I could refresh myself and get some food and rest before continuing on to Sydney. We did not exchange addresses. I would have liked to, but as John explained, he was married to an Australian and the jealous sort – mindful that her husband had plenty of opportunity to misbehave as he travelled the country. I pondered on the situation later. It seemed as if the Aussies eschewed the wicked ways of the inhabitants of the Old Country but to me, this did not seem like much fun. Hopefully things would look up in Sydney.

I decided to stay the night at the hotel as I felt close to exhaustion. I sent a telegram to Dorrie saying that I would arrive a day later than planned. I waited for my connection the following day in my room in the Majestic Hotel overlooking the Spencer Gulf, which led directly into the Southern Ocean. Although the sparkling blue vista before me bore no resemblance, I felt at last on the verge of discovering the real Australia – an Australia that would, I hoped, be like a version of the England which I now missed so much. Surely, Sydney would bear some comparison to London, with its sophistication and customs. The next day I would embark on the final stretch of my journey across New South Wales.

I still had over twenty-four hours of travelling ahead of me but, refreshed from my rest, I began to feel a faint twinge of excitement. I had fortunately procured a sleeper carriage, despite the fact that I had postponed my journey. The train left at noon from the busy train station junction at Port Augusta and would arrive in Sydney in the late afternoon of the following day. I felt buoyed up by the knowledge that my journey would soon end, and as I waited for the train to pull into the platform, looked about me with interest. Among my fellow passengers a few soldiers in full kit chatted in convivial groups, some sitting on their kit bags, perhaps returning from leave and bound for their Sydney barracks. For once, I felt relieved that I would not have to share a carriage with them.

Once on the train and settled, I ate my packed lunch and almost immediately took the opportunity to rest on my bunk. About seven o'clock that evening, just as I considered repairing to the dining car, the train juddered to a halt. Looking out into the golden light of the outback evening, I could see a railway crossing with the barrier lowered across the front of the train, surmounted by red lights over one side. Several uniformed officials surrounded the driver's cab, conversing with the driver. Two of the men then mounted the train and I heard them clattering along the corridor towards my compartment. I felt a little intimidated as one of the officers opened the door and I saw the insignia on his arms and shoulders and long, knee-height leather boots.

"Good evening, madam," he greeted me. I noticed that he did not remove his cap. He produced an identity card and put it in front of my eyes.

"Railway Transit Officer Corps," he continued. "We're investigating an incident, madam. We've had an army desertion. Have you noticed anything suspicious on the train? Has anyone approached you?"

I denied seeing anything out of the ordinary.

"I have had an exhausting journey from Perth, officer," I said wearily. "But if I should see any suspicious persons, I will definitely inform the guard."

The officer sensed my reluctance to engage and merely requested to see my ticket and passport. Without any further questions, he nodded and abruptly took his leave. About half an hour later, with the officers disembarking into the twilight, the train once more clanked into motion. We had crossed the border into New South Wales.

The hands on my little travel alarm clock showed a very late hour when I awakened from deep sleep. I had no idea what had woken me and drew back the curtains above my bunk. We had stopped in a station which was dimly lit by occasional lamps positioned at intervals along the platform. The effect was an eerie sulphur-like glow in the surrounding blackness. The train let off steam and I saw the guard jump down from the back of the train and gaze along its length. He strolled along towards the cab, whistle in hand. A sleepy station master looked out of his office and emerged to speak to the driver. Amongst the ornate Victorian decoration on the station buildings, I noticed a sign underneath one of the lamps, not long, I was sure, converted from gaslight. BROKEN HILL it read. Nobody alighted from the train.

I had nearly closed the curtain to return to sleep when I caught a movement out of the corner of my eye. In the half-light the soldier looked hardly more than a child as his face was momentarily lit by a lamp towards the back of the train. He looked familiar, as if I may have gazed at him briefly at the station in Port Augusta – perhaps camouflaged by others in a similar uniform. The brief instant it took him to glance towards the front of the train where the little group was gathered around the cab, jump down from the goods van and cross the platform to a fence at the back, seemed like a dream to me in my drowsy state. In a couple of seconds, he had scaled the fence, swallowed up by the surrounding darkness. I rubbed my eyes. Perhaps I had dreamed it after all, I thought, as the station resumed its midnight air of quietness. The guard jumped back onto the train as it slowly chugged out of the station and into the outback night, leaving the station master to his undisturbed rest.

The remainder of the journey left me with impressions of never-ending dry, flat plains, eventually reaching the farming country of western New South Wales, appearing almost as barren during these summer months. Finally, just after Lithgow, an announcement came over the loudspeaker that the train would shortly begin an ascent over the Blue Mountains, a part of the Great Dividing Range which also extended south to the Snowy Mountains, containing the highest peak in Australia, Mount Kosciuszko. Just two hours from Sydney, I began to notice my surroundings more keenly. It seemed that I stood on the cusp of reaching civilisation. As the train strained up the steep incline, I glimpsed deep gorges and valleys through the bushland. One could not, I mused, fail to be impressed with the immense efforts of the early pioneers who had first crossed these mountain ranges in the early nineteenth century, before Victoria had ascended the throne. From what I had seen, the country had an untamed and untameable enormity on which so-called civilisation had so far had little impression.

From Katoomba, a small mountain-top town with noticeably cooler and fresher air, the train began to descend through eucalyptus and scrub, among sandstone rocky outcrops, through numerous small mountain settlements. Finally, we left the mountains behind when the train crossed the Nepean River and arrived at Penrith. From here, I saw them clearly just beyond the town like a tantalising blue ridge, a contrast to the somewhat mundane appearance of the town visible from the railway. Thenceforth to the outskirts of Sydney, small townships appeared every few miles interspersed among open bushland, with Parramatta, a mere half hour from Central Station in Sydney, the only larger town on the route.

At Strathfield, where a short stop occurred to pick up a few commuters, I began to gather my possessions in anticipation of arrival. My long journey which had covered the width of the continent drew to a close and now I would, with huge relief, give myself over to my friend's hospitality. I felt close to exhaustion, but determined to appear cheerful and happy to be in Sydney. I examined my face in the mirror. I looked white and tired but I pinched my cheeks to encourage blood flow and combed my hair without disturbing the fashionable rolls I had formed over my forehead. These I tweaked into place and a little red lipstick completed my *toilette*. Again gazing out of the window, I noticed that the train had slowed and was crawling through the inner suburbs. As we passed through Redfern without stopping, another announcement came over the loudspeaker.

"Ladies and Gentlemen," announced the speaker in a pronounced Australian accent, "we will shortly be arriving at Central Station. Thank you for travelling with New South Wales Trains."

I noticed a strange building to the left of the track, which seemed to serve no particular purpose, of a particularly ornate Victorian gothic design, resembling a small acropolis. To the side of the construction appeared a sign announcing that it had been built by Australia's "first female architect." I felt fascinated by this anomaly and also impressed that a woman should have received such acclaim in an otherwise somewhat male dominated land. Perhaps hope existed after all, I thought, however slender.

Dorrie told me later that she had waited on the platform for a good fifteen minutes before my train pulled in. It wheezed to a halt slowly, as if befitting the momentousness of the occasion. I had already hung my head out of the window, gazing eagerly up and down the platform. On seeing Dorrie with her hopeful, expectant face searching along the carriages I yelled aloud, my voice turning into something of a screech.

"Dorrie! Dorreee! I'm here!"

Several people on the platform looked startled. Lavinia waved out of the window, and Dorrie finally saw the same dear Lavinia whom she had last seen in the autumn of 1939 again waving, but on a dreary November day in Southampton as her ship had slowly pulled away from the dockside on her way to Australia. She could hardly restrain tears of joy, rushing up to the carriage as her friend dismounted from the train. They laughed and hugged and started talking at the same time. Both women immediately noticed changes in the appearance of the other. While Dorrie looked more maternal and plumper to Lavinia, Dorrie saw in her friend the ravages that illness had wrought. She immediately determined that she would try to fatten her up with plenty of good, wholesome, Australian food.

"We went quite mad as soon as we saw each other and walked towards the wrong end of the station, the sort of thing we always used to do!" Lavinia wrote to George in her next letter to him.

The friends laughed. "Just what we used to do at Charing Cross!" laughed Dorrie. "Oh, it's so wonderful to see you, dear. Now, Roe and Brian are waiting at home. We'll get the train down. It's not far."

Laughing and talking non-stop, they made their way towards the underpass and the platforms to the southern suburbs.

Chapter 20

Brighton - Le - Sands

We celebrated Christmas Day 1942 in style. Eager to make me feel welcome and introduce me to Roe's family, Dorrie invited everyone to a traditional English meal with all the trimmings she could manage. The only absent member was matriarch Flora, who had a summer cold. With the temperature soaring into the nineties Fahrenheit, a concession to the climate seemed appropriate and the feast took place on the patio of the sun-baked and treeless back yard of the bungalow. This turned out an error of judgment around lunchtime, when the sun at its zenith beat down on the newly-developed housing estate. An awning projecting from the back of the house gave only partial relief. By that time, however, it grew too late and Dorrie too busy to re-set everything indoors. I had occupied myself with Brian in the bedroom. He had just woken from his nap and I dressed him in his Sunday best in honour of the day.

This, my first Australian Christmas, seemed to me about as far removed from the feast day imaginable, although we tried to recreate a little of the desired atmosphere. The previous evening, we had listened to *Carols from King's* on the wireless over a glass of sherry and a mince pie, almost moved to homesick tears by the timeless message of the opening carol. After much foraging in the local grocer's, we had unearthed the requisite fruity filling for the pies in the dark, dusty recesses of the store. We also made an attempt at decorations. We raided the neighbourhood, finding in native Australian plants such as bottlebrush and a prickly form of Christmas bush good alternatives to holly. The tinsel did not, however, have similar success. In the dazzling sunshine which flooded the living room it looked sad and out of place, not able to outshine its natural rival.

At noon, the family started to arrive for pre-lunch drinks while in the kitchen Dorrie wrestled with the roast potatoes, her face becoming a deep shade of scarlet. Roe had applied his expert baking experience to the progress of the "joint" by pressing the top to assess its resilience, a method he also applied to cakes and bread. We heard the car pull up outside and Roe, having only just regained his arm chair and newspaper, let out an "Ah!" and hastened to the window. He drew aside the lace curtains, exposing his view to the sight of the bakery's Ford, full of Gartrells, transported to Brighton-Le-Sands from the North Shore by his younger sister Marjorie. Short haired, trousered and competent, she took the wheel as confidently, if not more so, than Roe. Hearing the hubbub, in the bedroom Brian wriggled off the bed and trotted to the door on his chubby legs, one sock on and one off. I hurried to redress the balance before he ran out of the bedroom before I could stop him. We rarely had visitors. In the narrow hallway, chaos reigned, as everyone talked at once. Jean, the older sister, picked up the baby, who laughed and chattered and tried to tell her something about the toy car he had in his "sack" that morning, in reality a requisitioned pillowcase.

"Well! Hello little fella," she said to him in her broad accent. "What did Santa bring you, eh? A car! Well, I'll bet she's a beaut! Show me!"

She kissed him and put him carefully down, then Marjorie's turn came to pick him up. The toddler struggled against her hold, to get the toy for his aunt. Frank, the youngest of the clan, and a more diffident character, greeted his much older brother with a handshake. Roe laughed and chucked him under the chin, asking him what presents he had received. In the meantime, I held back, feeling somewhat overwhelmed by this sudden intrusion into the peace of the morning.

Dorrie appeared from the kitchen.

"Lavinia!" she said, seeing me on the outskirts of the group. "Have you been introduced? Roe!"

Her words were drowned out by everyone wanting to greet her at once. Brian wanted picking up by his mother at that moment to join in. Dorrie continued with difficulty.

"Lavinia! Let me introduce you."

Roe suddenly realised his omission and looked abashed, but not for long.

This marked my first introduction to an Australian family at close quarters apart from Roe, who seemed atypical. These carried themselves with well-dressed dignity, open manners and assertiveness. Jean immediately made herself useful in the kitchen with Dorrie, while Roe poured the drinks from the sideboard and Marjorie started a conversation with her brother and me about the war. Threats to Australia, she said, with the Japanese having invaded Malaya, now looked even more likely to come to fruition. Young Frank set to work on the table decorations, for which he had brought vivid-coloured flowers from the Northbridge garden. I felt caught off guard by their demeanour and a little out of breath. Both sisters had marked outward self-possession and frankness which as an Englishwoman I found disconcerting at first, but I found myself warming to them. I could see that their manner demonstrated an unconditional sincerity which I had not known before.

I learned that Dorrie had got to know the Gartrell family, and later Roe, through Jean at Red Cross meetings. Jean had not hesitated in doing her bit for the war effort from the start. Dorrie, I had gathered, soon found out when war broke out that it had become the "thing to do" and anyway it served the additional purpose of meeting people. Marjorie seemed no less active in life. As a trained nurse herself, she had stopped short of procuring a sister's post abroad like so many other Australian nurses of her generation. Ostensibly, she had let it be known that this was in order to stay at home with their mother but despite Marjorie's confident demeanour and incisive intelligence, I sensed an uncertainty, lying deep in her psyche.

Although they had bought the house two years ago, the yard still had the barren, utilitarian appearance of the new-build. Roe, religiously performing what he saw as his husbandly duty, regularly cut the grass but this marked the limit of his inspiration. He had trustingly left the finer design details to his wife. Dorrie had duly planted what she remembered, thinking to recreate an English garden - lavenders, violets, daffodils and hydrangeas, among others. These delicate blooms, despite much hand-wringing and profuse watering, promptly shrivelled up in the next scorching heatwave. Her efforts contrasted poorly with Flora's, who had over the years cultivated a shady and beautiful garden full of the most appropriate species of mature plants, trees and shrubs, surrounding lawns unusually lush for a semi-tropical climate. Although Roe seemed oblivious but would never have blamed her, I knew Dorrie felt the contrast keenly and, stemming from a sense of failure to adjust to this new, inhospitable land, had begun to resent her in-laws for their breezy competence.

Once they had all sat down at the table, Dorrie saw with satisfaction and pleasure that in spite of the inadequacies of the surroundings, the conversation flowed freely. At least, she knew, the food rated second to none. She had worked hard to prepare the lunch, alternating meeting the needs of her guests with that of the baby's. Roe beamed around the large group on the terrace and took a little more wine than usual. He chaffed with his little brother Frank, eighteen years his junior, who sat next to him and who was tasting his first beer. I guessed Roe never felt happier than when in the company of those he loved and he grew eloquent with jokes and reminiscences, his face flushed with pleasure. I, the guest of honour, sat conversing with the sisters at one end of the table, who displayed a lively curiosity about my experiences in Malaya. I had managed to recover from feeling overwhelmed by now but I had by no means returned to my former spirits from before the escape. I felt in many ways a different person – irrevocably changed by the trauma I had experienced.

"So do you think it was more difficult for you to get on a ship because you were a patient at the time?" Jean said, lighting up a cigarette. I saw before me a capable, shrewd-looking young woman of twenty-nine with a kindly interest in people.

"Yes, I'm sure that was the case," I answered, knowing that I should not smoke but eyeing Jean's cigarette just the same. "In Batu Gajah, for example, I was treated as a special case and evacuated with the staff, but the general practice was to hand the patients over to the military. I acted independently after that. Frankly, it was every man or woman for themselves. I still can't believe it has happened."

The sisters looked at each other. Marjorie helped herself to more turkey and asked me a somewhat sensitive question. It had been widely believed among the British in Malaya that the Australians constituted a "tough lot" and thought the British too accustomed to the servants they enjoyed in the colony. Marjorie did not identify as an Anglophile like Roe and I believe she saw in me, even after so short an acquaintance, an obdurate imperialist – with regard to Britain.

"So how do you like Australia, Val?" she asked casually.

"I don't suppose she's had time to take it all in yet, Marj," Jean interposed. She demonstrated a kindliness, unlike her more abrasive sister, and did not want the British opinion of them to have any basis in fact.

"Well, from what I've seen, which is not much yet...."

"Yes," interrupted Dorrie from the other end of the table, only partly hearing the conversation. "We're taking Lavinia up to the mountains after New Year!"

"That's right, dear," I said calmly. "I was just saying that from what I've seen, you have amazing possibilities here.... And I love your harbour!"

This remark definitely struck the right chord, as admiration of the harbour, with the bridge so newly built, seemed expected and appreciated.

"I adored working with the natives in Malaya," I went on confidently, pressing my advantage. "Would there be any opening for someone of my experience here, Marjorie?"

I had chosen a topic close to Marjorie's heart. I came to realise that for better or worse, she loved the country which had given her birth at grassroots level – the red soil of the outback, the heat, the flies and the native flora, fauna – and humankind. She planned to build a clinic for her "dear primitive" out at Haasts Bluff... She looked penetratingly at me and I could almost read her thoughts. Certainly, my experience, both in London and Malaya would prove useful, and I had the right qualifications. A nurse holding a diploma in health visiting would fit the desired job description for the peoples of the remote community nearly one hundred and fifty miles west of Alice Springs. She had visited with a nursing colleague last year. From what she had seen on that trip, the scanty population stood in desperate need of health education and weaning off the influences of the *kurdaitcha* or witch doctor. However, Marjorie wanted to try a new approach with the people of Haast's Bluff - in a spirit of optional professional care rather than paternalism. The old colonial attitude wouldn't do for her people[1].

"I must be honest with you, Val," she went on. "It's a harsh environment outback. Are you sure your health could stand it? Could be even worse than Malaya." She paused, looking out at the suburban garden, then went on. "I'd want a hundred percent commitment, Val. It would mean staying in Australia after the war, or the whole venture might fail. Come over to Northbridge one day and we'll talk it over. I'm planning something which might interest you."

Far from committing myself to anything as demanding as outback nursing, I spent the next few weeks starting my shorthand and typing course and gaining a general impression of the Sydney social scene.

"Sydney is full of smart and pretty women," I wrote in my eighth letter to George. "The only way to have any distinction is to dress irregularly and leave all one's make-up off because every girl is dressed up like a Paris model."

I still wrote to George regularly, not allowing myself to believe that he lived in any other way but fully fit and well. And I yearned to go back to England and the protective love of my parents, to find comfort in the familiar environment of home. Instead, knowing that Dorrie would worry if I appeared unhappy, I felt obliged to wear a cloak of cheerfulness. How weary I was of pretending! My dear friend tried very hard to make me feel welcome, guessing, because my appetite was poor, that I felt homesick as she did.

I slowly became accustomed to the Sydney climate. January being one of the hottest months, the sun beat down mercilessly into the little back yard and against the windows of the house. At night I often lay sleepless on my bed in Brian's room (the little boy had temporarily moved in with his parents, much to his delight) bereft of clothing, trying to catch a little circulating cool air. I sometimes imagined that I had never left Malaya and my bungalow, and lay within the ubiquitous mosquito net, and that any minute Mary or Tam would come into the room. Occasionally in the afternoons, if my attendance at college was not required, I would take Brian down to the beach in his push-chair, glorying in his strong, firm, tanned limbs, while Dorrie rested. If I had allowed myself to think long about it, it would have broken my heart to realise how nearly he could have been our son, mine and George's. I remembered the time I had thought I carried his child. How casually I had dismissed it then, when I had found out that I was not ..... Down by the sea, looking across the blinding white sands at the fledgling aerodrome of Mascot, I invariably thought of George. How he would have loved this coastline – the fine white sand and – on the bay itself, a deep blue calm.

But George lived and worked far away, back in Malaya where I had left him, perhaps in great danger. My only recourse seemed to write him the monthly Red Cross letters in which I never failed.

"Brian is two years old and we are now great pals!" I wrote in my

next. *"He's an absolute darling. He's a bit of a tyrant as most children are when they're the one and only, but we're getting him into shape. He now goes to bed at a reasonable hour and the other day I cut his hair. If only you could see him as I know how much you love children. He is so firm and tanned a lovely brown by the sun."*

As promised, on the Australia Day weekend, we drove up to the mountains, leaving Brian with Jean. Roe's Ford Prefect groaned up the steep inclines, while I sat in the back, watching Roe's broad shoulders hunched over the steering wheel. It seemed his usual driving position – he appeared almost to be egging the car on, as if it needed help. As I remembered from the train, the eucalyptus, bushes and spindly gums formed steep escarpments which plunged to the ground, hundreds of feet below. The tops of trees, resembling a false forest floor, appeared like masses of blue-green wool in a vaporous haze. Swaying in the back of the car and jerking with the gear changes, I began to feel queasy and felt relieved when we stopped at the Three Sisters lookout, if only for some fresh air. The view certainly took my breath away - the mountains of the massive dividing ranges reaching fold after fold around us and into the distance, imparting a feel of prehistoric timelessness. The silence surrounded us, profound and complete, the air pure and heady, to the open, cloudless heavens.

We had arranged to stay the night at the Carrington Hotel in Katoomba, where Dorrie and Roe had spent their honeymoon two years ago. For the married couple, although I knew they had no wish to exclude me, they had a chance for a holiday together – a second honeymoon. Watching the two of them strolling around, with Dorrie's arm through her husband's, I could not help but be reminded of my loneliness – more so than if I had come up here alone. I wrote to George in my next letter that I did not like "trailing about in a mountainous district with a married couple. I don't," I wrote despairingly, "want any holidays – just working or reading."

My mood at this time, although I tried to conceal it, was almost identical to that which I had suffered in Perth – a morbid melancholia which seemed to pervade my very being. I had disturbing dreams – a distortion of my memories of Malaya - George and I quarrelled all the time or he lived a long way away, or looked different - dark nightmares that immediately neutralised themselves by waking to another morning in Brighton-Le-Sands with bright chinks of sun penetrating the cracks in the thin curtains and the baby's chatter from the kitchen. Another morning of dwindling hopes. My life, I told him, seemed a mere existence and unless he came back, it would remain as drab as before I met him. Especially here.

"Everything is a replica one can get anywhere, plus an extra dose of gum, flies and bush, and you can keep those. It has a certain interest where zoology and botany are concerned. I think it has enormous possibilities provided enough capital can be obtained for manufacturing a modern metropolis with steel-souled inhabitants and electrical appliances for every form of domestic endeavour. As far as I can see, no-one wants to have anything to do with domestic affairs, reproduction is out and lovers of history and tradition are almost alienated. Life is intolerably dull with all the same stereotyped steel-lined modern minds."

I told him that I talked about him all the time with Dorrie and Roe - especially Dorrie.

"Nobody has shown the same interest in you as she has. I think it is because I mean so much to her."

I relived my life in Malaya with George as I told my friend about all the things we had done together. I "made him live," she said, with the way I described him. She knew I suffered and gave of her attention unendingly.

Although I appreciated my friend's hospitality, in reality I found their day-to-day life a little dull. Dorrie did not seem to have any friends for me to get to know and Roe was...

"....quiet, very cautious and never tips the elbow except on very special occasions. His sense of humour is rather slow in coming to the surface and needs a little encouragement. In contrast, I never remember you doing anything which savoured of the practice of angels, my darling. This is what excites me about you!"

Dorrie celebrated her thirty-fourth birthday at the end of April, 1943, the third year of her marriage. For once, she woke early – she had only dozed since Roe had quietly risen in the pre-dawn - and now she lay there, sinking into the deep silence of the house, broken only as the sun rose by early birdsong. She worried about Lavinia after her ordeal in escaping war-torn Malaya and fully understood her feelings of loss and homesickness. Lavinia had shown outspoken-ness in her opinions of Australia with Roe out of earshot, which at first had surprised her. After she had thought about it, she realised they confirmed her in views towards which she had groped herself - yet may not have reached but for Lavinia. Of course, Dorrie missed her parents and worried about them in this war. Roe had himself suggested a trip over, when the war ended...

From his little bed in the corner, Brian began to stir, and seeing her, although she feigned sleep, climbed down and trotted over to his parent's bed. Climbing in, Brian started to pat his mother's face and whispered in her ear.

"Mamma, I'm hungry!" the toddler lisped, his sweet baby breath and a few drops of dribble falling on Dorrie's cheek.

She drew the baby down and cuddled him closely, feeling his strong legs and velvet-smooth buttocks, a little chill in the autumn morning. She warmed them with her hands.

Roe brought home a bottle of white wine that afternoon to cele-brate his wife's birthday, which he presented to her together with some "Black Magic" chocolates. He departed from his usual routine by producing some bread and a cake from the bakery as well– a treat normally saved for a Friday – and a joint of beef purchased from a butcher acquaintance of his father. Although unaccustomed to a large meal and a late night during the week, Roe had stretched a point from his usual strict bedtime.

That evening, the three of them sat, unusually, in the dining room, with its walnut dining table, chairs and sideboard – a wedding present from Roe's parents. Dorrie had made the evening an occasion, not only in celebration of her birthday but also to cheer up her friend and had squeezed into one of her smart city dresses. Lavinia had managed to increase her shorthand and typing speeds – enough to obtain a job in a solicitor's office in the city. Next week, she would begin to travel into Sydney on a daily basis. Roe uncorked the wine and poured a little in each glass. He looked a little tired but jovial, as he raised his for a toast.

"This all looks very nice, dear."

He looked round the table from his seat at the head. Brian sat next to Dorrie in his high chair, allowed to sit up as a special treat.

"Many Happy Returns dear, and congratulations to Lavinia. Well done in getting that job. I hear you might be leaving us soon."

I took a sip of my wine, appreciating its cool, dry fruity flavour and contrasting warmth as it reached my stomach and crept through my veins. Dorrie and Roe rarely imbibed, and I missed the social conviviality I had enjoyed in Malaya where cocktails and spirits had flowed unceasingly. Rarely had I spent an evening with George which did not involve alcohol, usually in the form of whiskey. I smiled at Roe.

"It's been wonderful here with you both. But it's time I branched out into a working girl's life here. I've seen an advertisement for a room in a house near George Street with a few other girls." I tickled Brian under the chin and he giggled and stopped trying to climb down from his chair for a few moments. "And this chap can have his room back!"

Dorrie and Roe made the appropriate noises of disagreement, but even they could not deny that extended visits from guests often became irksome, even if that guest had narrowly escaped death or imprisonment at enemy hands.

After the meal, Roe went to sit in the loungeroom and listened to the nine-o'clock news on the wireless, while we cleared up. Brian had finally dozed off in his chair and been carried off to bed. I held up the wine bottle and looked at it. Half of it remained. I looked at Dorrie hopefully.

"How about you and I finish this, dear? We can sit down here and have a talk."

Dorrie looked rather horrified. If Roe had not sat in the next room she would have agreed, but from previous observations of his reactions when she had taken a little more wine than he, she knew that it would have been dangerous and could spark off a fit of bad temper in her husband. She did not want to spoil this day by having to cope with Roe.

"No dear, Roe would not like it," she said, putting the bottle in the refrigerator. "Perhaps we will finish it tomorrow with dinner."

I sighed. "Alright, dear." Hopefully, things would be more lenient living in the city and I could keep some liquor in my room....I sighed again. "Let's make some coffee then and we can talk anyway." I drew back a chair and sat at the table. "I wanted to have a talk, dear. I was wondering if you ever get homesick?" I contradicted myself. "Yes, I know you do. I remember you writing to tell me about it before, when I was in Malaya. England has been calling me home, Dorrie. Not only for the people, although this is definitely part of it. I have not met anyone here yet that I would like to call a friend."

Dorrie looked sad. "I know dear, and I haven't been able to help you much."

I saw the tears come into her eyes – more readily now than they used to, I remembered. I got up to give her a hug. It was her birthday, after all. I could not bear to see my friend unhappy with me the cause. "I've been trying to find out ways to return since I arrived but my father has told me on no account to tempt providence again by another sea voyage until after the war. I've had to tell them everything – about my illness and just how narrow the escape was. I haven't wanted to worry them before."

Dorrie felt relieved that Lavinia would not attempt anything foolish and quietly applauded Mr Coates for remonstrating with his daughter to exercise patience, in spite of her frustration. It seemed that she had not been completely honest with her parents while she lived in Malaya and Dorrie now saw, approvingly, that a new, more open relationship had sprung up within the Coates family. Whether she would admit it or not, her frail health had shown that she needed her parents' support despite her natural proclivity for autonomy. Nevertheless, she should now be settled for a while. For the time being, she stayed in a place of comparative safety, she now had a job, good friends in herself, Roe and the rest of the Gartrells if she chose, and had narrowly escaped Malaya with her life. Percy knew that Australia, despite its shortcomings in Lavinia's eyes, constituted a much more wholesome environment than Malaya with its comparative debaucheries reflective, if one wished to moralise, of the worst of British society. Well, now all that had come to an end, finished, perhaps for good. He had written to Lavinia that the war in Malaya had put him in mind of *Gone with the Wind* which he and Florence had seen at the Sevenoaks Odeon last year. "*It was prophetic as well as retrospective,*" he had written.

Percy reflected on examples from history, such as the ancient and corrupt Roman Empire and its overthrow, and although he did not write of this to his daughter, considered it not a bad thing that the British one should suffer a similar fate. The winds of change had swept through Malaya, the first of the British colonies to succumb, as the Japanese had swept through like a tornado. For the first time, I heard of the acute anxiety of Father and Mother as they had waited for news.

"*We were very worried during the invasion of Malaya,*" Father wrote, "*We had all our letters returned damaged by seawater! You can trust the Royal Mail to deliver letters no matter what, but you can imagine what we thought! What a relief when we got your cable from*

Perth saying you were safe and sound! We had been really anxious for three weeks. We had a cable from Ipoh and then Singapore, then nothing. We didn't know if you had got away or not. We were supported by our friends through all this. They were wonderful. Uncle Ernest wrote and said from what he knew of the Japanese he thought they would treat you well if they made you prisoner."

I continued to make plans for the future and for the time being I gritted my teeth. I had thoughts of working as a secretary in my father's business when I finally returned to England. Father expressed his doubt, although he had to admit help would come in useful. He and his brother Vic, who had been a partner from the start, didn't get on – although I felt that if I had to work with Vic I may not get on with him either. But, Percy wrote, how would I settle down to the humdrum way of life he had taken for granted for so many years, after my exciting times? I had mentioned George being involved if he ever returned and of a job awaiting him in the family business. This remained uncertain, but as a start, Father made me a business ambassador by giving me the assignation of investigating conditions in the Australian leather and glove industries. He had imported skins for some time, despite hold-ups during the war, and wanted me to send some samples.

In addition to scouting for Father, I became a fully-fledged Australian city girl in May 1943. I had regretfully abandoned, perhaps for good, the nursing vocation. It had become such to me, even though I had not become a nurse for purely altruistic reasons. Now, during my lunch breaks, I would walk from my solicitor's office in George Street to either Hyde Park or the cathedral close of St Andrew's to eat my packed lunch. I did not find the work for Dott and Crossitt arduous. In fact, my mind, while it guided my hands on the keyboard of my typewriter, would operate on different levels. On the surface, I played the part of the efficient secretary Miss Coates, while underneath, my thoughts would be busy in an ongoing dialogue with myself.

I will find George. I will go home; I will (perhaps) get my job back! Clatter, clatter, went the keys. "Good morning, Mr Crossitt!"

In the shared apartment I maintained a friendly but distant relationship with my flatmates. I made no actual friend among them. After work, I prepared myself a meal, then retired to the privacy of my room, to write letters or read. Having been accustomed to the empathetic characteristics of nurses, I found most of the Sydney city girls brittle, as I had suspected I would. As I had observed, they were immaculately dressed - presented as fitting citizens and workers of the new order, of an Australia entering its coming-of-age.

I had two letters from old acquaintances at this time, forwarded from Dorrie. The first, reminding me almost painfully of the past, came from an army major I knew simply as Bruce, now stationed in the north west of India. His letter contained news of people we had both known in Malaya. Not knowing the fate of many colonials, I had first heard from him the previous year, when he had told me of his late escape from Singapore via Sumatra. The majority of his friends had not escaped. He had met Molly and Howard soon after he had reached Bombay. He had gone bathing with Molly one day but he said she had a "fairly gay time" and he did not see much of her. In this latest letter, I learned that Molly had married in India, as had Howard. He had spoken with typical restraint about the conditions on Sumatra where he and several nurses had cared for wounded escapees. Brenda Macduff, a mutual friend, had been "simply wonderful – always bright and working hard." She and one Joan Quark stayed after Bruce and others had left, and while Bruce wrote that Joan had reached Bombay safely, no mention was recorded of what happened to the others. I found it difficult to assimilate the horrors at which Bruce had hinted, purely by omission. Somehow, we survivors had to carry on living.

Dear old Denyer I met in Sydney. Our shared experiences formed a bond between us as we picnicked in the bush one beautiful winter's day. Like me, circumstances had waylaid her in Australia after escaping from Singapore on one of the last ships to leave. Ever practical, she found a temporary sister's post in Sydney and waited to take up a more permanent one in New Zealand. Denyer had no close family or ties and felt as happy to settle there as anywhere. After we left Batu Gajah, she had promised Matron Holmes that she would look after me and I owed her a debt of gratitude. Denyer was one of the good souls of the world, who seemed to live to help others. Out here in the silence of the bush, where we had driven in Denyer's hired car, we reminisced about people we had known, many of whom were still missing or captured. We parted vowing to correspond but we both knew that we would probably never meet again.

At weekends, I would go down to Brighton-Le-Sands where I usually stayed the night with Dorrie and Roe. Brian was always over-joyed at my appearance and ran to meet me as I passed through the front gate. I felt happiest at these times that I spent in Brighton. Dorrie and I would walk with the push-chair down to the beach and watch Brian squeal with delight as he dipped his toes and splashed in the still-warm water of the bay. We treasured these times together. All too soon, as we knew, I would leave for home. It would be a wrench for both of us, but at the same time I knew the parting would increase Dorrie's homesickness. We pretended that these transitory days with their fragile peace, would last forever.

The second letter after Bruce's came from my old WREN friend Margaret. She had written in answer to one of mine, in which I had vilified Australia and the Australians, and had put forward in no uncertain terms my views on why Malaya had fallen so quickly. Margaret knew me well enough to know that my denouncements hid an unhappy woman. She had hit the nail on the head with her perception.

"Don't judge the Aussies on the way they speak or act, dear Val. You speak of steel-lined minds, from which I understand you mean soulless, but I am sure they are as kind, deep down, as any other human being once you get to know them. A "cockney" accent can conceal a heart of gold! "Good on" the Aussies (as they would say!) for being so smart in their beautiful city of Sydney. They're a modern

nation. We can't stay in the past, Val. Malaya was lost as much from our fault as anything you say the "natives" might have done or did not do. The world is changing, quickly now because the war has been a catalyst for change. A few years after the war you won't recognise it. We have to leave the natives to themselves and retreat, like the Romans did. Remember? Nothing lasts forever and we have had our innings."

I hated to admit that Margaret might have a point but I did not yet feel ready to give up on the empire. Surely something so far reaching could not collapse without trace so quickly. How could Margaret bear to speak of it so glibly? One could not alter one's entire belief system in the twinkling of an eye. I was on my way home and picked up a *Herald* at a little newsagent's on George Street. Later that evening after I had cooked and eaten, I took the paper to my room. The war news looked encouraging now. Following on from the Allied victories in North Africa, the invasion of Sicily and Italy had resulted in the downfall of Mussolini's government a few weeks ago. Germany, however, still acted as bellicose as ever and the length of the war still seemed uncertain. Glancing over the inside pages, my wandering eye stopped suddenly, caught by a news column with a grainy photograph. Instantly, my mind went back over six months to a deserted outback station at midnight, sparsely lit by yellow lamps. In the shadows at the back of the train a man had jumped down. I looked closely at the photograph and saw some similarity but was not certain. The incident had since disappeared from my mind like the dream it had seemed. The man still roamed at large, probably desperate by now and possibly involved in some criminal activity. They asked for any information which could lead to his arrest and court martial. After a moment, and with studied insouciance, I turned the page. I felt a curious detachment from the normal duties of a citizen and did not feel in any way obligated to provide information to the Australian government. They would probably say that I should have come forward at the time but in the excitement of my arrival it had slipped from my mind.....

The hazy memory of the deserter in military uniform led to an image of George in his, fresh from parade and hastening to meet me in Ipoh or Batu Gajah. I knew that I had to put my emotions aside and become as "steel minded" as the Aussies if I had any chance of finding him. I had a deep conviction that he lived, that he would never have gone without saying goodbye – that the vibrance of his being could not be so easily extinguished. I could not consider returning to England yet, until I had tried to find him through any means possible.

---

1. *Dear Primitive: A Nurse Among the Aborigines* by Marjorie Gartrell. Angus and Robertson, 1957.

Chapter 21

Finding George

I held fast to a determination that if George existed anywhere, I would find him. Only then could I abandon my search and try to come to terms with living alone. For occasionally, the niggling voice of reason intruded unbidden and unwanted, that surely if he lived, he would have attempted to contact me. This little voice increased in persistence the more time that elapsed from the beginning of the invasion of Malaya and I knew that if I allowed it to become too intrusive it would destroy my will to live. In a stubborn adherence to a kind of "positive thinking" ideology, I denied the negative and reaffirmed an illogical belief in a happy ending.

Everyone who knew me was aware that although I went through the motions of daily existence and appeared superficially to be cheerful, business-like and optimistic, I had merely adopted this persona as a fragile shell. I had designed the masquerade to fend off anyone who probed too deeply into the desolation which lay beneath. I filled the weeks full of desperate activity at the George Street solicitor's office where my apparent dedication to duty did not go unnoticed. Outside working hours, I spent some evenings alone in my room in the apartment but I had by now investigated the Sydney social scene and regularly went to the cinema and the theatre. I even thought about dating. In a matter-of-fact way, I knew I had to function and survive in the typical cliché of the British "stiff upper lip" manner at any cost. Perhaps wisdom could be found in this approach to life after all. If one allowed oneself to diminish to a broken wreck of a human being there could be no hope. So, I used all my strength to act as usual and explore all the channels I could think of in my search. Through the Malayan Club in Sydney, which I had joined to feel spiritually closer to the country and to those who had had similar experiences, I had met three sisters who used a short-wave radio in an attempt to contact people they had known in Malaya but who, like George, had now disappeared. Willing to try anything, I sent a message to George in the hope that somehow, somewhere, he would hear it. I almost felt as if I tried to contact a spirit.

Because I could not bear to contemplate that George may have died, I made a conscious decision to follow a course of action which assumed that he lived and probably as a prisoner of war. I busied myself accordingly, writing to Father for help with continuing the divorce procedure in the New Year of 1943. My dear parents, always with my happiness in mind, trailed up to London amid continuing threats of air raids to Temple Chambers, in the heart of London's legal district. Here they visited the offices of Hasleward, Hare and Co, the agents for George's much maligned "B&B", or Basset and Boucher of Rochester. Mr Hasleward, as Father described, bespectacled with a bald pate and barely visible behind a gigantic and littered desk, heard in some distress the news of George's incarceration. But there seemed nothing they could do to continue the progress of the divorce unless George could somehow smuggle letters out. I had to admit that I had never had a reply to my many letters, even through the intervention of the International Red Cross, who had managed to visit some camps. Mr Hasleward, notwithstanding, agreed to send an affidavit through me on the slim chance that George could get this signed and returned.

"All the while George is a prisoner, I do not see how the decree can

be made absolute," Father wrote in February 1943. *"But we have seen Mr Hasleward and the affidavit necessary to be sworn before the decree can be made absolute has been sent to you. If George can get it sworn by an officer who is a POW the case can go on but after that it is a year before George will be free to be legally married."*

I now know something I did not know in Australia in 1943. Even if George had remained alive and suffered incarceration, the war crimes committed by the Japanese in south-east Asia as yet remained largely unknown to the British public, who assumed that under the Geneva Convention, prisoners of war received good treatment by their captors.

The affidavit I received covered the history of George's marriage to Madge. George had served in the Royal Navy at the time and in 1938 Madge had certainly misbehaved with at least one other man while he was away with his ship. It all seemed hopeless, and had warranted the intervention of the Naval Welfare Officer. Receiving anonymous information, George had cut his wife's allowance, but his captain had advised him to increase it again.

A letter from the Red Cross in Geneva had followed hard on the heels of Father's letter. At first glance, my heart leaped, only for a cruel disillusionment to follow. To my knowledge, George did not have a middle name, but the letter referred to a George Raymond Powell, whom they had found "alive and well." I knew instinctively that it did not sound like George but a further letter from the Thai Tin Syndicate headquarters in London confirmed my fears of the mistake. In communication with the Foreign Office, their information amounted to this George Powell being an internee in Bangkok Internment Camp and a "missioner", which they thought might have been a misprint for "miner", but Australian and a Jehovah's Witness.

I laughed bitterly at this, and I felt George would have laughed too, at the irony of himself as a member of a religious sect. Later, alone in my room, I wept bitter and copious tears in anger and frustration. It proved increasingly difficult to carry out my search in Australia. Late the previous year, I had written to the Commonwealth of Australia Department of External Affairs which dealt purely with the affairs of Australians, who had assumed George an Australian. In those days I often had issues with communication (perhaps because of the state of my mind) and failed to include vital information in correspondence which I remembered later, such as the fact that George had British nationality and worked in the Federated Malay States. This department had wanted to know George's last known address in Thailand. It proved to be another dead end. I had forgotten to mention that George had not been resident in Thailand but acting under military orders, and they had misdirected me to another department for Thai residents.

What proved a confusing and exasperating quest redirected my thoughts to England as I remembered it. Although I could not imagine in 1943 how it had been transformed by war, it seemed the only way I knew how to think of it. It did not occur to me then that the powerful centre of empire which had existed in 1913 had finally suffered eclipse by two world wars, that the still-confident country I had known in the 1930's now struggled for its very existence, let alone as an imperial power. The process had already begun with the fall of Singapore, through the authorities' inability to give credence to the abilities and determination of other nations and peoples, despite their experience as colonial rulers. They never fully understood, or wanted to understand, their subject peoples. I shared this obtuseness with other British individuals. I refused to give credence to the accounts of hardship and gloom I heard in letters from my family and friends. If I did, I did not think it would last too long beyond the end of the war. Here in Australia, the few English people I knew thought much the same as I. It seemed unthinkable that England could come out of this badly. For hundreds of years, she had built up her resources and standing in the world to make her powerful presence indispensable. Despite my knowledge and interest in current affairs, I did not bring into account the crippling debts England had built up to win Churchill's war – which would affect generations to come, until the country could emerge into a new millennium – tattered but still proud.

It was mid-winter 1944 and I had arranged to leave Australia within a few days. On my last visit to Brighton-le-Sands I had walked with Dorrie, Roe and Brian down to Botany Bay and stood gazing beyond the bay to the Pacific Ocean. Roe had made a rare concession to accompanying a pushchair in public but nevertheless felt inordinately proud of his little family and nodded to acquaintances, chuckling at the waiting cars when we crossed the road to the beach, which had caught him holding one of Brian's baby bottles of orange juice. Embarrassment formed part of his jocularity. We had found a café on a terrace overlooking the ocean and bought tea and cakes at Roe's suggestion. He retained the habits of a baking family and never lost the taste for their confections. He too, as if mesmerised, gazed over the sea. The bay lay flat and calm, but beyond, he knew, would surge the breakers which he had spent his life challenging from the beaches of the city he loved and never thought to leave. The winter's afternoon was perfect. The sky stretched an almost cloudless, fathomless blue, reflected in the bay. Every object around held a startling clarity into the distance, as the blinding light accentuated every colour and delineation into stark relief. Everyone wore the statutory sunglasses and Brian's pushchair had a white sunshade attached. The baby had gone to sleep and Dorrie turned the chair away from the sun. Overhead, a giant striped umbrella shaded our table. No sound disturbed the peace but the soft plash of wavelets on the white sand and distant shouts from bathers, their voices carried away and lost on the breeze.

"Gee, it's a bit different from the English Channel, Val!" Roe remarked, with his customary, mildly spoken understatement. "Are you sure you want to go back?"

I put down the slice of cake I held and paused. Dorrie and I had spoken together at length about our mutual feelings of homesickness and what might lie in store both on a voyage and back in England. Of course, I had never intended to live in Australia and had left home with the intention of working at my beloved nursing profession in the gay colony of Malaya. My TB and the Japanese had changed all that. Dorrie of course, felt very sad at my departure. How could she be otherwise and how could she bear it? In our heart-to hearts, we had formulated a plan. My opinions about Australia and the Australians had reinforced Dorrie's yearning for home and she knew that she must try to persuade Roe to resettle in England after the war, whenever that happened. It could not last much longer. Already the Russian's counter-offensive gathered pace in eastern Europe and, following on from the D-day landings, the Allied invasion of France seemed on the point of liberating Paris.

I looked at Roe, his hair neatly oiled and brushed back from his broad forehead, already becoming reddened by the strength of the coastal sun. He belonged to a family settled here for generations. How would he survive in a country where the best that could be managed was a windy shingle beach and a steel-grey sea?

"I'm afraid I must go back, Roe. Poor Mother has been ill and she was never strong. She always depended on me and I have been away far too long. She suffered greatly at the time of my escape, as you know," I paused again. "And I must be on English soil to carry on my search." I looked at Dorrie and unseen by Roe, my friend gave a barely perceptible flicker of a wink in my direction, signifying her understanding. "It's been wonderful here with you both but I have to carry on with my life. All this," (I gestured around at the paradisiacal scene) "...is not real. I mean it IS real but it is not my reality."

Roe coughed and recrossed his legs on the other side. He looked at his wife then back at me. He did not understand this kind of talk. "Oh," he said, clearing his throat. "Well, you know you are very welcome to stay with us as long as you like if you change your mind. Dot will miss you, you know." He looked at his wife again, anxiously. "And Brian, of course." Roe fell to looking at his highly polished brogues, to which he attended every Sunday, without fail.

"I know dears," I said, more upset than I wanted them to see. Then I consciously brightened my expression for their sakes. "But let's not be too gloomy! The war will soon be over now and you can visit the Old Country. Won't your mother and father love to see Brian!"

I felt my pragmatism come to my aid. One must always just think of the next task to do. Life was a series of stepping stones, after all. One never knew what treasure may lie underneath on the way along. I knew the moment of parting would be hard and resolved to get past that point as best I could. I would have to summon all my strength for Dorrie and reassure her that the time would pass quickly until we met again. In the meantime, I entrusted her to Roe. In his inept and rather bumbling but sincere way, his love for Dorrie had no bounds and would have to serve as her strength.

I looked long over the shining sea and in my heart, I said a last goodbye.

It was a mellow, golden October afternoon in St James's Square. On one of those crisp, clear days which leave a lingering memory through rarity, I sat on a bench in the gardens and absorbed the sights, sounds and smells of London. Here in the garden, I sat alone. It drew on to late afternoon and the light began to fade but the nightly rush hour had not yet come. The continual hum of the traffic, the impatient hoot of taxis and the transient chat of passers-by the square were the background to my thoughts. I knew I took a risk by being here, for in what became the death throes of the Nazi regime, the deadly V-2 rockets, the descendant of the V-1 pilotless aircraft which had killed and wounded thousands in the capital and destroyed much property in the East End, had just started to be a menace. Despite the hardships though, for the time being I did not feel sorry to be home. Percy had met my ship at Southampton on a chill overcast day three weeks ago - feeling unmanned, I felt sure, by the tears of gladness which ran down his cheeks - but also profound relief that I had come through safely.

"Oh Father, how wonderful to see you!" I had hugged my father closely, smelling his familiar scent of Brilliantine cologne, Lifebuoy soap and a faint tinge of leather. "But where is Mother?"

"It's not one of her good days, I'm afraid," Percy explained. "She wanted to come but I told her it was better to wait for you at home. Now, do we have to wait long for your luggage? I think the boat train to Waterloo leaves from the Ocean Terminal over here."

Dear old Waterloo. I could hardly believe I was home. The voyage had lasted longer than usual, uncomfortable and treacherous. We had narrowly escaped being torpedoed in the Atlantic, and because of the scarcity of berths on ships returning to England, I had reluctantly shared a cabin with two other women with whom I had very little in common. When I said my goodbyes, I felt considerably relieved that I would never have to set eyes on them again.

After nearly four long years away, the sight of the old house in Hildenborough had been almost overwhelming. Everything looked exactly the same as I remembered and imagined so many times, especially after I had left Malaya. I had submerged myself in the atmosphere of the familiar environment with relief, spending most of the first few days, when I did not help Mother with the meals, resting in my old bedroom overlooking the garden at the back which Mother had joyfully prepared for me, accountable to no-one. I had felt distressed when I had first seen how frail Mother had become since I saw her last. I realised that I must take responsibility for a good deal of the worry she had endured which may have contributed to her illness but subsequent partial recovery when I returned home. I saw clearly that for now and for the rest of my parents' lives I could not in all conscience leave them.

I started and looked at my watch. It just came up to four and in St James's Square as the sun descended behind the plane trees, its dying rays glimmered through the autumn leaves, bright with gold and maroon. I shivered in the evening chill, pulling my overcoat collar up, still becoming accustomed to the colder climate of my homeland. I had come here on a mission for George. Sir Josiah Crosby, the British ambassador to Thailand until 1941, had granted me an audience in his club round the corner. Although he could very well have put the information in a letter, he had found my story interesting when I had written and had suggested afternoon tea in the Thatched House Club. As I approached the grand Georgian town houses and walked up the steps of the porticoed entrance, I felt not a little intimidated. The atmosphere of the interior, from the reception desk to the club rooms which I glimpsed through several doorways from the entrance hall, was one of stringently enforced silence. My feet, clad in black patent high heeled court shoes, sank into thick blue-patterned carpet. I caught a glimpse of myself in one of the many heavy gilded mirrors in the hall and felt glad that I had taken trouble with my appearance. The navy blue felt hat, fashioned with some height, balanced my face, and I had allowed a few dark curls to protrude on the sides of my carefully made-up face.

"Can I help you, Madam?" The imperious voice emerged from a small, smartly dressed clerk who stood behind the mahogany reception desk, pencil in hand, in front of a large ledger.

"I'm here to see Sir Josiah Crosby," I said, looking the clerk directly in the eye. "He is expecting me. Miss Coates."

"Coates, Coates….ah yes, Sir Josiah will be down presently."

I guessed he was in the bar. The clerk summoned one of the pages.

"Could you take Miss Coates into the tearoom, please? I will call him for you."

This last came directed at me. He picked up the phone, while a minion ushered me into one of the male preserves opposite. I felt conscious of many pointed glances in my direction over the tops of spectacles as I entered the large room which had the distinctly stale odour of cigarette smoke. Mainly elderly gentlemen sat sunk low in their capacious leather armchairs behind newspaper screens. I wondered if the appearance of women happened as a common occur-

rence in this sanctuary and decided in the negative. I felt relieved
when the page led the way to a seat at a table among several, overlooking St James Street. Now, I thought, I could look out of the
window and ignore the occupants of the room. I did not have long to
wait.

Josiah Crosby KBE, had been His Britannic Majesty's Envoy
Extraordinary and Minister Plenipotentiary to the King of Siam
(Thailand) from 1934 until the country fell to the Japanese in 1941.
As he crossed the room towards me, I almost rose, then decided at the
last minute to remain seated. His tall, now slightly stooped figure
moved lightly, despite his large frame, dressed immaculately in a grey
lounge suit. His face wore a mild expression, hiding, I guessed, an
astute but kindly intelligence. The features appeared unremarkable,
with a somewhat hooked nose and penetrating blue eyes. I guessed he
was in his mid-sixties and perhaps starting to fail in health. The letter
he had written to me in the February of the previous year had demonstrated a shaking hand, evident in his handwriting.

"You have caught me at a good time, my dear," the diplomat
began, holding out his hand in greeting. "Josiah Crosby at your
service. These days my time is more abundant. Have you ordered
tea? No?"

He raised his hand to the waiter but one was already approaching. I had expected to feel somewhat overawed at the prospect of a
meeting with this doyen of the British establishment but I need not
have had concerns. Sir Josiah put me completely at my ease and in
answer to his many questions on the way, I was soon, in my mind's
eye, back in Malaya, reliving that year from the January of 1941
which I knew I would never forget. I felt gratitude for his sympathy
and detected a certain respect in him on hearing about my escape
from Singapore and the subsequent voyage to Australia.

In reality, however, there seemed little he could do and he told
me everything he knew. In my heart, I had not held out much hope
that he would have known of George but perhaps he might have been
able to use his influence in some way. Just to speak to someone who

had lived there at the time made me feel closer in some way to George. He had managed to gain some access to the internment camp for prisoners of war in Bangkok, not having left there until August 1942, and as he had intimated in his letter, in the camp at that time one of the POW's went by the name of Mr G.R. Powell, an Australian whose home address was in Strathfield, Sydney. He knew of no other man by the name of Powell. I listened eagerly to Josiah's accounts of the conditions the prisoners lived under at that time. I did not know then that Josiah had spared me the worst facts about the Japanese treatment of the POW's and privately hoped that this nice woman's (as he saw me) fiancé had died. After the war I realised that although he had done his best to try to negotiate better living conditions for the men, he had been deeply shocked at what he saw.

As I rose to leave, Josiah stood and bowed with old-fashioned courtesy over my hand. As he walked me to the front door of the Club, he mused in his rambling way, and shook my hand again at the door.

"It's been a privilege, my dear. But if your fiancé is not in the camps, it's very difficult to know what may have happened to him. We can only hope that with time and better communication with the Japanese authorities, things may become clearer. Just keep probing, someone must know something. Incidentally, the Foreign Office is trying to arrange exchanges of as many British civilian prisoners of war in the Far East as possible. Difficulty arises because of the large numbers and the scarcity of shipping at the moment, you understand."

I walked down the steps into the bite of the October evening and hailed a taxi to Charing Cross.

Mr GR Powell was not the only namesake George had amongst the internees in prisoner of war camps in Thailand and Malaya, from Singapore to Bangkok, thanks to the not-uncommon surname and the large number of detainees. At the beginning of 1944 the Colonial Office had four George Powells listed, ranging from a merchant seaman of eighteen interned in Changi, to a forty-five-year-old dentist, also an internee in Changi camp. I often thought I stood in danger of losing my sanity, as the confusion slowly dissipated and only one or two possibilities remained. One of the listings from the Colonial Office caused me some disquiet, however. The Office had identified George correctly, but I did not bring their attention to the listing as the George I knew and loved and felt that some mistake had occurred.

Number one listing read: *"George Powell, mining engineer of Tekka Taiping Ltd, Perak, of whom no news has yet been received and whose wife is resident in England and had been hearing from her husband in Malaya up to the fall of that country."*

How dry, brief and exact the official correspondence had sounded to describe the life George and I had lived together, or rather did not describe. They made it sound as if George and Madge were a happily married couple and that George regularly corresponded with her, when to my knowledge this was not the case. If I took it at face value, I amounted to no more than a casual fling, a doxy, a dalliance, on a par with Gladys. The correspondence between them must have related to the divorce. But why did George have to write to her directly instead of through his solicitors, B&B, as would have been the normal procedure? The questions I raised seemed like a Pandora's box and I knew that I risked at least my peace of mind if I allowed myself to brood on what had emerged from my investigations. I realised then that I might never know the truth.

Later that evening when I reached home and sat down to yet another meal which my parents were providing for me, I knew that I could no longer take their love and concern for granted. I had recovered from the journey and my health was stable. There was no reason why I could not look for a job while I continued with my search. It would be over a year, however, a year of resolution in both my personal life and that of the world, before I began work. Mother's condition worsened during the winter months and her general health declined with an attack of pneumonia. She had, with immense effort, held herself firm until I had arrived home, but now that I had, she relinquished her remaining strength and allowed me, her daughter, to nurse her. I took over the running of the household in my usual resigned way, much to Father's relief. It enabled him to give more of his time and energy to his business and keep an eye on Vic, leaving domestic matters to me.

The Christmas and New Year celebrations of 1945, held in the typical modest, restrained style of the English middle class, was reinforced by the privations of wartime. The season enabled me to renew contact with many old friends of the family as well as personal ones, a pleasure and a comfort in itself. Often, I reflected on the changes the war had wrought on me since its beginnings, when I had travelled home only at weekends from London. January 1945 brought with it a weary hope of victory in a sad and subdued population. In November, I had visited the Foreign Office, in order to follow up some of the activities about which Sir Josiah Crosby had informed me - the exchange of POWs in concentration camps in the Far East and the necessity of keeping George's name before them, even though these leads appeared exhausted.

Finally, a letter arrived from the Foreign Office at the end of January.

"Madam, I am directed by Mr Secretary Eden to refer to your visit to the Foreign Office of 7th November 1944, and to previous correspondence regarding Mr. George Powell.

"At your request, a telegram was sent to the Swiss Consul at Bangkok, desiring him to question Mr. HR Belcher, interned there, as to Mr Powell's movements in December 1941. Mr Belcher informed the Swiss Consul that Mr Powell left Malaya by car on the 20th November 1941, in the company of another mining engineer. He was in Siam at the outbreak of hostilities and Mr Belcher left him at Kantang on 10th December 1941 with five other tin miners. A

Japanese intermediary has informed Mr Belcher that the six men were killed.

"Certain unofficial evidence has been received which gives some reason to think that at least two of the six men above survived. One of the men was mentioned in a broadcast from Saigon in 1943 as being in Japanese hands, while the other is believed by a member of his firm who escaped to be a prisoner of war in Siam.

"While, therefore, it would be unwise to place too great hopes on the chances of Mr Powell being still alive, it seems possible for the reasons enumerated above that Mr Belcher's informant was mistaken in stating that all six men were killed.

"I am to assure you that any further information which may be received will be conveyed to you with the least possible delay."

I received this with mixed feelings. For one thing, I did not trust the Japanese report, as, if they had intended to kill all six men, it would embarrass them to admit that two of them had fallen through the net and escaped the firing squad. It seemed, however, that the Foreign Office had at last sniffed out the right track, and all I could do was wait patiently for more news. In the meantime, with the Germans in full retreat, the end of the war seemed only a matter of time. On the 5th April, with the Americans having captured Okinawa Island, the last island held by the Japanese in the South China Sea, only a few days before, a final letter from the Foreign Office arrived.

"Madam, I am directed by Mr Secretary Eden to refer to the Foreign Office letter of 26th January 1945, communicating the information supplied by Mr HR Belcher in Bangkok, and to state with regret that further information which has since reached the Foreign Office has left little reason to hope that Mr Powell may still be alive. It has now been learnt that one of his five companions, who was believed to have sent a broadcast message to Australia from Saigon, is not in fact identical with the sender of the message. In view of this, the report referred to in the Foreign Office letter under reference that another of the six

men was believed to be a prisoner of war in Siam, is not thought to be based on sufficient evidence to justify the assumption that he, or any of the other five miners, are still living.

"It is much regretted that it is still impossible to supply you with more definite information.

"I am, Madam, your obedient Servant.......")

I did not travel to London to join in the VE celebrations a month later, although I tried to stay happy and optimistic for Mother and Father's sake. I did manage to attend some of the local celebrations which heralded in the new age. Perhaps I felt I had less to celebrate, as I had not, for the most part, suffered the losses and sacrifices of a country under constant threat of attack for the past six years. Resolutely, I compartmentalised my grief and disappointment over George and thought about my immediate future. The prospect of the new post-war age ahead excited me and I had new qualifications mostly untried in England. I still had the advantages of comparative youth. But unknown to Mother and Father, I kept a bottle of whiskey in my room to calm my late-night thoughts and a packet of George's favourite cigarettes, which I had often smoked in Malaya. The habits of a colonial, even a brief one, died hard.

Chapter 22

Years of Peace

I looked up from my perusal of the *Evening News*. I occupied one of a pair of winged armchairs placed equidistant on either side of the hearth, in which a small coal fire fitfully smouldered.

"Would you like any more celery, Father?"

Percy finished munching, with his few remaining teeth, a fresh, pale green stalk of his favourite vegetable. I looked at him with exasperated affection. Every afternoon at five, he insisted on this meal with similar accompaniments. If celery was not available, a boiled egg, slice of ham or a kipper would be substituted.

The old man, now in his eighty-seventh year, shook his head. He dipped his last stalk into the salt cellar deliberately but with a slightly trembling hand.

"No thank you, I still have plenty of bread and butter," he mumbled, hardly audible through a mouth with almost toothless gums.

Percy Coates sat in the front window of the Hildenborough house at his favourite gate-leg table, immaculately laid with a white embroidered cloth, for his ritual high tea. He sat alone. Florence had died four years ago – the present year was 1962.

I returned my attention to the newspaper. Continuing my lifetime habit, I closely followed world affairs and cut clippings on interesting items to put in my scrap book. I sighed, perhaps for the world, perhaps for my father or myself. The world never seemed at peace for long. Scanning over the article on the latest developments in the Space Race, I frowned when I got to a column reporting the possibility of Russian missile bases in Cuba. The relationship between the two great powers of the post-war era, the US and the USSR, had deteriorated over the past fifteen years or so. Perhaps the young and glamorous president known as JFK would be able to handle it without plunging the world into a war far worse than WW2 or indeed, one that anybody could imagine.

I shivered with a sense of foreboding, pulling my cardigan closer around me. Taking up a poker from the fireirons stand on the hearth, I poked at the meagre lumps of coal burning reluctantly in the grate as if I were fencing with a hated adversary. I had never become reaccustomed to the English climate. Sparks flew up as at last the separated lumps began to burn more brightly with tongues of flame licking each piece. October had only just begun after a disappointing summer, but the nights drew in noticeably earlier these last few days and the large, mainly unused rooms felt damp and chilly. I looked again at Father. Just the two of us remained now, each drawing support from the other. Mother had hung on by a thread for several years, as weak as a new-born kitten, but had finally succumbed to pneumonia during the cold winter of 1958. By all accounts, we seemed set for a cold winter this year, too. I had, I thought, better ask Mr Watson to supply us with some logs to save the coal.

Percy had pulled his napkin from under his chin, folded it and placed it carefully on the table beside his place. I went to help him rise and guided him with his walking stick to the vacant chair opposite mine. Every year he became frailer yet he never actually succumbed to illness. He would outlive me yet I thought, with filial pride, as I reflected that I now approached my mid-fifties. George had been slightly younger, but we were now past that age when we had

imagined that together we would look back to our years in Malaya.....
I resolutely halted my train of thought right there. I still thought of
George but without the acute sense of loss I had twenty years ago.

"Father, would you like another cup of tea by the fire? I think I
can just squeeze another one from the pot."

Percy placed his stick with great care by the side of his chair. He
looked at his daughter and saw her neat as ever in her turquoise
checked tweed skirt and matching plain cardigan, her hair cut short
now and greying at the temples but wispy and fly-away as always. I
never bothered with much makeup these days except for a dab of
powder and a smear of lipstick. He thought, unbeknown to me, that I
frequently looked tired and drawn, and he noticed the new lines
showing up on my neck and between my eyebrows. Only the smile
was still the same, lighting up the face with fun and compassion.
How grateful he was that I had come home even though he was sad
for me at times that I had never married. He would have liked grand-
children.

"No thank you, Daughter," he answered. "Can't you leave the tea
things? Mrs Roberts will be here in the morning."

"I will, Father," I said, appreciating his paternal consideration. "I
was just going to stack them in the sink."

I placed a tartan rug round Father's knees as he warmed himself
by the revitalised fire, then went over to the table with a tray. I carried
the few things Father had used through to the old-fashioned kitchen
with its shallow stone sink and wooden draining boards. Mrs Roberts
kept everything spotless. The old house was too big for just the two of
us but Father would never move. Later on, perhaps, I thought -
when.....

Percy's thin, quavering voice just managed to carry through to the
kitchen.

"Have you heard from Dorrie lately?"

I went back into the sitting room.

Dorrie, Roe and Brian had travelled back from Sydney soon after
the war in Asia had ended so dramatically. They had procured berths

on the *Stirling Castle* to face a country very different from the one Dorrie had left in 1939. As I had predicted, once the initial euphoria of seeing friends and relatives had evaporated and the hardship of daily post-war life dawned, it had not been an easy adjustment. Roe, I knew, soon began to regret leaving Australia as he faced the employment difficulties of the late 'forties. The long, hard winters took a toll on his spirits and he lived for letters from his family in Sydney. Nevertheless, in March 1948 their daughter Claire had been born into the melee of extended family members who lived at 41 Woodfield Road and as the 'forties graduated into the more optimistic decade of the 1950's with its idyllic summers, life became more tolerable, especially with the death of a rich uncle.

"I'm going down to Tonbridge for tea on Thursday, Father," I said. Dorrie wants to come up and see you soon and bring Claire with her. I said you would like that."

"Yes, yes, of course," said Percy. "But won't you be going back to that job soon? The one at the school?"

I had worked for three years part time as assistant matron at a boarding school in Tunbridge Wells which, as Percy's care needs increased, became exhausting, as I travelled on the bus to and from work. Mrs Roberts had stayed with Father during the day, but as he began to get out of bed during the night to the bathroom, I often had interrupted sleep. I had handed in my resignation nearly a year ago now, to stay at home with Father full time. I earned a little extra money for myself these days by typing and duplicating at home.

"Now Father," I said patiently. "You know I left Marsden House nearly a year ago. I was finding the travelling too much."

Percy looked puzzled for a moment, then remembered. "Ah yes," he acquiesced, and nodded sadly.

Although mainly content and in reasonable spirits for his age, Percy occasionally noticed that his once-reliable memory started to fail and it was obvious, even to him, that his mobility deteriorated. He felt a little disconcerted by these observations. He did not like to think that his dear daughter sacrificed her freedom to look after him.

He fell to rumination. How old was he now? Could he be about eighty? Let's see now, dear Florence had reached her eighties when she had died, but how long ago now that was he could not quite recall.... He felt himself getting drowsy...

I saw that Father nodded with sleep, his grizzled head falling onto his chest. Gently, I tucked the tartan rug more securely around his knees and then sat down in the opposite chair. I knew that an hour or so would pass before he would wake, then want to turn on the television set to the BBC for the evening news programme. I would watch it with him and whatever programme came after it until, after a light supper served on a tray in front of the television, I helped him to bed.

Percy still slept on the same side of the heavy mahogany bed he had shared with Florence all their married life and continued to occupy as a widower, never venturing onto the side which had been hers. On his bedside table stood a small brass bell, which occasionally he remembered to ring for me in the night when he wanted to use the bathroom, but often did not. I would wake up, disturbed by his furtive steps as he felt his way along the passage, and the soft click of the bathroom door as he tried not to wake me. Once, I had found him on the floor in the bathroom, miraculously unhurt except for some bruising, having slipped in a puddle of his own urine. I had managed to get him to his feet, feeling the familiar strain on my lower back, overworked from years of nursing on the wards. I expected similar occurrences nightly, knowing that there would come a time, not too far off, when I would not be able to cope. I already reluctantly looked into respite care in some of the local nursing homes.

Meanwhile, in front of the fire, I abandoned my newspaper and allowed myself the luxury of introspection. I reflected on my life – not only since I had been back home but the whole of it. If I had looked in from the outside – if I had been born a twin or with another self – someone who knew my most intimate thoughts (perhaps Dorrie? But no, not even she), they might have perceived whether or not I had used my innate abilities for the good of others. Why did this matter to me? Deep within, I had always known that my motivation had been suspect. But were not I and my contemporaries taught this principle as future wives and mothers, or if not so lucky, as benefactors in the female professions of teaching or nursing? Those in charge of us had drilled it into us, so that we no longer knew the difference between it and personal desires. Here I stood now, clinging to that principle of duty as I struggled alone, waiting for release from a just God. If I had brought George back from Malaya as my husband – if the Japanese had not invaded Malaya, he would have stayed with me, sharing the house with Mother and Father. He could have taken over the leather business which Percy had, for want of an heir, to sell out to Vic's family. I wondered sometimes whether my adversities were actually punishments, inflicted in some way for that early lack of sincerity.

Although I never liked to indulge in self-pity, I saw the hand of fate thwarting every effort to promote my own happiness as surely, I should be due. Or was I? My dearest wish had been a husband and children, but the Great War had created huge deficits in eligible men during the inter-war period, leaving the women of my generation either spinsters for life or forced to look further afield for partners. Dorrie had struck lucky and I had, following her example, seized my chance with Malaya, hoping, deep down, to combine a nursing career with a successful search for a husband. I had entered colonial social life with gusto, seeing some promise among the eligible men employed in vital industries such as tin and rubber which supported the war effort. But then George had bowled me over. Being already married, he failed to fulfil my criterion of eligibility. I had unintentionally scuppered my own chances.

Within three months of my arrival in the colony, my congenitally weak lungs had succumbed to tuberculosis. I had had less than a dozen weeks of the intoxicating whirl of work, parties, dancing - immersion into the vibrant world that was colonial Malaya. I had fought against my illness until I was forced to concede defeat and admit myself to hospital. But meanwhile, I had met George and still felt, from inside hospital walls, the exhilaration of being in love, of being in the sun, the sensuous feel of tropical warmth and the protective blanket of privilege in the life of a European among a ruling class. This brief interlude I would never forget.

It had lasted less than a year. With the threat of pending Japanese attack, George had suddenly left me in the hospital at Batu Gajah. Then, as now, I had found it almost impossible to believe that I would never see him again, that having reached my mid-fifties, I would in effect still be waiting for the miracle of his reappearance. I had found diversion in daily life, in meeting friends and in the jobs I had taken immediately after the war. But something within me remained unsatisfied. I had given myself completely to George, hoping that with this investment of trust in the surrender of my being, I would eventually find my reward. I still waited for that reward. The drama of the "Great Trek" as I called it, down the peninsular to Singapore and then the treacherous escape to Australia, had acted as a diversion from the perpetual inner ache of loneliness which followed. I had, effectually, divided into two people – the outer Val, brisk, efficient and cheerful – always ready to help her fellow creatures – and the inner one, which refused to die and lived on within me - the miserable creature to whom I only occasionally gave attention.

A year after the war ended, in January 1946, I had taken a job in the information bureau of the Malayan High Commission in Trafalgar Square. I had travelled by train from the tiny railway station at Hildenborough through to the outskirts of the capital. From Orpington, the evidence of destruction from the war showed clearly visible from the railway line – huge swathes of bombed out buildings giving an air of desolation which would take many years to heal. Even now, in 1962, although nature had covered some of the old bomb sites in its own inimitable way, the scars remained as a reminder of what had once stood there. Back in 1946, I had been horrified with the changes to the London I remembered before my departure to

Malaya. It presented as a desolate scene indeed, with which to welcome returning citizens.

The British had briefly returned to rule in Malaya after the retreat of the Japanese in 1945, forming the Malayan Union, which granted equal rights to any citizen born there before 1942. The information bureau at the Malayan High Commission provided me with a strategic position for keeping abreast with events in the Far East. I liked to think that my suitability for the job largely stemmed from my first-hand knowledge of the country, but in reality, I knew I had instinctively homed in on the ideal place to receive the latest information as it emerged and thence have more of a chance of locating George. Once again, my motivation had suspect foundations.

I enjoyed playing the part of a working city girl again. I renewed many friendships from before the war and "meeting in town" became the fashionable and fun thing to do. Lyons Corner House on the Strand turned into a favourite hang-out for my depleted remnant of pre-war friends. Margaret, having been discharged from the WRENS at the end of the war now worked for the Home Office as a secretary and we would often meet at Lyons or take our packed lunches to St James's Park and gossip. Dorrie, too, dressed smartly, would occasionally come up to "town" to relive her single working days and meet me in my lunch hour. During one of these we planned the outing.

The main edifice of the Norman castle on the River Medway at Rochester in Kent had always been well-known as one of the best preserved in England or France and a popular tourist attraction. I had not visited there as a child, as Mother and Father did not favour traipsing round ruins. Dorrie, who, in the summer of 1947 still relished being back in England, had been there before but after living in Australia wanted to revisit as many historical monuments as her domestic duties would allow. Many of them had just reopened after the war. Violet Raymond and Brian, now an English schoolboy of six years old in cap and blazer, accompanied us one beautiful Saturday in June.

I had sat in the sunshine with Dorrie on the green-painted bench in the park, munching on a salmon paste sandwich. We wore cotton summer dresses but made allowances for the uncertainties of the English climate by the addition of cardigans. I had rejoiced when she and the family had returned to England. Being with them in Australia had created a continuity of friendship and reinforced the bond between us.

"What a good idea, Dorrie!" I had enthused. "It will get me out of the house. It's so dull there at weekends. Father does a half day at the factory on Saturdays then plays golf, and Mother is always visiting someone. Will Roe come, do you think?"

"No, I don't think so. He works on Saturday mornings as well, you know, in the bakery. He's always rather tired on Saturday afternoons. I'm sure Mother would love to come though. Dad will be in the shop, of course. Saturdays are very busy on the High Street."

Dorrie's father, W.S. Raymond (known as Stanley), ran a shop on Tonbridge High Street, opening his watchmaking and jewellery business in 1900. His wife, Dorrie's mother Violet, usually assisted him with the customers at busy times but since Dorrie and her family had returned from Australia, she had preferred to spend the time with them. Now in her late sixties, she found the long hours on her feet in the shop very tiring. She grumbled at Tonbridge Station when the little party of four assembled at ten in the morning the following Saturday. It was more than an hour by train to Rochester.

"We'll have to get a car one of these days," she remarked to Dorrie. "Roe drives, doesn't he?"

Dorrie nodded. Wonderful as it had been to see her parents again after the anxieties of the war years, her mother's moods did not improve with advancing age. She was a strong and somewhat overbearing character and always wanted inclusion in family activities. A one-time member of the Temperance Society and a staunch Conservative, she disapproved of strong drink in all its forms and although her long-suffering husband had found his own way of coping, she had ruled her own family of three girls with an iron-like control. When she felt annoyed, her face flushed a livid purple, which it did now at the lateness of the train.

"Brian, stand still dear," said Dorrie.

Brian made engine noises and pushed his matchbox toy car up and down his grandmother's sleeve – a risky activity, given her deteriorating mood.

I, who had stood to one side with what I hoped resembled a benign expression, now intervened and took Brian off to look at another train standing in the station. Although Brian did not remember our friendship in Sydney, I could still see in him the little boy I had known, and our friendship had revived instantaneously.

At last, the train puffed into the station and we were underway, having a carriage to ourselves. Brian kept wanting to pull down the window cord and eventually got a smut in his eye, necessitating my administrations with the corner of a handkerchief. Once the medical emergency had been addressed and the patient convalesced in his own corner of the carriage with a comic and a packet of fruit gums, we adults could relax and enjoy the journey. We looked out of the window as the east Kent countryside rolled past. There seemed little sign here in the depths of the country that only a few years ago it had been torn apart by war.

The party decided by consensus to walk to the castle from Rochester Station. The air smelled sweet and refreshing after sitting for so long in a carriage with the distinct odours of sulphur and soot, and we enjoyed stretching our legs. The route took us through the centre of the picturesque town and past the cathedral. Mercifully, the cathedral and castle had escaped the worst of the bombing raids which had taken place but the evidence still showed in several ragged gaps between the buildings. The areas had been cleared and after three years, nature had begun to reclaim the remaining rubble, disguising the worst of its rawness by administering a healing covering of moss and foliage. The town, after two years of peace, now began to recover its former quaintness and attracted more tourists as local businesses began to reopen their doors.

By now, lunch time approached.

"I'm hungry," said Brian, gazing wistfully into a coffee shop.

The aroma of newly roasted coffee wafted out into the cobbled high street as the party passed. His grandmother, with her old-fashioned heeled lace-up shoes painfully tight, had some difficulties with the cobbles.

"Are you alright, Ma?' said Dorrie, looking back at her mother as they climbed the slope towards the gate leading to the castle.

I walked on ahead, enjoying the climb. I remained lost in my own thoughts for a while. A few evenings before, I had attended a spiritualist meeting with a friend in Tunbridge Wells, which I had found utterly absorbing. Unlike Dorrie, who, encouraged by family members who had espoused Christian Science had developed a growing interest in this movement, I had never, beyond lip service to Anglicanism, professed particular interest in any religion. The speaker in Tunbridge Wells represented the Spiritualist Church, which did recognise some aspects of the divine, but one particular aspect of the faith especially fascinated me - the alleged communication with the dead. I actually considered attending a meeting with a medium present and asking them to contact George. I realised that if they could not contact him, he may very well be alive.....

Dorrie, holding Brian's hand, waited for her mother to catch up. They had brought their own lunch and had planned to find somewhere to picnic within the castle grounds. The question of the hour was whether to eat before they explored the castle or afterwards. Dorrie rather thought that for the sake of peace and everyone's comfort, it would probably turn out better to find a good vantage point of the castle, have their lunch and then tour the castle when they were refreshed. "We'll have lunch when we get to the castle," she said to Violet and Brian.

Both looked relieved and with this brighter prospect in view, took a kindlier interest in their surroundings. They came in sight of the imposing, almost intimidating keep of the Norman construction, towering over the town below and dwarfing the little group of pilgrims who approached.

"About time," grumbled Violet. "My feet are killing me. These shoes haven't been right since I bought them. I'll have to take them back."

"It's too late, Ma," said Dorrie soothingly. "Perhaps they will wear in."

She refrained from saying that wearing new shoes on an outing when more walking than usual might be anticipated may not always constitute the wisest choice.

Violet, a woman born at the time Benjamin Disraeli had endowed Queen Victoria with the title of Empress of India, had not received education in thinking but rather had learned the qualities of acceptance and endurance. If she had, she would have realised that the balance of power in the household had shifted since her daughter's family had returned from Australia. It likely provided the reason, had she known it, for the anger she often experienced these days. She had grown into a woman, if not of great intellect, of considerable practical ability and forward views, and had embraced the more enlightened position many privileged women occupied at the turn of the century. She gave way to the younger generation somewhat grudgingly, a situation which would only get worse.

The little party approached the castle gate and stood for a moment admiring the sight of the castle, standing as proudly and as threateningly as it had appeared to its enemies in the thirteenth century.

"Lavinia!" Dorrie called me back to the fold.

I had walked around the castle mound to try to get a photograph on my box camera. I waved, carefully framed the photo and clicked the shutter, then started back to the group.

"Got a good one!" I said triumphantly as I re-joined the others. "The sun just came out as I managed to frame it."

I could see that Dorrie looked happy that I enjoyed myself today. Certainly, the sun and air refreshed my spirits and the ambience felt peaceful after the daily rush in the capital. Dorrie pointed to a wooden picnic table, erected by the Rochester Town Council to facilitate visitors. The council had placed several of these seating arrangements on a flat area at the top of the incline on which the keep of the castle sat, with advantageous views of the monument.

"Brian and Ma are ready for their lunch, dear," she said, indicating the picnic area ahead. "Shall we stop now and have a bite, then we can have a look round the castle?"

I willingly agreed as we climbed the slope together, puffing a little as we got to the top. Dorrie had to stop and assist her mother, who had become a little stout in her older age. She had insisted on dressing over-warmly for the June day in a summer "dust" coat, with her legs, afflicted now with the varicose veins she had acquired through hours spent on her feet serving customers, uncomfortably and warmly encased in thick support stockings. Dorrie, watching her, vowed to watch her weight as she got older.

I sat myself down next to Brian at the table, facing the castle and pointed out the various features to the little boy.

"Do you see those slits in the walls of the castle, Brian?" I pointed to the great walls, towering menacingly above us. Suddenly, I froze, staring ahead of me into a group of sightseers. Brian looked at me curiously.

"Auntie Val! What's the matter?"

I did not answer for a second or two. I felt the colour drain from my face as what I thought I had seen disappeared from view and did not re-emerge. Brian tugged at the sleeve of my cardigan, starting to look frightened. I did not think I could speak for a moment.

"Auntie Val!" Brian said again.

Dorrie, who sat opposite me, now looked over to see what bothered Brian. Violet, who helped to arrange the picnic on the table, seemed too engrossed to notice anything.

After only a few seconds, during which time had seemed to stand still, I recovered myself. The reassuring scene around me returned and I looked around at everyone, embarrassed. I smiled down at Brian.

"Nothing, dear, I just thought I had seen someone I knew."

Later during the meal, I had a chance to look over at Dorrie, who from time to time had been glancing anxiously at me. While Brian busied himself, alternately eating and playing once more with his matchbox car, I leaned over to her and spoke in a low voice.

"I'll tell you about it later, dear. I had a funny moment, but I'm alright now."

"Are you sure?" whispered Dorrie. "Do you want to carry on or would you prefer to rest here while we go up?"

"No, really, Dorrie dear, I'm fine."

I looked up the table at where Violet had taken charge of most of the food, keen for once to be in control.

"Violet, do you think I could have one of those delicious-looking oranges? Isn't it wonderful to have them again after the rationing?"

As the years passed, I had settled into my single life, for the most part living at home with Mother and Father. I took several temporary jobs of a clerical nature, involving shorthand and typing, bookkeeping or reception work. Wherever I went, I procured excellent references, which pointed to the dedication and willingness with which, apparently, I undertook my duties. In the late 'forties and early 'fifties, the south coast called me, perhaps because the atmosphere of the larger hotels in Eastbourne, Folkestone or Bexhill-on-Sea exuded a faded grandeur, a remnant of their heyday in the Victorian era. The retired military personnel who made their homes in these social and sociable microcosms found me a congenial representative of the establishment where they lived. I treated them with the respect they expected, always addressing them by their attained rank.

As these contracts only lasted for a short term, Mother and Father spared me for the duration and I could obtain an hotel room for a much-reduced rate. I would walk along the promenades in the evenings reflecting how similar these seaside towns appeared, all along the coast from Sussex to Dorset. I would look out to sea, past the shingle beaches, past the ubiquitous pier, past where the wavelets lapped on the shingle and then drew back, hissing through the pebbles as they ebbed. So few years in a lifetime had passed since I had looked over the Pacific at Brighton-Le-Sands but it had changed me forever.

By 1955 I had finished with the hotels, not finding the answer I sought in their faded gentility. I lived at home in Hildenborough for a few months, taking a bookkeeping job in a local garage and helping my parents more in the house and garden. Mother became increasingly frail and spent most of her mornings in bed and the afternoons wrapped in shawls, sitting in her favourite drawing room chair. Mrs Roberts tackled all the housework and laundry, while I took over the cooking and Mother's personal care. Father had now retired permanently from the factory, though he still took a keen interest in it from a distance.

Between my job and home responsibilities, my hands, for the time being, were full. But in my quiet moments I felt a presage of my life in the future – at times, an overwhelming sense of grief and loneliness came over me and at these times I cast around for an explanation, a support – I still dabbled in spiritualism and the occult, attending lectures, usually held in Tunbridge Wells, from well-known speakers in the field and occasionally going to a séance. The notion that presences could be summoned or manifest themselves interested me now in spite of scepticism in my youth. I would never have dreamed of discussing this with my parents or close friends but if George had died back in Malaya in 1941 would a slim chance remain that I had not seen the last of him? It comforted me in my quietest moments alone, that I might not actually be alone. At these times I grew close to something akin to a religious ecstasy as once more I persuaded myself that I felt his touch on my receptive body. It felt so real and I felt so alive, my skin sensitive to touch in every pore, that I could barely stop myself from crying out loud.

For back in the summer of 1947, at Rochester Castle, I could have sworn that among the tourists, another woman's arm beneath his, I had seen George. The vision had lasted only for the briefest of moments. Our eyes had met but then a chill had clutched my heart and descended to my stomach. The eyes of the man before me looked blank, expressionless, cold, like a dead person's. They gazed through me, as if focussed on something behind me, as if I were not of substance. The man had turned away and looked ahead, through to the back of the castle. The pair disappeared through the archway and must have gone through and out of the other side, because I did not see them again. This man had looked older and paler, without the tan, than George had looked when I had last seen him, like a man, prematurely aged, who had passed through the hell of a POW camp. His body, dressed in clean and well-pressed slacks and shirt, looked even leaner than I remembered and his hair contained much more grey. His demeanour had seemed more subdued, his personality smaller, than my George's.

Later, I had felt a little foolish, as if my eyes had deceived me. I had never seen him this way again, although I never stopped looking. I even briefly visited each eastern Medway town, remembering he had spoken of one, Gillingham or Chatham, I had forgotten which. I searched in vain. As time passed, it seemed more and more like a dream or a vision. For the man I saw had not been the George I remembered.

Chapter 23

Full Circle

In the days before Malaya fell, one last escape route briefly remained open through the archipelago to eastern Sumatra and from there overland to Pedang, on the west coast. By this time, there remained no possibility of evacuation by sea from Singapore as the Japanese ruthlessly bombed any departing shipping out of Singapore Harbour and through the Bangka Strait, as the tragedy of the *Vyner Brooke* had shown. The way across the jungle and swamps of Sumatra was highly treacherous, as the deaths of those attempting it demonstrated, but for a man like George Powell with his extensive naval experience, it would just fall into the outside realms of possibility, if he had survived, to navigate a small boat across the Indian Ocean to the refuge of the British Crown Colony.

George had settled down to wait with his platoon in Thailand, preparing for the invasion. At first, morale stayed high. He and two other men from the Thai Tin Syndicate were billeted in temporary quarters in Huey Yod, close to the Malayan border. Three others, including Jock and Ian, his former housemates, lodged in another guest house close by. The accommodation, befitting soldiers, was basic, but the locals seemed friendly and accommodating, anxious to look after the part-time volunteers who had come to defend them from an unpredictable enemy. For the short time before the invasion, the group of men joined the rest of their volunteer force in supporting the regular troops prepare the defences from the sea and underwent the usual drills and manoeuvres. In the evenings, as they always had, they drank the local bars dry and turned up the next morning for parade in a state which can only be described as short of the ideal, for a professional. The commanders tolerated it. The threat from the Japanese still remained uncertain and there seemed no way of knowing how long this state of limbo would continue for the men.

George wrote to Lavinia twice during this period, missing his visits to Batu Gajah hospital and her welcoming, loving arms, to which he hoped to return when this false alarm passed. He also wrote to his wife at home in Rochester, as he had always done from time to time. Not being an introspective man, he had not recently analysed his feelings for her, only still being concerned for her welfare. He knew, deep down, that the two of them were as good as each other, both passionate, headstrong and not too strict about morals when it suited them. Whereas with Lavinia he always had an awareness of having to be on his best behaviour with her constant reminders of her background, with Madge he could just be himself, and not feel inferior if he slipped up, as he always did.

During the night of the 7th – 8th December, everything changed. Suddenly, they no longer played at soldiers. The sinister dark shapes of large troop-carrying vessels appeared off the coast of Khota Bharu, and the alarm went out to His Majesty's dissipated forces that they should muster immediately to support the scanty defences on the coast. Although the bombing of Pearl Harbour had taken place that morning, the news had not reached all the commanders in Thailand, otherwise it seems likely that they would have been more on their guard. Shortly before midnight, Harry Belcher came tearing like a madman into Maggie's Bar in Huey Yod, waving a telegram. George sipped on his second "nightcap" and stood with Ian and the others at the bar, joking with the pretty Thai barmaid, who tried unsuccessfully to persuade them to leave. The vision of Harry advancing towards them almost seemed like a vision and in slow motion.

"We're being invaded, men! Back to your posts! The enemy is just offshore at Khota."

He left them to gather their weapons and equipment, although he had a sinking feeling that it was all too late. The enemy was already upon them.

The men stared stupidly for about two seconds, then gathered their wits and their weapons and ran hither and thither. They managed to keep together and followed Boucher to the transport. The short journey was like a nightmare. It seemed unbelievable that this should happen. Where had all the regular troops disappeared to - the air force defence, the intelligence corps? Too late, George wished that he had not had so much to drink. Whilst now, he felt comparatively sober due to the shock, the whiskey churned in his stomach and he felt an acid taste in his mouth. He turned his head over the side of the open truck and vomited copiously into the rapidly passing dirt road, not quite missing the sides. The other men looked away.

As they approached the beach, they saw before them a chaotic scene, lit by a half moon which periodically disappeared fitfully behind clouds. With the black shapes of the troop ships standing a few hundred yards offshore, the calm stretch of ocean between them and the beach was full of small boats which disgorged what seemed like large numbers of the enemy, many wading in the shallow water with some already ashore and advancing up the sand. Some were met with resistance from the machine guns of the first line of defences at the top, while some hand-to-hand combat took place further down, with the use of bayonets. It looked obvious to George and the rest of the Thai Tin group that they stood no chance.

George looked around and behind him. Some of the men were already fleeing and in disarray, seeing the position of the allied defence as hopeless. George managed to form the opinion, with his drink-addled wits, that it was unreasonable to expect the men to stand here and fight in this situation, poorly prepared and let down as they had been by their superiors. It was nothing less than a slaughter. Harry seemed much of the same opinion. He gestured to the six men to follow him. Everyone seemed too much occupied with defending themselves to notice the seven men edge themselves away from the melee and back towards the jungle. Silently, they penetrated deeper into the dense jungle which had encroached almost to the beach. Without speaking, the men, now acting by their wits, fell into a single file along an animal track, walking quickly but as silently as possible until they reached a small clearing. The noises from the beach behind them gradually faded.

Boucher, who had led the way, stopped. Ian, with a look of panic on his face, would have kept stumbling along in the almost pitch darkness, but Harry waylaid him with a hand on his arm.

"Easy now, chaps," he spoke in a half-whisper, wondering, as they all did, whether any of the enemy had penetrated this far inland.

"We can't carry on walking in this way without a plan. Let's stop and think for a moment."

He spoke with the authority he had become accustomed to exercising in his role of dredge master, keeping a team of talented but testosterone-fuelled men in order as they in turn controlled the coolies in the uninterrupted production of the precious metal. He could see that a few of the group acted instinctively, in survival mode, only too aware of their new status of deserters. He smelled the scent of fear from them and tried to avoid the wild, animalistic look in their eyes, lest he too should become incapacitated by panic.

"Anybody got a compass?" Harry tried to estimate their position in relation to the beach. He did not think that they had walked in a circle. Jock produced one from the depths of his shorts.

"Good. Now chaps, we obviously have to continue forward. I suggest we make for Kantang on the west coast of Siam. It's a fair-sized port on the Malacca Strait. It will be three days march. Once there, we can obtain a boat across the Strait to the coast of Sumatra. We're all engineers, most of us with seafaring experience, so it's possible. I'm not saying it will be easy. We have no food or water but we can forage and beg. I say we continue on for a few miles in the general north-west direction we're aiming for then camp down until daylight. Luckily, we have maps."

Over the next two days, the fugitives marched by day and camped in the jungle by night, always in the general direction of Kantang. In the morning of the first day, exhausted and weak from lack of water, they stumbled across a small village. Harry raised his hand for a halt as the sounds of voices came to the ears of the leading men.

"I'll take one other man with me," he said in a low voice. "George. Let's see if they can help us with food and water. Where there's a village there must be water nearby."

The remaining men watched from the surrounding bushes as George and Harry approached one of the huts. They had left their packs and weapons with the other men to appear less threatening. An old man, wizened by age, sat in the early morning sun outside on a cassock, his thin, brown bare legs emerging from a loin cloth in a squatting position. He saw the men immediately, emerging from the jungle, but they felt glad to see that he did not react in fear, although he eyed them unsmilingly. Both Englishmen smiled as they approached and bowed. Both Harry and George had a working knowledge of Malay and, hoping that the two languages had some similarity, tried a greeting. Thankfully, the villager appeared to understand the gist when the two men asked for food and water. He called in a quavering voice towards the open doorway of the hut and a middle-aged woman appeared, looking, as the Englishmen noted, well-nourished and dressed in a long cloth wrapped around her body like a sari. By this time, villagers from some of the other huts had emerged and stood watching the men. Several children ran around, their faces dirty but appearing content and well fed.

After much misunderstanding and gesture-accompanied explanation on the part of the miners, the sari-clad woman and her elderly father held a long discussion, during which the rest of the miners appeared gingerly from the cover of the surrounding trees and approached the group with what they hoped resembled friendly expressions. Harry introduced them in the approximation of Malay he had used before. More gestures and explanations ensued, but eventually the woman of the house disappeared into her hut and came back with an earthenware pitcher of water. Thankfully, with profuse bows, Harry passed this around to the others and then drank himself. With relief, their thirst was quenched with the sweet tasting water, cold and fresh. The woman pointed to the edge of the group of huts and said something Harry did not understand.

"She said 'Sungai'!" said Ian. "It means "river" in Malay." Either the woman knew Malay or the word was the same in both languages.

"Good," thought Harry. At least they would be able to fill their canteens and if this woman had any food, it would see them to the end of their march. They searched through their pockets for money and pooled some resources. Jock gave the total to Harry, who offered it to the sari woman. She looked at her father. The old man waved his hands in a negative gesture.

The men, their stomachs full of the food the villagers had managed to produce between them, slept more easily in their makeshift camp that night. That first day, their eyes and ears fully alert for signs of the enemy, they had made good progress and expected to arrive in Kantang via the jungle route during the third day. It seemed so easy to lose track of time but it had been the night of 7th-8th that the invasion had occurred, therefore they would be at their destination on the 10th. On the morning of the 10th, within sight of the coast, they discussed their final plans. Harry strongly suggested that he should go ahead for reconnaissance, leaving the rest within sight of the shipping masts of the port, standing up against the sky and jungle. He would perhaps arrange to hire a boat, then come back for the others. It always posed a danger to be separated in a crisis but they had seen no sign of the enemy in days. It seemed unlikely now that they should come across them before they could escape.

The six men settled down to wait for Harry in a clearing near the edge of the jungle.

"My God," said George feelingly. "What I wouldn't give for a smoke!"

Jock felt in all his pockets and produced a stub from a cigarette he had begun in Maggie's Bar, the night of the invasion.

"Here, George," he said, offering his friend the stub.

George grinned and clapped Jock on the back. The two of them had become a little separated from the other four, who faced away from his point of view. Suddenly, the stub halfway to his mouth, George grabbed Jock and pulled him into the bushes behind them. Jock followed the direction of his gaze and the two of them saw the sun glinting on the barrel of a rifle, slightly protruding from the bushes. Behind it a small figure crouched, in an unfamiliar military uniform.

"Run!" hissed George in Jock's ear.

"The others!" whispered Jock, and would have gone back but George restrained him. The two of them, looking back as they fled the clearing deeper into the jungle, just saw a party of Japanese striding into the clearing. The four other miners, with their backs to the intruders, did not stand a chance. The last George and Jock saw of them, they were responding to the shouts of the enemy - the striding Japanese surrounded the four men who had their arms up in surrender.

As silently as possible without disturbing the undergrowth, the two men made their way deep into the jungle. The shouts and screaming of questions and orders from the clearing faded. Then a sinister silence ensued. Suddenly, a volley of gunfire rang out, the jarring reports echoing through the trees and dense undergrowth, startling the human and animal life who heard it. A general flurry and squawking sounded from the trees as the two escapees threw themselves down onto the forest floor and covered their ears with shock and distress, trying to block out the sound. They heard screams and then silence, a few moans and then again silence.

George and Jock kept their cover until nightfall. When they had come to their senses their basic need for survival came to the fore.

They drank a few sips of water from little pools surrounding the bases of jungle plants, and found a few berries and jungle fruits which Jock, who had assimilated the most knowledge of survival tactics from their army training, assured George could be eaten safely. Then they discussed what to do. The appearance of the Japanese so far from Khota Bharu had taken them completely by surprise. Either they had already covered the same ground the miners had, or else they had entered by the western sea route – via the port of Kantang towards which they were heading.

"We've just got to carry on our plan," said George, leaning back against the trunk of a huge wild rubber tree. He felt exhausted beyond measure and degraded, with his army fatigues stained with sweat and dirty from lying on the ground. His skin was caked with dirt and shiny with moisture. But to do otherwise than continue with the plan they and their dead colleagues had formulated was a betrayal. "I think we should avoid the port," he continued. "I say we find a beach further along the coast and get some more help from some of the locals. We have money – we need a boat to cross the stretch of ocean leading into the Malacca Strait to get us over to north Sumatra. The Strait is only a few miles across from southern Malaya but up here I'm guessing it's more like a hundred. So, we need some navigation instruments, maps and supplies as well. Don't worry. Unless there's a storm the going should be quite calm."

Jock looked doubtful but trusted George's seafaring knowledge. He too, could see no other way out. They needed to reach India via Ceylon and safety. He too had a reason to survive – a fiancé back home in Scotland who had waited patiently through the war and whom he had hoped to bring over to Malaya. He squatted on his haunches with his back to George and rinsed his hot, flushed, freckled face with some water from the leaves of a yukka plant nearby.

"What about them?' he asked, drying his face with his sleeve and leaving traces of dirt on it as he wiped. He gestured towards the clearing. "And Boucher? He'll come back and find them."

A silence ensued while they listened to the late morning jungle sounds – many strangely European-sounding birds reminding them of home filled the jungle with diverse calls. Just then, George thought he heard a pigeon cooing somewhere in the surrounding trees. The sounds calmed the men into a kind of torpor, compounded by the heat and exhaustion from deprivation and hunger.

"We can't wait for him," said George in a low voice. "The Japanese will have disposed of – the others – by now, I hope. Boucher will come back and find us gone. We could have left a note for him or a sign but we can't go back. It's too risky."

Jock got up suddenly, as if in sudden resolve. He grabbed his kit bags.

"Let's go," was all he said. He tramped off ahead of George. The latter wondered whether he was crying. He said nothing, but gathered his kit and followed his former housemate, skirting the port and travelling further north to a safe haven.

Margaret Powell, or Madge, as she had always insisted those close to her called her to distinguish her from her mother, who also went by the name of Margaret, smoothed her nylons so that the seam at the back looked exactly straight. In order to do this, she stood with her back to the bedroom mirror and glanced over her shoulder, taking in every detail of her floral summer dress, cut on the short side, which exposed a slim but shapely calf ending in her usual high-heeled shoes. She checked her mirror once more, seeing a handsome, regular-featured woman still young at thirty-five, and reapplied red lipstick to her full, sensuous mouth. George might disapprove in principle, she smiled to herself, but she knew that in reality he could never resist any suggestion of flashiness in a woman, although he protested the reverse.

George had not written often to her from Malaya - and then India, where he had eventually joined the Indian Army - goodness knows what he had been up to – but he had remained solicitous for her welfare and had kept up her allowance. She could not say that she had behaved like a model of a demure wife herself, come to that, but since she and John had parted, she had tried to maintain discretion with her lovers. She kept the latest one at arm's length to avoid any awkwardness if George reappeared, and she now expected her husband any minute. She looked out of the window at the neat Medway town street then went downstairs to the kitchen, where she put the finishing touches to the modest meal she was cooking. Since the war ended last September, the rationing had remained severe and using the black market was completely out of the question with her scanty allowance. She hoped he would not arrive too hungry but if he had not changed, they might not in any case have any need for food – at least for an hour or so.

The front doorbell rang with the Westminster chimes she had had installed. In less than half a minute she had covered the length of the tiny hallway and opened the door. She stood for a moment gazing at the husband she thought never to see again. Although tanned by the tropical sun which had faded during the voyage home, she could see by his expression that he had, indeed, fundamentally changed. She had not known this expression before. He looked much thinner than she remembered, but apart from that his face held a gauntness and look of defeat she had never associated with him. Perhaps though, this could be attributed to fatigue and he would regain something of his former self with rest and good food. She had not thought that he would have suffered like this. He had always seemed indestructible to her, always with that hearty male energy which characterised him. He spoke first, having taken in the way his wife looked. He was not surprised to see that she did not appear to have changed. But then, she had barely been affected by the war as he had.

"Hello Madge," he said. She opened the door wider for him and he put his bag down in the hall. Then he turned to his wife, kissing her on the lips. The kiss, however, was enigmatic, and to Madge unreadable. Perhaps, she thought, after all, they needed to talk.

Madge glanced at her husband, trying to judge his mood.

"George dear, if you're hungry, I have a meal ready," she ventured. "Come through to the kitchen and you can tell me everything."

"I'd rather wait a bit," George said, trying to reorient himself in the little English house with its narrow passageways and poky rooms. He felt large and ungainly as the walls of the house pressed in on him like a prison. The day had become overcast and grey and inside the house the outside light showed dimly. He shivered suddenly. He felt cold in the chill of autumn in his native land. It seemed hardly surprising that in the swamps of Sumatra he had contracted malaria and had lain sweating and delirious in the tent for weeks, nursed by the ever-faithful Jock, who on several occasions had despaired for his life.

The small "kitchen" which in that style of Edwardian house had once been home to a kitchen range where meals were cooked, now held a large table and chairs and was used as a dining room for the "scullery" adjoining, now accommodating the gas cooker and kitchen sink.

"Would you like a glass of beer, dear?" Madge was trying to anticipate her husband's needs. She pulled out a chair at the table for George, who sat down gratefully. She went into the scullery and quickly checked on the casserole cooking in the oven. George followed her with his eyes, watching the sway of her body and short steps as the high heels tilted her hips from side to side. The waist of the cotton dress was clinched in with a belt, emphasising a clinging bodice. George deliberately looked out of the window, at a view which only afforded the sight of the blank red brick wall of the house next door, above which a grey sky was just visible over the rooftops this dreary afternoon. The atmosphere hung, oppressive, the air steamy from the cooking.

Madge returned from the kitchen with his beer and a small glass containing a sherry for herself and sat down opposite him. She took a sip from her glass. It seemed hard to know where to begin. She had not seen her husband since before the war, shortly after their marriage, when he had left her here in their house in Gillingham, Kent, to re-join his ship. At first, she had tried hard to behave like a model navy wife but soon her loneliness threatened to drive her mad. Coupled with this, the inevitable male attention for an attractive woman living alone had proved insurmountable. She had taken first one lover and then another, her fall from grace eventually being reported anonymously to George. Hurt and furious, he had cut her married woman allowance, thinking spitefully that her lovers should support her now. She had promised him.....

The alcohol had a relaxing effect, warm in their empty stomachs.

"Thank you for your letters, dear," she opened, emboldened. "I heard from the solicitor in '42 and I didn't know what was happening. What was all this about a divorce, George? Is it true? You said nothing about it in your letters."

George lit a Navy Cut, blowing out smoke luxuriously and picking small pieces of the raw tobacco from his tongue. He offered the cigarette to her as of old, and she accepted it as a peace offering. He lit another for himself, tapping the end against the packet.

"I was seeing someone," he said. "I was far away from you, Madge. Malaya was like another world, another life. It's gone for good."

Madge nodded. She had heard nothing further from B&B and would have believed George dead if it had not been for his letters and the information from the Foreign Office.

The ice slowly dissolved between them, little by little. Over the course of the home-cooked meal, George clarified what he had scantily covered in his letters. The Foreign Office had regularly supplied her with information as to her husband's whereabouts, and she had replied to one or two of their letters, assuring them that she heard regularly from her husband, supplementing this information. Although George's letters had remained thin on information concerning his activities, he had never failed to reassure her of his concern for her welfare. He had come to realise that if this included lovers to warm her bed, so be it.

During the bleak, dreary English afternoon, George relived for Madge the mosquito infested swamps of Sumatra and the treacherous voyage from northern Sumatra across the expanse of the Indian Ocean to the southern tip of Ceylon. The land crossing of the paradisiacal island until they reached the narrow strait to India had been fraught with danger, as George and Jock avoided the authorities until they reached the Indian mainland. There, exhausted from months of semi-starvation and sickness, they gave themselves up with something of relief. Through it all, they had stayed together, supporting each other, each filling in what the other lacked. Only then were they separated as they faced court-martial and hard labour for eighteen months. Their sentence had been lenient as they had been volunteers at the time of the Japanese invasion. Following this, they had been recruited until the end of the war into the Indian Army as privates. There in Bengal, George almost found another Malaya but as an army private, with less freedom than he had when working for the Thai Tin Syndicate. He had served the minimum length of service, the ending of which almost exactly coincided with the end of the war, bar a few months.

George had realised, towards the end of his service, that he had become desperately tired of foreign parts and thought with longing of home. Occasionally he had thought of Lavinia as he became more settled in India and wondered where she had got to and what could have happened to her. His questions had soon been answered. The British colonies constituted a small world and he either met, or heard of, people who had lived in Malaya when he and Lavinia had been at the height of their affair and had escaped through various routes to India. He had heard about the fall of Singapore and the Japanese occupation of Malaya soon after arriving in Bengal and through the grapevine, knew that Lavinia had escaped safely to Australia. He knew too, that when the war ended, or even before, she would want to go home to her people. Gossip among the British expatriates had a tendency to travel fast, and he felt fairly sure that she would hear, at some time, that he had survived and lived in India. Otherwise, he thought, perhaps it was better that she should think him dead.

They made a fire in the grate in the little back sitting room as the early twilight closed in. Madge drew the green plush curtains over the sash window and turned on the standard lamp, creating a warm, golden world within. The firelight created fantastic shadows on the ceiling and walls. George sat in one of the armchairs and his wife curled up on the deep-piled hearthrug, leaning against him. An air of tranquillity pervaded the scene and he felt finally at peace. All through the long voyage from the sub-continent, he had dreamed of such an eventuality and letters which he had received from Madge indicated that after all, she wanted him home.

They did not speak. George sat still for some time, and they listened together to the crackling of the wood as the coal caught and formed a bed of burning embers. Then George lifted one of his hands and stroked Madge's hair in a tender gesture. She turned up her face to him and he bent forward to kiss her, this time with mounting passion.

The post-war era was one of adjustment for everyone and times were hard, at least for a few years. George had made a conscious decision to settle down as he conceded that his wanderlust may have contributed to the difficulties in his marriage. Now at thirty-four, he did his best to fulfil the role of husband and provider expected of him. Having the ability to turn his hand to anything, a range of jobs were possible for him and he applied to the fire service, which gave him and Madge stability as well as the frisson of danger and excitement he always craved. He thought it more than likely that by now, Lavinia must have returned home to Hildenborough, a mere thirty-five miles away on the other side of the county. In his more devilish moments, he rather relished the thought that his two women lived close together and easily accessible should he so take the fancy. But for now, he shied away from the complications he knew would ensue from any attempted contact with Lavinia. His needs were amply provided for and his life was comfortable and untroubled. Only in his fantasies did he give his imagination full rein....

Chapter 24

Letting Go

It was finished. The day after I had written the ending of George's story, laboriously peering over the page as I scrawled in longhand, I had woken early. Today was a Saturday, and I knew that I would be alone for the next forty-eight hours. Janet, as usual, had left my weekend meals in the fridge neatly covered with cling film and had emptied the dishwasher ready for me to stack the dirty plates. I ventured a glance at the window, trying to pick up a clue about the weather. I had left the curtains undrawn simply because I had become weary of the endless daily drawing and opening, marking the passing of time, sunrise and sunset, becoming, to me, more rapid and frenetic – like a cine film in fast motion. Spring had delayed its appearance this year with late frosts brutally stunting the new growth on the trees which framed my window views, as if to deprive me of the simple pleasure of a promise of summer through the glass.

I had woken prematurely, the light, propitiously bright, flooding the room, yet I still felt weary from the effort I had expended over the last few days, weeks and months. It had taken me too long to achieve the complete peace I had sought over the years. I had become distracted, yes. Perhaps in the distractions lay my real life, when I had the modest successes I refused to accept as achievements. I had called this consciousness my superficial self and not given her credit. Yet now I recognised that she had worth. It was she, who, in the beginning, had escaped from a burning Singapore; it had been she who had accepted that I would not be able to return to nursing and became, with a kind of angry impersonation, one of the best secretaries Mr. Crossit had ever had. Here in England, this being had followed the same path. After Father had died in 1970, I had moved closer to the cultural centre of Tunbridge Wells where I could indulge my literary interests and form the friendships of which I had despaired in the materially orientated world of Sydney. I had to admit I had had a varied life. Yet underneath it all the questions from the past remained in that other consciousness. I had to bring them both into a closer harmony.

Over the past few months, I had tried to make sense of the notes, diaries, newspaper snippets and letters which had lain in the suitcase in the dining room. Yesterday, I had packed everything away again, neatly and carefully, knowing that I had finished with the story I had written. I had made my will, getting one of old Mr Jevons' young partners to come out and undertake the business for me. I had left everything in the house, including these precious papers of my life, to Dorrie. It would remain up to her to decide what she wanted to do with them. She had children, making a wealth of possibilities for someone of a literary bent to make something of them if they wanted. My own family had under-achieved in the reproductive stakes, I acknowledged.

My tale had seemed fine up to a point, but, as in fact, one unsatisfactory loose end stood out - one that mattered a lot. Well, I ruminated, it was my life story and I could write it how I liked. Some people might be surprised, I knew, and I had surprised myself. It had transformed an autobiography to a work of fiction. The ending remained unknown and I could only guess the outcome. One thing had stayed on my mind for forty years. George had survived outside Malaya. But in what form? That day had passed a happy, mundane one – and one which I had enjoyed with Dorrie and her family, spending time in the country. It had seemed like a setting which would be the last place I expected to see a ghost from the past. I had, through ever despairing to reconcile with my grief, turned to spiritualism. Although I had never sought a medium's help in contacting him – perhaps fearing what may appear or happen - I had, perhaps amateurishly, tried myself. Instinctively, apart from my feverish longing and imaginings, I had known that the afterlife did not exist for me. I felt nothing but a wide, black void of nothingness. Yet I had seen something at Rochester, although over the years what I remembered in those few moments became dim with time and after a while I wondered whether I had in fact seen anything. One thing I remembered well. His eyes. They appeared vacant to the scene around, perhaps focussing on a past event, seeing but not comprehending. I had seen eyes like that since – on men who lived on as shells of themselves, who had witnessed things no person ever should. In those days we called it "shell shock". There was no cure. The body lived on but they did not.

And the woman. She had been a necessary appendage for George, for never had I known him without one. I could think of this with equanimity now, I realised. Time proved a merciful healer of all things, including the awful possession of sexual desire. Yet there had occurred one incident in which I had accepted the kind of man he was. Gladys. The woman on George's arm at Rochester might just as well have been me, or Gladys, or any one of the countless female faces raised towards him as they walked together arm in arm or looked up from his shoulder in the bed, as I had done. With Gladys, I had found the whole affair had liberated my senses. Never, I remembered, had I been so aroused during our lovemaking before, so that for a while I had had the conviction that the pinnacle of our pleasure had not passed without result. This kind of surrender on my part had been what he had craved from me. I had felt used, like a slut, like Gladys. It had been completely alien to everything I had experienced before, or been taught, yet every part of my body had felt responsive and completely alive.

When I had seen him at Rochester, had I felt disturbed by the woman? I had dismissed her as irrelevant, and I wondered if I had done so in an attempt to erase her from my mind and persuade myself that she did not exist, that George walked alone. Perhaps now, as with Gladys, here I could see proof that George had not fundamentally changed, that in my absence she stood in as a mere understudy. She looked a little like Gladys, I had concluded, when I thought about what had leant on his arm. I recalled the high heels, the red lips, the skirt on the short side, the clinched-in waist emphasising the breasts the woman had displayed with pride. Of course, it had been Madge. Through the succeeding years, I had known that he had gone back to her. For a long time, I could not understand why. He must, I reasoned, have changed more than I could imagine he ever could – become, in effect, a completely different person from the one I remembered. Shell shock could drain a personality into a walking corpse without animation or the desire or energy to make changes. What I had seen at Rochester could have fitted that description. Without any desire or ability to seek a different kind of life, he had meekly just gone home. His body, as it always had, perfunctorily fulfilled its duty as he had allowed his wife to looked after him. Madge, I reasoned, would organise his affairs so that they would be able to live comfortably. She had no need now to look elsewhere for physical gratification with George by her side. *But had I really seen him or someone I could imagine might look like him in later life?*

And why, I often thought, as my body aged and the vigour of youth abated, had I not been informed of his return by the Red Cross or the Foreign Office? I wondered seriously whether if either had known that my fiancé had returned to his wife to whom he was still legally married, I would have been informed. The Foreign Office may have filed his details by now and yet no, all the while a person was still missing the case would have to be kept open. A tiny chink of uncertainty still remained which we had both exploited, in our different ways. Then I had remembered the uncertainty and confusion over the names and numbers of the George Powells. Perhaps George had had a middle name after all, which he had given to the authorities in India, making of him yet another Powell to add to the list. I no longer cared any more. I only wished for closure and that, through a story that, like his memory, would fade with time, would eventually become real and accepted. If I lived much longer, it was quite likely that I myself would accept my own account as the truth. Already, now that the work lay finished, neatly stacked, on the dining room table, I found myself forgetting little things and names. Especially after a bottle of that delicious red wine Bill had got for me. I would look it out later this evening. There must be several bottles left. The freedom I had felt while I wrote felt quite intoxicating and I hardly knew whether this had occurred because of the audacity of my ideas or that bottle of heavy red wine I sipped to aid my composition. The old George, God rest his soul, would have chuckled if he had known.

The church clock had struck nine. Time I got up, I thought. The day stretched before me endlessly with its endless freedom of choice. Why I should feel I had more choice today, I could not say. Janet always made a special effort to appear unobtrusive enough, heaven knows. Yet nothing appealed more than an empty house for promoting freedom, even at my age. What would I do, that I could not if other people were around? Well, I thought, I could walk around naked if I had a mind. Not a bad idea at all. It felt warm enough. I reasoned that I might not even see the next bill come in, so resolutely kept the heating on all day, the boiler going into overdrive and firing up reassuringly, every now and again. I didn't bother with slippers and dressing gown, but took off my nightdress as I sat on the bed and felt the slight draught from the window cool and play over my breasts. I lifted them up, allowing the cooler air free access to their delicate underside. George had said that he had loved them, the pale pink of the nipples merging into the small mounds on which they lay, cheekily pointing upwards. Not having to answer the demands of pregnancy, they had never swelled and later sagged, unlike other parts of my body. I rose from the bed, and walked towards the landing mirror. Diffused light from the window shone full on the pale spectre that approached it. Underneath the breasts, as smooth and untouched as a virgin's, the white expanse of abdomen revealed a similar past. Smooth and still firm, the pristine surface unaffected by the burden of childbearing had waited a lifetime for the impregnation that had never come. I really must stop looking at myself like this, I thought. What would George have thought of me now? Was Madge any different? Her breasts would undoubtedly sag. She had at least one child before she and George had been married and perhaps more later with George.

I had long become familiar with the process of conception and childbirth, through study and experience. I had worked among the women of the London poor, seen how the process had victimised them and subordinated them into slaves of their own bodies, how they paid, sometimes with their lives, for their men's gratification, and often their own. Not that rewards did not come along the way in the fearful mother-love that came with birth, which I had witnessed and understood but never felt. All the same, I had not avoided it, although some did.

I would not bother with washing today and perhaps tomorrow. I liked my smell. After we had made love, I had loved to smell George's strong, male smell of testosterone, particularly pronounced at these times and mingled with the sweet smell of semen. How well I remembered this. I had not experienced this again to the same degree since. I began to become aroused, remembering, as I had often done before. Better get dressed, cover myself up, get some breakfast, or I would spend the day pleasuring myself and, although gorging to satisfy one appetite, neglect another.

This house had become entwined with my story, in my memory. Each room reflected a microcosm of the different parts. I thought over the different chapters I had written, as I threw on what I had on yesterday and took up my stick, starting towards the stairs. I made my way down carefully. It's alright at the moment, I thought, but God knows what will happen later. I didn't really care. I still preferred this freedom to kill myself, if I wanted. In a care home they would have protected me at all costs – more perhaps for their own benefit than mine. They would keep me alive to keep the money rolling in. But my life I kept sacrosanct, different. I had just managed to get to my room last night, and had thrown myself down on the bed, to fall into a virtual coma. Perhaps I had been celebrating the end of my book, or my life.... The downstairs smelled strongly of cigarette smoke, and I went to the French windows to open them. I had stood here, outside on the patio and in the kitchen with Janet and we had been talking about Duger.

Not for the first time, I wondered what happened to her. Had her inimitable love life finally caught up with her and left her a washed out, spent old hag? I had left her back in Denmark at a crossroads, at the outbreak of war. What a pity I could not write her story too. I had kept all her graphically descriptive letters for some reason. She had made an indelible impression on me as an innocent young woman with idealistic aspirations from which I had never recovered. I had loved reading her stories, of times never seen again. If anyone imagined that the sexual revolution had begun in the 1960's, the story of Duger proved them wrong. I had devoured her letters, yet when her exploits had ended in sickness – a recurrent Bartholin's cyst – and an unwanted pregnancy, I had begun to tire of her and perhaps judged her. I had acted somewhat hypocritically, living vicariously through her when, until George, I held myself back from the abandonment of all my principles and teased men to the point of distraction until they had begged.

The morning grew warm, early fitful spring sunshine becoming more settled and focussed on the suntrap of the patio. I decided to make toast and coffee, sit at the wrought iron table and soak up as much as I could. If nothing else, it felt wonderfully warming. I could turn off the central heating for a change, at least for a while. Ten minutes later, I sat back at my table, having grabbed a cushion for the wrought-iron seat on my way back through. The garden, like all my neighbours' uniform plots, was square in shape and landscaped around a central lawn, around the edges of which undergrowth and a few large trees, in summer lending shade over the grass, grew in abundance. Years ago, I had planted bulbs – bluebells, gleaned from the woods beside the common, daffodils and pansies, which now provided pinpoints of colour in the bare landscape. If I had lived here as a child, I would have loved to hide among these trees and look over the fence into next door's garden. Once, I had visited my neighbour's garden. Those seen from over a fence never looked the same as when you were actually in it. I hardly remembered the garden we had had in Tonbridge all those years ago but the Hildenborough house had possessed such a garden as this with its nooks and crannies. I sipped my coffee, savouring its rich, roast taste and took another bite of my toast, on which I had spread a generous smear of orange marmalade.

After breakfast, I looked in at the dining room, the scene of my endeavours over the past few months. It all looked unnaturally tidy. The suitcase still stood on the table, on which for months papers had lain strewn haphazardly. My old typewriter, brought out of its retirement and pressed into hard service once again, when I had the energy to leave my longhand and exercise my typing skills, stood looking forlorn and abandoned. Both waited for Bill to take them upstairs again. I must remember to ask Janet on Monday about it. I looked through the lace curtains and onto the street. Only what had seemed like a matter of days ago, I had seen people carrying Christmas trees, chattering couples and groups laden with shopping passing by. In the summer soon to come, cotton dresses would appear, happy faces, sunshades on pushchairs as the Southborough populace headed towards the common for cricket or the summer fete.

Why, I thought, do I not imagine myself seeing this?

The colourful painting of the *Narkunda* still hung in its corner reminding me that months ago I had wrestled with my chapter on my voyage to Malaya. It seemed almost as long ago as the voyage itself. Really, I definitely became confused, although I did not feel disturbed by this thought. Time merged itself into a jumbled medley of images and sounds from the past – all converging into one mass....

I spent the afternoon watching an old wartime propagandist film on the television in black and white, barely following the plot, if any existed, but enjoying watching how the actors spoke in the exaggerated accents of the upper class, their posturing and how the heroine gazed up adoringly at her man as if he resembled a god, breathlessly waiting for that kiss he would condescend to give her with her glossy red mouth slightly open. I wondered if her position had given her a stiff neck, the way she held her head so far back, obviously, I thought, because he was portrayed as tall as a mountain. I remembered the first time I had seen it, in wartime London. Had I behaved like this? I had probably thought the film "marvellous" and had gone home on a blissful cloud, deeply moved by its sentiments, even though I had become disillusioned with London life even then.

At five, with the closing credits of the film accompanied by a full symphony orchestra tinnily reaching the desired atmospheric crescendo, I decided on a gin and tonic as an aperitif before exercising my skills with the microwave. Janet had left explicit instructions on a small white label stuck onto the cling film of each meal at the high point of the centre of the dinner plate. Apparently, I had to heat tonight's dinner for four minutes on "high". I felt confident that, even in an inebriated condition, I would have few problems with these instructions. I hunted out a bottle of the red wine which had caused my rather disgraceful condition last night and put it at the ready, to go with my meal, opening the top to allow the wine to "breathe". I found my packet of cigarettes, noting that I had almost decimated a large proportion of the packet to accompany yesterday's binge. No matter. My lungs had managed to survive this far. Dear Dr Shelley in Malaya and the Perth substitutes had done an excellent job and more temperate climates and sedentary jobs had done the rest. I got out my little foot stool, set my drink on the table beside my chair and settled myself comfortably. I would just see "*Mastermind*", then heat my meal ready for the news. I chuckled a little to myself at the amusing thought that I followed Father's habits in old age in some ways, but certainly not with the temperance. On the show tonight appeared a history enthusiast who, coincidentally, answered questions about the Fall of Malaya as his "Specialist Subject". This should be good, I thought with glee. I'll see if the so-called "experts" have got their facts straight. So often, what now had the appellation of "history" had been recorded wrongly. I knew what happened, I thought. I have lived through it. Why didn't they ask me? *"Because, for one thing, you're a woman and not a don"*, came the answer, unbidden, to my mind.

After ten minutes, I turned the programme off in disgust. The cold presentation of facts was only half the story. History could never tell the true story – the colour, noise, smells and emotions of those who lived through it. The contestants glibly spouted facts from memory and the winner had settled smugly back in his seat. Probably a bank manager, I thought cattily. The veterans never went on *"Mastermind"*. I could not imagine George doing it. Again, no matter. I took a long drought of gin and tonic and inhaled at my cigarette deeply, noting how the effects of both complimented each other in a temporary wave of euphoria, which began as a warm glow in the depths of my gut. An ideal state for contemplation, or meditation...

I continued with the same train of thought in which several new ideas presented themselves. Madge. I thought about the woman on George's arm, which could have been me, or any woman. ("Everywoman"). George had seemed possessive, almost greedy, and the woman completely acquiescent. George and Madge – both as good, or as bad, as each other then. Why had Madge been painted so badly by George? He had had serial affairs, many simultaneously, while, although Madge's "gentlemen callers" could probably be counted on the fingers of one hand, he had strongly denounced her and had used the evidence he had acquired to instigate a divorce. Here I saw the famous "double standard" in action – one rule for women and another for men. I remembered that, when I had begun to see George, I had all but done the same thing, with "X". I had relished my time with both men, and knew that if I had felt sure that it would have been safe, I would not have hesitated to fuck them, and hard.

But then, times had changed since. But how different are they now, really? I thought. Witness the ridiculous antics the women had adopted in the film of the time, which I had watched only that afternoon. George had the prevailing quaint idea about women because he held the ideas of a man of his time and believed that only whores liked sex. This had formed his opinion of the character of his wife Madge. Yet his poor opinion of her begged the question: why had he married her? I had early on realised George's complex character; his unique personality and creative energy on the one hand – which I had fallen in love with, mingled with, on the other, a dreadful and morbid self-doubt, fuelled by the after-effects of alcohol. He may have thought Madge a fitting mate for this self-perception. He had seen me as almost unattainable except within the artificial, hothouse environment of colonial Malaya where sailors such as he could take a chance with a decent girl away from the constraints of home and family....

The chimes of Big Ben, signalling the introduction to "News at Ten" demanded my attention as intended. I had fallen into a happy doze, but became aware at that moment of a faint echo from the church clock, its chimes a little out of sync with its brother over thirty miles distant. I peered at the television groggily. Each chime announced news items of diminishing importance, the presenter's interposition sounding dramatic, urgent. Something very odd was happening. My thinking seemed crystal clear but the screen appeared blurred and a second screen appeared like a shadow to the side. I tried closing one eye to see if this helped. The ghost disappeared but the blurriness became even more pronounced.

"Val Coates, you're drunk," I said out loud. "This is a disgraceful state of affairs."

The news presenter seemed oblivious to my predicament and blandly continued with his broadcast.

"Better get to bed, old girl."

I managed to find the remote control down the side of the chair and turned off the television. I sat for a moment in the descending silence, broken only by a slight rattle as the refrigerator in the kitchen turned itself off. My head span unpleasantly and for the first time I began to wonder if I would make it. Groping for my stick, I found it at length propped against my little table and positioned it beside my right leg. With prodigious effort, I tried to rise, putting all my weight on the stick. Strange. Nothing seemed to be happening. My legs stayed put, refusing to budge. I experimented with moving my legs, wriggled my toes and noticed a difference between the left and right sides of my body.

"Oh God. No," I thought.

I had seen it on so many. I must get to the phone, and quickly. Why, oh why, had I not had an extension put in beside my chair?

With my right hand I felt the left side of my face and my heart sank. Even with my intoxicated senses, it felt numb, the mouth drooping, as if I had just visited the dentist for a particularly complex filling or extraction.

"Stay positive," I reprimanded myself. "Don't give up."

I made one last Herculean effort to rise, the phone in the hall like a beacon of hope. Even if I fell, I could crawl, I thought. It was no good. I crumpled like a marionette whose strings had gone slack and the mauve and yellow carpet ascended like a lift, to meet my eyes. I lay as I had fallen, sprawled on the carpet.

I must have blacked out. When I woke, although I had hoped I'd had a nightmare, I did not lie in my bed as usual and the same hopeless situation entrapped me. Trying out my limbs, I knew that the effects of the stroke had progressed and far from being able to crawl, I could not move at all. I had no choice but to await discovery and rescue. I heard the church clock in the distance striking three. I had no thoughts of the certainty of death because I knew that it was not certain, then. I would be rescued, taken to hospital and, with good treatment, make a recovery.

As the hours went on, night dawning into Sunday, I lapsed in and out of consciousness - as time elapsed, more out. I heard the laughter of children playing in the garden next door. Then voices outside the front door, a knock, the sound of the letter box being lifted and dropped as someone peered into the hall. I opened my mouth to shout but only a squeak emerged. Footsteps going away and then the telephone ringing just past lunchtime. I knew the time by the church clock, marking the hours through the generations, as it would after me, into the future.

"She looks so peaceful," said Janet.

Janet and Bill sat at the kitchen table. Bill was holding his wife's hand, alleviating the shock associated with an encounter with death. It was over. Janet had come in as usual with her own key at eight o'clock on this Monday morning, only this time no answering call came from the bedroom. The curtains had been drawn closed as usual in the lounge and it was then, as she turned from the light of the new day that she saw Val. She lay still, but trying in vain to remember any first aid she may have learned, Janet had looked into her face and touched her hand. The heating had still been on, but Val felt cold and she knew.

Since then, unlike Val's last days on earth, the house had seen a swarm of people, all maintaining the hushed tones of respect for the dead. Although she knew the act to be futile, Janet had called an ambulance but there had been little they could do. Val's doctor, a kindly man, had come to certify her death, taking a last look at his patient whom he had treated since she had moved to Southborough. He saw the wine bottle on her table, with a few dregs left in the bottom.

"She liked her little tipple, didn't she," he observed, thinking that it probably hastened her end in that quantity.

"Ever since Malaya!"

He put the death certificate on the table.

"I will inform her next of kin for the funeral arrangements," he said, reverting to practicalities. In the meantime..."

The doctor wrote down a number on a slip of paper and gave it to Bill.

"If you could call these directors, they will come for her."

He looked sympathetically at Janet. The help still sat at the table, white with shock.

"It's always sad, I know," he said. "Turn this infernal heat off, lock up, go home and rest as soon as she is gone. Life goes on."

Afterword

Pilgrim in Malaysia

In 2014, seventy-two years after Lavinia left, I followed in her footsteps. If the only Malaya I had ever known was to be found among the dusty, time-worn pages of another age, I might have laboured under the delusion that this is how it remained. I had to see for myself. In late March I left London to try life in Sydney, Australia, having reached something of a crossroad. I had retired from my job at Guy's and St Thomas' Hospitals the year before and lived in possibly one of the most disguised and restrictive old people's homes in the country since then. Whilst there, I had suffered the disintegration of an ill-fated love affair, before realising that I needed a sea-change, somewhere completely new and far away. My son and his partner had paved the way the previous year. Perhaps, I thought, I would just visit them with the option of staying.

Booking a Malaysian Airlines flight before two of their fleet unfortunately foundered in quick succession, I planned a week's holiday touring the peninsula *en route* for Sydney, making full use of the arduous journey down under. I had just completed the reading of Lavinia's archives and before I tackled the book, needed to put them in context – to breathe the same air, listen to the sounds she had -- the voices of the people, birds in their native trees - feel the same heat on my face. None of these things would have changed. Would I recognise it after immersion in the country it had been then? As I landed in Kuala Lumpur, I prided myself that through Lavinia, I saw and loved it as she did and did not see myself as a regular tourist.

I had booked hotels for a week, covering the extent of the Malaysian peninsular – KL, Penang in the north and Ipoh. Ah, Ipoh – where Lavinia had lived and worked! Surely there, I would recognise some of the places she had described. In heat and humidity which left drops of water on my camera lens and spectacles, I explored first the immediate vicinity of my central KL hotel. Amid the closely built shops, markets, stalls, vendors and the crowded streets, I could see few modern buildings in the neighbourhood. All must have been as she would have known it, the same chaos, bargaining and confusion. I stayed only two days before departing for Penang by air – to its main city, George Town. Here, I discovered the taxi drivers – a useful breed and my passport to knowledge of the country - everything from the cost of living to jobs and taking up residence. After my taxi driver in Penang, I never took public transport. He was one of the nine percent of persons of Indian origin – like all my drivers. Now, as in Lavinia's time, Malaysia is a conflation of ethnic diversities, all freely and competitively practising their traditions as Lavinia expressed it – "It's a noisy country on the whole". As my driver and I cruised the streets of George Town and beyond, he described the way of life in Penang and ergo Malaysia - how to get a job, a house and other necessities, making it sound so attractive that I almost decided to forget about Sydney and settle there. Perhaps, I thought, I could come back if Sydney didn't work out. To illustrate, he took me to see an elderly British woman who lived much better on her pension than she could at home. He revealed that he did her grocery shopping and generally popped in on her to check if she needed anything.

I have a vivid recollection of a modern, white high-rise apartment building, well-appointed and spacious but apparently in the midst of a building site. From the window, I looked out on anthills of workmen in hard hats; drills and mechanical diggers, all contributing to the inevitable din, despite double glazing. The taxi driver seemed quite at home and settled himself comfortably on the lounge suite. I did the same, having been introduced to his friend as someone keen to learn about life there for expats. The elderly woman, happy to talk to a fellow Brit, gladly explained that she had lived there contentedly and cheaply for a number of years but the cost and necessity of healthcare was such that she was obliged to return to the UK for treatment on the NHS. I mentally filed all this away for later reference.

Ipoh was my second and last stop before I returned to KL and my flight to Sydney. Lining the roads and stretching inland, where there had been rubber trees in Lavinia's time were now a certain species of palm tree, palm oil now the number one demand in place of the rubber and tin so badly needed in wartime. From the hotel, spacious as a palace, I booked a taxi for transport to the Cameron Highlands. I had heard of the tea plantations and the driver headed for the Boh estate, one of the best-known. We climbed into the cooler air, admiring the exquisite green vistas on all sides. The driver parked and let me out. I was free to wander at will, but he waited, strolling about on his own, enjoying his leisure. I stayed about two hours, tea tasting, buying souvenirs, watching the rolling green countryside unfold around me.

On the last day I homed in on trying to find Lavinia's bungalow. I had often wondered what happened to it and her things after she went into hospital, never to return. We visited the town hall for information and the three of us, the clerk, the taxi driver and I, pored over a map of the city. To my surprise, the street name she had written on the top right corner of her letters still existed in a sea of Malay names - Windsor Road, the only one which had kept its British name. I wondered at the fortunate coincidence but did not press it. Back on the road, the driver found it easily, but finding number four proved more complicated. Just off the busy main highway north, the street was an oddity, twisting and turning back on itself as if to hide its quarry - so that it was hard to make out the street numbers. Finally, I thought I had found the one – by itself, the style old, easily from her era, the garden overgrown. It did not seem occupied. Perhaps since Lavinia's time it had remained empty, full of ghosts, rejecting strangers. I like to think that. I took a picture but still wasn't completely sure.

The taxi driver had entered into the spirit of it as much as I when I told him the story of Lavinia. He had said the people of Malaysia would love the story. It is their country and their history as much as the Petronas Twin Towers. I should not forget them.

Claire Gartrell,
Wentworth Falls,
New South Wales, Australia.
22nd October 2023.

About the Author

Claire Gartrell is an author and academic. Since completing her doctorate at Oxford University, she has continued an exciting and varied life as a nurse in the south of France and then in the Blue Mountains of New South Wales, Australia. She currently lives in Sydney. *Lavinia's War* is Claire's first novel, and she is now working on a follow-up - a memoir of her own adventures and personal struggles throughout the 1970s, a story that has shaped this most unconventional life.